GILDED LOCKS

A DARK
GOLDILOCKS & THE THREE BEARS
RETELLING

VILLAINS OF KASSEL

LYDIA MICHAELS

CONTENT WARNING

This is a dark reverse harem romance featuring morally grey men who don't ask permission—they take it. Expect explicit sexual content, including anal play, voyeurism, dominance/submission dynamics, primal play, and consensual non-consent scenarios. Themes include captivity, forced proximity, psychological manipulation, power imbalance, trauma (including sexual assault of a secondary character), violence, and obsessive/possessive behavior.

If you need sunshine and safe words, this isn't your book. But if you're ready to surrender to three Russian bears who'll ruin you in the best possible way—welcome to the den.

—XO, LYDIA'S DARK SIDE

DEDICATION

For Ellie,
a friend who always wants the best for me and expects nothing in
return.
So I make the soup and protect you with the woo.
Love you, babe.
See you at the next coven circle.

GILDED LOCKS
Villains of Kassel

Dark Romance

Copyright © 2025 Lydia Michaels

PLAYLIST

Visit Spotify and listen to the music that inspired Gilded Locks as you read!

GILDED LOCKS
VILLAINS OF KASSEL

A scorching hot, morally grey reverse harem featuring possessive anti-heroes, forced proximity, primal dominance, explosive chemistry, and a heroine who refuses to break.

When runaway heiress Marigold Calder crashes into the forbidden Isles of Kassel during a blizzard, she's desperate for shelter. The isolated mountain lodge seems like salvation, until she realizes it belongs to them—three massive Russian brothers who own the most exclusive, and dangerous, private pleasure club in Kassel.

By Lydia Michaels

www.LydiaMichaelsBooks.com

CHAPTER 1
A BITTER DEATH

The rope seared through Marigold's frozen fingers as the boat pitched toward the banks. Ice-glazed planks shrieked their protest beneath the storm's relentless assault.

Each breath carved glass shards through her lungs, the arctic air so savage it crystallized her exhales before they could escape her lips.

The choppy water pitched her from one side of the boat to the other as terror pressed down on her like gravity. A frigid blast of ice sprayed forcefully from the waves, followed by a towering surge that rose from the raging surf. It knocked her off her feet the second it crashed into the boat, washing her back like wasted plankton and throwing her about as if she were as inconsequential as an autumn leaf lost in the wind.

She slammed hard into the boat floor, gasping as salt water flooded her lungs, whacking her shoulder against one of the bench seats. Bitter cold water drenched her clothes, turning her bones to brittle ice, pinning her weak limbs to the ground with impressive weight as the world turned over and another wave crashed again.

She was going to die.

Gasping and sputtering, she turned and gripped the rail before she was washed overboard. In the black, obsidian night, beneath the swirl of stars above, she thought she spotted life, but as she desperately tried to wipe the salt water from her frozen cheeks, she realized the rumors were wrong about the Isles of Kassel. Either that, or she was lost.

This frozen wasteland of jutting obsidian rocks and skeletal trees bore no resemblance to paradise. She must have gone off course.

Her phone died hours ago, around the time her lantern went out and the small craft nearly capsized. She only survived because she held on for dear life, letting the sea swallow the only possessions she had left.

No compass. No map. Not a dry stitch of clothes nor a match to start a fire. Tonight would surely be her last.

She knew death was a possibility when she escaped. She swore she didn't care if she lived or died, as long as she escaped the hell she'd been living in. But in the face of fear, she questioned her devotion, accepting that she'd massively miscalculated the length of this journey and she was much better suited for travel by limousine or jet.

Another bitter cold wave sloshed into the boat, and Marigold screamed in frustration, hoping her rage might warm her bones. Her fingers were numb and useless as she tried to get the water out of her craft. But she was no match for the wild sea.

Fighting back tears of fury, she shook with hypothermic tremors and finally admitted she was not ready to die. She'd suffered so much. This was her chance to break free and live. Why was life so unkind?

Wind whipped against her drenched, sagging clothes, but

no matter how she twisted and turned in the wet rags, there was no escaping the painful onslaught of cold death settling in.

"I hate you!" she raged to everyone who contributed to her suffering.

She screamed at the top of her lungs, only to have her voice give out like a hollow whistle, ravaged from the cold and strain on her body.

Kassel was supposed to be a modern-day Eden—lush emerald jungles thick with orchid-perfumed air and humid promises of sanctuary. Not this merciless tundra where death whispered through every gust of wind.

The stolen invitation crinkled inside the frozen pocket of her stolen coat as she wrestled with numb fingers to secure the boat's line, the false identity she'd stolen tucked against her thundering heart.

She was now Mary Langford.

Thank god she was smart enough not to keep the paperwork in her bag, or it would have gone overboard with the rest of her belongings. Not that it mattered now. She'd likely freeze to death by dawn and wash onto shore with a stolen identity in her pocket. No one would ever know the truth.

Not that it was a pretty truth. Her life had been good once, but after her mother died, everything went to hell.

Clutching her shivering chest, she closed her eyes, fighting back the threat of another anxiety attack. She couldn't afford emotions now. If she wanted to live, she needed to focus solely on survival. And Marigold would do anything to survive. *Anything*.

She branded her new identity into her memory during the last hours of daylight. The deeper she traveled into the sea, the more she accepted she was really getting out, and Marigold Calder was gone.

She read the ID, repeating Mary Langford's information over

and over again, each repetition a prayer she soon knew by heart. Marigold Calder was dead—buried beneath layers of deception and desperation. She was now Mary Langford. Innocent. Safe. Free.

She never expected her half-brother's hatred to go this far or demand this much from her. But every day brought new challenges, and she'd been forced to run harder and think faster than she ever dreamed herself capable of.

They tracked her across Europe, proving the nightmare would never end. But even on the days when her body ached and her fear reached unmanageable points, her survival instincts were still stronger.

Wind slammed into her with the force of a freight train, nearly hurling her sideways into the churning black water below. Her discarded designer heels—so laughably wrong for this hellscape, but all she'd possessed when terror drove her from London—skittered across the ice-glazed boat deck. The cashmere coat, so luxurious in its former life, clung to her frame like an icy shroud, useless against nature's fury.

Through the driving sleet, she squinted into the hostile landscape, amber eyes burning as they searched for salvation. *There.* Her breath hitched as a flicker of golden warmth pierced the darkness, barely visible through the storm's veil.

Her heart tripped into overdrive, chipping away the ice that lined the inner walls of her lungs. Light meant shelter. Light meant survival.

Plunging her hands into the black, icy water that sloshed over the floor, she searched for the tattered rope. Her frozen fingers locked down the moment she grazed its frayed edge, and she yanked hard, angling the rudder to steer her towards what looked like a jetty protruding from a black coast.

The sails were gone, and she wasn't sure how much of the

rudder remained. The waves curled and crashed, pulling her in, but away from the light.

Gone. The light was gone.

All she could see was rain and sleet and endless ocean. Had she imagined it?

"No! I saw it!" She searched the endless black and screamed, *"Help me!"*

Panic welled up inside of her until she thought she might drown from the desperation spewing out of her in growling profanities, but then she caught sight of salvation again.

"I see it!" She steered the rudder, fighting the urge to squint or blink.

Minutes wore like eons. There was no guarantee she would make it to shore. All she had was a distant light in the endless black to guide her. The horizon didn't exist. Everything was black. Just bitter cold, endless black.

"Come on!" she snarled, hauling the rope with all of her weight, fighting the current, and willing what was left of this wreckage to take her to shore.

She needed to stand on dry land again. Even if it wasn't the lavish Isles of Kassel, anything was better than dying at sea on this godforsaken craft.

She hurled her shoes and any other weight overboard, desperately trying to lighten the load. Drifting toward the light, she'd suddenly waft back with the current, so close yet so powerless. If she jumped in, she'd only have minutes before hyperthermia killed her or she drowned. Maybe that was her best hope.

Gray clouds blocked out the stars, hiding the moon and its guiding light. Looming waves gaped like wide yawns on massive inhalations. The ocean was a greedy pig that swallowed any earthly morsel whole, and she was no exception.

The closer she came to the light—to what had to be shore—the choppier the water became. Eyes wide, she saw the power of the black sea as it towered over her, building to terrifying heights, and the choice was made. Thrown overboard, the wave forced her down with little air in her lungs, pummeling her into the sea. A thousand icy blades stabbed into her spine as her air cut off and she swam wildly, too disoriented by the wake to know what direction was up.

Her lungs burned as panic left with her last breath of air. Churning bubbles tickled her frozen face as she kicked wildly toward what she hoped was the surface, and then...oxygen.

She gasped, her airways so tiny she could only sneak a scant breath past the fear clogging her throat. Her legs kicked as the churning waves blinded her. Choppy whitecaps forced her back down as her clothing tangled about her legs, tripping her on nothing.

In that moment, she knew the ocean was alive and it wanted to kill her. Its determination was nothing short of personal, and she nearly surrendered, thinking there might be some peace in giving up, but then her toe hit something hard and solid.

Slippery moss made it impossible to grip, and as another wave crashed over her, plunging her down into the jetties of rock and seaweed, her head bashed on something sharp, and the roaring wash of the sea silenced into a muffled hollow of nothing.

Gasping, she broke the surface as the copper taste of blood mixed with the briny water rushing into her mouth. Sharp jetty smashed into her with bruising force as the relentless waves beat her against the black shores. Breakers tumbled her hard, and she stopped fighting, needing a few seconds to simply breathe.

Drifting, gasping, savoring what were likely her last breaths, a calm washed over her. Perhaps she passed out for a second or a day. Time lost meaning in those last few seconds of life, until true salvation smacked into her.

The slice of sharp shells and barnacles abraded her skin. The pillar came out of nowhere, but as she squinted, she could see that the rotting wood once belonged to a dock that had nearly washed completely away.

A dock meant people. It meant land.

Rejuvenated by hope, she swam as hard as she could toward the battered wood. Another pair of pillars jutted from the surface, which meant the sea was retreating and the ground was rising. Her frozen toes kicked into cross beams below the surface, and she was soon leaping off the muddy sea floor and hurling herself onto wet, withered wood.

"Thank you," she wept, pressing her chest and cheek to the icy plank as broken sobs bellowed out of her.

Relief swamped her in heavy victory. She could have died then—in peace—simply knowing she made it. But she was a fighter, and fighters didn't give up.

Violently shaking, frozen to the point of dysfunction, she growled and forced her body upward. "Get up!" she yelled when her legs wouldn't cooperate.

Unsure where she was, but content she wasn't drowning in the miserable sea, she used the last of her strength to haul her lower limbs out of the water and fell to her back, panting as the stars came into view through the blurry wash of her tears and the salt of the ocean.

She wanted to lie there forever and never move again, but there wasn't much time. She wasn't out of danger yet. If she didn't find shelter and warmth soon, she was going to die.

Her legs trembled as she abandoned the dock's dubious safety for solid ground that proved anything but. The earth beneath her feet was more ice than soil, treacherous and unforgiving as the family she'd fled. But it was her lack of balance that threw her more than anything else.

Each weak step forward became a battle against the wind, determined to fling her back toward the water, back toward the boat that had been her only escape from hell. The light she'd spotted had been smudged out by the storm and bare trees.

Bent forward against the cutting gale, she lurched and shivered, the fog of her breath so thick in the wind she could only squint and blindly hope she was heading in the right direction.

One foot before the other. The mantra her mother had whispered during those long-ago panic attacks, before everything crumbled to ash. Before she learned that monsters wore Savile Row suits and carried ancient names.

The climb from the harbor transformed into an odyssey of endurance. Her numb, stockinged feet caught in patches of frozen mud and brittle undergrowth, forcing her to claw at bare branches that scraped her palms raw.

The metallic taste of blood flooded her mouth. From where, she didn't know. Didn't have time to check her injuries or time to waste breath on screams, and she had no misconceptions that she might be entitled to something better than this.

Crying was surrender, and surrender meant dying in this godforsaken wilderness. She would not die. She would live.

She was Mary Fucking Langford.

When she finally saw the light again, she nearly burst into tears. As she struggled up the steep incline of snow-covered rock, the light expanded into something impossible. Shelter!

Or was she dreaming?

The structure belonged in fairy tales, not reality. Maybe she was hallucinating. Maybe this was heaven.

She'd grown up in the shadows of mansions and estates, but never witnessed anything quite so cavernous and...gothic.

Was it a castle? Where the hell was she?

More importantly, was anyone home?

Something created that light inside. And light meant warmth.

Survival instincts drove her harder than logic ever could. The stone structure loomed against the storm-darkened sky like a sleeping dragon, its windows blazing like molten amber eyes watching her approach.

Gothic spires vanished into low-hanging clouds while iron fixtures gleamed dully in the intermittent lightning. Not merely large, this was architecture on a scale that dwarfed human ambition, all dark stone and soaring peaks that pierced the grey heavens above. Annexed wings sprawled across the landscape with the casual arrogance of absolute power. Its very presence was a challenge to the elements that dared to assault it.

What manner of god lived in a place like this?

Her teeth chattered so violently, the sound echoed in her skull like castanets. The cold had evolved beyond discomfort into something alive and predatory, prowling through her bones with glacial fingers. Hypothermia wasn't a possibility anymore. It was an inevitable certainty counting down with each labored heartbeat. She would likely die tonight, so her only hope was to minimize the suffering and die somewhere comfortable.

As she approached the looming castle, the high walls protected her from the spewing ice and frozen rain falling from the sky. It blocked the wind, convincing her this sanctuary was a gift, not a curse.

Before the massive entrance, she paused. The doors were carved from what appeared to be a single piece of midnight-dark wood, adorned with iron hinges that belonged in medieval fortresses. An enormous brass knocker shaped like a snarling bear's head watched her with metallic eyes that reflected her desperation.

Questions plagued her numbing mind. What if someone answered? What if they demanded explanations she couldn't provide without revealing the truth? What if they turned her away? What if they recognized the name she'd stolen, the identity she wore like armor, and turned her in?

The wind shifted, making the decision for her, shoving her against the wood with bruising force. Her ravaged hands found the massive iron handle, and when it turned beneath her desperate grip, she nearly sobbed with relief.

Unlocked.

CHAPTER 2

INTO THE TEMPEST

The heavy door surrendered, swinging inward with surprising grace, and warm air rushed out to embrace her like a lover's caress. The temperature difference burned her frosted skin, striking with disorienting force, making her vision swim as she stumbled across the threshold and sealed herself inside, cutting off the storm's howling rage.

Silence descended like a benediction as her flesh prickled, the comfort of heat quickly turning into a traumatic assault on her frozen limbs that made her shake uncontrollably.

Her ears rang in the sudden absence of wind and sleet, the quiet so profound it felt sacred.

"Hello?"

Only her voice echoed back.

She stood, dripping on black, gleaming marble veined with gold that seemed to pulse with its own inner fire. Above, a chandelier hung suspended like a frozen moment of violence, wrought iron twisted into thorny vines that cradled dozens of flickering candles.

Candles? Who owned fixtures like that in this day and age? She searched the floors and walls for outlets, finding none. The blend of primitive and luxury was unlike anything she'd seen before.

Someone was clearly home, as they took the time to light the candles above and on the candelabras scattered throughout the massive entrance. There must have been a hundred pillars blazing. But when she tried to lift a candelabra, she realized it was bolted to the ground.

"Is it gas?" Frowning, she examined the antique brass, warming her hands over the flickering flames. The modern touch was such a nuanced tribute to the dwelling's original style.

She looked around the gaping foyer. *Whoever lives here must pay a fortune to do so.*

Everything existed on a scale designed for giants. The ceiling soared two stories overhead, supported by wooden beams that gleamed like silk in the candlelight. Rich tapestries depicted hunting scenes that walked the knife's edge between beauty and savagery, while a staircase curved upward like a lover's spine. Even the banisters were carved with meticulous attention to detail, displaying wood chiseled acorns and leaves.

It was more than a castle. It was a modern-day medieval palace.

Heat seeped into her frozen flesh like honey into starved cells as her core temperature danced with death. She needed heat. Real heat. The kind that could resurrect the dead.

Aimlessly staggering, she searched for life. If there were candles, there might be a fireplace.

Her exploration led her into what could only be called a great hall, where stone walls rose around her like the ribs of some massive cathedral. Floor-to-ceiling windows stood as black mirrors, reflecting her bedraggled appearance with merciless clarity.

The lingering scent of burned wood and smoke lured her in as she rushed toward the smell, toward the most enormous fireplace she'd ever seen. It commanded every other detail into submission. Carved from obsidian stone and large enough to accommodate an entire elk, the hearth yawned before her like the mouth of some benevolent cave.

Iron fixtures held logs the circumference of small trees, but the massive space remained cold and dark. Her heart dropped like a stone through ice water. Of course, it remained unlit. This was someone's private kingdom, someone wealthy enough to build castles in the arctic. They were probably lounging on some Caribbean beach while their monument to excess stood empty and frigid.

But someone lit that chandelier. There had to be matches somewhere. Kindling. A switch to the gas. Something to resurrect this slumbering giant of a fireplace and warm her frigid soul.

She ransacked the heavy wooden cabinets built into the stone surround, her fingers still numb and clumsy from the cold, making every simple task feel herculean. Finally, in the third cabinet...*salvation*. Matches and a pile of birch bark that some thoughtful soul had prepared.

She gathered the materials against her chest and rushed back to the hearth. Stripping off her sodden coat, she shivered and focused, her trembling hands making it impossible to strike the match on the first or even the third try.

"Come on, you fucker." Another match snapped, and she growled through her chattering teeth as her body jolted. The tremors were getting worse.

"Light, goddamn it!"

The epic struggle to coax a flame infuriated her to tears. Her hands shook so violently she dropped several broken matches, and when she finally got a spark, it quickly faded like a dying star.

"Please, please, please," she desperately begged, cupping her quaking hand around the tip as a small flame came to life.

Marigold held her breath, leaning over the kindling as the flame kissed the birch bark. Relief breathed out of her, nearly destroying the little miracle, but the flame danced back, bigger as if fighting as hard as her to survive.

Air, it needed air.

Softly, she blew a shaky breath toward the wood, careful not to blow too hard. When it caught, she cupped the bark as if tending a sacred altar. Laughter bubbled out of her, spreading into a glowing smolder that scorched the dry wood, then quadrupled in size. Carefully, she laid it in the crevice of the smallest log and blew some more.

When real fire finally danced in the enormous hearth, the warmth and light bathed her like a holy baptism. She knelt as close as she could without getting burnt, letting the heat seep into her frozen skin while her clothes began the slow process of thawing.

For a moment, she indulged in the quiet warmth, shutting her eyes. But when she opened them again, the room now aglow from the crackling flames, her fingers were blue and her clothes still cold and sopping.

Warmth couldn't solve everything. She needed dry clothes.

It crushed her to leave the sanctuary of the marble hearth, but she wasn't out of the woods yet. Her garments clung to her body like icy chains as she forced herself to stand. Her bones and joints popped with objections, threatening to drag her back toward hypothermia's embrace.

Warm clothes. She needed to find warm clothes, then she could come back to the fire and sleep.

Shivering, she stumbled out of the massive room into the corridor, heat escaping her skin rapidly and bringing her dangerously close to death again. The ground floor revealed itself as a maze of common areas, each more opulent than the last. A dining room that could seat twenty like visiting royalty. Sitting rooms furnished with leather sofas and fur throws that probably cost more than most people's yearly salaries.

This was somebody's home. She was trespassing. But guilt be damned, survival trumped propriety every time. Hopefully, if the homeowner or a servant was home, they were merciful and not someone prone to asking questions.

Marigold wasn't sure how well she could lie in her current state, as exhausted as she was, but after coming this far, she'd do almost anything to survive. Personal items such as clothing remained elusive as she searched the house. Cabinets only hid dishes and strange, foreign collectibles that looked ancient and fragile. The curved staircase led her to the second floor, where corridors branched like arteries feeding the castle's heart.

She chose a door at random and pushed it open, revealing a sanctuary of masculine luxury. Dark wood and rich fabrics in deep burgundy and forest green created an atmosphere of controlled decadence. The bed dominated the space like an altar to hedonism, its frame carved with the same obsessive attention to detail that characterized everything else in this place.

But salvation lay in the wardrobe. Rushing over the threshold, she yanked the doors of the armoire open. Inside, she discovered exactly what her desperate situation required. Men's clothing, but that detail mattered less than the thick cable-knit sweater that would swallow her whole, the wool socks that could serve as leg warmers, and hanging in the back like a gift from benevolent gods, a fur coat that radiated more luxury than most people would see in a lifetime.

She stripped from her wet clothes with shaking fingers,

modesty abandoned in favor of survival. The sweater cascaded to her knees, sleeves dangling past her fingertips like a child playing dress-up. The wool socks transformed into thigh-high stockings. And when she wrapped the fur coat around herself, the sensation transcended mere warmth into something approaching rebirth.

The silk-lined fur was impossibly soft against her skin, and whatever magnificent creature had donated its pelt must have been enormous. The coat enveloped her completely, heavy and warm and scented with something masculine. Cedar and amber and something indefinably wild, reminding her of the untamed forests and hidden dangers she'd trekked to get here.

For the first time since fleeing Whitmore, she felt like she might actually live and allowed herself a moment of pride. Anyone who knew her would never imagine her capable of surviving what she'd been through in the last several months, let alone the last few hours.

She nearly laughed. Was she a badass? Maybe.

Up until recently, even she would have said that wasn't true. Marigold Calder was a sheltered appendage of her family name. But that wasn't true anymore. She was no longer Marigold. She was Mary Fuckin Langford, and she liked it.

Her stomach growled, disrupting her first true moment of cocky victory, then cramped with such fierce hunger that she doubled over with a sharp gasp. She couldn't remember her last substantial meal. Terror had murdered her appetite, but she wasn't afraid anymore. At least not to the degree she'd been. Now, it was all about survival and meeting her basic needs.

The kitchen, when she discovered it, existed on the same impossible scale as everything else in this strange palace, built from folklore as much as luxurious modern conveniences. If she was dreaming, she no longer cared. She planned to indulge in every opulent amenity she found.

Commercial-grade appliances gleamed like surgical instruments while the pantry could have stocked a gourmet restaurant. Unease teased at the periphery of her mind. If there was this much food, there had to be someone here. Maybe more than one someone. But she hadn't seen a single trace of life since she'd arrived. Only once-living-creatures, now stuffed and displayed throughout the great halls, watched her trespass this empty lodge.

"Don't judge me," she said to the stuffed fox staring her down from atop the cupboard.

Hunger outweighed her worry as she used the sweater as a basket to gather pilfered food.

She found bread—real bread, with substance and weight—not the processed, plastic-wrapped foam masquerading as nutrition in supermarkets. Whoever called this place home clearly didn't believe in half-measures.

Dumping her stolen items onto the table, she quickly unwrapped the packaging, taking frantic bites before even chewing what already filled her mouth. She groaned in satisfaction as the fresh food awakened the neglected taste buds on her tongue.

The cave-aged cheese wrapped in wax smelled like sophistication and privilege, nothing like the bland food they'd forced down her throat at Whitmore. The cold cuts tasted like they'd been cured by artisans who'd perfected their craft over generations. Her desperate, chilled hands carved off thick slices of cheese with a knife made for culinary masters.

Moaning almost sexually, she devoured the food, too impatient to make an actual sandwich as she stood at the massive granite table. She feasted, tearing into every offering like a creature possessed.

Her hunger ran deeper than missing meals. Weeks of barely eating while planning her escape. She suspected they drugged the food at Whitmore, so she abstained as often as she could manage while keeping her strength. Then, once she'd escaped, she'd spent days hiding from her family. Fear massacred her appetite. The closer she came to death, the less she thought about eating. This was the first time she actually allowed herself to feed a need other than basic survival.

When she'd finally silenced the worst of her starvation, her stomach cramped in a different way. Too much too fast. And the memories of the Whitmore facility weren't helping. She rushed to the sink, fighting back the urge to vomit, as she breathed through the onslaught of sickening memories.

She could still feel the orderly's hands on her as Willum's weight crushed into her. Smell the tang of his sweat over the overpowering scent of his minty gum. The disinfectant. The taste of rubber. The feel of being strapped down.

Marigold shoved her fist against her lips as bile rose, forcing it back down with the growing panic that accompanied her nausea. She didn't have to think about Whitmore anymore. She was free. No one knew where she was. She was Mary Langford now.

She needed a distraction if she planned to keep her food down, and she needed that nourishment in her body, so she decided to explore the rooms she hadn't visited yet. Brushing off her fingers, she carefully wrapped the cheese, bread, and meat, returning them as close to how she'd found them.

This place defied every expectation she'd harbored about wealth and power. The sheer opulence was staggering, but something else lurked beneath the surface. An edge to the luxury that she couldn't quite define.

Her wandering led her through rooms designed for adult entertainment, but the entertainment they had in mind was clearly sophisticated beyond her experience. One room was lined with bottles with labels written in languages she couldn't decipher, using letters never encountered. Another held furniture that didn't immediately make sense—chairs with unusual angles, benches with mysterious attachments.

It wasn't until she opened a door and found herself in what was unmistakably a dungeon that vulnerability slammed into her. Understanding slowly crystallized as she crept over the threshold.

The room was a study in beautiful darkness. Black leather and polished wood with fixtures mounted to the walls that looked both gorgeous and terrifying. Afraid to blink in such a place, she looked up at the chains where silk-lined cuffs dangled from the ceiling like jewelry. There were benches and crosses and devices she couldn't begin to identify, all crafted with the same attention to luxury and detail that characterized everything else in this mysterious palace.

This wasn't just someone's home. This was something else entirely. A private club, perhaps. The kind that catered to very specific tastes and a wealthier clientele.

Heat that had nothing to do with the fire or the fur coat bloomed across her cheekbones. She retreated from the room quickly, sealing the door behind her. But the images lingered, stirring something deep inside her that she'd rather not examine too closely.

Whoever lived here enjoyed power. Her mind declared the owner male, and once again, weakened by her female identity, she felt the infuriating stab of injustice. What if they were cruel? What if they caught her trespassing and decided to turn her in, or worse, punish her in that dungeon?

She couldn't stay here, but she also couldn't leave. Not yet.

The storm still raged outside, and she needed rest. For now, this strange place would have to do. But she wasn't sure if she'd willingly broken into a sanctuary or another prison.

The adrenaline that carried her through the night in her

desperate search for shelter was finally abandoning her, leaving her hollow and shaking. Exhaustion struck her all at once, crashing over her like a tidal wave. She needed sleep. Real sleep, not the fitful dozing she'd managed on the boat while nightmares chased her across dark water.

But she also needed a safe place to hide. Sleep would leave her vulnerable, so she searched for a resting place off the beaten path, following a hidden stairwell up to the third floor, where there appeared to be guest accommodations, though they were grander than any hotel suite she'd ever imagined. She tested the first bed—king-sized and topped with pillows that looked like clouds. But the mattress was too firm, unyielding beneath her weight like sleeping on marble. Too hard.

The second room held a bed that was even larger, almost throne-like in its proportions. But when she lay down, she sank so deep into the mattress she felt like she might disappear entirely. Too soft, like sleeping in quicksand.

The third room was different. Smaller than the others, though still larger than any bedroom she'd called home. The bed was proportioned for someone tall but not gigantic, and when she pulled back covers that felt like liquid silk and slipped between sheets that caressed her skin, everything felt just right.

The mattress supported her without rigidity, cradling her body perfectly. The pillows were soft but not suffocating, and the covers provided warmth without weight. Even the scent of the room was perfect—clean linen with hints of the same cedar and amber she'd noticed in the fur coat.

She should be ashamed of this massive trespass. Breaking into someone's home, consuming their food, wearing their clothes, and sleeping in their bed. But guilt was a luxury she couldn't afford. Tomorrow, she'd figure out where she was and decide where to go next. Tonight, she needed to sleep.

Despite her unshakable theory that the homeowner was

someone powerful and threatening, as sleep pulled her under, her last coherent thought was that she felt safer than she had in months. Hidden away in this strange palace, wrapped in luxury and warmth, she could almost pretend that the stone walls could protect her from the monsters she'd escaped. But then again, she had no idea of the monsters within.

CHAPTER 3

EYES IN THE DARK

Stone Volkov never slept through storms, a survival instinct carved into his bones by years of reading danger in shifting winds and atmospheric pressure drops that whispered of violence to come.

He stood sentinel in the surveillance room's ethereal blue-white glow, fingers wrapped around a warmed tumbler of clear Stolichnaya that had surrendered its chill an hour ago, but he sipped it anyway.

Turning back to the wall of monitors that transformed the space into a technological altar, his eyes narrowed. Each screen offered a glimpse into every corner of their fortress. Storms played games on the senses, waking ancient trees as the wind breathed life into ice-covered limbs. Illusions that could easily frighten little ones, but he'd grown up around far worse.

Outside, the storm raged with the fury of primordial gods denied their sacrifice. Inside, empty corridors stretched like arteries through the lodge's heart. Vacant rooms waited in patient silence. The great hall displayed its cold fireplace like an unlit funeral pyre, awaiting their next—

"What do we have here?" The motion sensor chimed softly, and his sharp, arctic glare cut to the upper screens with deadly promise.

Stone's brow furrowed, cold eyes flicking from one harbor camera to the next, his predatory instincts honed by years of eliminating threats before they could breach his sanctuary.

"What in fresh hell was this?" He zoomed in the lens, but the storm made it difficult to see small details.

The dock's weathered planks hosted an unexpected guest, small and shivering. A child? From where—here—at this time of night? Then he spotted the wreckage of what looked like a dilapidated boat that hadn't existed thirty minutes ago, bobbing against the waves like an abandoned toy in the distance.

"A castaway?" Whoever it was, they looked to be hauling themselves onto death's door. He glanced at the gauges. The temperature was below zero.

He was gathering his emergency rescue gear as the trespasser flailed onto the dock, flopping to her back and then falling completely still. He paused at the slight curves and long hair. *A woman?*

Interesting.

She looked half dead and would likely be fully there by the time he reached her.

No one approached this island uninvited. No one possessed the technology or connections necessary to sneak past their security. And no one could cross the choppy seas on a night like this without proper nautical gear and equipment. Or so he thought.

His fingers danced across the console, switching to thermal imaging trained on the trespasser. She was a determined little thing.

A single heat signature climbed the hillside, stumbling

through wind and sleet with the desperation of prey fleeing hunters. The figure moved too unsteadily, too frantically for the professional killers who occasionally tested their defenses.

How was she managing it? Her clothing was stiff and frozen, her balance off, and her feet were wrapped in cloth. Such determination had to spur from desperation. She was either running from something or aggressing toward something.

Stone reached for his phone to wake Hunter and Ash, but paused when the door camera captured the intruder's face, and the thermal readings hadn't prepared him for the reality of such desperate beauty.

She was vulnerability incarnate. Golden hair whipped around features that belonged in a museum. Those classical lines and ethereal beauty made his chest constrict with something he refused to acknowledge. Amber eyes looked up at the hidden camera, wide with desperation and flickering like precious stones held too close to a flame.

A woman. Young. Beautiful in a way that made dangerous men stupid and smart men reckless.

Stone set his vodka down with deliberate precision and leaned closer to the monitor, pale eyes tracking every nuance of her movements. She reached for the door handle, hands shaking so violently the tremor transmitted through the camera grain.

Taking pity on her the way one does a sacrificial lamb, he punched in the code. The other monitors showed the usual views—empty docks, silent forests, and in the distance, the glittering lights of the other isles. Even through the storm, he could make out the surroundings and saw no other incoming threats.

When the massive door opened, she stumbled across the threshold and practically collapsed on the polished floor. The foyer camera claimed her immediately. She stood, dripping, on marble that had witnessed centuries of Volkov power, her torn, stockinged feet wrapped in wet rags contrasting with her wet cashmere coat, marking her as either privileged or a thief.

"What the hell are you doing here, little one?" He zoomed in, noting the tremor of her eyes as her teeth noticeably chattered.

Their island was the furthest north, protected by fierce weather and bitter climates that devoured the unprepared. No way she made it here on that piece of shit boat.

Soaked to the bone, he wondered why she kept the wet clothes on. Perhaps she was sick in the head. Who knew how much time she'd been out there and how much she had left? He should help her, but instead, he merely watched her stagger from one room to the next, curious what she was looking for.

Maybe she was a decoy. A distraction.

His gaze quickly flicked to the other cameras, searching again for incoming threats.

Nothing.

Just her. She was either running from something or towards something. Maybe both.

He pulled his vodka closer and sipped, watching her discover the great hall with great satisfaction. "Ah, that's what you were looking for."

He reclined slightly, his mouth kicking up in a half smirk as he watched her search the hearth and nose around their private cabinets for kindling.

He chuckled. "Good girl. You're resourceful when you need to be." But despite finding the matches, her body shook so violently she couldn't seem to get the kindling lit.

He read her frustration through the grainy screen, grinning at her determination. When she flung off the expensive coat, his eyes widened. Definitely not a child. Her wet clothes clung to her like threadbare rags, translucent enough that he could see every vertebra of her spine as she kneeled before the hearth, hunched over the scraps of bark, fighting with matches to get them lit.

She drew back and stilled as a tiny flame flickered to life, then she blew delicate breath over the bark, spreading her creation, and her face came alive with hope.

"Poor little lamb," he said in a thick Russian accent as he studied her over the rim of his glass. "You nearly froze to death in the wild."

He should have called Hunter and Ash by now, but he liked having a chance to observe her in her unhindered state, before she realized she'd stumbled into the bear's den, before she understood she'd escaped death only to run into danger. And he liked having her all to himself.

"You should take off those wet clothes, little rabbit, before you freeze to death."

She confronted the mammoth fireplace like David faced down Goliath. Something tender stirred in his chest at her unbreakable resolve. Even when her body betrayed her with evident exhaustion and hypothermic shuddering, she refused to give up until she had the fire lit.

But she didn't last long once flames filled the enormous hearth. Stone found himself oddly proud of her resourcefulness, so he decided to give her a moment to bask in her small victory.

She lay down on the cold stone, visibly shivering as she curled onto her side, but she'd never get warm as long as she stayed in those wet clothes.

"Come on, little rabbit, you're smarter than that, aren't you?"

Her body stilled for a long moment, and he leaned forward in concern. Then she snapped out of her trance and forced herself up.

Looking back longingly at the raging fire, she staggered out of the great room into the hall. Her instability might be more than just the effects of the cold. A dry trickle of blood curled down the side of her face, but her hair covered the source of the injury. Perhaps she was concussed.

As she hobbled through the house, she moved with a rheumatoid gait, likely from the stiffness in her bones, but she also held her left shoulder as if it ached. She followed the corridors, scurrying like a mouse locked in the shadows as she tested door after door, seeking something specific, and moving on when she didn't find it.

When she reached Hunter's room, she rushed inside. She was damn lucky he wasn't there, or her little exploration would have ended abruptly.

Stone switched monitors and brought up the image as she ripped open the wardrobe and pilfered the armoire shelves. Arms full, she carried the stack of stolen clothes to the bed and stripped away her soaked clothes.

He should have been prepared, but there was no warning for what he would see. Long, delicate limbs leading to a pert little ass so ripe he wanted to sink his teeth into it. The feminine flare of her hips spoke of hardiness, but there was something utterly fragile about her tapered waist. He bet he could hold her captive in the span of his bare hands.

Her breasts, pale and full, hung like inviting fruit, fresh for the picking. Stone's mouth watered, and he swallowed just before her beautiful body was engulfed in wool. The sweater draped her like an ill-fitting dress. She pulled thick hunting socks up past her knees, further emphasizing her petite size.

She was... *voskhititelny*. "Exquisite," he whispered, letting his thick Russian accent savor the taste of the word as if he were tasting her. "Sit on the bed, little one. Show me more."

Unfortunately, that was the end of the show as she shrouded herself in an old fur coat he hadn't seen in years. It engulfed her from shoulder to shin.

Enchanted, he watched her bring the fur to her cheek so she could nestle in its softness. She closed her eyes and breathed deeply of the silk lining, and his jaw locked. His fingers curled against the desk, his nails scraping into the polished surface.

She looked around the room and, for a moment, her desperation disappeared. The start of a smile danced across her lips, then she doubled over in pain.

His brow knit with concern, but he saw nothing with her buried in fur and wool. Perhaps an injury he'd missed.

Brushing her hair out of her face, her skin glistened with a thin sheen of sweat. He glimpsed a deep gash on her temple and cursed himself for not searching her body more closely for bruises or identifying tattoos when he had the chance. He could rewind the feed, but she was on the move again.

"Where are you going now, quick little rabbit?"

Her strides were slightly steadier as she retraced her earlier steps with purpose. She was learning the layout of their home, which both bothered and impressed him. She saw rooms not open to the public, and he wondered why he hadn't yet notified his brothers that they had a trespasser.

The kitchen cameras revealed her desperation in stark detail, and he zoomed in once again. She devoured food like she hadn't eaten in days, tearing into artisanal bread and aged cheeses with the hunger of someone who'd forgotten that sustenance was a luxury, not a guarantee. This wasn't the practiced nibbling of a woman worried about her figure. This was survival eating, raw and honest and beautiful in its desperation.

She was running. The question was from what? Or whom?

Stone's fingers moved across the console like a pianist interpreting Rachmaninoff, switching between cameras to follow her exploration of their domain. She moved through the common areas with wide-eyed wonder that suggested familiarity with wealth but not with wealth like this.

The style of her earlier clothing, though torn and soaked, whispered of money, old money, inherited money, but her behavior spoke of someone unaccustomed to the kind of power that built private kingdoms.

This was no princess. This was a refugee.

Once her appetite was satisfied, she neatly wrapped the food and returned it to the cupboard.

"What nice manners you have." He chuckled. "Steal our food and clothes, but put them back sweetly."

He didn't mind her thievery because she was doing the hard part for him. Dry clothes, a warm house, and a full belly. It wouldn't be long before she crashed. And then she'd be at his mercy.

He followed her curious journey from one lens to the next. When she discovered the second-floor playroom, Stone's breath crystallized in his lungs.

"Careful, little one." He zoomed in to see her face more clearly.

She froze in the doorway, like a deer scenting predators, staring at the equipment and sensing the edge of danger it implied. The confusion painted across her features was genuine. She didn't understand what she was seeing. Not completely. But some part of her knew.

A flush of color that had nothing to do with the lodge's warmth flickered across her face.

Curiosity.

He leaned closer to the monitors, pulse quickening as he watched with a slow grin. "See something you like, *Zayka*?"

Her hand slowly reached out, only to still before touching a single surface. She backed out of the room slowly. Her palm pressed against the closed door for an extended moment, as if she wanted to understand but had to deny herself the time to explore in order to prioritize survival.

. . .

HE CHUCKLED. "COWARD."

He tracked her exploration to the third-floor bedrooms. The cameras were Stone's masterwork. High definition and night vision capable, positioned to capture every angle of beds that had witnessed pleasure in its most exquisite forms. He'd installed them personally, taking pride in the image quality that would make Hollywood envious.

Never had he been so grateful for his perfectionism.

She tested the bed Hunter preferred during club events, bouncing once and moving on with the decisive dismissal.

Stone grinned. "Of course, you'll want something softer for sleep."

The next bed was made for slow seduction and long cuddles, Ash's domain during parties. She sank into memory foam and wrinkled her nose like a cat offered substandard caviar.

"Sweet, little, precious rabbit. You're used to comfort, aren't you? I think I know exactly what you need."

He switched cameras and waited as his bedroom door opened. Despite his pleasure that his bed suited her taste, his jaw clenched when she pulled back the covers.

His room. His sheets. His private sanctuary, to which no one entered without an explicit invitation. His nostrils flared as she slipped between the sheets, wearing Hunter's sweater and his spare sable coat. The sight of her there, golden hair scattered across his ivory pillows like spilled champagne, sent molten heat shooting through his veins like liquid fire.

She looked like she belonged there. Like she'd been born to grace his sheets and warm his bed. The thought was so unexpected, so completely inappropriate, that Stone shoved back from the monitors as if they'd turned radioactive.

He snatched his phone, stabbing out a text to his brothers like he was declaring war.

GET DOWN HERE. Now.

Hunter's response materialized instantly.

WHAT'S WRONG?

There wasn't time to explain in detail. Showing them would be easier.

SURVEILLANCE ROOM. Now. Bring Ash.

Stone poured fresh vodka while he waited, keeping one eye on the monitor displaying the sleeping intruder and the other on the door. She'd curled on her side with one hand tucked beneath her cheek.

In sleep, she appeared fragile, breakable in ways that had nothing to do with physical strength. But he knew better. There was untapped strength inside of her, the kind borne of will and suffering more than muscle.

His fingers tightened around the crystal tumbler as heavy footsteps announced Hunter's approach. In the last second of having her to himself, he grieved and accepted that she would never be solely his.

"What is it?" His older brother filled the doorway like a flesh-and-blood natural disaster.

Dark hair tousled from working out, sweat still slick on his bare chest, and black cotton pants that slung low enough to display the roadmap of scars across his torso. Each mark told a story of violence survived and lessons learned in blood.

"We have a visitor."

"Someone dies tonight," Hunter growled in Russian, scanning for threats across the machines.

"Not yet." Stone gestured toward the monitor watching his bedroom. "There."

Ash materialized behind Hunter, his characteristic silence intact. Stone didn't need to see him to know he was there. He sensed him like a shift in atmospheric pressure that drops the temperature and kills the wind. Where Hunter was brute force and volcanic fury, Ash was controlled violence wrapped in deceptive calm. Ash moved with surgical precision disguised as meditation.

Glancing back to read his brothers' expressions, he took in Ash's dark jeans and a thermal shirt that outlined every muscle. His alert ice-blue eyes zeroed in on the screen despite the ungodly hour. "Is it a child?"

"No."

"A woman," Hunter said matter-of-factly.

Stone watched Ash's expression transform as comprehension dawned. "How did she penetrate the island?"

"Boat." Stone indicated the harbor camera. "She climbed up from the dock approximately ninety minutes ago."

"She? You're sure?"

"Positive."

Hunter's low growl dropped to a register that made smart people reconsider their life choices. "And you waited ninety minutes to alert us?"

"I had a handle on the situation."

Hunter approached the central monitor with predatory focus, the one displaying Stone's bedroom. The brand on his back, right shoulder glinted under the dim blue lights of the security feed. "That little thief broke into our house?"

"I didn't feel like digging a hole through two feet of snow."

His brother's molten eyes glared at him. "You let her in? A perfect stranger—"

"She was soaked to the bone. A minute longer, and she would have died out there."

"That's not the point. She could be dangerous."

Ash chuckled. "I think we can handle her, Hunter."

Stone rolled his eyes. Might as well get it all out in the open now. "She's also been consuming our food and stealing our clothes."

Ash squinted at the lump of fur surrounding her face. "Is that your old fur coat?"

Hunter growled.

"Just be glad she's sleeping in *my* bed. I've got the situation under control."

The three brothers stepped back from the monitors in contemplative silence, each watching the woman sleep and wondering what the next move might be. She'd kicked away some covers, and the sable coat had fallen open to reveal the elegant line of her thigh beneath Hunter's oversized sweater. The cascade of her hair spilled like gold, catching candlelight.

"She's exquisite," Ash said quietly, his voice carrying that dreamy quality that meant fantasies were crystallizing.

Hunter grunted in agreement. "Beautiful women are dangerous."

"No, not her. She looks like a fallen angel," Ash argued. "She's just a lost little lamb who wandered into a bear den."

Stone glared at Ash. Not a lamb. She was *his* rabbit. "She

wasn't aimlessly strolling about, Ash. The little *zayka* was desperate for shelter."

"An angel in a storm. Let's wake her up."

Hunter caught Ash's sleeve. "Angels don't commit breaking and entering." His black eyes were fixed on the monitor. "Angels don't steal."

"So maybe she's not an angel." Ash's smile could have cut diamonds. "Maybe she's something far more interesting."

Stone switched to thermal imaging replay, showing them her arduous approach to the lodge. "She was nearly dead when she arrived. Hypothermic. Starving. Desperate."

"Running from something," Ash observed, back to clinical detachment. "Or someone."

"Which means desperation drove her actions." Hunter cracked knuckles, the sound similar to breaking bones. "Desperate people make mistakes."

"Like trespassing on property belonging to men who always collect their debts," Stone agreed, leaning against the console with deceptive casualness.

"So we agree," Ash said. "Violating our sanctuary without invitation means one thing and one thing only. We aren't going soft."

"Agreed." Hunter's arms bulged as he crossed them over his chest.

Stone glanced at her defenseless form. Her breathing had finally found a peaceful rhythm, and tension no longer pinched her features. "So what's our response?"

Hunter's answer dropped like an edict. "Wake her up. Extract information about her identity and purpose. Then decide whether she lives or disappears."

"We could contact the authorities," Ash suggested without much conviction. That wasn't how they operated on The Island.

Stone's laughter roughened with disbelief. "And reveal

what? That someone breached our private club? The one that doesn't exist in any official capacity?"

"We handle this ourselves," Hunter decided with finality. "Like we handle everything else that threatens our domain."

Pragmatic as always, Stone pulled up the Doppler. "The storm won't break for hours. She's not going anywhere regardless of our intentions."

"Who says we want her to leave?" The question came from Ash, and both Stone and Hunter turned.

There was nothing Stone could do to help this golden-haired thief with her desperate eyes now that they saw her. She was as good as theirs. But thinking back to her determination with the fire and how battered she'd been from the cold, he knew she wasn't built for captivity. "What if she just needed shelter and a warm place to rest? We could just give her a place to catch her breath and let her—"

"She violated our rules," Hunter pointed out in his unbending militant tone. "You break it, you buy it. That's always been our policy."

"She owes us," Ash agreed with mastered casualness. "At least until the storm passes. We ensure she's... appropriately grateful for our hospitality, then we decide when and how we let her go."

"*If* we let her go." Hunter's grin contrasted with the storm of violence swirling in his dark eyes.

Stone switched camera feeds to display the storm still savaging the landscape outside. Wind howled around the lodge like hungry ghosts, snow and sleet turning the world into a frozen hellscape.

"She has nowhere else to go." Even if she could reach her shitty little boat, she'd never survive the crossing in these conditions.

"Trapped," Hunter murmured with satisfaction. "Little thief trapped herself in a predator's den."

Ash chuckled and rolled up his sleeves.

Stone checked his watch. Three-seventeen in the morning. "We wait until she wakes naturally."

"Why?"

"Because I said so." His protective instincts kicked in. "Let her believe she's safe a little longer. It'll make her shock that much sweeter."

"Fine. But we approach her together," Hunter ordered. "Then we introduce ourselves properly and explain the house rules."

"Sounds good." Ash left the room, and Hunter silently followed.

Stone remained in the surveillance room's electronic glow. He told himself it was for security purposes, to maintain vigilance against any additional surprises the storm might deliver. But his attention kept drifting to the bedroom camera, to the woman sleeping so peacefully in *his* bed.

He gave them his word they'd approach her together, which meant he was shit out of a bed tonight. With a sigh, he swept his vodka off the desk and lounged back in the office chair, crossing his hands over his broad chest. As he sipped, his finger clicked the mouse, zooming in.

She'd burrowed deeper under the covers, and something about her protective position made him wonder what had driven someone like her to risk her life. Whatever her reasons, she'd soon learn everything came with a cost.

THE AWAKENING

A cool breeze swept over Marigold, and she surfaced from sleep, stingily curling into herself, chasing the dream she'd just lost. A draft crossed her shoulders, and she frowned, reaching for the heavy coverlet.

"Get up." The sheet ripped from her body in one violent motion, exposing her to biting cold.

With a gasp, she bolted upright, heart hammering against her ribs with the frantic rhythm of a caged bird, as three massive figures loomed at the foot of the bed. Ancient gods carved from shadow and menace.

"W-who are you?" she sputtered.

"Who are we?" The blond one laughed.

A scream crystallized in her throat, emerging as a strangled gasp when the dark one leaned forward, planting a massive fist into the mattress with enough weight that her body shifted.

"You're in our house, little girl."

Her eyes widened as she took in their suffocating presence. They stood like motionless monuments, blocking every escape route with their imposing presence.

"Let's start with your name," the one with long, shaggy hair twisted into a knot on his head commanded.

"Mm—" She'd almost said Marigold, but caught herself. "Mary."

The side of the blond's mouth curled into a half-grin. "As in had a little lamb?"

"Y-yes."

Light filtered through the floor-to-ceiling windows, chasing away the night shadows and casting the men in the soft glow of dawn. Tall, broad, radiating danger. Every survival instinct she possessed shrieked warnings to run, but there was nowhere to go. No sanctuary left to claim.

Marigold scrambled backward like prey until her spine collided with the headboard. All three men watched her. One with amusement, another with something akin to concern, and the other like a predator eyeing its prey, as if he planned to eat her alive.

She tugged the oversized sweater down over her bare thighs with trembling fingers. The sable coat had fallen away while she slept, now trapped beneath her weight, and she must have kicked off the wool socks overnight. "There was a storm—"

"Did we say you could speak?"

Her trembling lips pressed tight, and she trapped them between her front teeth.

The blond one snicked his tongue, and her wide-eyed gaze jumped to his face. "Submitting that easily? Where's the fun in that? Go on, little lamb, keep bleating. Give us a chance to force your silence."

Her heart hammered hard enough that she felt it against the headboard pressing into her back.

"You're scaring her," rumbled the man on the left, his voice rough and dangerous and completely uncompromising. "That's my job." Dark hair fell across features that belonged on wanted posters, and when he smiled, his full lips stretched with barely restrained violence.

The third man maintained perfect silence, but his black eyes tracked every tremor that rippled through her body with the focused intensity of a mercenary. There was something terrifying in his stillness, something that hinted he wanted to be entertained and liked an element of surprise, much like a cat waited for a mouse to flee.

The long-haired one stepped closer to the bed with fluid grace. "Tell us why you broke into our home." His Russian accent was smooth as ice, and his eyes equally as sharp.

How far had she sailed once she got off that plane? Had she crossed into foreign territory?

He called it his home, but what if he meant more than the property? She thought about the dungeon downstairs. This wasn't some empty vacation house waiting for distant owners to return. This was a place of secrets. These men led very private lives, and she'd trespassed on their personal property. Slept in one of their beds.

She needed to get out of there. Preferably alive and in one piece. "The storm," she began, but the dark-haired giant severed her words with harsh laughter.

"The storm made you jimmy our lock?"

"It wasn't locked," she protested. "I swear."

The blond glanced back at the long-haired one who casually lifted a shoulder. He appeared the most civilized, but she wasn't fooled. She could see every muscle under his designer wool sweater. And his ice-blue eyes were unreadable as an arctic sky.

"Ah." The blond nodded. "So, because the door was open, you felt entitled to steal from us?"

"I'm not a thief!" The denial burst from her with more force than wisdom.

"No?" The quiet, threatening one finally spoke, his voice a

low rumble that vibrated through her bones and settled in places she didn't want to examine. With his fist still buried in the mattress, he could grab her leg in one quick lunge. "Then what would you call someone who enters a home uninvited, consumes the owners' food, wears their clothes, and sleeps in their bed?"

Heat flooded her cheeks like spilled wine. When he catalogued her transgressions so clinically, they did sound like theft. But what choice did she have? The alternative was freezing to death.

"I was dying," she confessed, lifting her chin with more defiance than she felt. "Would you have preferred to discover my corpse at your doorstep?"

The long-haired man's grin widened with predatory appreciation. "That depends."

"On?"

"How you're willing to pay for our hospitality."

Was this what they considered hospitable? It was difficult not to scoff, but she wanted to live. The tone of his statement made her skin crawl with dread and unwelcome heat.

"I don't have any money. I lost everything—"

"There are other ways." The man with long dark hair dropped his gaze to her legs as the blonde circled to the side of the bed.

Marigold's head snapped toward him like trapped prey tracking a hunter. His clean-shaven appearance did nothing to ease her tension. Every muscle in his body, all the way to his perfectly edged jawline, spoke of controlled discipline. Nothing about this man was unintentional, and something in his poised presence told her he'd witnessed horrible things in his life, things that would have made weaker men beg.

He stared down at her with cold-blooded detachment. "You've put us in quite the position, little thief."

"Don't call me that."

"What should we call you then?" The long-haired one moved close enough that she could see his eyes. They were the most exotic green she'd ever seen, like pine needles under ice. "We all know you're name's not really Mary."

Did they? Wait. How? That was impossible. Even as Marigold, people sometimes called her Mari. She instinctively reached for her pocket, forgetting for a moment that she'd changed clothes. Shit. Where had she left her documents?

"Lose something?"

Her lips hardened. "I'm Mary. Mary Langford." She tried not to tremble under their combined scrutiny. "I lost most of my belongings at sea, but my ID was with my clothes. It's here."

"Right." The quiet one said, but his acceptance felt more like an accusation. "And what brings Mary Langford to our little corner of paradise?"

"I told you. The storm—"

"Drove you to our island specifically?" The blond's smile could have cut crystal. "How convenient. Tell me, little lamb, how did you even know this place existed?"

The question struck too close to the dangerous truth. "I...I lost control. I nearly capsized. It's not like I planned this."

Her stolen invitation still rested in the real Mary's coat pocket, and if they found it, they would know her story was a lie, but it seemed safer than her original plan, if this was, in fact, the Isles of Kassel and by some miracle she made it to her destination.

"I'm not even sure where I am." She continued, forcing her expression to remain neutral despite the panic clawing her insides.

"So, you were just out exploring, on a bitterly cold night like last night?"

Of course, they didn't believe her. "I had no idea anyone

lived here," she said with manufactured lightness, brushing over their suspicions.

The dark-haired man moved to flank her other side. She was fully surrounded. "Exploring? In an ice storm that could have killed you, in designer clothes and heels that cost more than most people earn annually?"

They'd seen her clothes. Did that mean they also saw her paperwork? Her shoes must have washed up on the coast overnight. These men missed nothing, catalogued everything, and stored details like ammunition.

"I wanted to get away," she said, keeping her lies as near to the truth as possible.

"From?" the quiet one asked with clinical precision.

Marigold's pulse hammered in her throat hard enough to make her dizzy. They were too close, too observant, and too intelligent. The walls contracted around her, closing her in, making it difficult to breathe.

One foot before the other, Marigold. She pictured her mother's voice, waiting for the calm to push back her creeping panic. *You can do anything you—*

"We asked you a question."

Her calm receded with the fading memory of her mother's gentle support as they bore into her with the demanding question. But she was used to being bullied.

"Haven't you ever wanted a vacation?"

The blond one held a black duffel. "Maybe this will help you cut the bullshit." He extracted her stolen coat, still sopping wet, and dumped it onto the bed. "You won't mind if we examine your belongings."

She lunged forward, attempting to grab the coat, but the dark-haired man caught her wrists in an unbreakable grip. "Not so fast, Goldilocks."

"Get off of me!"

"Be still." His narrow stare dropped to her body. The corner of his mouth curved then flattened as he looked at her with those haunting green eyes, as if daring her to try his patience. He clamped her arms in one hand, passing her off to the silent giant. "Hunter, hold her while we look over her things."

The largest one gripped her wrists behind her back. She jerked forward, but his hold was unbreakable. "You can't do this!"

His enormous hand tightened until she feared he might crush her bones.

The green-eyed one with long hair laughed. "We can do anything we want, *printsessa*." His accent transformed consonants into weapons, Russian heritage evident in every syllable. "This is our house. Our island. Our rules."

She didn't know what was worse, the large one's silence or the other one's taunting. She looked to the blond for help, but he only crossed his arms over his equally broad chest. Their united front was clear. She was the intruder, and they were the law. She glanced back at the giant holding her, her gaze meeting fathomless black eyes.

She instantly dropped her stare.

Every inch of him was thick muscle, and he did nothing to hide his brute strength. With a torso like a tree trunk and arms built to crush, he could snap her in half without even breaking a sweat.

This one—*Hunter*, the one with green eyes had called him— wasn't like the others. He was worse. There was something utterly untamable behind his obsidian scowl. And when his glare narrowed on her, she stopped struggling immediately, recognizing when she was outmatched.

The heavy scruff around his jaw did nothing to hide the hard angles of his face, and his mouth never strayed from a flat line. His dark skin, marked by old scars, told a story of survival.

Nothing about this man was vain. He merely existed in the rawest form of masculinity she'd ever seen.

The casual way he restrained her with one massive hand demonstrated just how powerless she truly was in this place. He wasn't even breathing hard, wasn't even trying, while she squirmed like a fish on a hook.

The other one's molten green eyes settled on her face, as the giant's thumb brushed across the delicate skin of her inner wrist, then loosened enough for her to break free.

She stopped struggling, stopped squirming, and looked back at him in question. She was free. She turned to green eyes.

"What do you think will happen if you run, little rabbit?"

The blond glanced at the blizzard outside the tall windows. "In case you haven't noticed, there's nowhere to go."

My god, they were terrifying.

Cowering, she scanned their faces but found no sign of compassion. These men did not want her in their territory, and they were the only shelter for miles. "Please," she said, softening her tone. "I swear, I'm not a danger to anyone. I just need a place to stay."

"This isn't the Ritz."

Thunder rumbled outside the windows, and wind howled. A grey hell made of wind and sleet seethed on the other side of those stone walls. She came here for shelter and willingly walked into a cage, but there was truly nowhere else to go.

"There has to be a way. You have plenty of room—"

"Do not speak of what we have," the quiet one snapped in a thick Russian accent. "What we have is a pest in our home."

"I swear, if you just give me a few nights—"

"You're staying," Green Eyes said, contradicting the larger one, as if it wasn't even a question. "You trespassed on private property. Now, we decide when you get to leave."

His threatening promise landed like a gavel in a corrupt hand. "Until the storm passes?"

"Until we say you can leave."

"You can't keep me here forever."

"That's not your decision to make." The blond searched her coat pockets with methodical precision, withdrawing her soaked paperwork and dropping it into a pile on the bed beside Mary's license, a few crumpled bills, and the wrapper of her last snack. He looked at her expectantly when he finished his search.

A sense of violation raced through her, stirring up familiar, indignant fury until she snapped, "That's all I have."

"No, it's not," the green-eyed one dragged his stare down her body.

"What else do you want?"

"We want to know why you're really here." The quiet one reached over her to flip the identification card right side up, and she caught his scent—cedar and something wild that made her recall the forests they used to play in as children.

"I told you. I got lost."

Green Eyes cocked his head as if to silently tell her they all knew that was a lie. She looked at the blond, but he shook his head. When she glanced at the silent giant, she again lowered her gaze.

"We're going in circles." Green Eyes reached back to adjust the tie in his long brown hair, and her gaze drifted to his ridged abdomen, hardly concealed by his fitted thermal shirt. "What are you willing to do to make amends for your transgressions?"

"Transgressions?" Fear transformed into anger, and anger made her reckless. "I was dying! I needed shelter!"

"And we provided it." The rugged, dark-haired man's grip tightened on her upper arm just enough to remind her who controlled this situation. "Fed you. Clothed you. Kept you warm and safe through the night. That kind of generosity isn't free."

"I can pay you back," she said quickly, words tumbling over each other. "Whatever you think I owe—"

"With what?" The blond flicked the pile of trash on the bed. "This? A few bits of trash and a license I'm almost certain you stole."

"I'm not a thief!"

"Tell me this coat was yours." The blond lunged forward, speaking through gritted teeth. "Tell me where you bought it, how much you paid for it. I. Fucking. Dare. You. Tell us one more lie."

Ice formed in her veins as he held up the invitation and flicked the damp paper until it unfolded. The elegant cardstock was meant to be her ticket to freedom. Now, it served as the damning evidence that would see her punished, and possibly cost her her life.

"Kassel's Winter Gala," he read with the focus of a scholar. "A private invitation made out to none other than..." His eyes flicked up to meet hers with predatory intent. "Mary Langford."

The quiet one flipped over the plastic ID, and the three men looked at her. "Mary's a brunette."

"Haven't you ever heard of bleach?"

They laughed, taking a moment to relax as if this was all in fun—then she was on her back, pulled into the middle of the bed as they flipped up her sweater and spread her legs.

"Let go of me!"

They did, just as the one with long-dark hair chuckled. "Sorry, blondie, your honeypot says otherwise."

"Honey gold from crown to cave." The blond looked into her eyes with that cool arctic stare, tasting his lower lip. "A little thief and a little liar."

"I'm Mary Langford! I swear."

"I'll remember that." The blonde tucked the invitation into his pocket with a sense of territorial entitlement. "I'm sure you won't mind if we verify your identity with Kassel authorities?"

Panic clawed at her chest with razor talons. But wait... Did that mean she was in Kassel? She'd made it? Dear god, she was a badass.

"You seem impressed with yourself."

Her unintentional smile vanished. If they contacted the authorities, if they started asking questions, it would all be over. Her family would find her. Drag her back. Lock her away again, this time permanently.

"Please," she whispered, the word scraping her throat raw. "You don't understand."

"Then explain it to us," the quiet giant said with deceptive gentleness. "Start with your real name."

She stared into his cold black eyes but found no mercy. None of them seemed the least bit compassionate. And why should they be? She broke into their home, stole their food and clothes, told them lies, and looked nothing like the real Mary Langford. They held all the cards, and they knew it. But she couldn't give them the truth.

"I can't."

"Can't?" Hunter flashed his white teeth in a snarl. "Or won't?"

"Does it matter?" She was trembling now, and not from the cold. "You're going to turn me in anyway."

"That outcome depends entirely on you, little thief." The rugged giant released her arm, his massive frame caging her against the headboard. "We're reasonable men. We believe in negotiating."

"What does that mean?"

"It means," the quiet blond said softly, moving to drop a knee on the bed. He crawled close enough that she could feel the heat radiating from his body. "We're willing to keep your secret.

Protect you from whoever you're running from. And allow you to stay here." He trailed his finger up her leg. "For a price."

Hope fluttered in her chest, then quickly transformed into a shiver. "A price?"

"A steep price," he added, his words falling like guillotine blades.

The three men watched her with shared understanding. They'd calculated this outcome before approaching her. This was always the result they'd expected, and at no point did they plan to walk away with less.

"I..." She swallowed tightly, unsure what to say, but clear on what they were asking. Fearful she had no choice but to agree to their terms, she searched her mind for any other alternative.

"A stolen identity. Showing up in the dead of night. Kassel has very strict rules about unwelcome people showing up unchaperoned and uninvited." Those penetrating green eyes glanced at the weathered invitation. "You stole this, thinking it would be enough. Unfortunately, that's not how it works around here. There are consequences."

The blond trailed a finger down her leg. "You understand, don't you, *Mary*." It wasn't a question, but she nodded anyway.

"Yes."

The long-haired man leaned close to her neck and breathed deeply, with a satisfied growl. "Until your debt is paid or the weather breaks. But fair warning, if you run, you're only tempting us with a good chase."

"And we love a lively hunt." The one with blond hair grinned. "It's going to be a long winter."

"Does that mean I can stay?"

He shifted close enough that she could count the gold flecks in his ice-blue eyes. "*Printsessa*, didn't we just make that clear? You're not permitted to leave until we say so."

"But, you expect me to..."

Green Eyes grinned. "You'll do exactly what we tell you to do. When we tell you to do it. No questions. No arguments. No escape."

This couldn't be happening. "And if I refuse?"

His smile was as sharp as a scalpel. "Then we make a phone call."

"After the authorities come for you, it won't be long for whoever you're running from to follow. But, if you consent to our terms, we'll protect you from whatever enemy is out there." He pointed toward the window where the storm raged outside.

Protect her under circumstances where she had absolutely no control. "You aren't leaving me much of a choice."

"There's always a choice. Just like you chose this home, these clothes, and this bed. Now, you get to choose if you stay or go."

They wouldn't call it a choice if they knew what her other options were.

Marigold stared at the three of them. Massive, dangerous men who held her life in their hands. Did they realize how much power they literally had over her? She should never have lied about not knowing where she was going. She could have kept up the story of Mary and shown them the invitation. But hiding her intentions gave them all the leverage they needed.

She had no other choice but to give them what they wanted, but she wouldn't give them her secrets. She would stick with her story and demand they call her Mary, whether they believed her or not. She would do anything to avoid returning to where she'd been.

"What exactly are you asking me to do?" she whispered, the words barely audible above the thundering of her own heartbeat.

The quiet one leaned down, his face angled over her thighs, as he made a show of breathing her in. When he looked up at her with possessive arctic eyes full of chilling promise, he grinned and said, "Everything."

That single word carried the weight of her destiny. Outside, the storm howled like a living thing, but inside this room, she had gone deadly still. If she planned to survive these monsters she had to be courageous enough to let them devour her whole.

If she managed that, and managed to keep them from killing her or turning her in, she might actually make it to the end of winter. Then she could start her new life wherever she wished. But tonight, the real nightmare was just beginning.

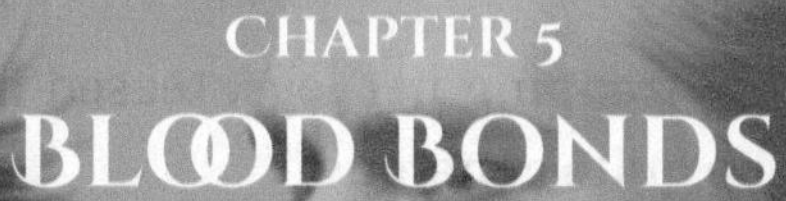

Everything.

The word echoed in the silence like a funeral bell tolling for her former life.

Marigold's hands fisted in the oversized sweater, knuckles bleaching white against charcoal wool. Her mind raced through impossible calculations. The storm outside that promised certain death. The men surrounding her offered something potentially worse. The only other option was to say fuck off and let them turn her in. But it would only be a matter of time before her family found her.

The blond lowered to the bed with the others, his pale eyes holding warmth but no mercy. "The question is, *printsessa*, are you intelligent enough to survive us?"

Something flashed in his cold eyes. A dare, perhaps. He looked at her as if he already knew all her secrets.

"I can survive anything that doesn't kill me."

His full lips stretched into a slow smile. "I'm counting on it."

His confidence in her put her strangely at ease. Of the three men, the blond seemed the safest. Or maybe she was just too desperate to face reality.

"We need to hear it from your mouth, little rabbit." The long-haired one watched her with that deep green stare. "Your full consent."

The blond, now trapping her legs, teased his finger higher. "We can actually be quite generous."

"Generous?" The word emerged strangled, disbelieving. "You're talking about—"

"Mutual benefit," he interrupted smoothly.

The silent one leaned back into the pillows beside her, no longer bothering to restrain her. She caught that intoxicating scent again, wild and dark. The less he said, the more intimidating he became to her.

"Lost, alone, perhaps on the run, in the dead of winter... You need protection," the blond said rationally. "We need entertainment."

A sound rumbled from the dark giant at her back like an avalanche racing toward her. "Entertainment. That's one way to describe it."

She glanced at him for a split second, and her eyes darted away. What gave a man so many scars on his face and hands?

"You don't even know what I'm running from."

"We don't care."

"Here, we're judge and jury on all that matters. If you work with us, we'll see that nothing bad comes for you."

Was it really that easy? She had no doubt they possessed the power to defend her in this fortress they called home. But was it nuts to trust them? They could also turn on her, lie, or trick her. "Why should I trust you?"

"You shouldn't," the scarred one at her back said, matter-of-factly.

His callous tone sent dread worming through her insides.

Then he touched her, and she stilled. "You should fear us. Not because we're bigger. Not because there are three of us and one of you. You should fear us because it's wise."

"Not to mention," The green-eyed one added, "that delicious tang fear adds to a woman's taste."

Unwelcome heat bloomed in her belly as hands tightened over her flesh ever so slightly. Around her hip, between her thighs, loosely framing her wrists as if to deliver an unspoken message.

"You want to push my hand away," the one with the green eyes taunted, voice thick with suspicious distrust.

It was a test. They told her the terms. Now, she had to honor them. She bet he loved scaring women with his enormous size and all those terrifying tattoos and scars. He looked like he'd escaped a Norse tribe.

She wouldn't give him the satisfaction of cowering, so she lifted her chin defiantly. Showing him she was stronger than she looked.

"Ah, there's that strong will I caught sight of last night." Those attentive green eyes teased her with mocking approval. "Chased in by the cold. I was the one who unlocked the door for you, you know?"

Because he took pity on her or because he saw her as prey and wanted to lure her deeper into his domain?

"What better option do you have?" the blond asked.

He studied her with the intensity of a predator scenting prey. She'd once read that when faced with a wild animal, like a wild bear in nature, the best thing to do was scare it. The minute a person ran, it became a game, and the bears always won.

She wasn't going to show them fear. No matter how much they scared her, she would not give them the satisfaction of knowing she was afraid.

She needed to show them she wasn't a weak little woman or

some pitiful concubine to pass their wasted time. "What exactly do you think I am?" she demanded, anger flaring despite her precarious position. "As a Langford—"

"Cut the crap." The blond rolled his eyes. "Rich girls don't wash up on remote islands alone. They arrive in private jets with security details and enough luggage to outfit small armies."

"Maybe I'm not that rich."

"Your coat disagrees." The blond held up the ruined cashmere, flashing the Hermès tag. "Or is it Mary's coat? I've never been great with names, *printsessa*."

Marigold's heart plummeted into her stomach. They didn't believe her. Now would be the time to admit her identity and belongings were stolen. She honestly wasn't sure if the lies were making matters worse or helping her. But she had the sinking fear that it was only a matter of time before they found all her secrets out. Then what would they do to her?

"You want to tell us the truth," Green Eyes said. "I can see it in your eyes, the desire to unburden yourself and be free from the lies." He caught her chin when she tried to look away, forcing her to face him. Face the truth.

She shut her eyes, and he let her go.

"Stolen invitation, stolen identity, stolen coat, probably stolen shoes. I wonder if she paid for the manicure."

These men noticed everything. The quiet one's gaze raked over her hands, and she instinctively curled her fingers to hide evidence of her privileged upbringing. "You're wrong about everything." Even to her own ears, her words lacked conviction.

"Are we?" The playful one at her legs lowered his chest, further caging her in at the knees. Heat radiated from his powerful frame. "Prove it. Tell us who you really are."

The weight of their combined attention pressed down on her like a physical force. Three pairs of eyes—emerald green, black obsidian, and ice-blue—all focused on her with laser intensity. They were waiting for her to crack, to spill secrets that would destroy the fragile new life she was trying to build.

She couldn't do it. Wouldn't do it.

"I told you my name. It's Mary Langford. I was visiting when I got caught in a storm."

The rugged one snorted with derision. "Bullshit."

"Hunter," the blond's voice carried a note of warning that could have frozen summer rain. "Leave it."

Hunter... How oddly fitting for a man who made her feel trapped since the moment she first saw him.

"Leave it?" Hunter's attention snapped to the blond with incredulous fury. "Every word out of that pretty mouth is a goddamn lie."

"That doesn't matter." The blond's tone was perfectly controlled, perfectly reasonable, the voice of a man accustomed to being obeyed. "She's here. She's agreeable. What difference does it make who she was before?"

Before.

The word hung in the air like smoke after the flame. Marigold realized that, to these men, her past was already dead. Maybe so was she. Even Mary Langford—or whoever she claimed to be—would cease to exist the moment she agreed to their terms. Agreed to be theirs.

What if this was merely them playing with their food and they never planned to let her go?

"The difference," Hunter growled, voice dropping with malice, "is that secrets are poison. What if she came here for a reason? Someone could be looking for her. We don't know who she's working with."

"Look at her." The handsy, green-eyed Viking said as he caressed her thigh, dragging his warm palm slowly upward.

"She's already agreed whether she's admitted it out loud or not. You guys are bickering about irrelevant bullshit."

Her thighs pressed together, stopping his hand from traveling any further. He stilled, their eyes locking in challenge. He could have easily overpowered her. Instead, he released her thigh and rolled casually to his side. "We all know how this is going to end."

"Stone," the blond said in warning. "Until she agrees, nothing is promised."

"Use your head," Hunter, the largest of the three, snapped. "She's making it too easy because she's hiding something. Stop thinking with your dick."

"You're paranoid." Stone glanced up at her with those penetrating green eyes. "There will be plenty of time to get to the truth. Our little thief isn't going anywhere. Are you, sweetheart?"

The endearment sent heat spiraling through her chest like liquid fire. He wasn't her ally, but he wanted her to believe he was.

She glanced out the window at the steel-wool sky, coarse and laden with dark clouds as the relentless blizzard locked her in. Stone's hypnotic touch returned to her leg, unraveling something inside of her as he traced small circles against her skin.

"Such a long winter..." he teased, tracing his finger higher. She should pull away, should be disgusted by his presumption. Instead, she forced herself to relax under the contact like a flower unfurling beneath the sun.

She needed them. And they wanted her. It was a steep price, but the cost of her survival.

Sensing her agreeability, his mouth curved with a slow grin. "You'll learn, in time, that I have ways of getting women to talk. Hell, I've even made a few drop to their knees and pray."

"Do we have your agreement?" the blond pressed, reminding the others, "Nothing happens without her consent."

How strange that they required such an intangible accord when they clearly held all the power. Their cards weren't on the table, but hers were. She was a body with a stolen identity, desperate to protect her secrets and willing to do anything to survive. They didn't care if she lay in a bed of lies, as long as she understood it was theirs and submitted to their absolute authority while under their roof.

"Ash asked you a question," Stone said, his green eyes taunting as his trespassing touch teased at the hem of her sweater.

She looked at the blond he called Ash. "I..."

She struggled to see a safer option. There was so much risk attached to their request. She didn't fully understand who they were and what—exactly—they wanted from her.

Hunter didn't seem as eager as the others. But they didn't seem to need his approval. His silent suspicion made her question her safety. None of these men pretended to be harmless, but Hunter seemed downright dangerous.

The blond's cold pragmatism hinted at depth. Perhaps he would be her safest ally. Though she would be a fool to trust any of them.

And the teasing one, Stone, he just looked like he wanted to devour her. "You'll let me stay?"

"On our terms."

"You have to agree," Ash pushed. "Full consent."

"For how long?"

"Until you change your mind. One whisper of the word stop, and it's over. You leave, and we go back to our long winter of hibernating."

"What about the police?"

"No loose ends," Hunter, the lethal silent one, stated matter-of-factly.

It was as much a promise as it was a threat. They would allow her to stay, on their terms. The moment she disagreed, she was out the door.

"Have you ever surrendered to a man, *printsessa*? Truly surrendered?" Ash's voice turned thick like honey. "Unburdened from choice to simply exist for his pleasure and yours."

She'd surrendered more than she ever wanted to admit, but there had been no pleasure. "Choice isn't a burden. It's a privilege."

"In some cases. But not in all. You *have* a choice, but if you choose to stay here under our protection, that will be the last one for a while."

One and done. "I have to decide now?"

"Yes," all three said at once.

The impossible decision they laid out positioned her like a chess piece already in check.

"She's tired," Stone murmured, his honeyed voice a mocking promise of safety. "Overwhelmed."

Ash dragged a long finger up her leg. "Why don't we start simple, *printsessa*?"

"Simple, how?"

His smile was soft around the edges, nothing like Stone's sharp grin or the chilling expression of the grizzly giant, who she now knew was Hunter. "You're sore. Exhausted. When's the last time you had a real meal? A hot bath? A chance to simply... breathe?"

The kindness in his voice almost shattered her carefully constructed defenses. He lulled her closer to acceptance with the promise of creature comforts.

When was the last time someone had offered to see to her well-being without expecting payment in blood or silence? Not since before her mother died. Not since the world revealed its true face.

It was transactional safety, but safety all the same—*If* they spoke the truth and kept their word. "Will you hurt me?"

The silence stretched.

The fact that not a single one jumped up with assurance spoke volumes. She lowered her gaze. "I see."

Ash patted her thigh the way a coach might tap a player's shoulder. "Food first. Then we'll discuss the small print." He stood and extended his hand with the grace of a prince. "Trust me, *printsessa*. We only bite when it's deserved."

She'd suffered the undeserved consequences of countless crimes she'd never committed. What if they found out about the things she'd done to survive? Would they bite then?

What if they turned on her when she least expected it?

Instinct warned, this was their nice side, despite her trespassing. As long as she was willing to work with them, give them what they wanted, she would be safe. Safer than she had been in some time. She didn't want to find herself on the receiving end of their anger.

"Come on, *printsessa*." Ash reached for her. "Let's take a walk —just the two of us."

As trusting as a lamb off to slaughter, she slipped her fingers into his warm grip and nodded. He firmly grasped her hand, gently pulling her to the edge of the bed. Stone and Hunter watched as she slid to her feet.

"There's a good girl." Ash tucked her hair behind her ear. "Looks like you could use some first aid, too. I have just the stuff."

Her hand fluttered to her temple where his gaze focused, and she felt the crust of dried blood. He pulled her hand away from the sore spot.

"Careful. If it starts bleeding again, you might need a stitch."

What the hell was happening? Why was he being so nice to her?

He wove his large fingers between hers and glanced back at the guys. "We'll be back in a while."

Silently, she let him lead her out of the room where she could breathe a little easier. She tested his honesty by cutting right to the point. "Why are you being so nice to me?"

"Turns out, I'm a nice guy." His accent wasn't as thick as the others', and she wondered if Russian was his native tongue or something he'd learned through association.

"Are those men your brothers?"

"As far as you or anyone else is concerned, yes."

That didn't exactly answer her question. "You're not Russian."

"Very good, *printsessa*."

"But your brothers are."

"Correct."

"And you're not British."

"Correct again." He released her hand and pressed his large palm to the small of her back, urging her through the door of a dark room. "I'm a Volkov. End of story."

His tone made it clear that the story was not a public one, but she imagined he'd paid his dues to adopt their last name and surrender his own. In some ways, bonds as loyal as theirs were far thicker than blood and water.

The lights flickered on, and she found herself standing in a large bathroom. "I'm afraid your sea adventures have left you a bit...odorous. There's soap and toiletries in the drawer. You have five minutes." He backed out of the room, and the door clicked.

She tested the gilded knob, only to find it locked. Wasting no time, she rushed to the standing shower and turned the golden handle to the highest setting of heat. Steam filled the room, and she quickly undressed.

The spray announced cuts and bruises she hadn't catalogued. Grime funneled down the drain, and her muscles unfurled under the warm water. She didn't have time to luxuriate, knowing Ash would be back in less than two minutes, so she quickly washed the dirt from her body and did her best to detangle her long curls—pausing briefly to appreciate the delicate citrus scent of the products. But when she tried to read the labels, they were written in a different language, with an alphabet she didn't recognize.

The door opened just as she was wrapping herself in a plush towel. She looked through the steam at Ash, nervously.

"Another sweater." He handed over the folded wool and turned his back. "We'll see about getting you some better-fitting clothes."

His respect for her modesty surprised her. "Thank you."

He turned just as the sweater fell down her thighs. Taking a step closer, he inspected her clean face. "You've had quite a journey." He lifted her fingers, noting how her nails had chipped and broken. He reached behind her and opened a drawer. "For your hair." He placed a wide-toothed comb in her hand.

Marigold had read stories about kidnappers showing kindness to their captives. It was a sort of grooming meant to condition them for other things. As she detangled her curls, she watched Ash's reflection in the mirror, but his focus was elsewhere. Only when she set down the comb did he meet her stare in the glass.

"Ready?"

Her mind screamed no, but she nodded anyway.

The kitchen was every bit as impressive in daylight as it had been during her desperate midnight raid. Gleaming steel appliances caught morning light like mirrors, granite countertops reflected her uncertain face, and windows offered stunning views of the storm-ravaged landscape. The world was buried in ice and snow, and she felt as if they were encased in time.

Ash moved through the space with proprietorial ease. "First, we play doctor."

She let out a startled squeak as he surprised her by hoisting her onto the cold counter.

He chuckled. "That'll teach you to run around bare-assed." He pulled open a drawer and removed a bottle of disinfectant, some gauze, and a tube of ointment.

"Are you a doctor?"

He laughed, ripping open the plastic casing around the gauze. "No."

Moving to the sink, he wet a folded dishcloth he found in another drawer. Gathering her hair, he twisted the damp strands securely behind her shoulders. "Hold still."

She did as he commanded, taking the moment to study his face closely as he attended the gash. He was possibly the youngest of the three, but also the most pragmatic. There was a gentleness about him. A nurturer beneath the beast.

Though his appearance—now that she was less terrified— wasn't beastly at all.

His body was thickly muscled, the kind of chiseled brawn honed from years of physical activity, but his eyes were soft and teasing when he watched her with that arctic blue stare. All sharp cheekbones and sea-glass eyes, his face seemed carved for sin yet tempered by a softness that betrayed something human beneath the polish.

There was something playful about him that the others lacked. She bet he had dimples when he smiled. He was beautiful in a dangerous, quietly devastating way—refined but ruinous. His short, blond hair had a tendency to curl at the ends, underscoring his lightheartedness rather than rigidity.

"You're not trembling anymore." Even the way he smiled—

lazy, knowing—felt like a secret meant only for her. "That's good."

Lost in thought, she could only silently stare, wondering how such angelic perfection could house a truly dangerous soul. Magnetic, masculine, and utterly impossible to look away from, this one was going to require careful caution because he was already gentling her with a false sense of safety she was smart enough to know didn't exist here.

"It's not too bad," he pulled away the cloth, and she sucked in a breath at the sight of blood. "That's just from cleaning it up. It's not as deep as I thought." He blotted gently. "What happened?"

So much had happened in the forty-eight hours, she couldn't remember what specifically caused that specific gash. "I bumped my head."

His ice-blue gaze met hers. "You don't say?"

"I don't know," she admitted, and he smiled.

"You're prettier when you tell the truth." He wet the cloth again and dabbed away the last of the blood.

Were her lies that obvious? "Do you blame me for wanting to protect myself?"

"No." Setting the cloth aside, he uncapped the disinfectant. "This might sting. Shut your eyes."

Her lashes lowered, and she wondered if it was stupid to trust someone who basically wanted to keep her as his prisoner. She sucked in a sharp breath through her teeth when he doused the cut.

"Sorry."

Idiot that she was, she believed him.

Pressing her lips tight, she tried not to twitch from the sting.

Warm air blew softly over her temple, and the pain receded. "Better?"

She opened her eyes and forgot how to breathe. He was

close enough that she could see the stubble under his skin. By night, his jaw would be covered in a golden five o'clock shadow.

He gently swabbed ointment over the gash. "This should help with scarring. You can keep it." He pressed the small tube into her hand.

"Thanks," she whispered.

"My pleasure...*printsessa*." He didn't back up or reach for the gauze. Somehow, he'd worked his way between her knees without her noticing. But now she was very aware of how close they were and that she wasn't wearing anything beneath the sweater.

"Ash..."

He smiled, and she was right about the dimple. "Say it again."

"What?"

"My name."

"Ash."

Silence stretched between them, neither one of them moving away. If anything, she might have leaned closer. Maybe she'd hit her head harder than she thought. Wasn't there a name for people who developed feelings for their captors?

Her eyes drifted past his shoulder to the butcher block stuffed to the gills with sharp knives.

He caught her chin, forcing her gaze back to his. "Don't go there. It won't end well for you."

"Is there any way this ends well for me?"

"I'm not your enemy."

"How can you say that when you know nothing about me?"

"I know people. Anyone can do terrible things when pushed hard enough. Who pushed you, *printsessa*?"

The urge to bare her soul took her by surprise. She couldn't be so trusting. Dropping her gaze, she broke eye contact.

"I see." He lifted her chin. "Here's what I do know." He

dragged a calloused thumb over the delicate bone of her cheek as if to emphasize how breakable she was. "If you turned on us, I know who would win." He pressed a finger under her chin, lifting her gaze to further meet his. "And so do you."

He was right. If she somehow armed herself against them—three to one—they would have her disarmed within seconds, and that would be the end of their kindness. But this wasn't kindness. This was captivity.

"Will I regret staying, Ash? If I give you what you want, will I eventually hate myself for it?"

"You never know." He shrugged and gathered up the trash on the counter. "Scrambled eggs?"

The intimacy vanished as if it had never existed at all. She remained on the counter as he pulled ingredients from the massive refrigerator with practiced efficiency.

"Or are you more of a pancake girl?"

"I'm not really hungry."

He shot her a look. "I thought we established you're prettier when you don't lie."

"What makes you think pretty is some monumental goal of mine?"

"Isn't it every girl's?"

"No."

He returned to the island and caught her shoulders in a gentle grip. "Pretty or ugly, we all need to eat. When's the last time you had a substantial meal?"

"Last night."

"Bread and cheese hardly constitute a meal." His hands closed around her ribs, and her spine lengthened as his fingers swept along the underside of her breasts. "You need to put some meat on these bones." He stilled, noticing her tension but not removing his hands. "Does my touch bother you?"

Her jaw trembled. What could she say? They both knew the

deal. She dropped her gaze again, but he didn't let her go. "Does it matter?"

"Yes, it matters." He held her without force, but also in a way that made his entitlement clear. "We're not interested in your suffering, *printsessa*."

She gave a subtle shake of her head, admitting his touch—as of this moment—was not as abhorrent as she'd assumed it might be. She could abide intimacy like this, though her tolerance did have its limits.

He moved his hands higher, now cupping her intimately enough that her nipples pressed through the wool between her flesh and his palms. "How about now?"

Breath tight in her lungs, she looked up at him with pleading eyes.

"You don't have to be afraid with me, princess."

Men loved to say things like that, but they would never know what it was like to feel threatened at the market or endangered by simple jogging with headphones in after dark.

He purposely held her breasts through the sweater, waiting for her to shove him away. "You want to say something, but you're afraid to share too much," he whispered, warm breath tracing over her cheek. "I love a challenge. Soon enough, I'll know all your secrets."

Cold slithered through her veins. That could never happen.

She met his stare, this time her eyes issuing the challenge.

He grinned and lowered his hand, sliding it expeditiously under the draping sweater in one swift move. "How about now?"

The heat of his palm teased upward, gentle and smooth. Other men had touched her far worse.

"Here's a crazy thought," he whispered. "What if you give us what we want and it turns out you enjoy it? What then, *printsessa*?" He grazed the soft curls at her apex, then dragged his other hand higher. "It feels good to surrender, doesn't it? No responsibility. No shame."

The heat of his hand closed around her breast, lifting the weight as he gently cupped her.

"You don't have to think. You only have to feel."

His thumb brushed over the pebbled tip, and she fidgeted ever so slightly, inadvertently pressing her body closer.

"There you go. Give in to the pleasure. Admit it's not all that bad to be ours."

Ours.

How could he touch her like this, then let them do the same? She tried to imagine Hunter's hands on her, and her shoulders hunched inward.

His hand disappeared the moment her body language shifted to uncertainty. He turned away from her so fast she swayed, slightly off balance.

"Breakfast." He cracked eggs into a bowl with the precision of a chef. "You need protein. Something to put color back in those cheeks. Scrambled or fried?"

As if summoned by his words, her stomach produced an embarrassing rumble that made him glance over his shoulder and grin.

"Scrambled eggs it is." He had no issue deciding for her.

She wondered if he'd honor her choice and give in to her preference if she spoke up. Tugging the sweater down to her knees, she watched him cook, fascinated by him despite her unease.

His movements were economical, precise, like he'd performed this ritual thousands of times before. Did they frequently find women trapesing around their halls in the middle of the night? Something about this seemed too practiced.

He whisked the eggs into silky batter as butter heated in a

pan. When he pulled fresh herbs from a drying rack in the corner, she wondered how any garden could thrive in this arctic wasteland. They must have trucks delivering goods, which meant trucks would also leave.

"You don't look like a cook," she said in an attempt to make small talk.

"What do I look like?"

She studied the strong line of his jaw and the golden hair curled at his nape. His casual strength was evident in every movement. "Dangerous."

"I am dangerous." He glanced at her, ice-blue eyes dancing with amusement and darker promises. "But I'm also practical. Can't survive on takeout forever. And we get very few deliveries out here over the winter months," he added, as if sensing her train of thought.

"Do you live here year-round?"

"This is our home—among other things." He slid perfectly scrambled eggs onto bone china and set the plate in her hands. "Eat."

"Fork?"

He shook his head slowly, as if daring her to disobey. "Use your fingers."

Was that because he was testing her, or because he didn't trust her around sharp objects? She wouldn't give him the satisfaction of a challenge. Plucking up a cluster of fluffy eggs, she popped them in her mouth and nearly moaned.

The eggs were creamy and rich with hints of fresh chives and something that might have been truffle oil. "Wow."

"I'm glad you approve." He grinned. "Now me."

She stilled, and understanding dawned.

Pinching another delicate cluster between her fingers, she slid it into his mouth. He caught her wrist the moment she tried to pull away, forcing her hand to stay there as he sucked them clean, his eyes watching her response closely.

When he released her, she continued to stare. No one had ever licked her hand like that.

"Keep eating, *printsessa*. It's getting cold."

To her, it felt warm. She tried to eat slowly, to maintain some dignity, but hunger won out. Within minutes, the plate was empty, and she was licking her fingers much like he had.

"Better?" Ash asked, his voice warm with approval.

"Much." She felt almost human again. "Thank you."

"Don't thank me yet." His smile held shadows that quickened her pulse. "It's time to test your commitment."

Before Marigold could ask what he meant, he took the plate from her hands and pressed her shoulder, forcing her to lie down on the countertop. "What are you—"

"Relax." He slid a dishcloth under her head. "I want to see if you're strong enough to follow through on your promises."

"Why?"

"Because we always do."

Her back flattened onto the cool marble countertop, and her heart thundered in her chest. All sense of safety gone.

CHAPTER 6

RELUCTANT SUBMISSION

Eyes wide, Marigold watched as Ash rounded the island, coming to stand behind her head. His thumbs found the knots of tension at the base of her neck, pressing with just enough pressure to make her gasp with relief.

"You're wound tight as a spring," he murmured, his breath warm against her ear as he leaned close. "When's the last time you truly let your guard down? Really let go?"

His fingers dug into her tired muscles, finding every sore spot and working it loose with careful precision. She'd been carrying tension for so long she'd forgotten what it felt like to let go of the pressure. But this was not the time.

"That's... that's not necessary," she managed, her voice breathy and weak.

When she tried to sit up, he pressed a stilling hand to her shoulder. "Isn't it?" His touch moved beneath her back, working muscles between her shoulder blades that were screaming for attention. "You're tight. Unrested. Running from something. Living on adrenaline and fear. That's no way to exist."

"You don't know anything about how I exist."

"I know you smell like desperation," he said quietly, the words sending electricity racing down her spine. "I know you sleep like someone who expects to be hunted. You flinch when anyone moves too quickly. And you lie to protect yourself."

His accuracy was terrifying. How could a stranger read her so easily?

"I wish you'd stop," she said, but the next muscle he pressed made her close her eyes and moan.

"Stop lying to yourself. You're not going anywhere. You know it. I know it. Hunter and Stone know it."

The mention of his brothers made her frown. His hands stilled on her shoulders. "That's the second time you tensed like that."

She couldn't make herself relax when she was so unsure of their true intentions. "Please... I want to sit up."

He released her, and she swung her legs around, not just enough to sit, but to hop off the counter. She thought distance would make her feel safer, but once on her feet his height only reminded her how much bigger he was.

"What are you running from?"

"I'm standing perfectly still."

"You know that's not what I meant. You've been running since you got here."

"You wouldn't understand."

"Then help me understand." He rounded the counter, his hands framing her face with surprising gentleness. "We invited you to stay. Do you think that's a common occurrence?"

"I wouldn't know."

"It's not. Trust me. Why are you so reluctant to let us take care of you?"

"You act like your offer is without condition."

"So what? Have you even asked yourself if the conditions are good or bad?" He waved an arm out, encompassing all the luxury that surrounded them. "You would want for nothing. Every craving, every thirst, every desire would be met. You would be safe from whatever has you on edge."

"In exchange for what?" she snapped. "There's a cost to surrender that men know nothing about."

He stilled as if she struck him. "Not all men." His thumb reverently traced the curve of her cheekbone. "Your desires would be met in exchange for letting us."

"That still doesn't answer my questsion. Letting you *what?*"

"Do whatever we want. It's that simple. We'd have you, protect you—"

"*Fuck* me?"

He smirked. "I know you're a brave girl, little thief." When she stiffened, he pressed a finger to her full lips. "Brave enough to risk your life for freedom."

She wasn't free if she didn't have free will. Sometimes, she felt cursed by fate. Certain other women had easy, normal lives with none of the suffering she'd known. "Why me?"

"You chose us."

"No, why am I the only woman—as you claim—to get an invitation like this?"

He didn't answer right away. After drawing in a deep, slow breath, he explained, "The winters are long on this side of Kassel. None of us take issue with isolation or the cold, and we entertain whenever possible, but this is different. This isn't for them, it's for us."

"Them?"

He grinned, but his smile didn't reach his telling blue eyes. "The ones we entertain. You aren't for them." His thumb traced the arch of her cheekbone again. "Just us."

"The three of you." He had to see how intimidated that would be to a woman in her position, of her size.

"You won't break."

"Maybe I'm already broken."

His soft chuckle was warm, soothing something inside of her with that misleading sense of safety. "I don't think so." He glanced down at her body. "You're small but hardy. Who's to say this arrangement won't also benefit you? See what it feels like to shut off your worry for a while. We'll protect you, Mary."

Her lashes lifted. It was the first time he called her Mary. But her satisfaction wasn't about finally fooling him. It was because she liked the sound of her name on his lips. Until she remembered it wasn't her name. He wasn't saying Mari as in Marigold. He was calling her by a stranger's name. And part of her was disappointed he was falling for the lie.

"I'm not brave," she whispered. "I'm a coward. Running away instead of fighting."

"Running takes courage, too." He leaned close enough that she could see silver flecks in his ice-blue eyes. "And courage is never without fear, *printsessa*. Run toward something that scares you. Run into the unknown with us."

Her lips tightened, but she was getting tired of shielding her emotions. "You're very good at this. Did they put you with me on purpose?"

"I'm here with you because I wanted to be alone with you." This time, there was no playfulness in his voice. "You see, *printsessa*, I've gotten used to getting what I want."

Her hips jolted forward, and a startled squeak escaped her throat as he cupped her bare ass possessively.

He quirked a smile that was part angel, part devil, that devastating dimple flashing like a dark promise hidden behind his tanned cheek. He lowered his head until his breath ghosted across her lips. His eyes closed, and he breathed deeply like some sort of wild animal. "I won't pretend I don't want you."

When he looked at her again, the intensity of his stare went beyond anything she'd ever experienced. "Ash."

"That's right. Say my name. Say it like a prayer. Let it be the first thing that crosses your lips when you can't take anymore, and you're begging for mercy." His smile curved and widened. "But you won't want it to stop. You'll be begging for it to go on forever—if you let me have control."

His hand slid under her sweater, fingertips between her ass cheeks. He gently pulled, spreading her in such a possessive manner that breath skittered past her lips. "Don't."

"Don't what?" The tips of his fingers only needed to shift ever so slightly, and he'd breach her.

"Do what you're doing."

"What am I doing, Mary? Tell me."

If he thought he could offend her modesty, he was wrong. "You're holding my ass."

"And?" He teased the crack, zeroing in on the tight little pucker. "Does it make your pussy wet, knowing I want to stretch every hole you have?"

All she had to do was walk away. She wanted to be the sort of woman who would slap a man for less, but she also wanted to see how far he'd push her. This wasn't just her test. It was his.

She swallowed, not confirming or denying.

"I bet those interior muscles are starting to clench." He leaned forward, trapping her earlobe between his teeth, sucking, licking, sending liquid heat to her core as chills raced down her spine. "Wanting to be filled..."

Her breath caught, and she shamefully moaned.

He released her ear and chuckled. "I've got you now, *printsessa*. Say mercy."

Her lips silently formed the word, but no sound came out.

"I didn't hear you." He dragged his touch between her legs, nudging her knees apart. She widened her stance. "Good girl."

Sliding a finger through her folds, he chuckled when he

found her slick with arousal. Mortification burned across her cheeks when he teased her open.

"Still think I'm hiding cruel intentions?" He curved his fingers, sinking his touch deeper until she leaned into him.

Her eyes closed at the unexpected gentleness. "Ash..."

"Yes?" He grazed his pillow-soft lips over hers, pumping his finger slowly through her shamefully slick heat.

"Ash, please..."

"Please, what, *printsessa*?"

She didn't know what she wanted. Her breathing turned heavy as she leaned into him, partially gripping his muscled shoulders for support, partially hiding her face against his neck in shame.

When he kissed her, it was gentle. Soft and careful, nothing like the brutal claiming she'd expected from a man like him. His lips moved against hers with infinite patience, like he had all the time in the world to learn the shape of her mouth and the feel of her body.

She gasped, losing the rhythm of the kiss, and clung to his sleeve. Thick, corded muscle twisted beneath her grip as he worked his fingers in and out.

"Getting braver now..." He rubbed and teased, more delib- erate than before, as if seeking that sweet release for both of them.

She should push him away. She should remind him she hadn't agreed to anything yet. She should try to maintain some shred of dignity. Instead, she melted into him like snow under an August sky.

Her hands fisted in his shirt, pulling him closer. Tension rippled through him, and she sensed him holding back in order to stay gentle with her.

"Once you give in, we'll show you things you never imag- ined. Things that make a woman's mind splinter into a thousand pieces while her body shatters like glass from the pleasure.

"You can't break what's already broken."

"No?"

"No." But what was wrong with her that she wanted him to try? She caught his wrist, edging him on, but he tore his touch away and turned her abruptly, backing her into the wall, his hand wedged between her thighs, two determined fingers pressing back inside of her. He kissed her with pure possession. Demanding that she prove she could take what he was doing and meet him halfway.

The kiss deepened, and she tasted the dark promises he kept. His tongue teased and taunted, making her stretch for more.

She gasped when his fingers struck a particularly sensitive nerve. Something between a growl and a prayer escaped his throat.

"Getting closer, *printsessa*."

He focused on her pleasure, driving his fingers into her as his thumb played cruel tricks with her clit, edging her toward climax and then making her wait. He knew what he was doing, dragging this out to make her beg.

"Ash, please... Don't tease me."

Dear god, was she actually begging this man to finish her? How was this her life?

"Say yes," he breathed against her lips. "Stay with us. Let us give you everything you need."

"I don't know what I need." She only knew what she wanted, and in that moment, his touch ranked number one on her list.

"I do. But you have to trust me."

His fingers delved and swirled, pushing her along that razor-sharp edge until she was mad with desire. Pushing the sweater higher, he forced her hand to hold the material at her ribs. He kicked her feet apart, widening her stance and causing her to lean into the wall.

She followed his gaze down, and gasped as he slapped her wet folds. "Soaking fucking wet and begging to come." Another slap followed by another startled gasp." Not hard, but fast enough to shock her. "Did you think it would be gentle? Easy? What fun is that?" He pinched her clit, and she grabbed his wrist.

Blue eyes flashed as he held her with that threatening stare, daring her to end this. The sharp warning was enough to keep him in control, enough to prove she didn't want to walk away. She stilled, his fingers unmoving, as the tightening pain spread.

"You trust me to know what you need. Trust us to take care of you."

"That's not pleasant."

"That's fear talking. Let the physical feeling process. Get control of your emotions. Don't let fear control you."

She breathed through it, and the sharp pinch transcended into liquid heat, melting her insides and burning her resistance to ash. The tension in her body noticeably softened.

"Very good, *printsessa*. You're only a few words away from ecstasy, now." He released his hold of her little bud and rubbed away the sting, teasing her with focused precision until she started to quiver. "Say it. Say you're ours."

God help her, she wanted to give in. Wanted to sink into his strength and let someone else carry the weight for a while. Wanted to believe that this beautiful, dangerous man could keep her safe from the monsters of her past.

His fingers sank deep, and he stilled, holding her on the precipice of something dark and unknown. "All you have to say is yes. Agree to be ours, and your worries are over."

Her spine stretched against the wall as he pressed deeper. "Ash—"

"Say it."

"I..."

"Say it. Submit. Why force us to be cruel when it feels this good to take it like a good girl. Don't you want to be a good girl, Mary?"

Her eyes closed in shame, but what other choice did she have? If this was her destiny, she might as well enjoy it. "Yes, I want it."

His lips pressed to hers, tongue dominantly taking control of her mouth as he smiled against her with ultimate satisfaction. "Very good, *printsessa.*"

He lifted her off her feet, hooking a strong arm under her legs as he carried her to a kitchen chair. He sat her on his lap, back to chest, and used his knees to spread her legs wide as he gave her privates another slap.

"Ah!"

"Be still. I want to show you something you'll never forget." His fingers wedged inside of her with absolute possession. Her slick folds were her body's shameful betrayal. Bunching the sweater in his fist, he held the material above her chest, exposing her bare breasts to the wide window.

Thankfully, there was only barren snow on the other side.

"Look at yourself in the glass, *printessa.*" He pulled her knees wider and fingered her faster.

She gasped and panted as pleasure built inside of her, needing a way out. The sounds her body made as he fucked his fingers into her should have mortified her, but she was too fascinated by her body's response to address the shame.

Leaning forward, her body bent with his as he reached for a glass bottle on the table. "This will help."

He doused her belly and thighs with what appeared to be

olive oil, then folded her legs upward, trapping them against her chest and under the hook of one strong arm. Her lungs compressed as he folded her like a pretzel. She'd been on the verge of climax, and she wanted him to finish her, but this position left her too exposed.

"Ash, wait."

"No. This is how it will be now." Fingers slick with oil, he fed them back inside of her, pumping faster and deeper until her climax ruptured into something all-consuming.

Her body tensed and spasmed, reveling in the fantastical finish, but he was far from done. He didn't let her come down. Instead, he pushed her higher, driving another orgasm out of her before the last fully left her.

It was too much. But he held her so tightly, folded on his lap, she couldn't get the words past her lips. Using the oil, he worked his touch deeper, purposely stretching her.

"Breathe, *printessa.*"

He was trying to fit all five fingers inside of her. "I can't."

"I can't hurt you if I vow to protect you."

"It's too much."

"It's not. Think of all the amazing things the female body can do."

He pushed his hand deeper, and panic took over. "*Stop! Stop! Stop!*"

His touch disappeared, but he held tight, as if afraid she'd bolt. "Look at me." The lash in his voice commanded her full attention.

Turning her head, she stared up at him in bewildered confusion.

"This is what you chose. If you walk away now, my brothers will keep their promise. You'll be in police custody within the hour. Your welcome, requires your full surrender to stay."

"I gave you my word, but what you're trying to do… It's too much."

"It's not. I'm trying to show you what it is to trust in the face of fear."

"There are physical limits—"

"And I'm well aware of them. Unless there's some sort of injury in your past that I'm unaware of, we've hardly grazed your limits."

"Physically, maybe, but mentally—"

"There is no *mentally*, not when you surrender. You trust us to think for you. About your pleasure and your safety."

"I can't surrender my free will like that. My body, maybe, but not my mind."

"Can I show you something? If you tell me to stop again, I will. We'll go find the others, and we'll begin arranging your transport home. You have my word."

Except she couldn't go home. "Please don't hurt me."

"Do as I say—*exactly* as I say—and there will be no pain."

Closing her eyes, she nodded.

"Good girl."

She gasped as he plastered her body on the flat surface of the table, using his dominating size to hold her down. "This will be a lesson you never forget." His hands traced up her arms until they folded over hers. He pressed down on her hands in a silent command for her to hold the position.

"You're scared. But I swear you're safe. Don't let fear steal this opportunity from you. You're so close to discovering a new sense of freedom. So close to safety. So close to feeling protected from whatever haunts you. You just have to trust us."

She shuddered under the gravity of his words more than she did from the weight of his dominant hold. His hands curved over hers, pressing her fingers around the lip of the table. "Hold the edge and don't move."

Tears welled in her eyes. "Why are you doing this?"

"To show you." He kicked open her legs, and more oil drizzled down her crack, sliding along her sex. Heat pressed into her back as he leaned close to whisper in her ear. "If you tell me to stop, I will. Everything will stop. We'll collect your things and never lay another hand on you. If that's your choice, we'll respect it. You'll become the magistrate's problem."

His fingers worked inside of her, soft and teasing like the way he'd started.

"Do you want me to stop?"

She bit down on her lips, trapping them between her teeth, and shut her eyes.

"Good, *printessa*. Very good." Deeper, he pressed, sometimes turning his pinched fingers in a corkscrew motion until he worked all four back inside. "You have to trust that we won't hurt you. That means truly understanding your limits."

She didn't feel pain. She felt fullness. Pressure. And panic.

When she gasped for breath, he sensed the presence of something other than pleasure. "Your panic's tricking you," he whispered, not backing off but gently smoothing a hand over her damp hair. "Breathe with me. In."

She matched his deep inhalation.

"Out." His hand continued to calm her as the other breached her sex in ways she couldn't fathom. "In." His voice was coaxing her away from that edge of terror where anxiety took hold. "Out." He waited for her breathing to settle, and then he praised her. "See how brave you are." He kissed her cheek. "Such a good girl." He pressed deeper.

Her fingers curled tightly around the lip of the table as a whimper escaped.

"Don't tense. Stay loose. Keep breathing." He added more oil. "The only thing preventing me from getting inside of you is your mind."

He kept his booted stance inside of hers, forcing her legs wide, the rasp of denim against her bare inner thighs a delicious friction that made her squirm. He rested his free hand on her spine.

"Feel your body stretching to accommodate me." He gently pressed and pulled, wedging his exploring touch deeper by small degrees. "I think you want to please me, but you're afraid to admit it, afraid to discover what that says about the kind of woman you are."

He was right.

"It doesn't have to mean anything beyond the fact that you're a good girl who takes what we provide."

There was so much oil, she could only feel the pressure. Deeper now, he rocked his knuckles inside of her. It should have hurt, but instead something strange unfurled, and her lips parted on a sharp gasp.

"You're feeling it now."

Every sensation was strange and new. Intensely over-whelming.

"Some would be shocked to see what a woman's body can handle. A fist. An arm. Three massive cocks."

She sobbed—the building pleasure refusing to be denied by silence. No idea how deep he actually was, she sensed his presence inside of her through every nerve ending. Her muscles contracted, and her body no longer obeyed her brain. Ash had become the puppet master. He held the strings and had complete control of her.

"I like when you make noise, *printessa*. It shows your control's slipping. Each startled gasp of pleasure's an invitation to take a little more."

A guttural sob escaped, borne of hedonistic confusion and carnal sin.

"That's it. Take it like a good girl for Ash. Nothing sexier than a woman's surrender." He pumped his fingers deeper. "Such courage. Do you feel it? Feel my hand inside of you? Feel the power of disarming the fear."

As he moved, her brain short-circuited. In and out, with slow, firm, dominating thrusts that drove her to her toes and rocked the table.

The sounds that escaped her were raw and primal, torn from depths she didn't know existed. The moment he gave her permission to speak, she couldn't shut herself up. Every thrust pushed a cry out of her, his masculine groans rumbling like distant thunder as she clenched around his invading fingers.

She felt him everywhere, rippling through her veins like fire that burned with erotic delight. His clothing rustled behind her, but she couldn't see him. He purposely held her in a position where she could only feel.

Her cheek rested on the table as he vehemently fucked his hand into her, but not painfully. He was not rough, but rather determined.

"Now, I want to hear my name from that pretty mouth of yours."

"Ash," she bit the word out on a moan.

"Again."

"*Ash.*"

"Louder."

"*Ash!*"

The guttural grunt from his chest should have warned her, but she wasn't prepared. He shoved the sweater up her back as his hot release spattered across her bare ass. The masculine scent of his raw arousal tripped her past that final layer of resistance until she was screaming his name in ecstasy on a string of profanities and confessions she had no way of stopping.

CHAPTER 7

HONEY & LIES

Marigold jerked as Ash placed a cold compress between her legs.

"Easy."

Confused as to how she was back on Ash's lap, she frowned at their surroundings. No longer in the kitchen, she wondered if she'd blacked out. "What happened?"

"I believe you caught a glimpse of euphoria."

Last she recalled, she was plastered to the kitchen table being fisted by this complete stranger. A weak smile ghosted past her lips as she murmured, "I did it."

"What's that, *printsessa*?"

She hadn't said stop. She submitted, and it didn't break her. But that sense of pride was something just for her. Veiling her satisfaction, she blanked her expression and said, "Nothing."

He pressed the cool, damp cloth against her swollen folds, but her body wasn't as sore as she'd expected. At least not there. Her legs, however, trembled, and her throat was ravaged from screaming. How had the others not heard them?

"Do they know what you did?"

"I'm sure they watched."

She stiffened. "What?"

He caught her chin in a gentle grip and angled her gaze toward the brass bear head in the corner. She'd seen the wall fixture in several rooms before.

"Wave, *printessa*."

Her lips parted, and she shifted to close her legs.

"*Uh-uh-uh.*" He held her thighs apart. "I'm not finished."

"Are they watching us now?"

"Someone's always watching." He slid her to the bed. The room was plain compared to the others she'd visited.

"Is this your room?"

"No. But it's connected to one of the better bathrooms." He disappeared through a door, and the familiar sound of rushing water met her ears. "Your bath will be ready in a few minutes. Do you need anything? How do you feel?"

"I feel..." *Strange? Violated? Enlightened? Confused? Unsteady?* "A lot of things."

"Trust?"

She met his stare. "Am I allowed to say no?"

He chuckled. "Of course. But your resistance to trust will only make your part that much more challenging."

Oddly, it was hints of his indifference that aggravated her most. "No, I don't feel trust."

"You will." He held out a hand. "Come."

He led her into one of the most opulent bathrooms she'd ever seen. White marble from floor to ceiling, and an enormous bathing pool in the center with a three-foot lip around the edge. It was something designed for gods.

Steam rose from the water as Ash set out towels, a robe, bath oils, and soaps, then poured bubble bath into the water. He swirled his fingers inside, and the scent of roses filled the air. "You can undress."

She searched the walls. Sure enough, a small brass bear head was mounted to the center of the vanity mirror, in clear view of the bath. She stared into the bear's eyes, hoping whoever was on the other end could see her disapproval.

She hadn't felt ashamed until she learned they had an audience. Now, she was humiliated. How could she willingly let him do those things to her?

Removing her sweater, she held it against her chest, protectively covering her front, turning her back to the tub so the cameras couldn't see her ass.

"Hell." Ash was on his feet and touching her in half a second. "What have you done to yourself?"

"What?" She turned and gasped when she caught her reflection in the mirror. An angry, black bruise covered her shoulder.

"I think you're past the point of ice, but I'll get some anyway. Let me help you into the tub."

He held her hand and helped her as if he were a complete gentleman, not a blackmailing pervert who just did unthinkable things to her.

She hadn't realized how sore her body was until she sank into the warm water. Her muscles sagged with relief as the heat wrapped around her.

"I'll be back in a moment with your ice. If you need anything..." He pointed to the brass bear.

He left her unsupervised, which should have been a relief. However, knowing she was never truly alone, she felt safer with him nearby.

A shadow passed by the frosted glass of the door—too tall to be Ash returning already. Her pulse quickened as the shadow paused, lingered, then moved on without entering.

· · ·

MARIGOLD SANK LOWER in the water, sheltering her body beneath the foamy bubbles. She groaned into her hands. How had this become her reality?

"Hiding?"

Startled by the deep voice, she jolted with a splash. Not Ash, but Stone. "Where did you...?"

He held out a large, fabric ice pack. "For your shoulder."

She hesitantly took the ice and draped it over the lip of the sunken tub so she could press her sore shoulder into it, her eyes never leaving Stone's emerald stare.

"Are you hurt?"

She shook her head, unsure if he was asking about her back, her temple, or other regions. Where was Ash? Did he know Stone was here?

Stone settled onto the lip of the tub and watched her. "You agreed."

She nodded, but hoped he didn't plan to take her from the warm bath to prove his authority the way Ash had.

"I watched you last night."

She gave him her full attention as she guided bubbles over the surface to better block his view of her nudity underneath.

"From the docks. Then, through heat tracking in the storm. How are your feet?"

His awareness of such detail surprised her. She just started to regain full feeling in them. She'd been able to stand and walk, but now little pricks of pain were sneaking past the numbness.

"I asked you a question."

"They're sore."

"Let me look at them."

"I'm fine—"

"That wasn't a question."

Too tired to challenge him, she lifted her leg. He cupped her heel and examined a few tender spots with the pad of his thumb, then set it back in the water. "Wash them well. After your bath, we'll wrap them."

She was a mess.

Stone, unlike his so-called brother, understood she needed more rest before she would be fully functioning. He pressed a button, and the water started to drain, but he turned the faucet on, refreshing the clouded water. "Soak for as long as you like. When you're finished, rinse off." He stood to leave.

"Th-thank you for the ice."

He paused at the door but only nodded, never looking back.

She waited a long time for Ash to return, but he never did. Maybe he heard Stone had brought her the ice for her shoulder and saw no need to come back. She disliked the disappointment that followed his absence, certain only a crazy person would miss her captor.

That's because you are crazy...

She shook off the taunting voice in her head and whispered, "I'm not. I'm not. I'm not."

Whenever her thoughts got too dark, she needed to move. She was still too overwrought to feel settled, and she didn't want to get too comfortable in a place that required her mind to stay sharp.

"Nice and big." She breathed in. "Blow it out small." She exhaled. "Just right," she whispered, forcing herself out of the tub and into the shower.

After she rinsed off, she examined her reflection, curling a lip at the brass bear every time she recalled it was there watching her. As she moved, she swore the eyes of the brass bear moved with her.

She glared at the frozen face. "Enjoying the show?"

Rolling her eyes, she turned, lowering the towel a bit so she could glimpse the full bruise on her shoulder. It looked worse than it felt. Until she touched it. Poking the dark skin definitely was not recommended.

Tightening the towel around her chest, she returned to the empty tub and sat on the marble perimeter. What now?

She didn't want to go back to the men, and she didn't know where she was supposed to wait. Should she rest? There was a perfectly tempting bed in the next room. Sleep was all she wanted to do at that moment. The days of running and struggling had fully caught up to her, and she felt dead on her feet.

Too exhausted to figure out a better solution, she lowered to her side and used the folded robe as a pillow under her damp hair. Maybe if she just closed her eyes for a moment, she'd figure out what to do.

Next thing she knew, she was being lifted against a rock-hard chest and carried through the hall. Glancing through her lashes, she caught a spattering of scars under a jaw full of scruff and stiffened.

Hunter gave an order in Russian that commanded her to be still without translation. Where was he taking her?

He carried her through the corridor and down the steps into a vaguely familiar room. He didn't put her down until he pulled back the covers. She recognized the armoire from last night.

"Sleep now." He pulled the heavy covers to her chin, tucking the edges tightly around her arms in a way that made her feel slightly trapped. The enormous bed engulfed her in heavy furs and silk.

But when he removed his shirt, her relaxed state shifted abruptly to panic. "Wait."

He stilled, one hand on his belt, eyes warning her he took orders from no one. Especially her.

Her gaze dropped to the scar on his back. The raised edges formed the familiar muzzle of a bear. That wasn't the mark of an injury. That was burned into his skin intentionally. She wondered if it was his intention or someone else's?

"Shut your eyes."

"But Ash said—"

"Ash isn't here." He unbuckled his belt and pulled the leather free with a slithering snap.

Her heart raced as he climbed into the bed beside her, his body over the covers.

"Please don't—" Her words cut off as his cold, black glare snapped to her face.

His laugh was gruff and dismissive. "*Mne eto ne interesno, prekrasnaya lgun'ya.*" Then, as if recalling she didn't speak Russian, he translated, "I'm not interested. I am only here because I don't trust you, *prekrasnaya lgun'ya.*"

He spoke as if she were a tedious inconvenience. "What does that mean, *prekrasnaya lgun'ya*?" She butchered the pronunciation.

"Beautiful liar. Now shut your eyes."

She did as he commanded, but sleep was impossible. Every breath from his lungs reminded her she wasn't alone and there was an enormous, wild, possibly-killer beside her. It also didn't help that she was naked under the covers in only a towel.

Weren't the cameras enough? Did he have to be so close she could smell him? Not that his scent was unsavory. But it was unique enough that she now recognized it as solely his. And he was the one man she didn't want to be alone with.

She rolled to her side and huffed.

"What is it?"

"Nothing."

"Do they pay you for lies?"

She glanced over her shoulder and glared at him. "They?"

"The men who sent you here."

"No one sent me here."

"Exactly what a spy would say."

"You seriously think I'm a spy?"

"I know you're a thief."

She was done arguing semantics. "Yes, I stole your clothes and broke into your house uninvited. I think I've already paid enough for my crimes."

His gruff laughter was terrifying. "Do you now?"

She snapped her mouth shut before she got into more trouble. "I just want to sleep."

"Then shut your mouth and close your eyes."

That sounded like a good plan.

She thought restlessness would keep her awake, but she'd awoken sometime later, well-rested and alone. Her dreams had been a chaotic wash of visions that made no sense. She'd been running through a wild forest, chased by three bears—a grizzly, a gorgeous while polar bear, and a black bear.

Her hand brushed over the covers where Hunter had been, finding the sheets cold. She searched the room for a camera, but didn't see a brass bear head.

Stone had claimed he'd watched her last night. Ash said there was always someone watching. Who watched her now?

Perhaps all of them. "Oh, god."

Mortification over her performance in the kitchen returned. She recalled stripping off her wet clothes and changing last night, certain she must have looked like a wet rat on death's door. Was this the entry to her slow death?

"Shit." She needed to think.

These men were thorough, and with the surveillance system around the house—*House? Castle? What the hell was this place?*— Regardless of the name, she needed to remember she had no privacy. They were most likely watching her now. Observing. Studying her every move to see how she thought and acted.

Sudden awareness washed over her like a chill. She would

only show what she chose to share. Just because she was their prisoner and...

She winced, not wanting to admit that she was now some sort of communal concubine. She was a prisoner. But so was the sultan's wife, the one who enchanted him for a thousand and one nights.

She needed to be smart. She couldn't show fear. And she wouldn't cower. Whatever these next few days brought, she'd face it head-on and deal with the fallout later. Eventually, the storm outside had to pass. And while they might be the only home for miles, they certainly weren't the only men in the Isles of Kassel.

The more agreeable she pretended to be, the more freedom and trust they'd allow. She could do anything for a short time. This wasn't her forever. If she played their little game, she'd eventually break free. Then, she could follow her plan to start a new life.

Aware she had an invisible audience, she sat up and ran her fingers through her golden hair, breaking up the tangled curls. When the blankets fell, exposing her breasts, she didn't bother to cover herself. The more comfortable she became with her nudity on her own, the less they could use it to manipulate her.

Sliding out of the bed, she walked naked to the armoire she had visited last night. Only this time, when she tried to open the doors, it was locked.

I don't trust you, beautiful liar...

Hunter made it clear he didn't want her there, yet he brought her right to his bed, to his personal space. Why, if he thought her a thief and a spy? She rolled her eyes and scanned the room for other dressers. There were three. Each one locked.

Slamming her hand on the surface of the last bureau, she chewed her lip. "Asshole."

Fine. He wanted to leave her without clothes? She'd manage.

Yanking the dark, silk sheet off the bed, she carelessly let the outer covers fall to the floor and wrapped the silk around her like a black toga, twisting the fabric into a sort of asymmetrical halter.

Pleased with her design, she left the room to explore the house, passing the next hour through an imaginary game of follow the leader. In each room she entered, she searched for the gold bear. When she found it, she made an ugly face at the beady little reflective eyes. By the time she reached the end of the second floor, she'd grown bored with the game and started flipping the bear the finger.

Where were they? So much for hospitality.

Irritated and antsy, she debated what to do next. She remembered the dungeon. That was the only room she avoided on her journey. What if they were there—awaiting her?

Her eyes turned to the long hall, as she debated continuing her search. But the game no longer tempted her. Not down that hall.

Her gaze jerked to the ceiling, where a soft buzzing sounded from the beaded chandelier overhead. She squinted at the peculiar black gem in the center. Then it moved like an eye—watching her—and she bolted forward, quickly moving out of view.

CHAPTER 8

MOUSE IN A MAZE

"She's up to something." Stone zoomed in, following her from one camera to the next as she walked briskly down the east hall.

Ash flattened his palms on the desk, too worked up to sit down. "What the hell was the point of making her agree if we're just going to leave her alone?"

Stone met his brother's bruised stare. "You better put more ice on that."

"Fucking Hunter." He pressed the frosty glass of vodka to his eye. "He always does this."

Stone laughed. "Right. This is exactly like the last time we took a woman captive," he said dryly, as if anything like this had ever happened before.

"You know what I mean. He always thinks he's in charge—"

"Shut up." Stone leaned forward. "She's going to The Cave."

Ash set down his glass and watched as she stared up at the camera planted above the door. "Wait until she sees what's on the other side."

"She knows. She was there last night."

His surprised gaze jumped to his face, but quickly returned to watching Mary. "What are you up to, little lamb?"

Her delicate hand reached for the knob, and she frowned. Jiggling it again, she kicked the door and let go.

"What the fuck?" both men said at once.

Ash growled. "Hunter probably locked it."

"Why?"

"Who the hell knows?" Ash snatched his glass and paced the control room. "This is bullshit."

"Chill."

"Fuck off."

"I mean it, Ash. You had no right to go at her like that this morning. You're already on thin ice."

"Now, I gotta hear shit from you?"

He sent him a warning glance. "We're still figuring her out."

"You guys act like she's some unsolvable puzzle. She's a rich little runaway looking for trouble."

"I don't think so."

"I do. Don't be so fooled by those big innocent eyes. She's no virgin."

Stone's nostrils flared as he ground his molars. "Well, you would certainly know."

Ash's low chuckle nearly earned him a second black eye. "She was sent here for a reason, Stone."

"You too, now? She's not a fucking spy."

"That's not what I mean."

Stone frowned. "What are you talking about?"

"What if she was sent here as a gift? For us?"

"By who?"

Ash shrugged. "The universe."

"Give me a fucking break, Ash—"

"I'm serious. We're always saying it would take a special woman to tolerate the three of us. What if we somehow manifested this?" He glanced at the monitors. "She could have fought me this morning, but she didn't. And I know when a woman's faking."

Stone lifted a brow. "Coercion and submission are two different things. She submitted because she's scared we'll turn her in. That confirms she's running from something. We don't have shit until we have her full story."

"Maybe this is the way to make her talk."

"By fisting her?"

"Trust. That kind of intimacy requires trust."

About to call Ash an idiot, he opened his mouth, but something held back his words.

"See, you agree with me."

He narrowed his eyes but couldn't deny there was some sense to his theory. If she trusted them, she'd eventually come clean. "There are other ways to figure out who she is."

"And Hunter has that covered." He shrugged. "We can go at this from multiple angles."

Stone sipped his vodka, watching as Mary followed the labyrinth of corridors from one wing to the other, like a lost mouse desperately trying to escape a lab.

When she reached the door of the grotto, heavy and sealed, she tested the lock. It opened with a tug, and her eyes widened as she stepped inside. Both men moved closer to watch the screen as Ash cued up the internal cameras.

Stone dropped back in his chair, elbows braced on the armrests, eyes fixed on the wall of monitors. The image flickered —grainy in the low light—but it didn't matter. He could see her.

She stepped into the grotto wrapped in a black sheet, the fabric draped over one shoulder like some pagan goddess caught between modesty and sin. Steam curled around her as she moved deeper inside, slow and uncertain, every shift of her body traced in shadow and silk.

The cavern looked colder through the cameras than it was in truth—stone walls, carved arches, the faint shimmer of condensation where heat met centuries-old rock—but he knew better. The air in there was thick, heavy with mineral vapor and cedar smoke. He'd designed it that way. A place meant to draw out secrets. To put people at ease and break down the last of their inhibiting walls.

She hesitated before the first pool, the dark water gleaming like liquid glass. Then she walked on, bare feet against warm stone, curls coiling tighter from the inescapable humidity.

She paused by the statues, fingertips ghosting over marble forms older than the country she came from. Every motion was careful, reverent, but he saw the tremor in her hand. The way she was fighting not to look over her shoulder.

His mouth curved. "She's learning."

"She knows she's never alone."

The cameras followed her through each chamber—the salt room, the baths, the long corridor where steam thickened to fog. She was silent, lost in the hum of dripping water and the occasional sigh that escaped her lips when the heat kissed her skin.

And then she reached the final door. The sauna.

Framed in the glow spilling through the ironwork, the black sheet clinging damply to her thighs, she looked like temptation carved out of night—something he could almost touch if he stepped closer to the screen.

Stone leaned forward, forearms on his knees, eyes narrowing as she pushed the door open and disappeared inside. The monitor filled with gold light and mist. It was the only place their camera lenses couldn't manage.

He exhaled slowly, the ghost of a smile tugging at his mouth as he stood, throwing back the last of his vodka and setting the crystal glass down with a definitive click. "I'm taking a walk. Watch the cameras."

"For what?" Ash yelled, but Stone didn't bother answering as he left the room.

CHAPTER 9

HEAT

Marigold eased into the lodge's sauna with a sigh that bordered on ecstasy. It was getting dark again, and she hadn't been able to find the men, so she decided to use her unchaperoned time for a little more pampering and self-care.

They didn't seem to care what she was up to anyway. She couldn't find a single trace of them, and, despite her photogenic taunting, she was starting to get worried something was wrong.

What if they changed their mind and decided to report her? Maybe they were with the police right now. Her nerves jangled at the thought.

She tried to guess if Ash could touch her like that and then betray her so easily. Maybe he already had. Perhaps that was why he'd never returned.

But Stone had come, and he'd been respectful and patient. Then Hunter. He wasn't someone who radiated manners, but he also didn't lay a hand on her.

She was being ridiculous and working herself up for noth-ing. She should be reveling in her privacy and grateful they left

111

her alone. Though she was never truly alone. Her gaze drifted to the wall where another bear watched her.

Were they watching her now? Questioning her motives as much as she questioned theirs? Heat enveloped her like an embrace, drawing out the last of her body's tension. Muscles loosened like liquid heat as steam rose from heated stones, filling the cedar-lined chamber with humidity that made her skin glow like polished ivory. She loosened the sheet twisted around her neck and stretched her neck.

The door opened with a soft hiss of escaping steam, and she opened her eyes, her pulse quickening at the sight of Stone wrapped in nothing but a towel.

"Mind if I join you?" he asked, as he settled on the bench across from her with fluid grace.

His broad chest and wide shoulders radiated controlled danger. Ropes of sinew twisted up his arms and sides. He was a chiseled work of art with a body that could literally kill. She couldn't help but stare at the lean muscle of his torso, the way condensation already beaded on his golden skin like scattered diamonds.

His green eyes tracked a drop of sweat that rolled slowly down her throat. "Enjoying yourself?"

"Do you want me to go?"

A staying hand pressed to her knee. "You're welcome to use the grotto as much as anyone else."

"Thank you."

"You're welcome."

His generous tone surprised her. "Do you share your house often?"

He met her stare. "What we share is conditional. Everything here is ours. Including you." His gaze dropped to her breasts where that rolling drop had disappeared. "But you're not to be shared."

She looked at him in stunned confusion and he caught his slip.

"I mean, shared between anyone but us."

The possessive words should have triggered her flight response. Instead, they sent molten heat pooling low in her belly like liquid fire. He'd been so distant the last time he visited her, or maybe that was just Stone. Precise. Calculated. Intentional.

"I'll be sure to ask permission before assuming in the future."

He frowned at her tone. "If there's something you need, we'll provide it."

She scoffed. "*Clothing* would be nice."

"Clothing isn't necessary for your purpose here."

Her molars locked. *Her purpose.* She wanted to punch him, though she'd probably only end up hurting her hand. As if sensing her urge, he smirked.

Her eyes narrowed. "You seem pleased with yourself."

"I have no complaints at the moment." He studied her for a long moment. "I was watching you again, this afternoon, as you explored."

"I figured."

"You tried every door but the front one."

She stilled, feeling guilty for a rule she didn't break and stupid for overlooking the most obvious escape from her captivity. "The storm—"

"Yes, snow can be quite treacherous for those not used to it, but that's not my point. Most people would have tried to run by now."

"Where would I go?"

"Exactly." His smile was sharp as arctic wind.

He stood, ladling water over the stones with practiced ease. The hiss of steam filled the small space, making the air even more oppressive. As the room fogged, giving everything a dreamlike feel. Rather than return to the bench across from her, he settled onto the bench beside her.

"You don't have to pretend with us." His fingers traced the line of her collarbone, following the path of moisture down to where the dark sheet tucked between her breasts. "You don't have to be perfect either." He hooked his finger and tugged, loosening the fabric. "Don't have to be polite. Don't have to smile when you want to scream."

"Why would I scream," she whispered.

"Not all screams are borne of terror." His hand cupped her face, thumb brushing across her lower lip with possessive gentleness. "Do you know what I enjoyed most about watching you last night?"

She shook her head as she stared into his emerald eyes.

"You weren't performing. This afternoon, you were different."

That was because she knew they were watching. They were always watching.

"I bet you've been performing your whole life. Playing a role someone else wrote for you."

She blinked rapidly, wondering why he'd make such a statement. Was she really that transparent. "Until recently."

"Ah," he pulled the sheet open. "I'm guessing that's when life changed. Am I right?"

"Yes."

"How?" Dew gathered on her warm skin, gathering and trailing down her body in a slow race with gravity. He leaned closer, licking up a drop that gathered by her collarbone. "I'm very good at uncovering secrets, little rabbit. All kinds of secrets."

As he leaned in to taste the salt on her fevered skin, his groan rumbled through her like distant thunder. He pressed her back to the warm cedar bench. Without invitation, he cupped her breasts in his large hands and kissed her.

It was nothing like Ash's kiss. Stone kissed like he was claiming territory, marking what belonged to him with absolute certainty. His mouth devoured hers with demanding strokes of his tongue, unforgivingly challenging her until she found herself responding with equal hunger.

The sheet fell away, but she was beyond caring about modesty. Stone's hands mapped her body with clinical precision, finding every sensitive spot and exploiting it ruthlessly. When she arched against him, gasping his name like a prayer, his laugh was dark with satisfaction.

"That's it," he murmured against her throat, his voice rough with desire and dominance. "Let go. Stop thinking. Just feel."

He shifted to kneel on the planked floor as steam swirled around them. He pressed her knees open, burying his face between her legs.

One deep lick and he groaned with masculine satisfaction. "I knew you'd be sweet like honey."

She gasped as his tongue darted into her, circling and teasing. Slick sweat coated her body as the heat made her dizzy. They were cocooned in a haze of swirling desire, so thick and drugging she stopped calculating consequences and surrendered to pure sensation.

Stone broke down her walls with methodical skill. Every gasp stole her senses. The heat of the small cedar room made it impossible to catch her breath. And the more she panted the less she could think—of reasons she should push him away, reasons why he was her enemy. It was as if the steam and his talented mouth were working together to put her under some sort of spell.

He didn't back off until she was boneless and quivering in his arms, wrung out and shaking with tremors from her intense release. He cradled her against his hard chest as they lay tangled together on the cedar bench.

"Note to self," he said as he stroked her shoulder. "You stop pretending when you climax."

"How do you know? Maybe I was faking—*Ouch!*" He pinched her ass.

"That was not faking. A man knows."

"They all say that."

"I know."

Strangely, she believed him. She didn't think she could fool Stone. He was too observant and too thorough. He was also very good with his tongue.

"We've been in here too long."

She was feeling a little more breathless than usual, but she assumed that was the result of her orgasm.

"Come." He eased her up and unlatched the door. "I want to take care of those feet—" His words cut off as Hunter rounded the corner.

She shifted behind Stone to hide her nudity. How had she forgotten the dangers of this place so quickly?

Hunter's expression wasn't one of arousal or satisfaction. There was something cold and calculating in his amber eyes, something that made the blood freeze in her veins.

"Hunter," Stone said in warning, drawing his glaring eyes away from Marigold. "Did you need something?" Stone's tone held an edge of challenge.

"We have intel."

Stone reached a hand behind his back as if to assure her she was safe. "We can discuss it later."

"We will discuss it *now*."

His gaze fixed on her with predatory intensity. "Facial recognition is a wonderful thing."

Marigold tensed. They had her picture from the surveillance

cameras. They could have found anything. Panic rose inside of her. This was it. This was where everything fell apart.

"She's connected to an old friend of ours." Hunter's grin was feral as his eyes locked on hers with laser focus. "Someone who has a score to settle."

CHAPTER 10

SINS OF BLOOD

The temperature plummeted. Stone's protective hold transformed to iron restraint, his muscles coiling beneath sweat-slicked skin with barely leashed violence. Marigold tried to back away, but he jerked her to his side. The tender man who seduced her moments ago was effectively gone.

"Just fucking say it," Stone's voice was deadly quiet, each word carved from arctic ice. "Who is she?"

Hunter's smile brimmed with malice. "Marigold Elena Calder. Twenty-four years old. Daughter of the late Evangeline Calder and that bastard Harrison Calder. Half-sister to—"

"Jordan Calder." The name spat from Stone's lips like a curse as he shoved her away.

Marigold's blood crystallized to ice as she stumbled into the wall. "I can explain—"

"We don't want more of your lies!"

She drew back at the barely contained violence in Hunter's voice. When she looked to Stone for help, he looked away in disgust, only to glare at her with dark accusation. "Is Jordan your fucking brother?"

"Half-brother." But why did they hate him? Knowing Jordan, he could have done anything. "We're no—"

"No more lies!" Hunter snapped, his expression shifting from cruel to something far more dangerous. "There's been a change of plans."

It was clear they harbored hatred for her half-brother, and she knew all about that. What wasn't clear was what this now meant for her. So she ran.

"*No!*" she yelled as Hunter snatched her off her feet, too fast for her to get away. His fingers dug into her ribs like talons.

"Hunter, wait!"

But he ignored Stone's warning, dragging her into the hall. She kicked and fought, but he was too powerful.

"Your brother's about to get exactly what he deserves, little liar." Hunter's voice was gravel and broken glass.

"*Stone, help me! Please!*"

But Stone only watched as Hunter dragged her off.

The way he called her a liar made her stomach lurch with dread. This wasn't the teasing endearment Ash had used or the possessive claim Stone favored. This was an accusation. A condemnation. A declaration of war.

"Hunter, please," she whispered, desperately trying to reason with him.

He covered her mouth with his enormous hand, blocking her nostrils and making it hard to breathe through her panic. Her muffled scream didn't make him loosen his hold any more than her clawing. So she bit him.

"Fucking bitch!" He turned into a random bedroom and

threw her onto the bed. She sprang to her feet, bolting to the far side of the room where several pieces of furniture separated them. He slammed the door, locking them in what might as well be a tomb. "A little over a year ago, your dear brother attended one of our events. Uninvited. Unwelcome."

Just like her, she thought, wondering if the irony would be her death sentence.

"I didn't know that." She mirrored his steps, desperately trying to keep her distance as he closed in.

"We never allow uninvited guests past the front door, but he had friends who vouched for him, so we... accommodated his presence."

She jerked as Stone pounded on the door. "Hunter! Open the fucking door!"

Hunter's breathing had gone shallow and harsh, each exhale carrying the weight of barely contained fury. Stone continued to pound on the door.

Marigold searched the walls for a camera and found one above the bed. "Do something!"

Rage radiated off Hunter in waves, a hatred so deep and cold it made her bones ache with sympathetic pain. She didn't know what Jordan had done, but she always thought the worst where her half-brother was concerned.

"He was only supposed to observe," Hunter continued, his accent thickening with every step as he rounded the bed. "Our rules are crystal clear. First-time guests observe. They learn. They *earn* the privilege of participation through respect and understanding."

"*Hunter.*" Stone pounded, but his voice sounded almost... broken. Then the pounding stopped.

She felt the moment Stone abandoned his rescue and left her there to fend for herself. "Please..." she begged, certain he could kill her without even breaking a sweat.

Hunter's obsidian stare bore into her with untethered hate. "You deserve to know exactly what kind of monster shares your blood. What kind of poison runs through your veins."

"Please," Marigold begged, backing into the wall.

"She was a child."

"I'm not like him!" She closed her eyes, covering her ears.

He snatched her wrists, ripping her hands away and forcing her to listen. Panic spiked as his strength dominated her into submission. He twisted her body, pulling her away from the wall. "First, he drugged her." The words exploded from Hunter like artillery fire, each syllable designed to destroy.

"I don't want to hear this!"

"Tough!" He pinned her hands at the base of her spine, forcing her body to bow forward as he spoke directly in her ear. "Our sweet, innocent sister. Eighteen years old, as gentle as summer rain, fresh as morning dew, and he fucking drugged her."

"No," she cried, shutting her eyes as if she could somehow escape what was coming.

"Then, he took what he wanted and left her bleeding and broken in a room that was supposed to be her sanctuary."

The world tilted sideways, reality fracturing like glass under pressure. Marigold was once again drowning. Once again, on that cold slab, being strapped down, forced to tolerate the unthinkable.

"Big breath in...." Her mother's voice echoed from a distant corner of her mind, but her heart pounded louder.

"Blow it out small..." Hands. She could feel their cold hands pushing her down.

She pulled her hair as her mouth and eyes squeezed shut, already tasting the rubber as she tried to breathe *'just right'* like her mother had taught her.

She could smell the disinfectant on the floors, taste the

sweat on her lips. *"Big breath in..."* But phantom hands were all she could feel. Pushing. Pulling. Until every breath was shallow, cold, and wrong.

"Get off me!" she screamed, opening her eyes to find red carpet not linoleum.

Hunter's voice was a blade against her throat, sharp enough to draw blood. "He drugged a girl barely out of school."

She panted. Her mind breaking under the weight of fear.

"Raped her."

Reality splintered. Was this real? Or was this a hallucination? There were three. But now there was only one. She gasped, every shallow breath hiking up her anxiety until she was in a full-blown panic attack.

"Not only did he leave her in a mess of his own making, he left her pregnant and traumatized, going back to whatever hellhole spawned him."

Pregnant. The word hit her like a physical blow, driving the air from her lungs as the door burst open.

"Hunter, get off of her!"

She was thrown onto the bed, too afraid to do more than cover her head. Russian expletives exploded from each of them as Hunter was thrown into a wall. This was too real to be a hallucination.

She pinched her arm, validating that everything taking place around her was real.

"Have you lost your fucking mind?" Ash shouted.

Marigold flinched when he placed a gentle hand on her back.

"Are you okay?"

She cowered away from his touch, unsure who she could trust. They were all liars. Like Jordan, the golden son who could do no wrong. The perfect heir to the Calder empire.

"I'm sorry," she cried.

"Not yet, but you will be," Hunter threatened.

"Enough!" Stone shoved him back.

"Why should we protect her from the truth?" Hunter snarled at his brother. His black eyes found her. "Our sister lost the baby at twelve weeks. She attempted suicide twice before that. After the miscarriage, she stopped eating, stopped speaking, stopped being our bright, beautiful Katya."

Katya.

Their sister had a name, a face, a life that Jordan had destroyed with casual cruelty. And Marigold shared his blood, carried his DNA, bore the same family name that had become synonymous with the suffering he caused.

"Now, it's our turn to make things even." He lunged for her and she screamed, scrambling off the bed and running to Ash.

"Stop!" Ash curled his body around her trembling body. "What the fuck, Hunter? Get control of yourself!"

She sucked in a jagged breath, then another. Her mother's voice couldn't penetrate her panic. "Please..." she begged. "I swear, I didn't know. I'm not lying."

Hunter's tone was as cold and unbending as ice. "Not lying like you swore you were Mary Langford?"

She twisted in Ash's arms. "Jordan is everything wrong with my family," she sputtered. "Everything I was running from. If I'd known what he did—"

Her words cut off as his hand closed around her throat. Ash and Stone shouted for him to let go, but when they touched him, he shoved them away with merciless force.

"You'd what?" Hunter's grip tightened as he towered over her with the presence of an avenging angel. "Turn him in? Testify against him? Make him pay for what he did?"

She tried to pry the fingers around her throat loose,

desperate to make him understand. *"Yes!"* The word tore from her throat like a battle cry. "Yes, absolutely, whatever it took—"

"Lies!" he bellowed, shoving her into the wall. "Calders can't be trusted. Deceit's written into your fucking DNA."

"Hunter!" one of the brothers snapped, but she couldn't see past his looming presence. Lack of oxygen was making it difficult to hear.

"I'm not like him. I'm decent. That's why I was trying to escape." Tears burned her eyes as she sputtered for breath. "I hate him," she rasped. "He's the reason I'm running!"

"Why?" Hunter demanded, his fist knotting painfully in her hair. "I want the fucking truth."

"Because I know what he is." The confession stuttered past her lips on a narrow wheeze. "I knew about the women he brought home. I saw how they looked afterward. Hunter... please." She clawed at his unbreakable grip and wheezed, "You're choking me."

"How did they look?"

She flinched when the brothers tried to pull him off of her, his unbreakable grip jerking her around by the neck like a ragdoll. Blackness bled into her periphery.

"Broken." She gasped for air. "Empty. Wrong."

"Hunter, you're killing her!" Ash jumped on his back, fisting his hair.

"Your brother is a cancer," he seethed through gritted teeth. "A poison on this earth."

"I... know." The words pushed painfully past her bruised larynx as her eyes closed.

He snarled, then Stone shouted something in Russian, and her body crumpled to the floor. Air rushed into her lungs like fire. Painful coughs sputtered past her ravaged throat. Her vision tunneled into a narrow keyhole of black as tears blurred her vision.

Stone tried to help her stand, but her legs collapsed. "God-damn it, Hunter, you could have killed her!"

"Big loss."

Stone helped her sit up as Ash's large hand rested on her back. She heaved for breath. Hunter might have let her go, but she still felt his grip around her throat. Her body still radiated with the fear he instilled.

"There are other ways to deal with this," Ash snapped.

Hunter seethed but something in Ash's voice held him back. They exchanged a look that spoke of years of shared pain and protection, decades of trauma that dated back long before Jordan slithered into their lives.

Hunter wanted to take his vengeance out on her. Marigold knew then that this man had killed. Her life meant nothing to him, and she was his next target.

Gripping Stone's arm, she pulled herself up off the ground so as not to look weak. "If you kill me, you'd be doing Jordan a favor."

The room silenced as her body swayed under the remaining dizziness. Clinging to Stone's shirt, she used his body as a shield. Ash's hand slipped into hers, offering additional support.

"Hear her out."

They looked at her expectantly. May the truth set her free. "Jordan convinced my father to have me committed."

Hunter glared at her with unfiltered distrust and barely contained rage.. "Committed how?"

She looked to Stone and Ash, but neither was her friend. Her protectors were not willing to risk themselves.

Fine. She was more than used to handling things on her own. And she'd learned long ago that men were always in it for themselves before anyone else.

Lifting her trembling chin, she stared into fathomless eyes. "It was a private facility. They called it behavioral modification."

The truth tasted like bitter shame, burning her mouth like acid. "They left me there for months, claiming I was hysterical, unstable, and delusional. But that wasn't true."

"Is anything out of your mouth true, little liar?"

"I know what my brother really is. And when I told the truth, they punished me."

"Why didn't they believe you?"

"They swore Jordan would never hurt anyone. They thought I was making up lies because of jealousy. They said only a sick person would make such heinous accusations about family."

"You said he was your half-brother."

"Yes. But to my father, he's the first born son. I'm nothing compared to Jordan in his eyes."

"Charming." Ash watched her like an equation he needed to solve.

"Yes," she agreed with a bitter cold. "Misogyny runs deep in the Calder lines."

"And what about your mother?"

Pain engulfed her heart. She bowed her head. "My mother passed away while I was committed."

A moment of silence passed as she fumbled with the bottomless regret of missing those last goodbyes. *Big breath in...* Deep down, she believed her mother fought to keep her out of that place, but she was no match for her father. And in the end, the fight might have been what killed her.

"Yet here you are," Hunter sneered. "Free, on the same island your brother had no business visiting, lying about your identity, trespassing through our home, and stealing our things."

"You don't understand—"

"*Because you've been feeding us bullshit lies since you arrived!*" Hunter roared as he slammed his fist into the wall.

"I had to lie!" This time, she didn't cower. "They had no plans of letting me out of that place! They would have let me rot inside those white walls. Do you know what it's like to have your freedom stripped away so completely that you can't even choose your meals? I had to swallow whatever pills they fed me, wear soft clothing, stare through barred windows. And when I tried to reason with them, they doubled my dosage and turned me into a walking zombie. If I threw up the meds to keep my senses, they..."

"What?" Stone asked. "What else did they do?"

She rubbed her temples, remembering the way they strapped her down and made her bite into the rubber mouth guard.

"There's nothing wrong with me." Her voice turned small as she rubbed away the feeling of having her wrist strapped down. The sensation of five orderlies pinning her to a gurney as she fought with all her might. The indignity of having her clothing tugged and her privates exposed, all so they could get her to submit. And then came the shocks.

The first was always the worst, when the body was still engaged in the fight and every muscle went taut. It was an unwinnable battle, yet she instinctually fought them every time —until she couldn't.

Sometimes she felt them removing the head gear and pulling away the mouth guard. Other times she saw them as if through a dream as they lifted the padded cot onto another surface and wheeled her back to her room.

Afterwards, she was always still. Not numb, but too over-taxed to truly feel the reality of life for a bit. Her tongue was too tired to move, and her eyes stayed unfocused for days. It was as if her spirit were forced outside of her body and her flesh only held bone to cage whatever remained of her mind.

She didn't have the words to make them understand every-thing she'd survived. "It was hell on earth."

"How did you escape?" At Ash's quiet question, she straightened and blinked back to the present, forcing those horrific memories away and digging deep for courage.

"I was visiting family, home for the weekend."

"I didn't know hell sanctioned field trips."

She glared at Hunter. He was right, of course, but that wasn't the point. "Only for well-behaved patients." Which she was not. "Jordan brought a friend home that weekend. A girl." She couldn't claim the girl was a woman. "She looked barely sixteen."

Hunter hissed what could only be a swear word in Russian, as Stone turned away, rubbing the back of his neck. Ash was the only one not to break eye contact. He wanted the truth and intended to have all of it.

"I tried to help her," she confessed truthfully. "You have to believe I'm not like him."

"How did you try?"

"When Jordan was preoccupied, I told her to leave, but she had no interest in going anywhere. She wanted to be with him. Jordan caught me trying to force her out the door and lost it. He called my dad, then they contacted the facility. They were already looking for me."

"Because you weren't allowed to leave in the first place."

"Correct. Jordan..." Those final moments had been her last familiar glimpse of her family. "He said that would be the last time I ever saw home. He promised to have me committed for the rest of my life."

The walls were closing in on her. Just the thought of wasting away in that place for a lifetime left her claustrophobic and terrified. She still wasn't safe. These men could turn her in, send her back to that waking hell, and sentence her to rot for the rest of her life.

She was suddenly very tired, as if she hadn't slept in months.

"So you ran," Stone said, with something approaching understanding in his voice.

"Wouldn't you?" She met his emerald eyes without flinching, and he gave a subtle nod.

"Why did you come here, to Kassel?"

"I needed to go somewhere they wouldn't think to look. I'd heard how exclusive the Isles of Kassel were, and when I found the invitation it seemed almost serendipitous. I'd once heard Jordan mention that he couldn't go back, but I had no idea why. I just figured anywhere he wasn't welcome was safe."

Ash studied her, rubbing his chin. "Care to explain who Mary Langford is?"

"She's the daughter of a member of Parliament."

"I ran her name. She's never been a guest here. Her invitation wasn't issued by us. Who invited her?"

"I don't know. I never met her face-to-face. There was a gala at the country club the night I ran. I went there, hoping Jordan wouldn't make a scene if he followed me. I stole her coat and purse when I was looking for a disguise in the coat check—"

"Clever little thief," Ash said with a smirk.

"Yes, I can be. Anyone can be, if their circumstances are bad enough. I used her phone to arrange a flight with her documentation. No one ever questioned me. I didn't see the invitation to Kassel until I was in the air on her family's private jet."

"So you stole a coat, a phone, her ID, and an aircraft. Impressive," Stone chuckled.

"This isn't fucking funny," Hunter snarled. "Where did you get the boat?"

She hesitated, not wanting to get the only person who helped her in trouble.

"I asked you a fucking question!"

"A woman." She jolted with panic, trying to recall the order of events. "It all happened so fast. Agents were waiting at the tarmac when we landed. I wouldn't have escaped if not for her."

"Who was she?"

"A flight attendant. Someone who works for the Langfords, I suppose. She recognized my desperation and took pity on me. She told me where the boat was docked and where to find the hidden supplies."

"You risked your life."

"Maybe. But I'm alive. I don't think they know where I am. Unless you plan to report me."

Hunter growled. The truth hadn't softened him one bit. "Your family's debt is yours to bear."

"But I didn't do anything!"

"*Your blood destroyed ours!*" Hunter roared. "There will be consequences!"

"Hunter," Ash snapped. "Take it easy. She obviously didn't know what Jordan was doing. And when she found out, she tried to stop him."

"Not good enough! He should know the pain we suffered, be forced to watch his sister break the way we watched ours."

Marigold's heart leapt in fear. "If you hurt me, he won't care. You'd be doing him a favor. I'm a threat to Jordan. I know the truth about the real monster he is. He wants me gone."

"Then we'll send you back to him."

"No—"

"Don't tell me no!" Hunter snarled. Stone caught his shoulder before he could touch her again.

"You have to relax, man."

Her vision blurred with unshed tears. "I may share Jordan's DNA, but I'm nothing like him."

"Prove it," Ash challenged, giving her a look that said she

needed to convince them quickly, because there was no reeling Hunter in. "Tell us how to find your brother."

Her shoulders curled inward, and her spine pressed into the wall. They were asking her to go against her family.

She didn't care about betraying Jordon, but her father would never forgive her for turning against her own blood—despite all the times they turned against her, dismissing her truth as lies and abandoning her in that hellhole of a facility to rot until they fully fried her brains and turned her into a breathing corpse.

"I can try," she finally said in a small voice.

Hunter's smile was sharp as a blade. "Your brother has been very good at disappearing these past three months. Trying won't be good enough. Either tell us how to get to him, or we send you back to the clinic and use you as bait."

"He would never visit me—"

"He'd have no choice. Your condition would be too critical to ignore."

"Fucking hell, Hunter," Ash snapped, pulling her protectively to his side.

Marigold's heart hammered against her ribs. "I don't know anything about his personal life. Jordan's always been an extremely private person."

"You know things we don't. The kind of car he drives. Who his friends are. Where he spends his free time."

"I really don't."

"You're lying again."

She might know some things, but not much. "I can tell you what I know, but, like I said, Jordan has always been a private person."

"We'll want to know everything you know." Stone said, stepping closer to look her in the eyes. "His habits. His friends. His weaknesses. Every dirty secret you have is now ours."

"Just like you're ours." Hunter reminded, looming over her

as she stood shoulder to shoulder with Ash and Stone. "Understand?"

This was her only choice—if one could even call it a choice. But even as she nodded, Marigold couldn't shake the feeling that she'd just signed a different kind of devil's bargain. These men didn't just want information—they wanted blood. Her family's blood. She was now their greatest asset and an accomplice to whatever they planned.

CHAPTER 11

MARKED FOR THE TAKING

Marigold's legs wouldn't move as Stone nudged her toward a dark room. She knew this room and couldn't force herself to go in there.

"What are we doing here?"

"Finishing what we started," Stone pushed the door open. "You remember The Cave."

It had been locked earlier. He brought her here for a reason. No longer on her own terms, her curiosity died. "I don't want to go in there."

"I didn't ask." He flung her over his shoulder, knocking the wind from her lungs.

The gentle possession she'd experienced earlier was gone. Everything about him had changed since learning who she was. Even his handling was more demanding, more desperate. Whatever sense of safety she'd had was now gone.

"You said you wouldn't hurt me."

"You said you were Mary Langford." His fingers dug into her ass as he yanked her down and set her on her feet. His pale eyes were wild as they met hers. "Now, we negotiate from a position of complete truth."

The implications hung between them like the blade of a guillotine. She wasn't just their captive anymore, or even their willing participant. She was their weapon against Jordan—and weapons, she knew from bitter experience, were meant to be used.

"We can do this the hard way or the easy way, Goldilocks."

She scowled at the childish nickname. "What's going to happen to me?"

"Everything. Things too dark to name. Things that exist without names."

He was one of the kinder ones, she'd thought, but now, all signs of any gentle nature were gone. "Please," she whispered, searching his eyes.

He turned her to face the room and marched her forward. "I love to hear a beautiful woman beg, but let's wait until you really mean it."

What did that mean? "Are you going to hurt me?"

"Not all pain is unpleasant. And, even when it is, it only makes us stronger. If you're going to work with us, we want to get you into tip-top shape, Goldi."

"Don't call me that."

He laughed and gave one of her blonde curls a tug. "You don't get to decide what we call you."

He flipped a switch that kicked on lights further down the narrow space, showing off just how cavernous the room was compared to the other enormous bedrooms in the house. Several soft surfaces existed. Button back couches with velvet, jewel-toned upholstery, stripped poster beds with only satin sheets, chaise lounges, round octagonal chairs for multiple people to rest, odd benches, and padded bolsters. And there, on the farthest wall, was the large wooden X.

"Times to play."

"Can't we—"

"No. You either submit or we return to plan B."

Plan B was sending her back to her father. Back to where her brother could find her. Her brow creased as she measured her options. What if Jordan's wrath was the easier route?

No. Jordan would punish her. He vowed to silence her one way or another, and he would never see her interference as anything other than a betrayal and an attempt to ruin his life.

Stone caught her chin and forced her to meet his gaze. "Look at me."

She blinked rapidly, feeling on the verge of tears.

"You're stronger than you realize. You made it here on that pile of drift wood in the freezing cold. But now, you have to prove your loyalty. Tonight won't be easy and I need you to prove to not just me, but Hunter and Ash, that you're committed to the task. Committed to us."

"Why does it have to be difficult?"

"Because choices like this are not conscious. They're borne of blood, sweat, and tears."

"Blood?" Her stomach dropped and she swallowed. "Please," she begged. "I already told you I'd cooperate."

"Yes, and that's what this is. A test of your word. You will cooperate and give me—us—exactly what we want."

Her insides shook as she tried to imagine what that might be. "I won't break my word."

"I want to believe you but, so far, you've only proven that you're a liar. So I'm afraid I'll need a bit more convincing."

A lone tear trickled down her cheek, and he swiped it away with such contrasting gentleness she had the urge to rush into the shelter of his arms. He sensed her need, and took the choice from her, pulling her close and hugging her tight.

His lips pressed into her hair and he whispered, "Hush now. Tears will only make me want more."

Her fist tightened in his shirt. She wanted him like this. Safe. Protective. Gentle. But that wasn't how this would go.

"Enough now." He abruptly turned her away from him and stepped back, leaving her shivering before him. Bare. Exposed. Unguarded.

He moved to the wall and opened a cabinet. Various items dangled from bronze hooks, and he sorted through the rack like one might drag a finger over a bookshelf of their fondest stories. He selected a long, reed-thin leather crop, and she staggered back.

"What are you doing with that?"

"Relax."

"How do I do that when you're holding a horse whip?"

"You do it with self-discipline."

She wasn't feeling very disciplined at the moment.

"If you run," he said as her eyes darted back to the door, "I'll catch you. And when I do, I'll be hotter, which means I'll likely whip you harder. If you submit now, it won't hurt as much." He stroked his hand over the reed-thin whip and took her hand, opening her fingers to feel the weight. "You'll learn to relax, not because I mean to dismiss your fears, but because I know it's easier when your body stays nimble." He swatted the whip across her palm and she gasped, closing her fingers in a protective fist.

He casually stroked the leather-wrapped whip, never breaking eye contact. "You'll learn to trust us, Goldilocks. You'll come to discover that when you're obedient and well-behaved, life will operate more in your favor. You'll also learn—because I sense your opposition—that we enjoy a challenge. Whether you give us one or not, the outcome will be the same. Your submission is a requirement. The level of pain is up to you." He paused, using the folded leather tip of the crop to lift her chin. "Trust my advice is meant to make things easier, not harder." He turned away. "Keep your eyes on me."

She looked at him with a mixture of desperation and hate.

He pointed the crop toward the wall where a bolster stood in front of a padded bench. "Kneel for me." When she didn't move, he swung the crop against the leather bolster, jolting her into motion, but she couldn't bring herself to kneel. What sane woman would surrender to a beating with a horse whip?

"On your knees, Goldilocks."

She was frozen, paralyzed with shock that he actually wanted her to voluntarily submit to a beating. "I can't—*Ah!*" The whip struck into her thighs fast and sharp. She dropped to the bench.

"Head down." He pressed her shoulders forward and pulled her arms back. "Hold your ass open so I can see when you tense."

She was trembling so rapidly she could hardly make sense of his directions, but he didn't wait for her to obey. He merely positioned her the way he wanted and told her to stay.

The folded tip of the crop traced slowly down her spine, tripping over each protruding vertebrae. "Say the word and I stop. We can have you back to your family by midnight."

He moved behind her, folding his body over hers and pressing into her with his impressive weight. The bulge of his denim clad erection pressed over her ass as he ground into her hands. Warm breath teased her ear. "The word...is *stop*." He ground himself harder. "Do you want me to *stop* and send you home to Daddy, Goldilocks? Is this too hard?"

She shook her head, unsure if she was allowed to say no.

He pressed her harder into the bolster with the weight of his rocking hips. "I asked you a question, little thief."

"I don't want to go home."

"Good." He released her and backed off. "Then let's begin."

The whip came down on her thighs, leather singing through the air before the sharp kiss of impact bloomed into burning heat. She yiped under the swift force and reflexively jolted, her natural instinct to escape pain more powerful than her force of will in that moment.

"Stay," he commanded, as if speaking to a dog. His hand pressed her shoulders back down, his fingers brushing her hair toward the floor. "Hold that ass open like I showed you."

He gave her cheeks a warning tap and she quickly obeyed—rewarded with another swat. *"Ah!"*

"Try not to tense." He kept to striking the fleshy parts of her thighs and soon the sting transcended into a warm burn. There was the bite of leather, then the strange sense of release that followed.

""Good girl. Let go of your ass now, and turn your hands palm up. Keep them at the base of your spine and don't move."

Her legs were shaking, and she needed the bolster to hold her upright. She did as he instructed and gasped when he struck her ass. Twice. Three times. Four. He kept going until she lost count. Then he adjusted her arms outward, as if she were stretched on a cross. He turned her wrists to expose her soft palms and then whipped them as well.

Her entire body vibrated with an electric tingle, similar to the buzzing numbness she suffered after the shock therapy. She didn't move when he finally stopped whipping her. Nor did she look to see where he went, but she sensed him walk away and heard him opening more cabinets and drawers.

Furniture squealed as he dragged a heavy table in front of her. She looked up through bleary eyes and watched as he placed several objects on the table. One was a glass bottle, but she couldn't read the label. Then he set down a small silver object. One end was tapered like a spade, the other had a knob with a diamond.

Beside the diamond object, he placed a cord covered in balls of all different sizes. The width of each ball increased, graduating from small and slender on one end to thicker on the other.

Besides that, he placed a pitcher of water and a glass. On the other side of the glass, he lay down a long thick—

Marigold's eyes widened and she struggled to sit up.

"Stay."

She hated when he spoke to her like an animal. "That's not going inside of me."

"Incorrect. All of this is going inside of you." He filled a glass of water and stood before her at the bolster. "Head up."

Her shoulders were weak from tensing. He pressed the glass to her lips and tipped it so water rushed into her mouth and dribbled down her chin. Her nipples hardened at the cold drops and she moaned in distress.

"Swallow all of it. I want you fully watered when I get you nice and wet."

He held the back of her head and forced her to drink the entire glass. She gasped for breath when he finally stepped away.

Eyes wide, she watched as he lifted the ornate bottle and pumped several drops of what she assumed was oil into his hand. He then reached for the knotted plastic rope and rounded the bolster. She instinctively tried to follow him with her eyes, but he shoved her back down.

"Time to hold your ass open again." Cold oil drizzled down her spine as he massaged it between her crack. "Nice and wide, so I can see."

Her palms tingled from the whip, which made her grip clumsy, but she tried to work with him, believing what he'd said earlier about staying relaxed.

His finger found her tight hole and pressed.

"Wait, wait, wait!"

He paused, but left his finger partially penetrating the tight muscle. It was enough to scramble her thoughts. "Do you want me to stop?"

Stop meant home. "I..." Shit. *Shit!* Panic welled inside of her, but she couldn't back out now. She just needed a moment to mentally prepare for what he planned to do. "I've never done anything like this before."

He chuckled. "Gotta love a virgin ass. You won't be able to claim the same tomorrow." His thumb pressed all the way in and she screamed.

He held it there, waiting for her to accept the intrusion and figure out that screaming only made things worse.

"That's better," he said when she silenced.

A fevered sweat broke out over her skin and her breasts stuck to the damp leather of the bolster as she panted. Heat trailed up her spine as he stepped closer.

Still hard as a rock, he bent over her and whispered, "Soon, it'll be my cock in your ass."

She closed her eyes in shame, knowing he spoke the truth.

He pulled his thumb back ever so slightly, only to wedge it back in again. "Very good. I think you like having your ass filled."

She didn't. It was awkward and mind scrambling and overwhelming in a way regular sex simply was not. As soon as he withdrew his thumb she gasped in relief. Pressing her cheek to the cool leather, she caught her breath.

He returned to the table, then moved behind her again.

"Please..."

"Ah, yes, such a pretty beggar. Give me a *'pretty please, Stone'*, and maybe I'll give you what you want."

She doubted that, but she was desperate. "Pretty please, Stone."

"Now, that wasn't convincing at all." He chuckled and drizzled more oil down her crack. Ensuring her hands had a tight grip on her ass, he aligned the first bead of the plastic rope with her ass and pushed. "Just a little ball."

She was instantly aware of the intrusion and certain it was only going to get worse.

"Take a breath."

She did and he used that moment to push the next bead inside of her. She stared forward with wide eyes, no longer able to keep her head in a resting position.

"Remember what I said about relaxing."

"I can't."

"Your call."

As if any of this was her call. Another bead sank into her and she groaned through gritted teeth.

"It's getting tight now, isn't it?"

"Now? It's been—*ah! Mother fucker!*"

He chuckled, the sound dark and excited. "Just a few more."

"I can't."

"You can."

"No, I—*Ahhh! Fuck, fuck, fuck, fuck! Get it out! Get it out!*"

"Hush," he stopped, cupping her jaw and angling her head back, so his mouth pressed close to her ear. "Breathe. It's for your own good."

She was delirious. Shaking her head, she squeezed her eyes shut. "I can't."

"You can. You need this."

"Why?"

"Because." His grip gentled, sliding loosely to her throat. His warm breath teased her cheek, which was damp from tears she didn't recall shedding. "There are three of us, Marigold. What did you think we meant when we said you were ours? Did you think we would always take turns? Some of us aren't good at waiting."

"Please, Stone," she pleaded. "It's too much."

"It's barely anything. Calm your mind. Don't let the panic overtake you. Stay in control of your emotions. Don't let them control you."

She whimpered but he was right. If she calmed down and pushed away the fear, it wasn't so bad.

"Beautiful. See how well things work out for you when you take my orders?"

"I hate you."

"I don't blame you. If not for this, you would have found a reason eventually." The moment he touched the beaded cord, she felt a slight juddering movement throughout her entire body. "Deep breath."

She inhaled, and the next bead nearly stole her vision. Sweat beaded at her temple as he moved quickly, pressing the last three beads inside of her.

A strange hum broke the silence, and it took her a moment to realize that incoherent muttering was coming from her.

Stone had come to stand in front of her again. He stroked the damp hair from her temple and pressed a kiss to her head, his voice a low rasp as he whispered into her ear, "I can only imagine what they're thinking as they watch you submit so beautifully. They're probably hard as granite and jealous as hell that I got to you first. I wonder if they'll be able to stay away."

A whimper of distress left her throat, but she was too distracted by the overwhelming intrusion to form words.

"There, there, little thief. It won't stay this way for long. I only wanted to show you what you could handle. Do you want it out?"

She nodded.

"Say please, Stone."

"Please, Stone."

"Very well." He moved behind her and gently repositioned her hands into a resting position on the bolster. This made the beads a little more tolerable. "I think this one's too big." He pulled and she felt immediate relief. But there were still several inches inside of her. "Oh, no. I think I've taken too much. That one's too small now that I've stretched you."

"*Fucker!*" Her objection turned into a guttural moan as he inserted more beads inside of her. Then he started to tug gently, not removing the rope, but stirring all sorts of sensations.

"Ah, I think that one is just right." His free hand reached between her legs with clinical precision, and he penetrated her with one long finger. "Feel that, Goldilocks? You're all wet with honey, and this big bear loves honey."

The pain had moved into something else, something she couldn't quite name. It wasn't a pleasure, but it also wasn't anything she was in a rush to stop.

"That's it. Give over to the sensations. Your body belongs to us, now. No need to think or rationalize or waste a single breath on shame. Just feel." He breached her pussy with another finger. "So tight." He twisted his fingers and tickled her taint. "That's the beads. Imagine what it will feel like to have two cocks inside of you like this."

Her body shivered beneath his touch as he adjusted the beads again, now moving in tandem with his fingers. She was on the precipice of something wicked. Something earth-shattering.

"That's it. Let me hear you. Let my brothers hear what a good little slut you are for your masters."

Part of her wished she had the strength and cleverness to bite him, but what he was doing to her felt too good. She needed the reward. So close. Just a second longer and she would—

His touch disappeared.

"You fucker!"

He laughed at her fury. "You didn't think it would be that easy, did you?"

"I was right there?"

"No. You were on the cusp of something underwhelming and passing. I plan to give you much, much more." He refilled the glass of water and brought it to her lips. "Drink."

This time, she welcomed the cool water. Her throat still hurt from Hunter, and her mouth was dry from moaning. She swallowed down every drop.

"Good girl." She watched as he placed the beads back on the table and collected the oil and the small diamond knob. "This should be cake, now that we've proven what you can take."

She had to agree with him.

"Head down."

She obeyed without objection. She even held her cheeks open so he could insert it quickly, grunting as he pressed the plug all the way in. It only reached the length of maybe two of the smaller beads on the rope, so she adjusted quickly.

"What a fast learner you are. Time to move." He lifted her off the bolster before she was ready, making her that much more aware of the plug. He set her down on the mattress, dressed in only a satin sheet. "Down on all fours."

She looked back at him in question. What was going to happen once she got down there?

"Should I get the crop?"

"No." She moved into position. A sharp and sudden buzzing disrupted the silence.

He kneeled behind her upturned ass—still hard as a rock but no longer wearing pants—and tapped the enormous black, silicone vibrator to her clit. She sucked in a breath and leaned into him with a moan.

"Greedy little slut. Not yet." He moved in front of her, his engorged cock heavy and hard. He stripped off his shirt and tossed it to the floor. Just like Hunter, he had the mark of a bear on his back, right shoulder. "Relaxing time is over. Unless you want to stop." Her eyes widened as he kneeled before her. "No? Good. Open wide."

She looked up at him, but he gave her no chance to object. His fingers knotted in her hair, and the second her lips parted he was shoving into her mouth. She let out a muffled moan, not used to the position or anything quite his size.

Stone was thick. Thicker than her wrist, but thankfully he was average length. Still, when he seated himself at the back of her throat, she gagged because he hadn't given her enough time to prepare. Her eyes watered and she let out a garbled moan around him, but he didn't back off.

"Go ahead and cry. I'd love to see that."

She held his stare, understanding he would give her no quarter. When a single tear seeped from the corner of her eye, he noticeably shivered.

"Fucking stunning. Those lips were made to suck cock." He wiped another tear as she glared at him. "Are you angry? Want to say something to me?" He withdrew. "Go ahead. Tell me to stop and I will."

"Asshole."

He chuckled and thrust his hips, burying himself deeper down her throat. This time, when she tensed, he pulled back, giving her the briefest chance to catch her breath before shoving to the back of her throat again.

He fisted her hair, instructing her to open her mouth so he could slide effortlessly in and out, fucking her face until he was satisfied. He dragged the swollen head of his cock over her lips, mixing her saliva with tears, and then pushed back in again.

She had a hundred hateful names to call him, but when he

finally pulled out, she only collapsed onto her arm to rest and catch her breath.

He slapped her ass. Hard. "Did I say we were finished? Get your ass back up here."

Her limbs shook as she rose again to her hands and knees. He kneeled behind her. She recognized the sound of the oil pump, and then he was pressing into her, not with his cock, but with the long vibrator.

"You'll learn what it's like to have every hole filled." He thrust a few times and held it deep inside of her. "Not to scare you, but that's smaller than Hunter."

The thought of Hunter anywhere near her intimate parts terrified her. That image only made it worse.

Stone returned to kneel in front of her, his body stretched over her to hold the vibrator inside her as he crawled closer, stroking his engorged cock.

"Now, suck it like a good girl, and make me come."

Again, she barely opened her mouth before he plunged into her, nudging the back of her throat. He had to go deeper in order to grip the vibrator properly, then he was thrusting quickly in and out of both ends.

"Eyes on me."

She looked up, her eyes watering as he slowly fucked her mouth with deliberately deep strokes. The corners of her lips stretched tightly and she struggled to accommodate him.

"Relax your throat and tip your head back. Stop trying to maintain control." He tugged her hair, angling her head back. "Loosen your jaw and your mouth open wide."

As soon as she relaxed her jaw, everything changed. He was sliding in and out with ease, and the long dildo was pumping into her pussy, sending tremors to her clit and vibrating the diamond plug wedged into her ass.

"That's it." His words shifted from English to Russian as he thrust his hips faster. "More. Give me more. Show me what a good little slut you are."

She was an object for his pleasure. He pushed and pulled. Thrusted and tugged. She only had to stay upright and open and he did the rest.

When his fingernails grazed the raised welts from the crop, she screamed around his cock, and he twisted the vibrator, increasing the speed. He thrust forward and held himself inside of her, buried down her throat as the vibrator pushed as deep as it could go.

The vibration was too much. She couldn't bear any more, and this time, when she screamed, her pussy clenched and spasmed.

"Dirty, little thief. You stole that one."

He ripped the dildo away and tossed it onto the bed. Shoving her to her back, he climbed over her. The plug pushed deeper, and she gasped.

"Open your mouth." He shoved into her mouth, pressing her back deep in the mattress as he gripped her tits and fucked them hard. "This...is...what...happens...to pretty...little thieves." He drew back and jerked his flesh in a tight fist. "Keep that mouth open and show me your tongue."

She did as he commanded, and hot jets of come splashed over her teeth and lips. His flavor seeped into her mouth as his release rushed past his stroking fist, covering her cheeks and forcing her to shut her eyes, finally.

The room stilled and silenced, only the sound of his ragged breathing remaining. Stone had become all she could hear, feel, and taste.

She flinched when his gentle lips pressed to hers. "Very good, Marigold. I think you've proven yourself."

She nearly shattered under his tender praise.

He took so possessively, so completely, his control was inescapable. All of his playfulness vanished in the face of the rough and demanding animal that hid beneath his surface. There was something dark inside of him, something that wanted to degrade and mark her.

"Do you hate me?" She despised the neediness in her voice, but she needed to know.

"I hate your brother."

That didn't answer her question, but she supposed that was as close to the truth she would get. "So do I."

He sighed. "I believe you."

Tears welled in her eyes as relief washed over her. "You do?"

He nodded.

He might have an urge to punish her. But there was something else there. Something she realized at the peak of her fear when he guided her. They would also protect her.

Stone could have broken her skin. He could have left permanent scars. He could have really hit her and broken bones. But he didn't.

He took. He used. But he also gave. He showed her things about herself she could have never discovered on her own. And she responded with equal desperation, proving her loyalty through the surrender he commanded.

"I didn't say stop."

"No, you didn't." He pulled her close, mindful of the plug still penetrating her ass. "You were brave." His lips pressed to her temple. "And loyal." He kissed her shoulder. "This is where our brand will go." He kissed her shoulder again. "Just like ours."

"Yours?"

He rolled off the mattress and sauntered back to where he'd left his pants. "I saw you looking at it." He flashed his shoulder so she could openly see the brand of a bear. "Did you want to feel it?"

She sat up on shaky limbs. "You want to burn me?"

He looked down at her and frowned. "This mark is a great honor."

"That mark is a brand. I'm not a piece of livestock."

"But you are our property."

"You can't brand me!"

"We can if we choose."

Disgusted, she crawled away from him and winced when she accidentally fell on her ass.

"Careful." He reached for her leg.

"Don't touch me!"

He paused and scowled. Then he ignored her order and dragged her close, flipping her onto her belly. "I'd planned to be gentle, but not with that attitude." He pulled the plug out, and she gasped, cool air hitting her overheated flesh in a shock that made her whole body clench.

Rolling away from him, she wrapped her arms around her waist protectively and pulled her knees to her chest.

"Are you hurt?"

Her body was surprisingly fine after all she'd been through. Sore and exhausted, but not hurt. Her feelings, however... That was a different story.

"I asked you a question."

"I heard you."

The room stilled, and she braced for another consequence.

"You don't speak to me like that."

"Or what? Will you shove something up my ass? Or better yet, brand me?"

His glare turned ice cold, but rather than respond, he pivoted and walked out of the room, slamming the door and leaving her there. No blanket. No towel. Not even clothes.

She realized then that his abandonment was her punishment. And she hated that she felt his angry desertion in the pit of her soul.

CHAPTER 12

CRADLED FROM THE WRECKAGE

Stone stalked into the hall, fists tight and shoulders heaving. He shouldn't have done that. He could have been more gentle with her, more patient. Christ, it was clear she hadn't done anything like that before and she'd more than pleased him, meeting every command and submitting even when it cost her in pride. So what if she bristled at the thought of being permanently marked? So had he, back in the day.

"Fuck!"

"Problem?"

Stone spun to find Ash leaning casually against the wall, watching him. *How long had he been standing there?* "Why are you lurking in the halls?"

Ash's brows shot up. "That was some show. Bet her ass is sore tomorrow."

She was probably sore right now. "Glad you enjoyed it."

"I'll enjoy it more when it's my turn again."

All three of them were possessive due to their past. Growing up with nothing did that to a man. Now, they had everything, but old habits die hard. "You're next. She's not ready for Hunter yet."

Ash chuckled. "Think she'll ever be?"

He pressed his lips tight. "She's not a virgin—"

"No shit."

"But she's inexperienced." Something Stone should have kept in mind. "She's going to need some time to recover. Don't go too hard on her."

"No harder than you, my brother." Ash moved toward the door of The Cave.

"What are you doing?"

"Just checking on our little thief before she robs us blind." He paused and studied Stone for a moment. "Why? Problem? I assumed you were done."

He should be. He walked out on her for a reason. He didn't play with brats and he could always tell when women were entering into a bratty stage. But he knew better than to abandon a sub after rough play.

Stone rubbed the back of his neck as Ash waited. "Nah. You go. You're better at the aftercare anyway. I have shit to do."

He closed his hand over the knob.

"But Ash..."

"Yeah?"

"Give her time to...recover. I was tough on her."

"You got it."

THE DOOR OPENED and Marigold's entire body went taut with tension. Her gaze shot over her shoulder and she stilled. Not Stone, but Ash.

He shut the door and paused, holding his hands out, palms

up, like she was a skittish animal. "Easy. I just came to check on you."

She turned back to the shirt she held, the one Stone had left, and continued to wipe her face. It was Stone's and she hoped she was ruining it with stains.

"No, don't use that," Ash said, moving to an ornate cabinet on the wall. He pulled a hand towel from the drawer and opened a closet that turned out to be a washroom. Water briefly ran, and then he returned, crouching down to the mattress to kneel before her. "May I?"

She dropped her hands into her lap and nodded.

Gently turning her chin, he carefully washed her face. The cloth was soft and warm. "He really got you."

Shame churned inside of her, and she turned away. No amount of washing would wipe away her sins at this point, so what did it matter?

Sensing her distress, he stood and held out a hand. "Come with me."

She hesitated, unsure if she could take much more.

"Please," he said in that peculiar way that made her feel safe.

She placed her hand in his, and he carefully pulled her to her feet as if sensing the weakness in her legs. If Stone was right, Ash and Hunter watched everything he'd done to her. She had no secrets left.

More shame swirled in her stomach.

"Lie down." He pointed to the antique four-poster bed, much taller than the low mattress on the floor.

She hesitated. If he expected a repeat performance, he was out of luck. She was dead on her feet and on the verge of collapse. "I..."

"Trust me." He took her choice away and nudged her down to the mattress, forcing her to ease onto her side. Then he surprised her by crawling behind her and pulling her close. "Just relax. I'm only going to hold you."

Confused, she blinked at the wall covered in strange sexual paraphernalia and wondered why he was, once again, being so nice to her. He held her so gently, her mind finally stopped questioning. She gave in to the unexpected comfort, her greatest fear in that moment being that he would take it away.

Part of her feared this was a trap, but her fraught heart and tired body were so in need of gentle contact, she was too weak to resist. And wasn't that pathetic? Desperation filled her eyes with unshed tears. This man—this stranger—was the only source of affection and safety she had left, and she wasn't even sure if he meant to betray her.

Her family didn't want her anymore. She'd been running for days and living in survival mode for months, only to become the captive of three wild men. Strangers from a different culture in the isolated, barren tundra where no one could get in and no one could get out. And they wanted to not just ruin her in every way imaginable, but wreck her in the process.

A sharp gasp slipped past her lips as a sob unexpectedly escaped.

"Shh, I've got you." Ash's hand rubbed gently up and down her bare arm.

Pressure built in her chest and throat as an avalanche of reality crushed her. The fear and worry built up, needing an exit, and she couldn't hold it in any longer, despite pressing her eyes and lips tight.

A high-pitched squeal hummed from her throat as sobs built inside of her like steam building inside of a tea kettle without a valve. The world came back in pieces.

First, the trembling. Deep, bone-rattling shivers that had nothing to do with cold and everything to do with the raw, flayed-open feeling Stone left in his wake. Her backside and palms throbbed where the crop had bitten deep, phantom sensations of the toys pressing into tender flesh left an unfamiliar ache she couldn't rationalize.

Her throat ached for many reasons. Hunter. Stone. They were all awful. Even Ash. She wasn't naive enough to believe he honestly cared about her wellbeing. He was obviously being nice to her for some other reason. Soon she'd find out, and for that she'd need her strength.

But she was out of strength at the moment. She was weak and wrung out in every possible sense. And to top it all off, she couldn't escape the needling sense of shame stabbing into her with every conscious thought.

Her entire being was a raw, exposed nerve. And she couldn't contain her confusion anymore.

"Hey," Ash whispered, concern softening his voice. "Everything is okay."

But it wasn't. Nothing was okay. She was lost and confused and afraid of where this nightmare would leave her in the end.

She could have fought him, but she didn't. She begged Stone to do all those terrible, beautiful things to her. He pulled out her submission like a secret she had no idea she'd been keeping. A rational person would hate what he did. But some shameful part of her enjoyed it.

Until he mentioned branding her. Then she only felt stupid. How utterly foolish of her to think he was meeting her as an equal. She was his play thing. A possession to use and destroy. He wanted to brand her body, burn her flesh, and abandon her to deal with the wreckage.

Would the abuse stop there? What if they went further than disfiguring her? Why had she thought this was better than confronting her father and brother again? She was insane to stay here with these men. She needed to leave, and she needed to leave now.

"Easy, *Zayka*." Ash's voice rumbled against her temple, warm honey in comparison to Stone's arctic cold. "I've got you."

Again, she surrendered.

"That's it. Just relax and let me hold you like this. Give your-self time to process. Permission to feel whatever you're feeling right now."

The word permission loosened another knot inside of her and a shaky breath tugged from her lungs.

"It's okay to cry, *Zayka*."

What was that word, *Zayka?*

Ash gently stroked her arms and back as she wept silently, shaken by how much emotion this ordeal had stirred loose inside of her. As she allowed herself the long overdue chance to weep in the shelter of his arms, time moved differently. Her thoughts were thick like molasses, then sharp and vicious like shattered glass.

She tried to replay everything Stone had done to her, but it was a blur. One moment, she'd been furious and terrified, then she was suspended in that exquisite nowhere, nerve endings singing to whatever symphony Stone played into her body.

Now, she was here. Alone with Ash.

He would hurt her too, if she gave him time.

And after Ash, would come Hunter. She shivered at the thought.

Ash rolled to his back and pulled her closer, tugging a silk-lined fur over her shoulders. "Comfortable?"

She didn't want to answer. Answering felt too much like consent.

But she reveled at the security of his arms, the way he cradled her close. Curled in Ash's hold like a broken bird, wrapped in silk and fur that smelled of cedar and sin, she was as safe as a fool could be.

His massive hand smoothed down her spine, mapping each

vertebra under the blanket. Not sexual. Not demanding. Just...
there. An anchor when everything inside her threatened to float
away.

"Would you like to talk about what happened?"

In that moment, words were foreign things, too heavy for
her tongue. A whimper escaped instead, small, wounded,
embarrassingly needy.

"Shh." He shifted, cradling her closer against the furnace of
his chest. "You don't have to talk yet. Just breathe until the inner
storm settles."

The command was gentle, but it was still a command.

Her body obeyed without thought, lungs expanding to
match the steady rise and fall of his. In. Out. In. Out. Each
breath pulled her back from that razor's edge of lunacy she
sometimes worried she might have passed. Maybe the doctors
at the clinic were right. Maybe she was prone to delusions.
What if she really needed those pills and that awful electric
shock therapy? At least then, she didn't feel like she was spinning undone.

At Whitmore, they claimed her panic attacks were further
evidence of her instability. Perhaps they were right.

Being gaslit as much as she'd been in the past year left her
with a pockmarked memory. Events blurred with delusions and
memories lost all tangible ties to reality. Maybe she imagined
the worst of it. Maybe they were actually trying to help her.

But then she recalled Jordan's rage and the way he slammed
her head into the wall, spittle coating his lips and spraying in
her face with every profane threat.

And at Whitmore... She could still taste the rubber. She
could feel the orderly's weight pressing into her... Taste the
blood... Smell the urine...

"I've got you, *printsessa*. Just breathe..."

She frowned, her thoughts occurring on a delay. Ash said to

breathe until the inner storm settled. He said it as if he'd felt what she was feeling, as if he'd been in her position before. But that was impossible. Men like Ash, Stone, and Hunter could never fill a submissive role. They were dominant predators through and through.

But somehow he knew she was battling an erratic storm inside.

She curled tighter to his side, her mind as wild as the ocean and his stability the breaker she needed to crash upon. A new sense of shame awakened as she accepted this existential appeal he held. Danger masquerading as safety. Logic couldn't deter her from feeding that need for comfort and playing into the lie. It felt good to be held. That was all that mattered. The consequence would eventually come, and it might be the worst yet, but her short sighted heart needed this tenderness now.

She could face the fallout later.

"Ash..." she whispered his name like a prayer, a plea that he be careful with her delicate heart.

"I've got you."

Stone showed her where pleasure and pain blurred into something transcendent and terrifying. Ash blurred something far more dangerous. He was teasing her with intimacy and fake acceptance. He was pretending he cared. And her battered heart had been through so much, she was falling for it, even while consciously recognizing that it was all an act.

But the way he held her went beyond courtesy or surface concern. It felt sacred.

She was too emotional for this. Too vulnerable. Stone had taken her apart with surgical precision. Stripped away every defense, every pretense, until she was nothing but raw need and desperate submission. He'd pushed her to places that should have frightened her, places where her mind went quiet and her body became an instrument for him to master.

Beautiful. Necessary. Dangerous.

But what Ash was doing seemed worse.

Stone left her in pieces, and Ash was collecting all the scattered, sharp edges to put her back together again.

She tried to pull away, but his palm pressed her back down to his chest. "Not yet."

Was he getting something out of this as well?

She feared he might get aroused, but there was only one way to find out, and she wasn't going there. He had to have something to gain, some ulterior motive for treating her so gently when it was apparent none of them trusted her.

His touch stayed steady, grounding, while her psyche knitted itself back into something resembling wholeness. She must have drifted off in his arms, because she stirred when she felt him slip out from under her body and try to replace himself with a pillow.

Leaning up on an elbow, she looked at him through blurred eyes. The glass in the tall windows was now dark. How long had she slept?

He returned to the bed with a glass of water. "Thirsty?"

She actually wasn't since Stone had made her drink so much to stay hydrated, but she sat up anyway. When she reached out with shaky fingers, he gently brushed her hand away and pressed the glass of water to her lips, supporting her head. The cool liquid soothed her raw throat, each swallow a small act of reclamation.

"Good girl." The praise wrapped around her like warm silk, different from Stone's cutting approval but no less potent. "Such a good girl for us."

Fresh tears burned her eyes. The thrill of his praise was quickly tinged with shame. She couldn't mistake their possession as softness or affection. These men wanted to harm her. They were not her protectors.

But the tears wouldn't subside. They weren't from pain or fear, but from the overwhelming vulnerability of being seen like this. Trembling. Needy. Cracked open and spilling over with emotions too big for her body.

"Let the tears come." Ash's thumb traced softly across her damp cheek, the gesture impossibly tender for hands that could snap her neck without effort. "You were so strong for him. So perfect. But you don't have to be strong right now."

More permission. What was wrong with her that his authorization intensified her feelings? He had no power over her mind, yet his words gave her the freedom to feel every emotion honestly.

"Let it out, *printessa.*"

His words broke something loose inside her. Sobs wracked her frame, ugly and cathartic, while Ash held her through each one. He murmured praise in Russian and English, voice a constant rumble that vibrated through her bones. His hands never stopped moving —stroking her hair, rubbing feeling back into sore limbs, tracing soothing patterns that pulled her consciousness back into her body.

"I don't understand why I'm crying."

His soft laugh was teasing. "No? You've been through quite a bit."

"But I'm not a crier." She wiped the embarrassing proof of her fragility away, only to have more tears fall. "It's infuriating."

"I've watched men three times your size break down far worse from far less. It's the paradox of playing with strong power dynamics. The rougher the play, the softer the landing needs to be."

Was that it then? This was all a result of what Stone had done?

He hadn't just played with her body, he toyed with her mind, scattering her psyche like dandelion seeds into the wind.

She hadn't shed a single tear while he put her through the motions, but his abandonment afterwards and Ash's attentive care were her disgraceful undoing.

"It's perfectly natural to feel emotional."

She accepted his reasoning and nodded. "Thank you." *Ugh,* and now she was thanking him?

But without Ash gathering those pieces, without this careful tending, she'd be left fragmented. Suspended between spaces. Lost in a fall back to earth that could turn transcendent experiences into trauma.

"You're almost through it now, *Zayka.*" Ash tilted her chin up, ice-blue eyes scanning her face with an intensity that made her feel precious. Cherished.

She looked up at him and sniffled. "What is *Say-kah?*"

He chuckled. "*Zayka.* It means little rabbit."

She smiled.

"You like that?"

"It's better than little thief."

"I suppose it is." He rewarded her with one of those rare smiles that transformed his face from dangerous to devastating. "Though, I'm not so sure you have the heart of a small creature. Especially when I sense the mind of a *printsessa.*"

She smiled, trusting the compliment and not looking further for hidden meaning. His words gave her strength in a way that repaired her and helped her feel grounded again.

She glanced up at him. "What happened to your eye?"

"It's nothing."

It wasn't nothing. He'd had it before the fight with Hunter, but she still suspected he was the source. "Did Hunter do it?"

"I deserved it."

She wanted to ask if it had something to do with her. "Why?"

"Because I took something I shouldn't have." He shifted and let out an exhale. "Think you can eat something?"

The thought of food made her stomach turn. "I'm not hungry."

"That's because you're still coming down. It's important you enjoy some creature comforts." He tucked a lock of blonde behind her ear, letting his fingers trail over her collarbone and dangerously close to her chest. "Water. Food. Warmth. Touch."

Her nipple hardened, and she snuggled closer. Dear God, was she leaning into his touch?

He gazed at her questioningly, his hand no longer moving.

Her lips parted, but she wasn't sure if she wanted to whisper a plea or apology. "I..." Her lashes lowered in more shame. Living in a facility for the mentally ill didn't make her feel half as imbalanced as a few hours in this house with these men. "I'm sorry."

"Sorry for what?"

Pulling back, she put some space between them and closed her arms around her chest, hiding her aroused breasts. "I don't know. I'm...confused."

He gently pried her arms away. "Don't hide yourself." Softly, he dragged the back of his knuckle between her breasts. Goosebumps rose on her flesh and her nipples pulled tighter. He watched her carefully. "May I?"

His request threw her off. She was theirs. They had full authority over her—or else. The ice around her heart softened and she nodded ever so slightly.

Slipping a hand under her knees and behind her head, he lowered her to her back. Warm breath tickled over her neck as soft hair teased her skin. First, he merely nuzzled her breast with the side of his nose and groaned. He traced the tip of his tongue slowly, swirling over her curves and building anticipation. He was delicately teasing her, making her want his mouth even more.

When he finally closed his lips over her nipple, she sighed in sweet relief. Her body arched and her legs slowly scissored as pressure built low in her belly. Those soft kisses were perhaps some of the gentlest kisses she'd ever been given.

Then his teeth loosely trapped the tip of her nipple his tongue swirling decadently against her flesh. She moaned and instinctively ran her fingers through his soft hair, but he caught her wrist and pressed it into the mattress, holding her hand down as his fingers formed a sort of manacle.

"Is this too much? I know you're tired."

"No," she rasped, through with the shame and leaning into the pleasure.

"Good." His mouth closed over her nipple, and this time he applied more pressure, sucking deeply until something dark unfurled inside of her. She arched and moaned, but then the pleasure shifted and there was a bite of pain.

"Ah! Ash..."

He pulled back only to climb over her, capturing her other hand and pinning her arms overhead. "Too hard?"

"A little." The way he'd been doing it had felt soft and delicate. "But I..."

"You like it a little rough?"

She nodded, confused by the pull of two polar opposite sensations. Her mind wanted gentleness, but her skin needed the ache. She wanted soft kisses with teeth, gentle petting with scraping nails. "I can't get a handle on my emotions."

"You don't need to make sense of them right now. You only need to feel." He kissed her tenderly. "Who do you belong to, *printessa?*"

Something turned in her stomach and her soft expression fell.

"Don't be scared. Just answer the question. Who owns your body?"

Me! She wanted to scream. But she understood this was her reality. Her penalty and price for their protection. "You do."

"I've been very gentle with you, haven't I? Kind and patient..."

She swallowed, wondering how stupid she must be to have gotten into this position with him, naked, beneath him, with her arms pinned over her head. Now, he was going to collect his dues. "Yes."

"You're thinking too much." Shifting her wrists into the hold of one hand, his finger traced the space between her brows, barely touching. "Stone makes you shut down. Hunter makes you fight. But me? I make you think."

He was right. He broke down her walls and found her soft underbelly. She was most vulnerable with Ash, which meant he was the most dangerous despite feeling the safest. "I don't know what you want."

"I want to play with you. Nothing too intense. I'd planned to leave you be, but..." He glanced at her breast. "You're quite the temptation."

He released her hands and she automatically started to lower her arms.

"*Nyet.*" He pressed them back down. "I want you still. Mine to play with and explore. Understand?"

He traced a finger slowly over the swell of her breast and her breathing turned labored. "Y-yes."

"Good, *printessa.*" He stripped off his shirt and tossed it to the floor.

Ripples of muscle stacked neatly along his trim torso and ropes of thick sinew corded his tattooed arms. He bent over her, teasing her lips with his, so their breath mingled.

"You worry too much. You don't trust us. I know it's too soon. But in time, you'll see. We're nothing you need to fear."

His mouth teased featherlight kisses down her throat, so tender and hypnotizing. He touched her in all the right places, removing the strain in her muscles and replacing her anxiety with yearning.

"Kiss me," he whispered, and she eagerly gave in to his command.

His tongue skated delicately over hers.

"*Nyet.*" His thumb dragged slowly over her lips. "When you kiss me, you kiss me like you mean it." His hand closed loosely around her throat, not applying pressure, but implying how easily he could snap her neck if he wanted to. "Like your life depends on it, *printessa*."

This time, when his lips grazed hers, she angled up and sealed her mouth to his. He groaned in satisfaction and deepened the kiss, his tongue stroking over hers with possessive claim as he stated without words how attracted he was to her.

When they broke apart, they were both panting. "That was much better, wasn't it?"

"Yes," she confessed.

"I like intensity. Whether we're cuddling or fucking, I expect you to be uninhibited by shame or pride or whatever else is filling that head of yours. I want everything raw and unfiltered between us. Honest. Understand?"

She nodded.

"Good." He glanced down at her chest. "You don't fear me. Why do you think that is?"

But she did fear him. Unlike the others, Ash knew how to get inside of her psyche. "You're...different. You weren't mean to me like the others. You're patient."

Laughter rumbled in his chest. "Stone has patience. He just

uses it like a weapon. Hunter…" Ash shrugged. "Hunter doesn't believe in patience. He believes in now."

Was he actually opening up to her? The more she knew about them, about what made them tick, the more likely she was to survive them. "And what do you believe?"

"I believe in watching. Your body language tells me everything I need to know."

"That's very clinical."

"No. Clinical is Stone counting your breaths to calculate exactly when you'll shatter. This is reverence. I won't be satisfied with obedience alone. I want your trust."

She lowered her gaze. She could never trust them. The moment she did, she'd be lost. They wanted to hurt her family. She couldn't overlook that, no matter how horrible Jordan was, they would always share DNA. Therefore, they would always resent her for her sibling's crimes.

"You're overthinking again."

"I'm not a doll who can just lay here—"

His hand covered her mouth. "That sass is what got you in trouble earlier."

Something hardened inside of her. She bit his hand and he ripped it away, hissing out a swear in Russian.

He examined the bite mark and threw his head back, laughing with true amusement. "She has teeth!"

"And I bite."

His grin turned smoldering. "So I've learned." He surprised her with another mind bending kiss that left her off balance. He didn't fully pull away, as he whispered over her mouth, "One day, you'll trust me enough to take you apart, because you'll learn how incredible it can feel when we're broken into pieces. How freeing."

"I'll never—"

He pressed a finger to her lips. "You will, because you'll

believe with all you are that I will put you back together after. You will learn to trust me, *printessa*."

"Stone didn't—"

"Stone is Stone. I am Ash." He cupped her face, thumb tracing her cheekbone. "I like learning which pieces fit where. Which ones make you gasp. Which ones make you beg." His voice dropped, honey over gravel. "I like finding the sharp edges you didn't know you had."

"That sounds..."

"Dangerous?" He smiled, and there it was, that flash of something predatory beneath the gentle exterior. "We're all dangerous, *printessa*. I'm just better at hiding it."

Which made him the riskiest one of all. At least with Hunter she knew what she might be getting. And Stone had shown his true colors. But Ash was a mystery in many ways, curious but gentle, demanding but patient.

"Always thinking." His hands slid down to her throat, not squeezing, just resting. Possessing. "When Stone pushes you, it's because he needs your submission. When Hunter takes you, he'll demand your surrender. But when I touch you?"

Her pulse hammered against his palms. "What do you need?"

"Your trust." He leaned down, lips brushing her ear. "Complete. Absolute. The kind that lets you close your eyes and know I'll catch you. The kind that lets you say yes without knowing what you're agreeing to."

"That's terrifying."

"Yes." He pulled back to meet her gaze. "It should be. I'm just as broken as the rest of them. But we all fracture in different ways." His smile was slow, wicked, nothing like the gentle giant facade he wore so well. His hands tightened just slightly on her throat, enough that her eyes widened and her breath quickened.

"I'm broken too," she confessed.

"No, you're only bruised. A woman who doesn't know her own limits yet. But I can enlighten you." His lips traced her throat, settling on her hammering pulse. "And I'm *going to*. Slowly. Carefully. Until you understand exactly what your body can do."

He lifted her hand and gently kissed her palm. Only then did it occur to her that she wasn't prying him off of her. She'd kept her hands exactly where he commanded her to put them.

Ash traced his tongue over the fading welts marking her palms. "Did it hurt?"

"Not really."

"But you thought it would, didn't you?"

"At first. Honestly, the anticipation was worse than the strike."

"See? It's a mind game that manifests in physical play." He reached between their bodies and unsnapped the top button of his jeans, pulling the zipper down slowly until the heated weight of his engorged cock rested heavily on her body. "Like now. You're wondering why I just did that. *Is he going to fuck me? Force me to suck his cock like Stone did? Will he shove it in my ass now that I've been so beautifully broken in?* I'm sure those and a hundred other questions are running through your head, *printessa*."

Heat bloomed beneath her skin as a flutter of anxiety tickled her chest.

"Quiet your mind." Ash's command cut through her spiraling thoughts. "Whatever you're thinking, chase it away." He leaned close and whispered in her ear so only she could hear. "He's probably in his office right now, hard as stone and sick with regret, wondering the same things you are. Let's let him worry for a while."

He drew back and winked at her with a conspirator's smile, playing good cop to Stone's bad cop. She wanted to play with him, if only to make Stone pay for abandoning her and threatening to brand her.

"You're intrigued by the thought." Ash grinned.

"Maybe a little."

"You want to make Stone pay?"

She shrugged, afraid to show how deeply he'd upset her. "Who cares about Stone?"

Ash arched a brow. "Careful. He can hear you."

"Good."

"Feisty little rabbit. Let's see how fierce you really are. It's time to come apart."

"Wha—" He kissed her, harder and more demanding than before.

"Such a sexy mouth." He delved deeper, taking, stealing, forcing her to meet him stroke for stroke. Then his fingers knotted in her hair and tugged, exposing her neck. "Hair like spun gold."

His mouth closed over her throat, sucking hard enough to leave a mark. He cupped her breast, massaging as he dragged his thumb over the turgid tip.

"Such beautiful ivory skin. So easily marked." He trailed his mouth higher and sucked again, pulling back with a pop to admire his work. "Already showing traces of my desire for you."

He scooted lower, and captured her nipple in his mouth, teasing the tip with gentle nibbles and fast flicks of his tongue. But like before, his touch turned more intense the longer he played.

"Ah!"

"Yes," he purred, "Let my brothers hear you, *printessa*." He returned to sucking, hard and concentrated over the tender tips of her nipples. She shifted and squirmed, but that only edged him on.

"Please, Ash..." she begged, needing him to stop or do something.

He sat back on his thighs, pinning her at the hips under his weight. The swollen head of his cock peeked from his open jeans, pointing at her accusingly as pre-cum glistened from the slit. Then he caught her nipples between his thumb and forefinger and she screamed.

He smiled like a sadist, waiting for it to sink in that screaming got her nowhere. When she quieted, panting and glaring up at him, he flashed his teeth with amusement.

"Now, you're learning. Breathe through it. Breathe into the pain. Any second now, you'll feel a wash of pleasure."

As if conjured by his words, a flush bloomed from her chest, creeping through her blood as her eyelids lowered. Her breathing steadied as the pain subsided, replaced by a euphoric wash of pleasure.

"Now, take your hand and make me come. When I do, I'll let you go."

She awkwardly reached for him and stroked.

"Not like that."

She stilled. "How?"

"Hold it tight. It should feel like I'm inside your pussy. Grip it so it feels like fucking. Hard and fast. Don't stop until your fingers are dripping."

It was hard to concentrate with him pinching her nipples, but she managed to do as he commanded. He was thick and long, and every few strokes she could feel him pulse under her touch.

"Good, *printessa*. Keep going. Get used to serving us, and we will spoil you rotten." He flexed his hips, fucking himself into her hand. "Every day, I want you drenched with desire. I want you to keep your word as much as I keep mine. You'll learn to trust my promises, rely on them. Do you trust me yet?"

She risked disappointing him with honesty. "No."

"No?" Shock widened in his eyes.

Had he expected to sway her so easily? She pushed him on purpose, hoping to burst the safety bubble that gave the impression he was somehow her protector. She needed to shatter the illusion, not just to punish him, but to punish herself for being so gullible when she knew better.

"Deep down, you're no different than Stone or Hunter."

Fury flashed in his eyes, and he released her nipples. She screamed as blood rushed into the tips.

He fisted her hair, yanking her head back as he growled in her face, "Is that what you think?"

Tears pricked her eyes, but she didn't cower. "Yes!"

He shoved her legs apart and penetrated her in one hard thrust. "If I'm as awful as Stone, why are you soaked?" He ground his pelvis against hers, and she shoved at his shoulders. "*Nyet.*" He forced her arms to her side. "I demand truth between us."

Seething, she mocked, "*Nyet.*"

He chuckled. "You are a little brat, *printsessa.* So spoiled to think you can bite the hand that feeds you. Maybe leave a souvenir for you." He rocked his hips. "And then, when you fall in love with that little souvenir, we'll finally let you leave. But not with my child."

It was the cruel side of him she suspected, but she took no joy in revealing it. "You're a bastard."

"Because you wanted me to be. I showed you kindness, and you poisoned my compassion with your own distrust."

A tear seeped from the corner of her eye and he caught her jaw, forcing her to meet his stare.

"What is it about kindness that scares you? Do you like this cruel side of me? Does it take away the sense of blame?"

She was done playing games with him. She just wanted this to end. "No."

"That's right. Because the blame is in your head. Not once did I shame you for your actions, but that voice in your head never stops, does it?"

"No."

"I know how to quiet it, but you won't let me. Trust, *printessa*. That's what it takes to silence our demons."

She shut her eyes, hating how exposed he made her feel. How ashamed of the things she felt for these men, and the pleasure she took from their punishments. "I don't know how to trust."

"Because someone betrayed you." He lifted her jaw. "Open your eyes. Who do you see?"

Her lips pressed tight, and his grip tightened in warning. "Ash."

"That's right. Ash. Not Stone. Not Hunter. Not anyone from your past. Don't ever compare me to another man again. Do you understand me?"

She blinked rapidly as more tears started to flow. "Yes."

He released her face and pulled out of her. "An unnecessary remark when we were having a perfectly nice time together." He repositioned her, with her arms at her side and her legs pressing together as they were. "Now, let me keep my word." He bent forward and softly suckled her nipple, soothing away the pain he'd caused.

This time, there was no urgency, no authority. They came together in passion, her urge to ease her confused mind and his need to soothe away any pain he'd caused. She reached for him without a command and stroked him through long, drugging kisses.

"You taste like salty tears, *printessa*."

His mouth trailed lower, scattering delicate kisses over her throat. He sucked and licked her breasts as she stroked him to completion. And when her fingers were dripping and her belly was wet with his release, he didn't stop.

The hard muscles of his abdomen pressed into her sticky belly as he made a feast of her. Sucking. Licking. Marking her. Playfully nibbling and biting her.

It went on so long, he stirred something inside of her, soft and light, like a summer breeze whispering through trees. The delicate ripple of deep pleasure built into a gasp.

"Yes, *printessa*, give in to it." It may have been a command, but he spoke so softly it sounded like a plea and she shattered. "Beautiful."

Stunned that anyone could do that to her by only touching her breasts, she stared at him. He bent and kissed the sensitive tip of her breast, tasting the salt of her fevered skin as she arched beneath him. "This is the part where you rest in my arms, trusting me to hold you safe."

The son of a bitch played her. She couldn't even hate him for it, because in the end, he held her like she needed to be held, and his gentleness overshadowed the painful lesson. She needed someone she could trust. It was the only way she would survive this place when some days she wasn't even sure she could survive herself.

She leaned into him, showing him the trust she was still unable to verbalize.

Ash grinned, clearly pleased with himself, and pulled her tighter against him. He didn't just tend to her body. He anchored her mind. Preventing the drop that could turn submission into shame, and pleasure into regret.

"I'll never touch you in a way that leaves you hurting." He pressed a hand to her heart. "A sore ass, perhaps, but I'll never hurt you here."

She nestled into his strength, relishing the promise,

pretending for a twisted moment it might be one he'd keep. "Thank you."

He sighed and kissed her head, rather than question if her gratitude meant she was learning to trust him. She was going to need time. Time to recover from past betrayals and time to see if he would truly keep his word.

Of the three men, Ash was the first to give her kindness. If it was truly genuine, she wanted to give him something in return. But he was tricky. He didn't want her pain, or pleasure, or complete surrender like Stone. He wanted the intangible and sacred—her trust.

Where Stone abandoned her out of frustration, Ash held her through a storm. Without this bridge back to herself, Stone's gift, her unburdening, felt like theft. But Ash put her back together again.

"You're not like the others," she whispered, regretting her earlier accusation.

He stilled then pressed another gentle kiss to her head. "Rest now," he whispered, pulling her tighter into his side.

Safety.

Her eyes drifted closed, exhaustion pulling her under like a riptide. But this time, she didn't overthink it. Didn't fear it. Because she was cradled from the wreckage, safe in Ash's arms.

CHAPTER 13

A TEMPTATION TO TAME

Marigold awoke in a different bed in a different room, disoriented and confused. Layers of fur blankets weighed her down. She sat up, hair falling over her shoulder as she looked around.

Alone. Finally.

She studied the room, but didn't recognize the space. The furniture lacked the luxurious, masculine feel of the other bedrooms. Instead, this one had a feminine air to it. Exposed ceilings with pale honey planks and dark beams formed a star overhead, a beautiful contrast to the crystal chandelier hanging from the center over the king-sized bed. But this was no ordinary bed one could purchase online. The posts were raw birch, knotted and twisting upward, a natural work of art that made Marigold feel like she was waking up in a mystical fairytale.

Her nose twitched. The room might look like a fairytale, but she smelled like a bridge troll. Slipping out of bed, she quickly rushed to the door she hoped was a bathroom before someone noticed her nude form sprinting across one of the surveillance cameras. She was sure there were several hidden in the room. Otherwise, they would have never left her alone.

The door indeed hid a bathroom, equally feminine as the bedroom with a claw-footed antique tub, and a vintage dressing table facing an ornate oval mirror.

"Perfect."

She set the faucet to warm and let the tub fill as she nosed around for toiletries. To her surprise, the drawers were stocked with unopened products. Female products.

Was that a twinge of...jealousy?

No, she couldn't be jealous.

What did she care if other women had stayed here? However, the uncomfortable pinch persisted, evoking a sense of petty suspicion towards the females who might have stared in this mirror before.

She withdrew several unopened bottles and a packaged toothbrush. As the tub filled, the bathroom warmed and she doctored the water with oils and salts. The moment she sank into the warm bath, she moaned.

"Yessss...." She allowed herself several minutes to simply soak and take in the lavishness of the stunning room.

It didn't take long for her to find a brass bear head, looking directly at her. Unsure who watched on the other end, she lifted a hand from the water, stuck out her tongue and popped the middle finger.

"Do you think you're funny?"

Water sloshed as she jolted and looked back at the door, but she was all alone.

"To your right. The lamp."

She looked at the accent table where an apothecary assortment of perfumes and salts sat on a gold tray. Hidden at the base of the lamp was a small speaker.

She looked back at the bear and narrowed her eyes. "Pervert."

"Guilty. Did you sleep well?"

Only then did she realize it was Ash on the other end. His easygoing tone gave him away. "Yes. I don't remember getting here."

"You passed out. Stone put you to bed."

"S—Stone?" She didn't like the thought of him touching her while she was unconscious.

"Relax. He was a perfect gentleman. And feeling rather sheepish for his earlier tantrum. He carried you up while you were sleeping. It was the least he could do."

"Oh." She believed Ash, her nerves at ease again.

"Shit. I have to take this call. Enjoy your bath, *printessa*."

He stopped talking, but that didn't mean he stopped watching or listening. She pictured him in a dark room filled with monitors. Or maybe it was through their phones. Could they all see her? She slouched lower in the water, still on edge at the thought of having an audience.

When she finished washing, she brushed her hair to one side and tied it back with a blue satin ribbon. Then she returned to the bedroom, surprised to find a sweater dress laid out on the bed that hadn't been there before. And it was just her size.

She glanced around nervously, making sure she was alone before checking the label. Definitely women's.

"How frequently do they host hostages here?" she muttered, pulling the dress over her head. It was loose-fitting and fell just to her knees. "Ooh!" She spotted a tall pair of suede boots on the floor beside the bed. Brand new and just her size!

She pulled them on, dragging the zipper up slowly. The butter soft suede went to her thighs and had a tiny gemstone in the heel that looked like smoky quartz.

She examined her reflection in the mirror. It was the cutest she'd looked in months and the closest she'd felt to normal since that horrible day they sent her away.

Paranoia set in. Why were they spoiling her? They hated her. This had to be some sort of trap. As much as it killed her, she removed the boots and put them back beside the bed.

"Don't they fit?"

She spun toward the door, but was still alone. She padded barefoot to the bedside lamp, but didn't see a speaker. "Ash?"

"What was wrong with the boots?"

She continued to search for the speaker. "Nothing."

"Then why did you take them off?"

She shrugged. "I don't know."

"You clearly liked them. Were they too small?"

"No." She lifted a perfume bottle and checked the bottom. "Where are you?"

"Too big?"

"No." She searched the door frame unsure how small a speaker could be.

"Then what?"

"I just didn't want them."

"Liar."

Giving up her search, she snapped, "What do you care anyway?"

"The lodge gets cold. You should have something on your feet. Besides, they looked sexy on you. But more than that, you liked them. I saw how excited you got when you put them on."

She hated how much she liked knowing he thought she looked sexy. "I just don't want them."

"They were a gift."

"No, thank you."

He sighed and she swore it came from the left side of the room. She lifted a vase of flowers, but found no speaker.

"Marigold, gifts are gifts. No strings attached."

She pulled open a drawer but it was empty. "Everything here has strings, Ash."

"Put the boots on."

"No."

"It wasn't a request."

She glared up at the bear camera. "You just ruined them." Walking back to the bed, she put on the boots, but without the pleasure she felt the first time she tried them on. "Anything else, *Master*?"

"Watch the attitude. We don't take well to bratty behavior, as you've learned."

"Well, I don't take well to bossiness."

"Last night you did."

She pressed her lips into a firm line. "What am I supposed to do now?"

"Whatever you want."

She stilled. Seriously? "Aren't you afraid I'll get into trouble?"

"If you do, we'll see that you're properly reprimanded. I'm on duty a few more hours, but Hunter and Stone are around. Go exploring."

"Duty?"

"Work."

"What do you do?"

"Nothing that concerns you. I want you to go right to the kitchen and eat something before you do anything else."

Food sounded like a good idea. Her belly felt hollow, and she couldn't remember the last thing she ate. "Okay."

"Be good, *printessa*. I'll be watching."

She rolled her eyes and mumbled, "I bet you will."

In the kitchen, she concocted a small plate of bread, cheese, and some fancy jam she found in the cupboard. As she sat at the table, frequently staring at the bear cam beside the clock on the wall, she wondered about her hosts.

The house—or lodge as they called it—was state-of-the-art luxury wrapped in primitive strength. The castle-like exterior would hold up for years against the tundra-like conditions outside. She'd always thought the Isles of Kassel were tropical, but she supposed she was wrong. Or maybe the islands were just that big that they spanned different climates.

When she finished her lunch, she washed the plate and put it away. Opening the industrial-sized fridge, she set the jam back on the shelf where she'd found it. When she closed the heavy door, she jumped.

Hunter stood a foot away from her, glaring like she'd just robbed him.

Her heart jolted from calm to erratic as she took another step back. "Ash told me to eat."

He grunted and opened the freezer.

She took several more steps back.

Paying her no mind, he pulled a frosted glass bottle out and set it on the counter beside two small glasses, then caught her by the sweater. "You stay."

She didn't want to stay. She didn't want to be anywhere near him. Just looking at him now, made her aware of how her throat still ached.

"Sit." He pointed at one of the upholstered stools at the island.

Reluctantly, she slithered onto the seat and tugged her sweater dress down to her knees.

Hunter filled the two glasses with what she suspected was vodka. She kept her head down and studied him through her lashes.

He had to be ex-military. Ordinary men weren't built like that. His face was a mixture of chiseled, hard angles and scars.

He rolled his neck, deliberate and slow, each little pop breaking the suffocating silence.

"Drink." He pushed a shot glass in front of her.

Marigold lifted the glass with a shaky hand and sipped. Yup, definitely vodka. She took a minuscule sip and set the frosted glass down.

"No, drink." He demonstrated by throwing his shot back and slamming down the empty glass.

She only ever did shots on her twenty-first birthday and that had not ended well. "I'd rather sip—"

"Did I ask? Do as I say."

Her hatred for him grew. Lifting the glass, she took a deep breath and tossed the contents back, sputtering as the icy fire rushed down her throat. Her eyes instantly watered. "Oh, God, that's awful."

He refilled her glass and pushed it forward. "Drink."

"Seriously?"

He shot her a look that proved he was very serious.

Discouraged, she lifted the glass and hesitated. Two shots and she'd be drunk. Maybe that would be best. Reluctantly, she chugged it down and groaned.

When he refilled it again, she begged, "Please, no more."

"Drink."

"I can't."

"Either drink it or I'll shove it down your throat myself."

She pulled the glass closer and whispered asshole under her breath. Before she saw him move, her face was pressing into the counter. He had her bent over and pinned by the back of the neck.

"Do I look like someone you should fuck with?"

"Get off me!" She growled, but his hold only tightened.

A draft teased between her legs, reminding her she had nothing on under her sweater dress.

"Let me make this perfectly clear, so there is no misunderstanding in the future. You are nothing. Everything you touch, eat, and breathe belongs to us. We own you. Disrespect me again, and I'll throw you out in the snow and let you freeze to death."

She stilled, because he was that terrifying. She believed him. She believed he'd let her die in the cold and forbid his brothers from saving her.

"Please..." she whispered. "I'm sorry." Fear choked her as she understood how helpless she was against him. He could do anything to her, and she was powerless to stop him. "Please don't..." The air chilled around them. "...don't hurt me."

He let go, but she stayed bent over the counter, afraid to move.

"Get up."

Pushing herself back, she slouched in the stool and drank the shot. Hunter poured two more shots for himself and swallowed them down in quick, practiced gulps. "I'm not interested."

She kept her eyes on the ivory countertop.

"Understand? Fucking you would be a punishment for both of us."

She should be relieved, but such harsh rejection held so much revulsion she felt like the world's worst pariah.

"Say you understand. When I speak directly to you, you respond."

"I understand."

"Good." He opened a drawer and pulled out a notepad and pen, sliding it to her. "I ask the questions, and you write down the answers. Start with your brother's phone number."

Her hand trembled as she lifted the pen. The vodka had made her thoughts heavy and she couldn't recall the last few numbers. "I can't remember—"

"I'll wait until you do."

The pressure to write something only added to her distraction. In the end, she put something down but was only partially sure it was right.

"I want the names of all his schools and employers."

"Since high school?"

"Since birth."

Over the next hour, she wrote down every detail she could remember about Jordan. Several times she reminded Hunter that Jordan was older and not her full brother, so there were parts of his past she simply didn't know, but he didn't care. In the end, her treachery filled six pages, detailing every identifying trait of Jordan in blazing betrayal. Her family would never forgive her.

When she set down the pen, Hunter collected the notepad and left. She let out a breath she felt like she'd been holding for more than an hour.

No matter how many times she tried to settle in, something always came along to remind her she was the enemy, the unwanted captive they had to feed and could fuck at will. This wasn't home. It was her prison. She couldn't figure out if the wise response was to accept her fate and surrender, or do whatever she could to escape.

She needed to escape his lingering scent, escape the way she could still feel him on her skin.

Sadness shrouded her every step as she wandered through the halls. The house was quiet and isolated. Sometimes it felt like she was all alone. But she was never alone. Someone was always watching.

Time didn't exist here. The clocks were merely a decorative reminder that life moved on outside of these walls that both protected and imprisoned her. Her sleep schedule was so messed up, she was often taken off guard by the setting sun, sometimes pausing to decide if it was dusk or dawn.

Perhaps it was the vodka that put her in such a haze. But more likely it was the compounding trauma she'd suffered finally taking it's toll.

"I'm not crazy," she whispered, wandering down a narrow hall that opened to a wide corridor.

She found Ash in the lodge's library an hour before dawn, reading by lamplight as another storm exhausted itself outside. Relief flooded her. Of all the men, none should put her at ease, but for some reason, Ash did, so she knocked softly at the door.

Without glancing up from his novel, he turned a page and said, "*Printessa*, come in."

Floor-to-ceiling windows revealed the first hints of grey light bleeding across the horizon, and for the first time since her arrival, the world beyond the glass looked almost peaceful.

She stood in the doorway, a moment longer than necessary, simply taking him in. He'd changed into dark jeans and a thermal shirt that clung to the lean muscle of his torso, but there was something softer about him in the quiet morning light. Less predatory.

"Can't sleep?" he asked, still not looking up from his book.

"How did you know it was me?"

"Your scent." He glanced up with a slight smile. "You smell like fear and flowers. It's... distinctive."

She moved into the room, trailing her fingers along leather-bound spines of ancient first editions that were probably worth more than most people's cars. "What are you reading?"

He held up the book—thick, Russian text she couldn't decipher. "Dostoyevsky. *Crime and Punishment*. Seemed appropriate given recent developments."

"Is that supposed to be funny?"

"Dark humor is how we cope in my family." He set the book

aside and patted the space beside him on the leather sofa. "Come here. You look like you're about to shatter."

She was. The events of the past few hours had left her feeling like glass stretched too thin. One more shock and she'd fragment completely. But something about Ash's quiet presence drew her forward until she was curled against his side, breathing in his masculine scent.

"Tell me about the facility," he said quietly.

The words hit her like a physical blow. "What?"

"You said they committed you for eighteen months. For trying to protect other girls from your brother." His arm tightened around her shoulders. "Tell me what that was like."

"Why?" She pulled back to look at him, searching his ice-blue eyes for some hint of his motivation. "So you can decide if I'm damaged enough to be trustworthy?"

"So I can understand what it cost you to be here. What it cost you to choose us over them."

The gentleness in his voice almost undid her. When was the last time someone had asked about her pain without wanting to use it against her?

"It wasn't a hospital," she said finally. "Not really. Whitmore was private. Exclusive. They protect the secrets of their benefactors at all cost."

"I assume your family is one of those benefactors."

She nodded. "Wealthy families need places to send inconvenient relatives. I just never expected to be one."

"Inconvenient how?"

"I ask too many questions. I see things I shouldn't see and refuse to smile and stay quiet while others are getting hurt."

"Yet you honored our convictions, even at the inconvenience of others."

"Yes." She cuddled closer to his chest, focusing on the steady beat of his heart beneath her palm. "Family image is everything to my father. He never loved me the way he loves Jordan."

Ash waited patiently as she gathered her words.

"I tried to tell them I hadn't done anything wrong and that Jordan was the dangerous one, but Jordan is a master manipulator and an even better liar. They said it was only for a while, but then the days turned into weeks and the weeks into months." Pain engulfed her heart. "When my mother died, and they wouldn't let me leave, I lost it."

"How?"

"Screaming, fighting, basically threatening to burn the place down if they didn't let me go to the funeral. I know Jordan talked our dad into keeping me away on purpose. He wanted to hurt me."

"And he succeeded."

"Yes." She lowered her head, always questioning if she would have controlled her emotions if they might have let her attend the viewing. Closing her eyes, she let the endless regret seep through her.

"What happened after that?"

"They kept me medicated. Heavy sedatives that made me foggy, so foggy it became hard to think. They told me I had a psychotic break."

"Did you?"

She lifted a shoulder and let it drop. "I don't remember anything like that, but they kept me so medicated, I'm not sure. I was angry, but I think—based on my circumstances—that was a normal emotion."

"Sure."

"Since then, I've been unable to trust my own thoughts. I even question my memories."

"Trauma can do that to a person."

"They said my delusions about Jordan were symptoms of severe mental illness."

"What do you feel in your gut?"

"I know what he is. What he did to your sister only confirms my instincts. Jordan's a predator."

He looked away, and the library chilled. "So you know better."

"I know what I saw before they had me committed. The girls he brought home. The way they looked afterward. Broken. Confused. Regretful. Jordan knew I was on to him, so he convinced my father to send me away."

"Why didn't your father question his accusations?"

She bit her lip. "I've always had anxiety. When I was young, I'd have attacks. My mom used to talk me through them, because my father couldn't understand what was happening. He doesn't like inconvenient emotions. Jordan said my behavior was getting worse. He played on my father's fears of social ruin and convinced him I was a danger to the family's reputation."

"And your mother?"

"She tried to stop him. But she couldn't get through his fear. He needed to protect the Calder name, and my accusations about Jordan were a threat." She let out a breath. "After that, every time I tried to tell someone, tried to make them understand, they'd increase my dosage."

The memories came in flashes—white rooms, white uniforms, white pills that turned her thoughts to cotton. The taste of chemical compliance on her tongue.

"How long before you stopped fighting?" Ash asked.

"Six months." The admission felt like failure. "Six months of being told I was crazy, that my memories weren't real, that Jordan was perfect, and I was sick. Eventually, I believed them."

"But not completely."

"No. There was always this voice in the back of my head, so

small I could barely hear it, whispering that they were wrong. That what I'd seen was real." She looked up at him. "Does that make sense?"

"Perfect sense." His fingers combed through her hair with gentle precision. "Gaslighting is a weapon, *printessa*. They tried to steal your reality. But some part of you refused to let go."

The understanding in his voice made tears prick her eyes. "Once you're there and they realize your family has no interest in letting you out, they move you to a different floor. The rules are different there. The rooms aren't cleaned as often. The food's not as fresh. And the orderlies... Well, they follow different rules, too."

"Tell me."

She didn't know where to start or how much he wanted to know. In a way, if felt like a relief to unburden herself to someone who might actually care, someone who could spare an ounce of compassion for all she'd suffered. However, self-preservation kept her silent. If she told him, he'd know her darkest secrets and see her truest shame.

She thought about the bars on the windows that cast prison shadows across their beds. About the orderlies who enjoyed their power a little too much, who found excuses to conduct *'wellness checks'* that left the female patients violated and cowering.

"There was one orderly," Marigold whispered, her eyes trained on the bookshelves ahead. "Willum. He only worked at night. And when he made his rounds, he'd..."

Her mind jumped to the last time she tried to tell on Willum. The doctors said she was having more paranoid delusions. They increased her medication until she could barely form complete sentences. That made Willum's job a lot easier.

Ash's jaw clenched, muscle jumping beneath his skin. "What happened?"

"It doesn't matter."

"It does. I can see it still has power over you."

"I was one of the lucky ones. My meds were strong. I couldn't feel or think. In a way, I'm grateful. My roommate wasn't so lucky."

Ash hissed a sharp Russian profanity. "What did he do to her?"

"I don't know. But afterwards, she found a way to break a mirror in the bathroom. They're supposed to be shatterproof, but she somehow got it to break. They put her in a padded cell and gave her a strong sedative. But she hid a shard of glass without them seeing. Hid it for weeks." Marigold's voice cracked. "I woke up one morning and she was just... gone. Blood everywhere. They told us she'd been transferred, but I saw them wheeling out the body bag."

"Fucking hell." Ash pulled her closer, his arms becoming a fortress around her trembling frame. "How did you survive it?"

"I learned to play their game. To be the perfect patient. Compliant. Medicated. Grateful for their help in overcoming my delusions." The words tasted like poison, but she swallowed down the fear and pushed herself to go on, to finally unburden herself. "I smiled when they praised my progress. Thanked them for saving me from my own mind. Let them believe they'd broken me completely."

"But they hadn't."

"No. I was planning. Waiting. Learning their routines, their weaknesses." She took a shaky breath. "Willum liked me. Thought I was... *grateful* for his attention. He started giving me privileges. Longer visits to the library. Access to areas I shouldn't have been able to reach."

Ash went very still. "What kind of attention?"

The question hung in the air like smoke. Marigold closed her eyes, remembering hands that shouldn't have touched her, promises whispered in the dark about special treatment for cooperative patients.

"The kind that made my skin crawl," she said finally. "But also the kind that gave me leverage."

"Leverage how?"

"I had to get home. Patients on my floor rarely got to leave, but Willum had a master set of keys." She swallowed hard, tasting shame and desperation. Tasting blood. "All I had to do was show a little gratitude."

Ash's breathing went shallow. "What did you do?"

"What I had to do." The words came out flat, emotionless.

He turned her chin, forcing her to meet his stare. "Is he still alive."

"No."

She waited for judgement, but his expression only showed comprehension. "Then you ran?"

"I ran. As soon as the shifts changed, I was out the door. I stole clothes from the laundry, money from the office safe, and I took a bus back home. My father thought I had approval to leave. By the time they reported me missing, I'd already had the fight with Jordan and running for my life."

"He was going to send you back to Whitmore?"

"Or worse." She recalled how terrified she'd felt, trying to find a safe place to hide where someone wouldn't turn her in. She trusted no one. She was hunted and Jordan would not stop until he made sure she was no longer a threat. "He won't stop until he finds me. Until he silences me permanently."

Ash was quiet for a long moment, processing her words. When he finally spoke, his voice was rough with emotion. "You did what you had to do to survive. To escape. To protect another girl from your brother's depravity." His hand cupped her face, forcing her to meet his eyes. "You're a fucking badass."

Tears pricked her eyes at the fierce pride in his voice. "I'm damaged."

"Regardless, your ours now." He kissed her forehead with reverence that made her chest ache. "You survived hell to end up here, with us. That's not a coincidence. That's fate."

"I don't believe in fate."

"One day, you will." His lips found hers, soft and sure. "Believe that we'll keep you safe. That we'll make them all pay for what they did to you."

The kiss deepened, and Marigold found herself melting into his warmth. His gentle seduction was comfort that reached beyond the flesh. His understanding wrapped her in warmth that soothed away bone-deep pain.

Ash lifted her, carrying her to the thick rug before the fireplace. His movements were unhurried, reverent, like he was handling something precious and fragile. When he lay her down on the soft fur carpet, she felt like a goddess being worshipped by her most devoted follower.

Deep, languid kisses put her in a drugged trance, and when he pressed his fingers inside of her, she was drenched for his touch. He stripped away her sweater, leaving her only in her boots. Hot kisses trailed down her torso, lower and lower until he was licking into her.

He took his time, but also pushed her. She traced her hands over his broad shoulders as he opened his pants and stared down at her. "I'll erase the memories of any man who touched you before."

There was so much she had yet to learn about him, but she believed, if anyone could erase her pain, Ash could. "Please."

He pressed deep, staring into her eyes as he forced her to take every powerful inch of him. Shallow breaths constricted by the position forced her mind to stay present as he purposely let his weight sink into her. It was a good pain, the kind that made it impossible to forget who touched her.

"Feel how deep I fill you, *printessa*." His hand pressed over her belly, just below her ribs. "Here. Deep. All the way inside of you."

"Yes."

"No matter how many times I break you, I'll always put you together again. Remember? Trust."

She nodded, unsure how she'd come to trust him so quickly, but unable to deny the fact that she did. "What if some parts of me are too broken to fix?"

"*Nyet.* If they truly broke you, you never would have made it this far. To us."

He made love to her slowly, thoroughly, with a patience that spoke of infinite time and infinite care. His hands mapped every scar, every tremor, every place where trauma had left its mark. And where his touch lingered, the pain seemed to ease, replaced by warmth and belonging and something that might have been love.

He kept his eyes on her, watching her responses and studying her tolerance when he gripped her throat or pulled her hair. He liked manhandling her. Liked when he made it hurt because he liked kissing the pain away and putting her back together again.

When she shattered in his arms, it was with tears streaming down her face—not from pain, but from the overwhelming relief of being truly seen. Truly accepted. Truly cherished despite everything she'd been forced to do.

When they lay tangled together on the rug, watching flames dance in the hearth. Marigold confessed, "I like being with you."

He shifted to hold her a little tighter, but said nothing. The storm outside had finally broken, leaving the world washed clean and new.

"Maybe you're exactly what I needed, someone sturdy enough not to bleed from my rough edges."

"I have rough edges, too. We all do."

"I like when you put me back together again." She stared at the flames and laughed to herself. "Humpty Dumpty sat on a wall…"

"If you're expecting all the king's horses and all the king's men, I'm afraid you'll be disappointed. I only share with my brothers."

His words were playful, but also realistic. She shivered at the terrifying thought of Hunter. "What if I don't want to be with them."

He drew back to look at her. "Don't be foolish, *printessa*. We can be very accommodating, but the rules are clear. To stay, we require your full consent."

She tightly swallowed. "But Hunter hates me. He told me himself he has no interest in touching me."

He pressed her head back down to his chest. "Eventually, that will change. Do yourself a favor and accept that which cannot be avoided."

She sat up. "You can stop him."

"Why would I?"

His question stung. "Because we…" She looked down and frowned. "Don't you care about me?"

"Yes, but Hunter's my brother."

"So?"

"So, we have an understanding. I won't betray him."

"Even if he plans to hurt me?"

"He won't."

"He already has! Just tonight, he slammed me into the counter and threatened me. He's cruel and—"

"Enough."

Stifled by his sharp command, she stared at him in shock. He cared about her, but would never put her before his brothers.

"I'm such an idiot," she whispered, pushing herself off the floor.

"Where are you going?"

"Away from you." She tugged on her sweater. "Do me a favor, next time you want to fuck me, just do it. Leave out all the emotional bullshit, because it's giving me a migraine."

"I've been nothing but upfront with you, *Zayka*."

"And stop calling me that. I'm not a little fucking bunny or whatever the hell that means."

"Rabbit."

"Whatever." She snatched the ribbon that had fallen out of her hair and tied back her curls. "I'm not some skittish little animal who runs and hides and I'm not some helpless princess waiting to be rescued."

"I never said you were."

"Yes, you did." She crossed the library and yanked open the door.

"Do you always get hysterical after sex?" he yelled.

"Go to hell." She stepped into the hall and let the door slam, but when she abruptly turned, she crashed head-on into Stone's granite chest.

"Well, well, well." He steadied her. "Where are you running off to?" Bending closer, he stiffened her neck. "Smelling like sex."

She swatted him away. "Get away from me."

"Doesn't work that way." He crowded her towards the wall. "Ash has been hogging you."

Her pulse leapt when he tugged playfully at a long curl.

"Cracked you open like an egg," he continued, his gaze tracing attentively down to the toe of her suede boot. "He's good like that. Knows how to get the difficult ones to open up."

Ones? "He's not as smooth as he thinks."

Stone laughed and glanced back at the library door. "Lover's quarrel?"

"Something like that."

He moved closer, barely touching her but caging her in with his body all the same. "Part of you is enjoying this, aren't you?"

"No."

"Lying little thief. I think—"

"Stone." Marigold's spine stiffened at the unexpected lash of Hunter's voice.

Stone scowled back at his intrusive brother, who appeared at the end of the hall, but quickly returned his focus to her. "I'm busy."

Hunter didn't seem to care. "Meet me in the *berloga*. Bring Ash." He walked away, and Stone sighed.

"We'll finish this later."

Once again, she questioned if Hunter was some sort of alpha or leader to them. Why did he have such command over them?

Stone backed away and thumped his fist on the library door twice. "Hunter wants us in the *berloga*."

Ash opened the door, appearing surprised to find her standing there with Stone. He met her stare but said nothing as he exited the library and moved in the direction Hunter headed. Stone followed. Once again, abandoning her and leaving her utterly alone.

This time, she planned to make good use of their absence and use her unchaperoned time wisely. She rushed into the library, searching the shelves until she found the book she spotted earlier.

It was a small, cloth-bound English/Russian dictionary, worn from use but stiff from sitting. The spine creaked as she forced it open to the B's. Turning the thin pages quickly, she searched down the double columns with her finger for the word *berloga.*

"*Berloga, berloga*—Ah." She frowned as she read the definition. "Bear den." She glanced back to the door and frowned. "*Bear* den?"

Since they had already convicted her of being a thief, she decided to borrow the book a little longer. Exiting the library, she quietly headed in the same direction the men had gone. Her boots clicked on every tile, and the high ceilings had the acoustics of an amphitheater announcing her every step.

She paused in the open foyer and stared at the front door. She could leave. Now would be the time, while they were off in their little bear club doing God knows what. She took a cautious step toward the door and hesitated.

For once, it wasn't snowing and the sun was shining over a flawless bed of white, the distant trees encased in ice. Time froze. She'd have several hours of daylight to figure out somewhere else to hide.

Would they chase her? Catch her? Punish her?

Of course they would.

She'd given them everything they needed to go after Jordan. The next step would be to force him out of hiding, which might lead him here, back to them, back to her. If Jordan discovered where she was, he'd send her back to Whitmore—or worse.

She backed away from the door. The truth was, Jordan scared her more than three terrifying men. She was at their mercy, but also—she admitted—under their protection. And that awareness made her alliance clear. She was no longer on the Calder side. She was now working with them.

The realization stunned her. Was she actually choosing this? Choosing to stay here with them?

She glanced down at the book in her hand. Why would she care to learn Russian if she didn't intend to survive this place?

On some subconscious level, her mind was already made up. She wasn't going back, and if this was her chance to run, there was a reason she wasn't taking it.

Consciousness of her choice caused a subtle shift inside of her. She'd been playing this game all wrong. Used to living in survival mode, ricocheting off every command like prey driven by hunters. No matter which way she turned, another predator awaited. They liked the hunt, but she was tired of living on the run.

Her fear gave them power over her. The more she cowered and let them intimidate her, the more they would take control of her life. And she didn't escape one prison to enter another.

Marigold straightened her shoulders. She needed to start paying better attention, being more aware. She was a part of this, whether she liked it or not. And she would not allow her life to turn into one long line of consequences.

Like black ice underfoot, every step she'd made toward stability had sent her sliding toward the subsequent collision. But she was learning. Her awareness was sharper. She might not have total autonomy here, but she wasn't powerless.

In that moment of stark realization, she decided to reclaim some of the power she had lost. This might be their territory, but she was the catalyst. They needed her as much as she needed their protection.

Marigold pressed her palm against the cold window, watching her breath fog the glass. What if, instead of fleeing back to whatever banal life awaited her beyond the frozen forest, she'd claimed her place at their table?

She wouldn't just hide here. She'd choose here. A home.

No, not a home. A fortress. A *berloga* of her own, where three apex predators stood between her and anyone who'd dare hunt her. If they trusted her, Jordan could send a hundred men and they'd never get past the front door.

Here, wrapped in fur and stone and masculine possession, she was untouchable. Not because she was weak, but because she was *theirs*.

The world beyond these walls wanted to silence her, cage her, break her. But inside this frozen sanctuary, she could be both precious and powerful. Protected and desired. They'd kill for any woman they believed was theirs. Fiercely protective, she saw how deep their loyalty went for their siblings. It went beyond any loyalty her own brother ever showed for her.

That was how family should behave. Family protected all members, not just the precious male heirs. The second they turned on her, abandoned her to that horrible facility, they ceased being her family. And now, she needed to claim a new one.

Why would anyone hold onto a false sense of loyalty for a family that wanted to destroy them?

These men offered protection, and they would honor their word. She'd seen the conviction in Ash's eyes, felt it in Stone's calculating gaze, tasted the resolute promise in the fear provoked by Hunter's barely contained rage. Three guardians who'd tear the world apart before letting anyone touch what they claimed.

The Russian textbook weighed heavily in her hands. Not a burden, but a key. She didn't have to be their captive. She could become their treasure.

She stared out the window, letting her warm breath fog over the frost locked outside. Not restrained, but protected. They were her shield. Like the ice-wrapped birches bending beneath their crystalline armor, frozen in a shell of glass, she was safe here, protected from the brutal wind and those who aimed to harm her.

This place, this unpredictable, harsh place, hid moments of

hope. *Preserved*. Waiting beneath the surface for the right moment to bloom.

It was the first time in months that she gave herself permission to exhale. She didn't have to figure out the next ten moves until she was ready. They offered her sanctuary, a place where she could heal. This was her moment to decide exactly who she wanted to be.

Not a thief. Not a liar. And not a skittish little rabbit. She was Marigold Calder. Her status might have fallen from that of an heiress to a woman on the run, but she made it far enough that she could stop fleeing and start strategizing.

She delivered the book to the room she'd last slept in, claiming the space as her own. Apparently, she wasn't alone.

When she entered, the bed was made and there were more fresh flowers in a vase on the nightstand. Where did they find flowers in a blizzard?

That wasn't all that changed. The drawers were now filled with clothes. Sweaters, jeans, and even silk lingerie.

She lifted a lace garter belt and laughed to herself. "Aren't they presumptuous?"

The question was, which one did this? Was it a group effort or the doing of one brother? Her money was on Ash. It was time to get some answers.

She paused at the door, only to backtrack to the closet. Flicking on the interior light, she gasped. Rows and rows of designer shoes, all in her size.

There were definitely perks to living with three bearish men. They might act like possessive wild animals, but this was a sign they could be tamed.

Encouraged by their show of acceptance and gesture of good will, she grinned. She'd learn their language, their rules, their games. They wanted to possess her? Fine. But possession ran both ways.

Three dangerous men who thought they'd caught themselves a frightened little rabbit. They had no idea how far she'd go to get the life she deserved. She was done running. Done being prey.

She would mark them as surely as they planned to mark her. Stone with his icy control, Ash with his deceptive gentleness, and even Hunter, with his brutal need, she'd figure them out in time. Solve them like a riddle, until they were as dependent on her as they expected her to be on them.

As she walked down the hall, her mind went to Hunter. He was going to be her biggest challenge. He was too rough. Stone was too cold. And Ash wanted to be just right, but he could be just as aggressive and possessive as the rest of them.

Regardless, they were all hers.

No more cowering. She wasn't going to wait for them to decide her next move. She was going right into the den.

CHAPTER 14

BERLOGA

Ash growled at his brother. "Your plan puts too many people in danger."

Hunter held up a silencing hand and they stopped arguing. "Someone's outside the door," he spoke in thick Russian, eyes set to kill.

Stone stood from the table and yanked open the door, revealing Marigold's petite form on the other side. "Looking for something?"

She showed no contrition at being caught eavesdropping. On the contrary, she lifted her chin and sauntered into the bear den as if she owned the place.

Hunter scowled. "This is a private meeting."

"About me and my family. I think I'll stay." She dropped into the empty chair Stone had vacated at the foot of the table, meeting Hunter's challenging glare as he sat opposite her at the head.

Ash sat back and rubbed his jaw. This was an interesting twist he hadn't seen coming.

Hunter flipped the leather portfolio shut. "I don't know what you think you're doing—"

"I'm getting caught up," she cut him off.

Stone met Ash's stare and arched a brow. Folding his arms over his broad chest, he leaned into the wall, close enough to overlook any notes spread across the table—should they come back out. When Hunter glanced at him, he shrugged.

"Do you think you can protect your brother by being here?"

"I have no interest in helping Jordan after what he's put me through."

"Why should we believe you?"

Hunter might not be convinced, but after everything she told Ash, he didn't need further convincing. Jordan Calder was a piece of shit, and that facility he committed her to was its own crime ring. The other's didn't realize it yet, but once Jordan was handled, they still had work to do.

He would never understand men who preyed on women and took without consent. The world was an endless playground full of willing victims who got off on power dynamics. The waiting lists for their parties were miles long, and they certainly weren't the only pleasure club around. But they were the most exclusive and private. Point being, permission came in many forms, so in his mind, stealing it was never okay.

"Will you be so eager to watch when I'm beating your brother to a pulp?" Hunter growled.

Marigold didn't flinch as she held his stare. "I don't need to see that, but I also don't plan to stop you. How you handle him is out of my hands, but that's not why I'm here."

"And why are you here?"

"Well," she uncrossed her arms and rested them casually at her side, a position that said without words she was open for negotiation. "I've done some thinking. I want to kill the old

Marigold Calder and become someone new. And you're going to help me."

Hunter scoffed. "Why should we help you?"

"Because I've agreed to give you everything you asked for, and now you owe me."

His laugh was cold. "We don't owe you shit."

"You will. I've agreed to your terms. I'm here. I'm yours—for now."

Oh, she was getting sassy. This was not going to go over well with Hunter.

"I'll continue to play the agreeable little prisoner, but in exchange, I want you to help me recreate myself. Marigold Calder is dead."

"You aren't playing the prisoner. You *are* the prisoner."

"Really? Twenty minutes ago, I could have walked right out the door and left. Your security sucks."

Hunter looked at Stone and gave a subtle nod. Stone approached the table, showing Marigold his phone. "We're always watching, Goldilocks. I can lock any door with the press of a button. One code, and the entire property's on lockdown. You wouldn't have gotten far." He pocketed his phone and returned to leaning casually against the wall.

"Regardless, I didn't run. You don't have to keep me locked up. I've decided I'm willing to stay. For a price."

Intrigued, Ash leaned forward to rest his elbows on the polished surface of the table. "You do realize, if you do this, you'll never exist in polite society again. No job, no credit, no connections. Every door that ever opened because of the Calder name will slam shut." He kept his voice gentle but implacable. "You'll be completely cut off from the only life you've ever known."

"That's fine. They exiled me from that life months ago. I don't fit there anymore. I want to live on my own terms now."

Stone smirked, evidently impressed. "Where has our little *zayka* gone?"

Marigold met his gaze. "I killed her."

He glanced at Hunter. "I'm fine with her staying."

Hunter looked at Ash. "You?"

He shrugged, never one to show his hand. "What difference does it make? We're going to do what we want either way."

Hunter narrowed his eyes. "Fine." He moved to the bar with predatory grace and refilled his glass. When he returned to the table, he didn't sit. Instead, he stood dominantly over Marigold, fists planted on the surface as he caught her up to speed. "I've been monitoring your brother's communications. He plans to return to Kassel."

"When?" Stone, as always, kept to the facts.

"It's unclear. But I expect to know more tomorrow."

Hunter's smile was sharp with anticipation the moment Marigold's mask slipped. The fear that flashed in her eyes at the mention of Jordan coming to the lodge confirmed Ash's suspicions. Her brother scared her—perhaps more than anything else, including them.

"You have nothing to worry about," Ash said, hoping to relieve some of her fear. "He won't get near you."

She looked up at him with those big, vulnerable eyes, and relief rushed through him. He liked how she wore her courage, but he also loved when she went soft and deferred to him as one of her protectors.

"We'll keep you safe," he promised.

"Thank you."

Stone's brow shot up. Her change in attitude didn't go unnoticed by any of them.

"The transcripts I hacked from his cell confirms that he thinks you're here. He's bringing a lawyer, a private security consultant, and enough legal documentation to have you declared mentally incompetent and returned to Whitmore permanently."

The words hit Marigold like physical blows and she flinched. "So this isn't a rescue mission, but a recapture one. I'm not surprised."

"The only person getting captured is Jordan. You're just the bait."

"He's playing it off as the concerned brother, claiming you were kidnapped," Stone said quietly.

"My innocence makes less clean-up for the family."

"True. But according to his texts, he plans on exploiting your *'condition'*."

"He wants to expose me as mentally insane, which ensures no one will ever believe me if I continue to talk."

"Exactly. He plans to find you, then claim this was another 'psychotic episode,' claiming you need immediate psychiatric intervention. He looks like a hero and you look like the deranged charity case."

"How altruistic of him to concern himself with my care."

"We all have a role to play," Ash said. "We make him feel welcome. Let him think he's in control."

"Until he isn't," Stone added with cold satisfaction.

Owning the most exclusive pleasure club in the world taught them several things. The lodge was more than a house of hedonism. It was a psychological dungeon built to manipulate and twist people so far from their comfort zones that they lost touch with reality.

Without a graceful landing, guests could leave with more trauma than they carried in. Thankfully, they were experts at mitigating aftercare and seeing that everything under their roof was safe, sane, and consensual. But not for their enemies. Jordan Calder was getting a special brand of care when he arrived.

"Your brother likes to break things," Hunter said. "Beautiful, innocent things. He gets off on the power, the control, the moment when something pure becomes corrupted."

"So we're going to show him what it feels like to be the one without power," Stone finished, his smile revealing a vicious taste for vengeance. "Without control. Without any way to escape what's coming."

She shifted in her seat, and Ash watched as she processed this information, waiting for any sign of objection. She had to understand their intentions. They planned to break her brother the same way he'd broken their sister.

"When?" she whispered.

Hunter checked his phone. "Soon enough, but we'll be prepared."

Stone checked his phone. "Full moon, perfect weather, excellent visibility for what we have planned." His grin was feral. "Plenty of time to prepare a proper welcome."

"We should warn you," Ash said. "When he gets here, and our cards are revealed, what comes next won't be pleasant. What we do to men like your brother... It's not pretty. It's not gentle."

"And once we start," Hunter's voice carried a clear threat, "we don't stop until they're completely broken. You might hear things you can't unhear."

When she only nodded with understanding, the three of them exchanged looks of approval. A new respect was born in the den that day, one that made him realize Marigold was much stronger than they initially thought.

She also had a dark side to her that pleased Ash. All three of them had a fucked up past. Marigold made four. Maybe she was more fitting for them than they realized. He wanted to see just how depraved and dark she could go when this shit with her brother was over. As a matter of fact...

"Are we done?"

"You have somewhere else you need to be?" Hunter snapped.

"Yes." Ash stood and grabbed Marigold's hand. "Come with me."

Stone's gaze followed him as he pulled Marigold out of the room, but he didn't waste time explaining himself.

She tripped out of the room as he dragged her past the threshold. "Where are we go—" Her words cut off as he slammed his mouth over hers and walked her into the wall.

"You were quite impressive in there." He unbuckled his belt and lowered his zipper. "You're fucking sexy when you're brave." Snatching her hand, he folded it around his cock, gripping her fingers and showing her how fast he wanted her to pump. "It's fucking hot watching you take on Hunter."

"He doesn't scare me."

Ash chuckled. "Sweet, little liar, we both know that's not true. But you're getting braver, and that's good. If you don't put him in his place, he'll eat you alive."

The door opened, and heavy footfalls approached. "Bring her over here," Stone said, already peeling off his shirt.

Ash grinned, holding his pants up, bending to lift her onto his back. "Up you go."

Marigold yipped as Ash hoisted her over his shoulder and followed Stone into the closest room. He tossed her onto the bed.

"Get her arms."

She bounced and scowled. "Hey!"

Stone had her wrists bound before she could object. Ash removed her boots and hooked her ankles to a spreader bar, making it harder for her to flail and kick. This was one of the guests' playrooms, equipped with all kinds of fun surprises. When he hooked the spreader bar to the pully system suspended from the ceiling, he had her legs in the air with one firm yank.

"What are you doing?" she gasped, at the mercy of their care.

Stone shoved Ash out of the way. "It's my turn." He shucked his pants and climbed onto the bed, dragging her thighs closer and pulling her arms tight. "Hold on tight, *Zayka*." He sank a finger inside of her. "She's already soaked."

"That's because she likes when we're rough as much as she liked when we're gentle, don't you, *printsessa*."

"Stop!"

The room stilled at the unexpected safe word. Ash cautiously stepped forward. "Marigold."

Her breath was labored as she looked at him, then to Stone. "You owe me an apology."

Pride swelled in Ash's chest, and he had to hide a smile. Clever girl, calling Stone out on his bullshit.

"For?"

"Stone," Ash said in warning. He was well aware he'd fucked up by walking out on her before. If he wanted the right to touch her again, he owed her this much.

His brother grimaced but eventually gave in. "I'm sorry I walked out on you, *Zayka*. It was wrong, and won't happen again. Next time, I'll control my temper."

"Thank you."

He watched Marigold's eyes widen as Stone shoved his fat cock inside of her. His brother groaned in ecstasy, taking a moment to simply savor the way her body welcomed his.

Ash rounded the bed, pissed Stone hadn't removed her sweater dress before tying her up. He opened the nightstand and found a set of safety scissors. "We don't need this anymore."

"What are you doing?" she gasped when he cut into the wool and then tore the shirt open, exposing her breasts.

"Opening my present." He pinched her nipples. "Remember how much fun we had yesterday? Bet you're still sore." He bent to suck the tip of each one, leaving both hard, wet, and a deep shade of pink. "Doesn't she have the nicest tits you've ever seen, Stone?"

His brother grunted and rocked into her hard. The pully system left her dangling at his disposal. "I'd love to see them clipped."

"Great idea." Ash rummaged through the drawer until he found a set of clamps. Ripping open the package he held them up for Marigold to see. "What do you think, *printsessa*?"

Her eyes went wide. "What do you think you're doing with them?"

"You know exactly what I'm doing." He climbed onto the bed just as Stone smacked a heavy hand on her ass that made her cry out.

"She's got a hell of a set of lungs on her." He spanked her again.

Ash focused on his task, getting her nipples nice and wet as he teased the first gold clamp over the turgid tip. When he cinched the lock into place, she gasped and scowled.

"You'll adjust." He aligned the next one and had it locked into place in no time. "How's that?" he gave her tits a little swat.

"Tight," she said through clenched teeth.

"Good. That's how it should be." He threw his leg over her and crawled forward, not stopping until his knees slid beneath her sprawled arms. "Take this." He pressed a red ball in her hand. "Hold onto it tightly. If anything we're doing feels like too much, you drop the ball. Understand?"

She looked at the ball in her fist and back to him with wide eyes. "What are you going to do?"

He shoved his pants low on his hips, and rose over her, gripping the headboard. "I'm going to fuck that sexy mouth of yours until I come down your throat. Open up, *printsessa*."

"Wait—"

It was all the invitation he needed. Wet heat engulfed him as Stone increased his thrusts.

"You're going to have to do better than that," Ash said, gripping her hair and forcing her to look at him.

"*Mmmm!*" She screamed around his gliding cock, eyes wide and brow furrowed.

"Sorry, I couldn't understand you."

"I think she asked you to fuck her face harder," Stone joked.

"That's what I thought." Ash pressed deeper, holding himself at the back of her throat. His hand moved from her hair to her larynx, where he could feel the bulge of his intrusion. "Breathe."

Her nostrils flared, and her eyes glistened with unshed tears.

"Very good, *printsessa*. Now swallow." He moaned as the pressure of her throat constricted around him. "Now, relax and keep that pretty mouth open until I come."

A slap sounded behind him and she gasped, opening her mouth wide.

Ash bucked his hip, pumping in and out with rapid thrusts. The sounds were music to his ears, on the verge of choking as pleasure moans battled with sounds of exertion as he thrust his thick cock down her throat. When the tears started to fall, he nearly came.

She looked at the ball clenched tightly in her fist, but she hadn't let it go. If anything, her grip tightened.

"Eyes on me."

She looked up at Ash and he stared down in awe as she took every inch of him again and again. "You like having two cocks inside of you?"

"Just wait until there's three," Stone said on a grunt. That meant he was getting close.

Ash forked his fingers through her hair and fisted those thick curls. "Give me more tears, Marigold. You know how I love to watch you break."

She moaned around his pistoning flesh as he tightened his grip. Tears pricked her eyes and quickly fell. He grunted in pleasure, holding nothing back. And just as he heard Stone groan through his release, Ash let himself go.

"Swallow it." He drew back, pumping his fist over his cock as the last of his release sputtered across her swollen lips.

"*Asshole*," she growled and gasped, the moment she could speak.

Stone slapped her ass and laughed. "No one's denying that, little rabbit. But use that word again, and it'll be your asshole paying the consequence."

Ash climbed off of her, and she drew in a deep breath. Her nipples were swollen and dark red. "Now, for my favorite part."

Stone withdrew and rounded the bed on the other side of her. "You should see how hot her pussy looks, pink, puffy, and dripping."

"That's how it's going to look every day from now on." He winked at Marigold, but she narrowed her eyes.

Still, she made no objection to their plans.

Had she truly accepted her fate that easily? She had to know by now, after everything she confided in the library, that if she genuinely wanted to leave, he'd see that his brothers let her go. They weren't in the business of holding women against their will.

"I'll get the left one," Stone said, pinching the clip of the sliding loop that locked the nipple clamp.

Ash looked at his brother and grinned. "One."

"Two."

They both looked down at her full breasts. "Three."

Marigold cried out. Every muscle in her arms pulled taut against the binds, and her legs flailed, still in the spreader. He and Stone dove forward, sucking hard on her tits as her cries quickly turned to moans.

He could feel the slight pulsing against his tongue as the blood returned to the tips. Stone reached between her thighs, rubbing her clit. Her hips undulated and her toes pointed as muscles in her toned thighs jumped and bounced.

"See, two men is better than one." Ash moved from her breast to her mouth, kissing her deep enough to taste the lingering flavor of his release. "Did you like having Stone's cock stretch your tight pussy?" he whispered against her mouth. "You sucked me off so good. And now look at you, ready for more."

Stone rubbed her into orgasm and her cries of pleasure ricocheted from the walls. By now, Hunter had to know what they were up to. No way he couldn't hear them. But thankfully, he sat this one out. While Marigold seemed to have found her courage, she still wasn't ready for Hunter.

As if following his train of thought, Stone teased, "I think it's time we call our brother in." He withdrew his hand from her trembling thighs. "She's drenched enough that he won't split her in two."

Ash dragged a finger over her swollen lower lip, unable to resist teasing her. "You want Hunter's big dick in you?"

Her chin trembled. She didn't say no because she was stubborn and determined to prove herself, but she was still uneasy around Hunter, which was smart. He'd give her a few more days to mentally prepare for—

"He's on his way."

"What?" Ash's gaze jumped to Stone.

Stone tossed his phone aside. "I texted him."

Ash looked back at Marigold. There was no going back now. Joke was on him. He'd only been teasing her, but now Hunter was—

The door opened and Marigold stilled.

"We got her all ready for you," Stone said, slapping her lightly across the pussy.

She jumped, and Hunter's gaze leapt to her face, then her swollen nipples. He glared at them both, then looked down at Marigold. "Are you in any pain?"

Her head shook ever so slightly. He tugged the binds and snapped, "You two, out."

Marigold's gaze flashed to Ash and he registered her panic. He wasn't in the mood for another fight, but he couldn't leave her like this with him. "Uh, Hunter, we invited you—"

"I said out."

He inwardly cursed, but climbed off the bed.

"Ash," she called to him, voice tight with panic.

He bent to kiss her softly and whispered low enough so only she would hear. "He won't hurt you. Be brave, *printsessa*."

"No." She jerked at the binds. "Don't leave me here! Don't you fucking leave me like this!"

Snatching his clothes off the floor, he snapped, "Come on, Stone."

Marigold wrenched upward, confined by her binds as she shouted promises to never forgive him for abandoning her. "You swore you would protect me!"

And he would keep that promise, hanging outside, watching the surveillance on his phone until Hunter was through. But he still felt like he was leaving her to the bears. In a sense, he was.

As soon as they were alone in the hall, he shoved Stone. "What the hell's the matter with you?"

"What?"

"I was teasing about Hunter. She's freaking out."

"She was fine."

"Idiot! She was not fine."

"Well, she was going to have to face him eventually."

"She's terrified. I promised to protect her."

"Get over yourself, Ash. We all agreed she was ours, split equally between the three of us. Hunter isn't going to hurt her."

"She doesn't know that."

"Well, she'll learn. She set the terms as much as us."

He looked back at the door, wondering if he should go back in and face the consequences. "Fuck."

Stone cupped a hand to his shoulder. "She has a safe word, Ash. And she knows how to use it."

Unless fear paralyzed her vocal cords.

He dialed into the surveillance feed. "I hope you're right."

CHAPTER 15

YA NE MOGU DYSHAT' BEZ TEBYA

The door closed, and Marigold's gaze shot to Hunter. Her heart pounded in her chest like a wild tribal drum. How could they have left her here—alone—with him.

A low, cold chuckle rumbled from his broad chest as he crossed his arms, only further accentuating how massive he truly was. "They think you've accepted your circumstances. They think they claimed you. But you still flinch when I walk in a room."

Her pulse leapt when he pushed off the wall and sauntered closer to the bed. Bending at the waist, he made a show of sniffing her, scenting her like an animal. She could only imagine what she might smell like, freshly fucked, drenched in semen and sweat, tied and exposed, helpless against his inspection.

She closed her eyes as heat crested her cheeks and mortification burned through her.

"That fear?" He whispered, closer than he'd been a second ago. "It's mine. And I'm not sharing it with anyone."

Necessity forced her to open her eyes. She didn't trust him, didn't know what he intended to do to her. "I thought you weren't interested."

"I'm not."

She hated that his rejection still stung. It didn't matter how much she feared his touch, it bothered her that she couldn't make him want her.

He loosened the rope and adjusted the pully so her legs lowered to the bed. "Stone thinks he owns your submission." He unlatched the ankle cuffs. "Ash believes he has your passion." Moving to the headboard, he loosened the binds at her wrists. "But I'll have something they never will. Your choice. And I'll wait as long as it takes for you to ask me. To beg me."

Marigold sat up, but never took her eyes off him. He prowled around the room like a caged predator. Mapping every inch, commanding every corner. No matter what room Hunter entered, he owned it. Claimed it.

Scooting back toward the pillows, she shifted to her knees and drew her torn sweater dress together to hide her body. "I don't beg."

"We both know that's a lie." Noting her protective posture, he scoffed. "Relax. When I take you—*if* I take you—you won't be exhausted from them." He opened a drawer and removed a folded towel and a custom-wrapped bar of artisan soap, tossing both on the foot of the bed. "You'll be fresh. Aware. Present for every second." He paused to let that sink in, then said, "Clean yourself up. You reek of sex, and we have work to do."

When he left the room, she sagged with relief, letting out a breath she'd been holding since he walked in. Lifting her sweater, she sniffed her skin and drew back. He was right. She reeked of sex.

Gathering the soap and towel, she slipped into the attached bathroom. It wasn't as elegant as the one in her room, but it was still state-of-the-art and gorgeous. The second the water hit her breast she hissed. Her nipples were sore and swollen. She wondered how long they would stay hard from the clamps.

She showered quickly, but didn't know what to do about clothes. When she exited the bathroom in a towel, Ash was waiting by the bed.

She stilled at the sight of him, relieved then furious. "You left me."

"You okay?"

Crossing the room in fast strides, she ignored him. "Go away. You're good at that."

"Hey!" He caught her arm. "You know the rules."

"This isn't about rules. This is about you playing a joke and losing control. You think I can't tell when you're teasing me? You never meant for Hunter to get involved."

"You're right. But what was I supposed to do?"

"What is this power he has over you and Stone? Is he, like, your leader?"

He scowled. "Fuck no. We don't take orders from anyone."

"Except Hunter, apparently."

"If you knew him, you'd get it. Sometimes, it's easier just to skip the argument with Hunter. Besides, I knew he wouldn't hurt you."

"What gave you that impression? The choking? Or was it when he shoved me down on the counter and threatened me?"

"We promised to protect you. We keep our word. And Hunter would never hurt an innocent woman."

"That's not how he sees me." She wasn't going to explain the terror Hunter inspired. He should know from simply watching his brother's animalistic actions. "I need clothes."

"So go get them."

She frowned, annoyed by his indifference. "You're so annoying."

His brows lifted. "I'm not your servant, Marigold. If you're going to live here, you're going to have to learn how to take care of some things yourself."

"So much for all that tender aftercare bullshit," she snapped, snatching her boots off the floor.

"Wait." He caught her arm again, before she could get out the door. "Did you like having us both inside of you?"

"Oh, my God." She tried to yank her arm out of his grip, but he didn't budge.

"Did you?"

Her face burned with evidence of just how much she'd enjoyed being tied up and taken by both men. "That's what you care about?"

"Yes. Your pleasure's important to me."

She rolled her eyes. "I liked everything but the blowjob."

He backed her into the door, using his body to overwhelm her. "Liar."

"Guess you'll never know."

He tugged the towel loose.

"Ash, don't." The towel fell to the floor, and the heat of his clothed body burned into her skin.

"Let me make it up to you." His lips teased the sensitive slope of her neck as he nuzzled her shoulder, gently cupping her breast.

"I hate you." She sucked in a sharp breath when his thumb treaded lightly over her abused nipple.

"Sore?"

"Yes."

"Poor baby." He bent his head and licked over her swollen nipple ever so tenderly.

Her breath hitched as he pulled the tip into his mouth with extreme care. She was suddenly grateful for the support of the door as she let her head fall back.

"See, you can't hate me. I'm the one who understands you. I

see you, Marigold. The real you. You can't blame me for wanting you."

Her eyes closed as he placed tender kisses over her breasts and teased his fingers between her thighs.

"Are you sore here?" He gently slithered a finger inside of her heat. "Was Stone's big cock too wide for your pretty pussy?"

No one had ever spoken so crassly to her or discussed sexual acts with such casual ease. She smirked. "It's bigger than yours."

He chuckled, scraping his teeth over her flesh. "I won't deny it. Just wait until you see Hunter's."

"Don't bring him up."

"Will you fight him? Tell him no?"

She honestly didn't know how she would respond when that time came. Hunter was twice her size. She was no match for him. "Unlike you, I keep my word."

"That's because you're a good girl." He dropped to his knees, spreading kisses over her hips and lower belly. "And I kept my word. Hunter didn't hurt you. I was watching the whole time."

Her lips parted as he pressed her thighs apart and cocked her hips forward. He took a long swipe with his tongue, and she moaned at the first lick. Then, he delved deeper, and she shut her eyes.

"That's it. Let Ash take care of you, *printessa*." He gently stroked his fingers in and out of her as he sucked softly on her clit. It shouldn't have been enough to push her to orgasm, but he was so skilled with his mouth, she found herself climaxing on his tongue in no time.

He growled and laved up every drop, urging her to do it again.

"Ash..." She ran her fingers through his soft hair, pulling him closer as he speared her with intoxicating strokes of his tongue and fingers. She called out his name, breathless and panting for more.

Her knees softened as every muscle twitched and danced from her toes to the top of her spine. Next thing she knew, she was on the floor, with Ash sliding into her.

"You do this every time. You say nothing will happen and then…"

He kissed her to shut her up, his hips driving slowly as he fucked her deep. She didn't know how anyone could have such stamina. Just as he was about to come, he caught her wrists and pinned them over her head.

"Look at me." He thrust slowly, deeply. "Look what you do to me."

She watched as he came apart. The intensity. The passion. The awe. So many emotions danced across his beautiful face as he finished inside of her.

Only when he was done, did he release her wrists and drop to rest his head on her chest. "Fuck. I don't think I'll ever tire of being inside of you."

She sighed, irritated by how easily he could get her to forgive him. Part of her still wanted to be mad at him. "Now, I have to shower again."

"No."

She sat up on her elbows. "Excuse me?"

"Leave it. And no bottoms. I like the thought of it dripping out of you."

"Ash—"

"It's an order."

She wondered what he'd do if she refused. She also wondered what he'd do if she obeyed. Would it drive him wild to see his release glistening on her thighs? She couldn't deny getting off on the thought.

"Okay."

He helped her up off the floor. Giving her a slight twirl, he inspected her body for rug burns and hickeys.

"I love seeing my marks on your skin." He traced an especially dark hickey from yesterday, met her stare, and pinched her nipple.

"Ash!"

He cupped her breast and kissed her. "My little *printsessa*." He opened the door and took her hand. "Let's go find you some clothes."

"Wait, my towel."

"You don't need it." When she hesitated, he pulled her forward. "Let them see how regal you truly are."

What was this hold he had over her?

She walked back to her room wearing only a blush. No doubt Stone and Hunter enjoyed the show from whatever vantage point they had.

Once dressed in a skin-tight mini dress Ash had chosen, she followed him back to the bear den. He'd gotten a text from the others that told him to hurry, so she twisted her hair into a messy bun of curls and rushed after him. She wasn't letting any of them ditch her after all they put her through today.

"You could have let me find shoes."

"You look cute in the socks."

The socks were thick wool that stretched to her mid-thigh, about six inches below where the dress stopped. There would be no bending over in this outfit.

When they reached the den, she'd hoped to find out something new, but it was just a lot of shop talk and logistics. She ended up dozing off on the sofa by the window and when she woke up, Ash and Stone were gone.

Marigold groggily sat up and stilled when she realized Hunter was still working at the desk. "Oh."

"Enjoy your nap?"

"Um…" She brushed her fingers over her lips and sat up. "Yes." Slipping off the couch, she tugged down her skirt, but not before Hunter got a glimpse of what was underneath.

His head remained bent over his work, but his eyes followed her every move.

"I'll just…" She edged toward the door. Why was she explaining herself to him? She rushed out of the den and back to her room like a scared little rabbit.

Lights that were usually off were suddenly on. And music pumped softly from hidden speakers. She frowned at the pre-party ambiance and wondered where the others were. Several vases of fresh flowers had been set on surfaces throughout the house. And the furniture smelled of fresh polish.

She visited the room where Stone had taken her the day before. A steady thump spilled into the hall, alerting her that someone was in there. Then she heard heavy masculine grunting between each beat.

She entered the dungeon-like room they called The Cave silently, her eyes combing over every shadow and apparatus, until she saw the source of the sound and her lips parted. There, on the far wall, stood Stone. He faced away from her, his back a map of swollen muscles and sinew. Sweat glistened on his tanned flesh as Ash swung a whip, several feet long, into his back.

She gasped, as the whip snapped over Stone's back. Ash turned and stilled. "You shouldn't be here."

Eyes wide, she looked up at Stone's splayed body in horror. *"What are you doing to him?"*

Stone's shoulders bulged and heaved as he caught his breath, arms suspended overhead. "What the hell, Ash?"

"Sorry. We have company."

Stone craned his neck, but couldn't quite turn. "Who?"

"Marigold."

She rushed to Stone. "Are you okay?"

"He's fine."

"I wasn't speaking to you. And why do you have him tied up like this?"

Ash caught her arm when she got too close. "You can't be here right now."

"Let go of me." She looked back at Stone, as he hung his head and caught his breath. The bunched muscles of his back glistened under a sheen of sweat, pulsing with each labored breath.

"You want to chime in here, bro?"

The room silenced except for Stone's heavy panting. "Go."

"But—"

"He said go."

She stepped back at the lash in Ash's voice.

She didn't understand why he was hurting him. Had he broken a rule? A whip seemed such a harsh punishment. She couldn't just walk away and do nothing. "Stone?"

"Please, Goldilocks. Just go."

She blinked hard under the weight of confusion and retreated to the door, shutting it softly behind her. The crack of the whip sounded, and she flinched as if it stung her own flesh. She rushed away from the door, overwhelmed by how twisted things could sometimes get in this place.

Alone and unsure what to do with herself, she went to the kitchen, where she searched the tall wine fridge and selected a vintage chardonnay. Sometimes, when life got overly complicated, the simplest solution was a glass of wine.

She took the glass to the library and sat down with her Russian dictionary. By the end of the glass, she made it to the B's. Not much was sinking in—mostly because her thoughts were distracted with worry for Stone—but she was starting to notice patterns in the language.

The door opened, and Hunter stepped in, so focused on whatever he came to find, he didn't notice her curled up on the wingback chair by the window.

Book on her lap, glass in her hand, she stayed perfectly still and watched him search the shelves. For once, he didn't radiate intimidation. He was calm and as unthreatening as a grizzly wandering the woods. Like every room he entered, this became his natural domain.

He pulled a book down, so utterly uninhibited in his quiet habitat, so relaxed. But the moment he turned away from the shelf, and spotted her, his disposition changed.

His gaze froze on her like a predator spotting prey. An invisible wall erected between them. A hierarchy of the food chain that announced where they both stood.

She opted for cuteness. "Hi." She waved nervously. Maybe it was the wine. Sober her would piss herself at such a threatening look.

He obviously hadn't realized he had an audience. "I was just getting..." He caught himself mid-justification and scowled. Hunter wasn't one to explain himself. He lifted the book. Some Russian title she didn't recognize, and then looked down at her lap. "What are you reading?"

Her cheeks heated. "I was...trying to learn your language." She shouldn't feel embarrassed for wanting to understand them better, but for some reason, admitting her efforts left her feeling incredibly self-conscious. "I was bored," she adapted, diminishing the value she placed on fitting in with them.

He crossed the room and tipped the book to read the cover. "That won't help you."

"I know. It was just a way to pass my time."

He turned away and searched the shelfs. In the corner, where some reference texts collected dust, he pulled down an old hardcover and blew away a cloud of grime. "Here."

She cautiously accepted the book but frowned at the cover. Even the letters were unfamiliar. "I can't read this."

"You can. It's how I learned English."

She cracked the spine, and the scent of aged paper tickled her nose. The yellowed pages smelled of vanilla and time, each one filled with handwritten notes in the margins—some in English, others in Cyrillic script that looked more like art than language.

"You wrote these?" Her finger traced one of the annotations, careful not to smudge the faded pencil marks.

Hunter dropped into the chair opposite her, the leather creaking under his weight. "When I was much younger." He leaned forward, elbows on his knees, bringing with him the scent of smoke and something darker—the snowy outdoors maybe, or just him. "Ash taught me. Then I taught Stone."

The admission cracked something open between them. Hunter, volatile and brutal, had once been a boy struggling with foreign words just like her.

"Could you teach—" Her words cut off, the request escaping before she could stop it. A blush crept down her throat. "Never mind."

His dark eyes flickered with surprise, then consideration. He dragged his chair closer, one massive thigh brushing the edge of her seat where her bare knee showed from under her short dress. Recalling that Ash was the last one to touch her and what Hunter had said about her coming to him fresh, she self-consciously tried to cross her legs.

He noticed her posture shift and studied her for a moment, either trying to understand why her position turned from open to closed off, or he already knew.

Her heartbeat doubled as nervous energy rushed through her. "I'm sure you have more important things to do."

He turned the page, ignoring her objection as he pointed to

a passage. Small scars marked his knuckles, and his nails were clean and cut to the quick. Heat radiated from him like a furnace as he leaned down, his warm breath causing the small hairs at the back of her neck to rise.

"The alphabet first." His voice rumbled differently when he wasn't angry, deeper, richer, like aged bourbon. He dragged his finger over the foreign letters. "This letter," his finger pointed to a symbol that looked like a backwards R, "makes the *'ya'* sound. Like the end of *'Россия.'*"

"*Rossiya*," she attempted the unfamiliar sounds, each syllable clumsy on her tongue.

"No." He moved closer, and lifted her fingers to his lips, the scruff of his hard jaw sending shivers down her legs. "Roll the R." He demonstrated, the heat of his breath heating the palm of her hand. "Feel it here." Without warning, his fingers pressed lightly against her throat, right where the sound should vibrate.

Her mind leapt to memories of him choking her, and she wondered how this could be the same man. Her pulse hammered against his fingertips.

"*Россия*," she tried again, hyperaware of his skin on hers.

"Better." His hand lingered a moment too long before pulling away. "Next letter."

For the next hour, Hunter transformed into someone she didn't recognize. Patient when she expected frustration. Gentle when she anticipated roughness. He corrected her pronunciation with careful touches, fingers trailing beneath her chin to adjust the angle, a palm against her ribs to demonstrate proper breathing. Each contact lasted seconds but burned for minutes after.

"This word," he pointed to something scrawled in the margin, "means 'yearning.' But not in the manner of wanting food or sleep. It's..." He paused, searching for the English equivalent while absently dragging his finger over her bare knee. "Soul-deep wanting. The kind that leaves you hollow."

"*Toska*," she whispered, testing the weight of it.

His gaze dropped to her mouth. "Тоска," he corrected, his voice going rough. When she glanced up, he continued watching her mouth with an intensity that made her stomach dip and flutter.

The room had grown warm despite the frost coating the windows. Or maybe it was just her, burning up from the inside out every time he shifted and pressed against her ever so slightly.

She'd never been so hyperaware of a man's proximity. Every time his scent wrapped around her, masculine and wild and utterly Hunter, her IQ dropped another notch.

"Try this phrase." He flipped to a dog-eared page, his arm brushing the swell of her breast as he reached across her. "'*Ya ne mogu dyshat' bez tebya*.'"

She fumbled through the phrase, butchering the pronunciation, and stopped at his low chuckle. Was that an actual laugh from Hunter? The sound was as warm and as rare as summer snow.

"Sorry. I'm not good at this."

"You're thinking too hard. Feel the words instead." His hand covered hers on the book. "Like this. '*Ya ne mogu dyshat' bez tebya*.'"

His mouth was so close, each consonant teased across her skin like a caress. The words flowed like thick honey from his lips, intoxicating and smooth. She turned her head to watch his lips form the sounds, mesmerized by the way his language transformed him. Gone was the growling beast. In his place sat a man who'd once been young and innocent, a boy with dreams and ambitions that manifested in the margins of this text while he learned to survive in a foreign place.

For the first time, she saw him as human and believed him capable of empathy. "What does it mean?" Her voice came out breathless.

His eyes met hers, darker now, pupils blown wide. *"I cannot breathe without you."*

The air between them crackled. Charged. Electric. Her body leaned closer. Hunter's hand, gentle but firm, pressed against her sternum, stopping her.

"Nyet, Lisichka." She understood the word no and sank back, embarrassed all over again by his rejection. He stood, putting distance between them.

"I'm sorry."

He muttered something in Russian that was far beyond her comprehension. "My fault."

They both knew that was a lie, but she appreciated him freeing her from blame. "Hunter..."

He stilled. It was the first time she'd addressed him by name.

When he turned back, his eyes blazed with scorching intensity.

"Thank you...for teaching me."

He hesitated, then finally said, "You're welcome."

She feared the moment he left the library would be the last time she ever saw this side of him. She wanted to make sure that didn't happen. "Will you help me again?"

He stepped toward the door, hands clenched, jaw tight, muscles tensing. But he nodded. "Keep practicing. Your pronunciation needs work."

"I will."

He looked back and nodded. "Good girl."

They both stilled. Why did that phrase drill right to her core. She held his stare, wishing she was clean for him, regretting that she'd let Ash convince her to—

"I have a call to make." He pivoted toward the door, and then he was gone.

Breathless and burning, her hand closed around her throat where the phantom pressure of his fingers still lingered. The book lay open in her lap. She traced the words he'd written as a boy and reached for her wine but the glass was empty.

Slamming the book shut, she left the library and returned to the kitchen, stealing the bottle and taking it, along with the book, up to the privacy of her room.

CHAPTER 16

LISICHKA

Hunter stalked through the halls, blood running hot, hands still trembling from what he'd almost done. His room lay at the end of the north wing, far from the others and exactly how he needed it.

The heavy oak door slammed behind him.

Home. It was a sanctuary as much as a predator's den.

Exposed wooden beams stretched across the ceiling, dark as old blood. The walls were made of raw stone, interrupted only by a massive window that overlooked the frozen forest. No curtains so he could see any threats coming head-on.

The only one he missed approaching was the little blonde currently testing his control. Stalking to the window, he stared out at the choppy sea, wondering how anyone so fragile could manage that on the scrap wood she called a boat.

But she wasn't fragile was she? There was something determined under that ultra-feminine surface. A survivor. Maybe even a moral compass. The longer she was here, the harder it became to form a connection between her and Jordan Calder. She was nothing like her filthy brother.

He gripped the thick custom-built bed frame that dominated the adjacent wall. A hand-carved bear face growled back at him with a lethal stare. His gaze dropped to the black sheets and pelts.

He'd gotten too close. Shared too much. He should have never given her that book. The language barrier was a form of protection, a wall she couldn't penetrate, and he'd just given her the fucking key.

What did it matter if she wanted to learn Russian? Why did that trigger some endearing response in him? She was a thief and the sister of his enemy. She was not to be trusted.

Speaking of which, he withdrew his phone and opened the surveillance app, scrolling through the various feeds to search for her. She was no longer in the library.

He dropped into the leather chair that faced the fireplace, worn smooth from years of sleepless nights, he propped his booted feet on the bearskin carpet and used the tracking filter to find any movement. The servants were downstairs, existing like silent shadows. Katya was reading a book, safely tucked away in her private wing. Ash was seeing to Stone's aftercare—*Ah...* There she was, in the kitchen.

He watched as she snatched an open bottle of wine and carried it out. Tracking her journey, he fed his twisted obsession with her a little longer.

Lisichka. He'd called her little fox. The word had escaped before he could cage it, soft and possessive and entirely too revealing.

The motion sensors tracked her path from the kitchen to the bedroom they assigned to her. He should stop. He didn't need to see anymore. He'd seen enough. The way she'd looked at him, hungry and trusting and a threat to every fucking wall he'd built around himself.

Instead, he sank deeper into the chair and watched her infiltrate his private home like she belonged there. Her ease bothered him. How dare she feel so entitled to their personal domain. She had no clue how deeply the three of them valued their privacy and how privileged she was to earn an invitation during off-hours. The only reason he agreed to let her stay was because he believed in keeping friends few and far between while keeping enemies close enough to kill.

Shutting herself into the bedroom, she pressed her back against the door and twisted the gilded lock with trembling fingers. Did that make her feel safe? Little did she know he had every key.

Her body language lacked the confidence she exhibited over the last hour. Now, she appeared shaky and nervous. A clever little fox on the run from a big scary predator, running back to her foxhole because she wanted to feel safe again. From him. From this world she'd thrown herself into with zero caution.

Foolish little fox, signing over her soul and committing to things she couldn't imagine.

That thin piece of wood wouldn't protect her from any of them. Nothing could.

She tilted the bottle back, her throat working as she swallowed several gulps. She appeared just as triggered as him by their last encounter.

Wine dripped down her chin as she pulled the mouth of the bottle away and gasped. She wiped her full lips with the back of her hand. No grace, no performance. Just a raw glimpse of her actual state. A woman unraveling.

He'd done that to her.

No, she'd done that to *him*.

Hunter had sought the library for solitude but found her instead, curled up like she belonged there. The earnest frustration on her face as she tried to meld two of the most challenging languages in the world stirred something familiar and forgotten inside of him.

Those lost memories slammed into him hard enough to recognize the need in her eyes, that desperation to adapt and fit in, to survive. It was the first time he saw traits in her that resonated with him.

And that subtle connection carved straight through his walls. He'd been there. He recalled his own frustration, fear, and doubt from a time when he needed to make the best of a difficult situation. He'd struggled with the language, worried the words might never make sense. But he needed to learn English. His survival depended on it.

Like hers. Only she needed to learn Russian.

Now, she was doing the same. She wasn't playing games or drifting through the days here with naive trust. She was calculating angles. Strategizing. And he admired her effort.

She could have gone to the sauna or swam in the pool. She could have leisurely read a novel or watched television. The atrium was beautiful for indoor walks. But no. She'd used her free time to better her situation, asking nothing of anyone else, and taking the initiative all on her own.

And damn it all to hell, that told him more about the kind of woman she was than anything else so far.

"Resourceful little fox," he muttered, webbing his fingers over the screen of his phone to better read the expression on her face.

She set the book on the nightstand with careful reverence, fingers lingering on the cover. His chest tightened. That book had been his lifeline once. His loyalty toward Ash was cemented in that uphill battle as his good friend patiently taught him word by painful word as the world burned down around them.

He owed Ash an apology for the other day. He'd been out of sorts and unwilling to accept that they might benefit to having the sister of Jordan Calder in their home. Seeing Ash touch her... it unlocked emotions in Hunter he wasn't in the mood to face, and Ash walked face first into his fury.

Hunter was still debating if he could trust her, but the longer she stayed the thoughts of punishing her for her brother's crimes made less and less sense.

Marigold disappeared into the bathroom and he switched camera views. The wine bottle sat abandoned on the dressing table.

He should look away but he didn't. He clicked to the lens angled at the claw-footed tub. He zoomed in on her face, noting the divot between her cinched brows. Her motions appeared frantic and flustered, as if she were on the verge of tears.

She stripped off the long socks and skin-tight dress with urgent movements, not sensual but desperate. He frowned, wondering why she appeared so agitated.

As the tub filled, she stepped into the shower alcove. Confused, he switched lenses again. Clouds of steam made it difficult to see as she scrubbed at her skin under the shower spray. Nothing happened between them, yet she seemed to be washing a memory away.

Did he disgust her so much that the mere thought of him almost touching her needed to be scrubbed from her skin?

His jaw clenched. She'd been the one to lean into him. Those big brown eyes begging for him to taste her. Or so he'd thought.

He went back to the library feed and rewound, stopping at the moment she edged closer. Yes. It was there. Clear as day. So why was she furiously washing away her sins?

Holding his thumb on the reverse control, he sped backwards through their interaction. Then it was just her, sitting in the library, sipping her wine. Peaceful. Alone.

Where had she come from?

He followed the cameras, retracing her steps. As she walked

in reverse through the hall, her expression appeared distressed. She looked back and chewed her lip. Through the kitchen, where she'd stolen the wine. Back, back, back he followed until —"Bingo."

She'd walked in on one of Stone's sessions. He replayed the brief encounter, turning up the volume to hear what she said to Ash. She thought he was hurting Stone, but Hunter knew better. Stone needed weekly sessions to keep his demons at bay. They all had secret coping mechanisms that ensured they didn't snap in mixed company. The whip was part of Stone's.

He went back to the camera in her bathroom, returning to the present feed. The shower shut off. She wrapped herself in a towel and padded to the bathtub. Steam rose from the taps, fogging the mirror, but the overhead camera caught everything. The way she sank into the water with a sigh made him question if he'd ever know such comfort.

Her eyes fluttered closed as the heated water embraced her. She appeared calmer now. Serene even. Had she washed him out of her system that easily?

She used her toe to adjust the taps, turning the rushing water off. He zoomed in as she closed her eyes again. Those lips... Even as she'd butchered his mother language, he'd been enchanted by her mouth, watching her pink tongue caress every syllable as she took instruction from him so well.

If he'd kissed her in the library, with those beautiful Russian vowels still on her tongue and his fingers caressing her pulse, he would have taken her there on the floor. Would have made her scream his name in both languages until she understood the only word that mattered.

Moy. Mine.

But she wasn't his. Couldn't be. Not when rage still poisoned his blood every time he looked at her. Not when he didn't know if he wanted to worship her or—

Her hand drifted beneath the water's surface.

Fuck.

Hunter adjusted the intercom controls, turning the volume all the way up so he could hear her soft breathing over the gentle lapping of water.

He should shut it off. Should walk away. He could bury himself in a hundred beautiful women at a moment's notice. He just had to make a call. But every other option held no appeal. He only craved one woman, and she was his enemy's blood.

Her breath hitched, barely audible through the speakers. Her other hand gripped the tub's edge as her body arched subtly. Beautiful. Hungry. Alone.

Like him.

The water lapped gently with her movements. Her lips parted on a silent gasp, and he found himself leaning closer, chasing sounds too quiet to catch. Wanting to know if she thought of his hands or someone else's.

He'd purposely put his mouth close to her ear earlier, whispering words he'd never said to another woman. *Ya ne mogu dyshat' bez tebya.*

He'd done it to get a better whiff of her hair and to see how her eyes might dilate. She didn't disappoint, and he'd instantly sat back, taking the book to hide how her response to his nearness made him instantly hard.

Her breathing quickened again. The little thief was stealing an orgasm. In all the excitement, they'd forgotten to set that rule, so he supposed this was fine.

He watched, unblinking, as her reach shifted deeper and her narrow shoulder lifted ever so delicately.

Close now.

So close.

Her head tipped back against the porcelain, exposing the

column of her throat where his fingers had pressed. Where her pulse had hammered under his touch.

Then, soft as snowfall, she whispered, *"Hunter..."*

The world stopped, and his phone creaked under the weight of his crushing grip. He couldn't think. Couldn't breathe. That was his name on her lips as she came undone.

His name, like a prayer.

Or was it a confession.

He didn't care. It was his name. She breathed it out as if she could taste him on the mere sound.

Hunter's thumb jammed into the power button and his screen went black. "Fuck me."

But the damage was done. She'd shown her cards.

He'd thought she was washing away his touch, but that wasn't it at all. She was doing exactly what he'd ordered her to do. She was getting clean for him.

He growled and pressed his palms against his eyes until he saw stars, but he could still see her. Still hear her raspy voice as she called his name.

"Fuck!" He was on his feet and out the door before he could remember why this was a bad idea. At the moment, the few rules he kept were lost and he had no desire to find them. He only needed to find her.

CHAPTER 17

UNLOCKED

The water had gone tepid around her, but Marigold couldn't bring herself to move. Her body still thrummed with the aftermath of release, muscles liquid and languid. She should feel ashamed. Should feel guilty for whispering his name like a prayer into the steam.

The lock clicked and her eyes flew open.

The gilded handle on the bathroom door turned with deliberate intent, and her heart slammed against her ribs. She'd locked the bedroom door. She was certain of it.

"Who's there?"

The ivory door flung open, and she sloshed back against the wall of the tub, cool air rushing in, hitting her overheated flesh and raising goosebumps across every inch of exposed skin.

"*Hunter.*"

He filled the doorway like a storm given form. His obsidian eyes burned molten in the dim light, fixed on her with an intensity that made her sink lower in the water.

"What are you doing in my bathroom?"

He stepped inside, looming like a lethal threat about to destroy her. "*My* bathroom."

She sloshed to the other end of the tub. "Get out!" Her voice cracked with indignant pride.

He prowled closer, graceful and deadly, moving like an agile giant, each footfall silent on the marble floor, despite his heavy boots. "You called for me."

"I did not—" Blood drained from her face. Had he been watching her? Spying? Her gaze dropped to the water as mortification burned through her veins. "You bastard."

"That might be true, but I heard what I heard."

"You heard wrong."

"Liar." The word rolled off his tongue like a caress. He crouched beside the tub, one massive hand gripping the porcelain edge. This close, she could see the pulse jumping in his throat, could smell the pine smoke and raw masculinity that clung to his skin. "You whispered my name like you were tasting it."

Shame scorched her cheeks. He couldn't know what she'd been thinking. Couldn't have known what she'd done. Her gaze shot to the bear camera.

"Yes." He affirmed, not needing to follow her gaze to track her line of thought. "I watched the whole thing."

The realization hit like ice water.

"Heard every breath." His gaze tracked down her throat to where the water barely covered her breasts. "Every word."

"You had no right."

"I have every right." He reached for her, and she pressed back against the far side of the tub.

"Don't."

"You're mine to protect. Mine to watch." He extended his hand, waiting. "Mine to use."

"You rejected me." Not once, but twice. "You'll do it again. You're only doing this to punish me."

His hand froze inches from her skin. Something dark flickered across his features. "Not all punishment hurts."

"Well, rejection does. Play games with someone else, Hunter. I'm not interested."

His name on her lips, even in anger, was an aphrodisiac for the soul. "This time, I won't reject you."

"No."

He stilled, then stood, furious she'd think to deny him after giving herself to her brothers several times over. "That's not a word I abide from you." He plunged both arms into the water and lifted her out as if she weighed nothing.

"Let go of me!" Water sluiced off her body, soaking through his shirt, dripping onto his boots, and sloshing onto the floor.

He gathered her against his chest, walking her out of the warm bathroom. "We're past the point of resistance."

She gasped as cold air awakened her wet skin, instinctively curling into his warmth even as she fought to get free. "You animal!"

He carried her to the bed and tossed her down unceremoniously, then stepped back. The handmade birch frame creaked as she scrambled for the blankets, her shaking limbs radiating fury as she wrapped her body in white fur.

"I hate you!" she snapped.

"You're clean now." His voice had gone rough, accent thicker. He undid his belt, pulling it slowly through each belt loop so she fully understood where this was going. "Fresh." He toed off his boots. "No trace of them on your skin."

She clutched the furs tighter to her chest. "Why are you doing this now? You said you didn't want me. You said you wouldn't."

"Our circumstances have changed." He circled the bed like a predator stalking prey as he stripped off his shirt.

"Does this have to do with Jordan? Did something happen?"

"Leave his name out of this."

"How can I, when you plan to punish me? And I don't know what I did wrong!"

"Not wrong. It is what it is. Here we are. You called my name." He lowered his zipper. "Maybe it was a mistake. Maybe you regret it. But in that moment, as you fed your fingers into your tight heat and brought yourself to climax, it was *my* face you imagined. My hand. My touch. My name you whispered as you came." He caught her ankle and hauled her to the edge of the bed. "Tell me it wasn't and I'll leave you be."

She lay flat on her back, staring up at him in terror. The heat from his skin burned into hers. She couldn't deny it. She'd touched herself, and in that moment, wished it was him. But she wanted the gentle giant from the library, not this unhinged version from her nightmares.

"Hunter, please." She placed a staying hand on his chest, surprised when he stilled. "Why are you here? What do you want?"

"Everything." He caught her under the knees and yanked her to the edge, pulling her legs apart.

"Wait!"

"Your fear..." He growled. "I already told you it's mine. It won't stop me. It only edges me on. I want to taste it in your arousal when I devour you."

"Why does it have to be scary?" She panted, desperately trying to find the man she'd witnessed in the library. "I know there's a softer side to you."

"A man has many sides, but at the core, we're all hiding an inner beast. Whichever side you get, they're all me. And when

I'm done with you, you won't know where terror ends and pleasure begins."

Her thighs clenched involuntarily. "You said you weren't interested."

"I said you would beg."

Indignant fury burned through her as she glared at him. "You had your chance."

He threw his head back and laughed. "Is that what you think?" He moved on her so fast, pinning her arms beside her head and forcing her back to arch. "Every second that you're here, in my home, is another chance to do what I want with you."

The fur blanket slipped off her chest, and his gaze fell like a physical caress over her breasts, tracking the drops of water that trailed from her skin. Tension filled the room, so thick she could barely breathe.

"Hunter!"

He stilled. "Say it again. Softer."

She panted, gentling her voice, "Hunter..."

He grinned, his gaze traveling slowly over her exposed body like a hungry caress. "Look at you." His voice dropped to a gravelly whisper. "Shivering. Scared. Perfect." He was closer now, close enough that his body heat reached her. His gaze pinned her in place as much as his unbreakable hold. "Enough with this game, *Lisichka*. We will ease the tension so we can both breathe normally again."

His thick accent cast an intoxicating spell on her.

"It's better that I come to you now, while I still have a shred of control left." He leaned over her, dragging his nose along her breast and breathing her in. "Admit that you want it, too."

"I'm scared."

"Yes, sometimes I even scare myself." His gentle hand moved in complete contrast to her erratic heart. "Beg, and I'll end all your suffering, *Lisichka*. Just say one pretty word, and I'll show you things you've never imagined."

The Russian endearment shouldn't affect her. Shouldn't make her stomach flip and her skin flush. "What's *Lisichka?*"

"A clever, little fox." His hand lifted toward her face, hovering just out of reach, then he trailed his fingers softly over her throat. "Foxes are thieves. And I think you stole my sanity today. The little I had left."

She could feel the heat radiating from his palm, could imagine how it would feel against her skin. Rough. Warm. Possessive. The space between them crackled with possibility.

"Do you plan to hurt me?"

"*Nyet*, but that's not the right question, little fox."

He was right. She wanted to get it over with—this inevitable outcome was the only thing keeping her from fully accepting her new life. "Will there be pain?"

"Perhaps. Pain is unavoidable. It's proof we're alive." He glanced down where the blanket gathered over her hips and frowned. "You're very...petite. I'm not. Some pain is to be expected."

She studied his dark stare, searching for hidden cruel intentions. The friction of their chemistry alone was abrading her nerves.

She'd wanted him since she left the library. Continued fantasizing about him as she washed her body clean. Then, when she touched herself, it was his face she imagined, his fingers she pictured slipping inside of her. It wasn't an accident when she uttered his name.

Now, he was here.

"Touch me." The words escaped before she could stop them.

His hand dropped immediately. "That wasn't begging."

Frustration and need tangled in her chest. He stood over her like carved stone, everything she wanted just out of reach. The blankets slipped lower when she arched toward him, and his eyes tracked the movement with laser focus, but still, he didn't move.

"What do you want me to say?"

"The truth." His voice had gone deadly soft. "Tell me what you thought about in that tub. Tell me what made you say my name."

Heat flooded her cheeks. "You already know."

"Say it."

She pressed her thighs together, trying to ease the ache building between them. He noticed, of course, his eyes darkening, and his hands clenching into fists.

"I thought about your hands." The admission scraped her throat raw. "Your scars. How they felt on my neck. How they might feel in... other places."

"Continue."

"Your mouth." Her voice dropped to barely above a whisper. "How it sounds when you roll your Rs and how it might sound to hear you say my name."

"*Marigold...*" he said, with deliberate slowness, letting the R roll over the G into the long, lulling L.

Her eyes rolled shut. It was better than she'd imagined.

"You like when I say your name?"

"Yes."

He made a sound low in his chest, not quite growl, not quite groan. "Keep talking. Tell me more."

She stared through her lashes at him. "I thought about..." She swallowed hard. "I wondered if you'd be rough, or deliberately gentle. If you'd take your time or devour me whole."

"Which did you decide?"

"Both." She sensed a side to him very few saw. She believed he'd once been gentle, but life had made him hard.

"Which do you want?"

"Do I have to choose?"

His brows lifted. "You want me rough?"

"I want you honest. I want the real you, or nothing at all."

He moved then, faster than she could track, lunging over her, still not touching but close enough that his breath ghosted over her lips.

"Beg me." His voice commanded obedience. "Beg me to touch you, and I'll end this misery. I'll ruin you so thoroughly that you'll never try to wash me off again."

"I..." His words settled over like a chill. But then she frowned. "What are you talking about?"

"I saw you, in the shower, scrubbing your skin. You thought you could wash me away, but you can't get rid of me that easily, *Lisichka*. I'm in here." He pressed a finger to her forehead.

"That's not what I was doing."

"I watched you."

"But I wasn't..." She looked away. Why was she telling him this? "Never mind."

He caught her chin and forced her to meet his stare. "What then?"

Her lips pressed tight. "Ash. We were together earlier today, and he..."

Understanding dawned and his expression hardened. He drew back, now standing at his full height. "I see."

"You're upset."

"No."

"You are."

"You belong to all of us."

That might be what they agreed, but he was still pissed. Hunter was more territorial than the others. "I did it for you. You said you didn't want me after them, that I should be..." She recalled how much she needed to get clean when she returned to her room. "I felt filthy."

"You regret being with Ash?"

"No, but I wanted to be fresh. For you."

His nostrils flared as he studied her face. "For me?"

She nodded. Pride warred with need, but need was winning. "I don't know why. You're not even nice to me."

"I'm not easy like my brothers."

"None of you are easy. But I'm trying, Hunter. Truly, I am."

He stepped closer. "That is why you want to speak Russian."

"I'll never speak it like you, but I'd like to understand it better if I'm staying here."

"You honestly plan to stay?"

"You've left me little choice."

"There's always a choice, *Lisichka*."

"Well, I prefer this prison over the one my family chose."

"Not a prison. A fortress. It's a privilege to be our guest."

"I believe you. But not if you want to hurt and punish me."

"You're braver than you realize."

Her lashes lowered.

"Marigold." He delicately traced a finger over her cheek.

For the first time, she truly felt the loss of herself in the mix of surrendering her family and past. "When this is over, that might not be my name."

"But it is your name. Don't let them take it from you when they've already stolen so much."

"How did you...?"

"Ash."

She looked down, embarrassed. "I'm not crazy."

"No one would blame you if you were, after what they put you through."

"You say that now—"

"I mean what I say. Today, tomorrow, a year from now. We don't expect perfection, but we do expect you to be truthful. That's what it means to be ours."

She couldn't take any more of this man. "Please." The word came out broken.

"Please what?" He leaned closer, lips nearly brushing hers. "What do you need?"

"Touch me." She said, stronger this time. "I need you to touch me." She wanted him to make her irrevocably a part of this place so she could start her life over.

"Let me hear you beg."

She made a sound of pure frustration. He was going to make her say it. Make her bare her soul for him.

"Please, Hunter." His name tasted like surrender on her tongue. "Please. I'm begging you. Touch me, taste me, take me. I don't care how. Just make me yours."

Victory flashed in his eyes for a split second before his control shattered completely.

His mouth crashed over hers, not gentle but not cruel. He kissed her like he was claiming territory, teeth scraping, tongue soothing. His hands slid up her calves with devastating slowness, spreading her legs wide.

"Moya *Lisichka*." The Russian endearment rumbled against her skin. "My little fox. Do you know how many times I've thought about breaking my own promises to touch you?"

She couldn't answer. Could barely breathe. His hands had trailed up her thighs, thumbs tracing patterns that made her shake. He pushed the blankets away, revealing every inch of her.

His fingers traced higher, and she shivered. He pressed her knees into her chest, putting her most secret places on full display. "Look how you glisten, ready for me alone." He bent down, and dragged his tongue through her folds. "Untouched."

She gasped when he grazed her clit.

"I'm going to fuck your tight pink hole so hard you'll feel me inside of you for days." He pressed a finger inside of her, purposely reaching as deep as he could. "You'll be exhausted when I'm finished. If you sleep, I'll fuck you while you dream. And when you dream, you'll feel me inside of you. That's how deep it will be, *Lisichka*. I'll always be in you."

Her breath jutted out as he pressed a finger to her ass.

"Every inch of you will know the feel of my cock." He pressed his fingers deep inside of her and held. Her moans pitched when he teased a sensitive spot. "Three times as deep as I am now."

"Hunter..." He was edging her closer to that pivotal place, but dragging it out. Teasing her. "Please."

A low rumbling chuckle escaped his throat. "Greedy little thief. You already stole from us today."

Her attention snapped to his face. "No, I didn't."

"You did. When you were in the bath, touching yourself, you stole an orgasm. No more, *Lisichka*. Your pleasure is ours to give. You come see me or Stone or Ash when you need attention. Understand?"

"Are you saying I'm not allowed to touch myself?"

He twisted his fingers, reaching places inside of her she could never manage on her own. "That's exactly what I'm saying." His other hand pressed flat on her lower stomach, applying enough pressure to heighten the sensation of his exploring fingers. "Besides, your little climax was nothing compared to what I can give you."

Her breath hitched as he demonstrated, pumping hard and fast, hitting nerves she never reached before. "Wait, wait, wait!" She gasped, overwhelmed by the sudden onslaught of intense pleasure, but she was powerless to stop it.

He took ownership of her body. Drove her to heights she could never manage on her own, places other men had never cared to journey. She was merely a passenger, a victim of sin and service, an instrument he played like a master, and as she reached one explosive finish after the other, crying out profanities that slurred into incoherent prayers, he got her to sing.

The aftershocks rippled through her like endless electric zaps. Every nerve was so alive and firing, the simplest caress made her twitch and gasp.

"Very good," he praised, trailing the tips of his fingers over her wet thighs.

She was drenched flesh and sobbing pleasure, mindlessly malleable.

"The way you looked at me in the library..." He kissed the words into her flesh like brands. "So trusting. So curious. I wanted to bend you over that chair and show you exactly how those Russian words should sound when you scream them."

A whimper escaped as his hands tightened on her thighs, holding her steady as he worked his mouth higher.

"But this is better." His teeth found the sensitive skin of her inner thigh, and she gasped. "Now, you're mine by choice. Every time I make you come apart, you'll know you asked for it. Begged for it."

He pressed her thighs wide and looked up at her, the raw hunger in his eyes enough to steal her breath. "No place to run now, little fox."

"I'm through running," she whispered and his control evaporated.

He surged forward, taking her with his mouth. Tongue probing as his lips closed around her sensitized clit. She screamed when the pleasure was too much to control, but he didn't back off. He drank her in, growling and gripping her with bruising force as he demanded another and then another from her.

She lay in a panting puddle of lust, as every nerve ending sizzled with a steady pulse, so rapid her body became a live wire and he became its master. Capturing her mouth in a kiss that tasted like possession and promises, he whispered Russian secrets against her flesh. His hands were everywhere at once, learning the body he'd studied through cameras, claiming what she'd freely given.

"Beautiful." He growled the word against her throat. "*Moya.* Mine."

She arched into him, desperate for every delicious contact, craving the friction, desiring every torturous touch, trusting his teasing would only lead to pleasures beyond her imagination.

He obliged, pressing her damp body against the cool furs, the pelts silky against her fevered skin. His mouth traced a path of fire down her neck, across her collarbone, lower still.

"Say it again." He commanded between kisses. "Say my name like you did in the water."

"Hunter." It came out as a moan.

"Again."

"Hunter, please..."

He rewarded her with his teeth, just sharp enough to make her gasp. His hands mapped every curve, every hollow, as she writhed and begged. He took his time, thorough and devastating, until she was nothing but wild sensation and raw need.

"Look at me." He tilted her chin up, forcing her to meet his molten gaze. "I want to see your eyes when I enter you. I want to watch you break just for me."

She couldn't look away. Couldn't do anything but feel as he took ownership of her body. Every touch was a claim. Every kiss a brand. He was rewriting her at a molecular level, replacing every other memory with just this, just him.

"Please." She didn't know what she was begging for anymore. Release? Mercy? Life? "Hunter, I need you inside of me."

"You beg so pretty." He punctuated the words with a nudge

of his thick cock, showing her just how tight his entry would be. "You're mine now, *Lisichka*."

Her breath pulled deep, filling her lungs as he filled her with his all-encompassing possession. It was vastly different from being with the others. With Hunter, she had to be present. He commanded it, not just with his eyes or the way he held her face insisting she look at him, but with his touch. Every thrust was pure intention. Every gasp driven from a place deep in her soul that never spoke before this moment. Before him.

When the world finally shattered around her, she screamed his name, babbling in tongues just like he'd promised. He held her through it, whispering Russian endearments against her skin, each word of praise sinking into her bones like truth. She never felt so protected in her life.

"*Moya*." He breathed the word like a repeated vow. "Mine."

She could only nod. Her mind was beyond words, beyond thought. He redefined her, as promised.

"No going back now, *Lisichka*."

An agreeable hum was all she could manage.

"You'll never be rid of me. Never stop feeling my hands, my mouth, my claim on every inch of you." He kissed her again, softer now but no less possessive. "This is just the beginning, *little fox*. Now that I've tasted you, that hunger will never go away."

His promise should have terrified her. Instead, it filled her with an unfamiliar sense of security she had no comparison for. He would devour her, again and again, but he'd also protect her from any enemy. She was his now, and that meant no one—save his brothers—could lay a hand on her.

CHAPTER 18

A GLASS CAGE

As the men worked on their plans and preparation, Marigold explored the many hidden rooms of the lodge. She toured a wing she'd never visited before and discovered a stunning solarium.

The glass-walled sanctuary overflowed with impossible greenery and radiant blooms that somehow thrived despite the arctic climate outside. Orchids preened in beaming jewel tones, so vibrant she had to touch petals to assure herself they weren't fake.

"They're magnificent, aren't they?"

Spinning sharply, Marigold gasped in the sweet, humid air and backed into a large palm. "Who are you?"

The girl—because that's what she was, barely past her teens with features that belonged in a Renaissance painting—sat curled in a white wicker chair, a book forgotten in her lap. Dark hair fell like a curtain around her face, with eyes the same emerald green as Stone's, flecked with molten gold that dimmed and brightened with every emotion.

"I'm Katya Volkova. And I assume you're *her*." There was a touch of wonder in her voice.

She moved closer, drawn in by her fragile grace. "I'm Marigold. Though I suppose you already know that."

"My brothers warned me that you were beautiful." Her smile was tentative, like she'd forgotten how to use it properly. Brief and gone before truly there. "They also told me who your brother is."

"*Half*-brother."

"They said you're estranged now, that he sent you away and you managed to escape."

Marigold nodded. "That's right. When I tried to stop him from hurting someone, he had me committed."

"Because you knew what he was."

Another nod paired with a small step forward. "He's evil. What he did to you…"

She held up a delicate hand, so small and fragile. "I'm stronger than people realize."

"Still. No one should have to suffer that way."

"True." Such a small word to carry so much weight. She waved a hand, inviting Marigold to settle into the chair across from her. "I come to this room to read, and to escape. Winter can be quite a prison around here. The solarium helps me remember that change will come.

The humid room buzzed with hidden sprinklers and small insects. It was as if they trapped a tropical summer within a bitter tundra. "I suppose this is where the flowers come from."

"And the produce." She pointed past the archway lined with draping wisteria. "There are more gardens that way. Everything we serve is farm-to-table, regardless of the season."

Marigold leaned forward, angling her head to see the next room, but trusted Katya's word. An awkward silence expanded between them. She folded her hands on her lap, no doubt wondering what they might have in common.

"Why did you escape the facility?" Katya finally asked. "Was it simply because you didn't want to be locked away, or were there other reasons."

"There were other reasons." A knowing look passed between them.

Katya nodded. "I was sent away, too. But I had a choice in the matter."

"How long?" she asked gently then said, "Do you mind talking about it?"

"I don't mind. Six months. It was a private facility in Switzerland. Very discreet, very exclusive." Katya's laugh held no humor. "My brothers wanted the best care money could buy for their broken little sister."

"You're not broken."

The words came out with more force than Marigold had intended, but she didn't regret them.

She'd heard that particular lie too many times, had it whispered in her ear by orderlies who thought emotional damage was something that dehumanized a soul, as if her values could be medicated away.

"You sound like my brothers."

"Well, that's because I hear it from them too."

"Before... everything... I used to love the gatherings," Katya said softly. "Not here—my brothers kept me away from their business. But I'd attend the masquerades on Isola Verde." Her laugh was bitter. "Their parties were beautiful on the surface. Venetian masks sipping poisoned wines, secrets traded like currency."

"You've been to the other islands?"

"Most of them. The Nakamura gardens are actually stunning if you visit during the right season. And Björnholm is beautiful when it's not hunting season. The Björn family has a daughter my age. Was my age. She doesn't speak anymore." Katya's fingers trembled on her book. "That's what these islands do. They take things from you piece by piece until you're not sure what's left. My brother's never wanted that sort of crime here. They take pride in making sure every guest abides their rules."

Marigold lowered her gaze. "Until Jordan."

"Your brother was never meant to be here. Hunter will never forgive himself for allowing him through the doors. But it was my fault for venturing out of my wing during a party."

"None of this was your fault."

Katya visibly drew in a deep breath, but remained outwardly calm. "It's hard to imagine what I was like after. What I became. All of my innocence vanished in a blink. I was so ashamed, so afraid of what they would say, who they might blame."

"Did they blame you?"

"Never. I think, on some level, my brothers' devastation runs deeper than my own. They saw it as a personal failure on their part."

She could imagine as much. All three men prided themselves on being great protectors. To have their little sister attacked right under their roof, in this fortress they called home, it must have been an incredibly humanizing moment for all of them.

"Life has a surrealness about it after something like that," Katya continued. "Like a living dream. Or a nightmare." She laughed without humor. "Sometimes I think I'm going crazy, lost within the strange thoughts running through my head."

"I know what it's like to live in an unfathomable reality," Marigold whispered. "I know what it's like to question yourself so much that you lose your grasp on life. Truth loses meaning, and lies carry a tangible weight. It's like you're falling every day, through time with no landing in sight."

"Yes."

"You can't trust your mind."

"But you feel it. Here," Katya said, resting a hand on her chest.

Marigold nodded. "A fragile thread of a lifeline."

She recalled how some days, her mind was so fried and her drug-induced haze was so heavy, she lost that thread back to reality. Days slipped by, without hope, and with every passing minute, she'd lost her grip on the truth, the likelihood of her staying in that hellhole forever grew.

That's what happened to the residents there. They once cared, but over time, it became easier to give up. They would rather surrender to numbness than push through the fog to fight for their freedom.

It was the first time she found herself able to think about her time at Whitmore without the creeping panic she usually felt. "The more they tried to help me, the more I felt myself slipping away."

"Sometimes, grief is so personal, we can only help ourselves," Katya said. "It seems almost impossible to pick ourselves up when we're at our lowest. I've learned patience like I've never known, and my brothers remind me every day to give myself grace."

Marigold smiled at the image of the boys speaking with Katya in such a supportive way. She knew a side to them Marigold had yet to meet, a side she desperately wanted to know. "You're lucky to have such kind, protective brothers."

"I'm grateful for them every day. They never doubted me or blamed me for what happened. At the clinic, they said I was having delusions. Trauma-induced paranoia." Katya's fingers twisted in the silk of her dress. "They said memories aren't reliable after too much emotional stress."

"But you knew better."

"I knew what he did to me." Katya's words were barely a whisper. "I knew how he smiled while he... I couldn't move, couldn't fight, couldn't even scream. By crippling my other senses, he made my mind that much sharper. I'll never forget what really happened that night."

Marigold's chest tightened with familiar rage. "I'm so sorry he did that to you."

She smiled, but it didn't reach her green eyes. "I typically stay in the east wing when they entertain. Stone vets everyone on the guest list of every event, but somehow he got past their checkpoint unnoticed. When they realized he was here without the proper vetting, Hunter let him stay."

Marigold's heart pinched for Hunter, imagining how much he must blame himself for what she went though.

"He wasn't with the other guests when he found me. He also had everything he needed to do what he planned." Her laugh was cold. "To think, I wasn't even special."

Marigold's blood ran cold. "How did he do it?"

"Something in my drink. One moment I was laughing at his jokes, thinking how charming he was, how lucky I was that someone so sophisticated was paying attention to boring little me." Katya's voice cracked. "The next moment I was drowning in my own body, aware of everything but unable to do anything to stop it."

"I'm so sorry, Katya." Her redundant apology felt so inadequate, but they were the only words Marigold had. Leaning across the space, she placed a hand over hers. "I'm so fucking sorry he did that to you."

Her palpable sorrow gave way to a slow smile. "You swear like my brothers."

"There are three of them and one of me. Swearing helps my street cred'."

She laughed, the sound as melodic as chimes in a breeze. "You should hear them when they think they're around people who can't understand Russian." Katya's smile grew stronger. "Though I bet you understand more than they think you do."

"I'm trying. Hunter gave me a book and he's been helping me practice."

"Hunter? That surprises me."

"Why?"

"He's not the most tolerant."

"Oh, I'm well aware." She thought back to the last time she was with Hunter, and how exacting he could be. "But I think he has a soft spot for me."

"From what I hear, they all do."

Marigold's cheeks heated. "I suppose it's strange for you to imagine the three of them with one woman."

"Not really. They do everything together. It's how they got the nickname *The Three Bears*."

"You're kidding. People actually call them that?"

Katya laughed and nodded. "When we came to Kassel, they said all the islands were occupied. The Northern Isles were considered *undesirable* due to the long winters and harsh climates. They had been abandoned for nearly a century. Stone said it reminded him of Mother Russia, so we moved in that day. I was just happy that we were back together again."

"Were you separated?"

A startled look danced across her beautiful face. "Didn't they tell you?"

"No." It occurred to Marigold that she'd been so focused on surviving the present she only let herself think of the future. "We never talk about their past."

"It was terrible, what they survived. I wasn't there, but

when they came back to me they looked nothing like the boys who left."

A chill chased up Marigold's spine, despite the tropical temperatures. Outside the glass walls, snow still dusted the white landscape, but inside, everything was warm and green and alive. "Where did they go?"

"It was an expedition. Our father had thought it would be a good idea to toughen them up on the North Sea. But their vessel was commandeered by a cargo ship occupied by pirates. They were transported to Libya, where they were sold with other refugees and exploited in underground fights."

"They were trafficked?"

Lines of compassion formed deep grooves around her emerald eyes. "Hunter was determined to survive. His body count was unfathomable."

Marigold sucked in a harsh breath. "He actually killed people?"

"He's not proud of it. He was oldest. Those years shaped him in ways he'll never undo. He had to be terrifying to protect Stone, and then Ash."

"Is that where he met Ash?"

She nodded. "Ash nearly died. If not for Hunter's protection and after care, he wouldn't have made it."

It was no wonder their bond was so strong.

"But Stone had it the worst," Katya continued. "He was smallest, and used as bait. He'd always been docile, which is probably why they chose him. The bait fighters were restrained until training time. Then, they were used to hone the killer instincts of the more aggressive fighters."

"Oh, my God." Her heart plummeted as her stomach turned. How could anyone be so brutally cruel?

"Sometimes, Stone still needs to feel the bite of pain to function. They almost broke him."

That must have been what she walked in on the other day. And, of course, Ash would value aftercare above all else, especially when his brothers were the reason for his survival. "I had no idea."

"No one, outside of this family, truly knows what happened. They just know that our loyalty runs deep. My brothers will do anything to protect those they love."

"Like you."

"Yes. And you."

Marigold's gaze snapped to hers. "They don't... I mean, I'm... We're not..."

"You understand they've never, in all their lives, allowed another female to live here."

"But I found things. Clothers. Products."

"Overnight shipping knows no limit. Stone's an impulsive midnight shopper who suffers insomnia."

"You're saying they bought all of that stuff for me?"

She nodded. "They're very generous."

"I don't know what to say."

Katya reached for her hand. "Them opening up, letting you in... It's special, Marigold. Please don't hurt them."

"I have no intention to."

"Even when your brother gets here? It's not easy to turn your back on family."

"He turned his back on me, first."

Katya's full lips pressed tight. "Are you afraid?"

"Terrified," Marigold admitted. "But not of Jordan. Not anymore. I'm afraid of what seeing him will do to you."

"They won't force me to see him. But if I choose to... I'm stronger now—and smarter." She straightened in her chair, lifting her dress to expose the knife tucked into a thigh holster strapped to her leg.

Marigold could see echoes of her brothers in the set of her jaw as much as her quiet confidence. "Will you use it?"

"If I have to. He'll never put his hands on me again." She covered her legs. "Last time, I was a naïve little girl. He killed that little girl and left me to bury her."

"Your brothers will see that vengeance is served."

"And then some. I know they would burn the world down for me." Katya's smile was soft with affection.

Marigold shook her head, still reeling from all she'd learned. "Thank you for sharing all of this with me. It helps."

"Does it?"

She nodded. "At first, I thought they couldn't possibly understand what it feels like to have their choices stolen. To be reduced to a victim. Helpless. Trapped."

"Now, you know differently."

"I do. I also know that they would never keep me here against my will."

"No, they wouldn't. They also wouldn't punish you if you wanted to leave. But I hope you stay."

"I plan to. I just want to get past this next part and focus on a brighter future."

"Me too."

"Tonight, we take our power back," Marigold said fiercely.

"Will you watch and tell me—"

Heavy footsteps echoed in the corridor, cutting off Katya's question. Both women turned as Stone appeared in the doorway. His pale eyes immediately sought Katya, scanning her with the protective intensity of a guardian angel.

"How are you feeling, little bird?" His voice, so cold when he spoke to others, went warm as honey when addressing his sister.

"I'm fine. Marigold and I have been getting acquainted."

Stone's winter-green gaze shifted to her and then back to his sister. "I hope you've been making her feel welcome."

"She has," Marigold said, before Katya could answer. He'd been avoiding her since she found him strung up in the dungeon with Ash.

Katya stood gracefully, moving to her brother's side. Even standing, she barely reached his shoulder, but there was nothing fragile about her confidence. "I like her, Stone. She understands."

"Good." Stone's arm came around his sister with careful gentleness, as if she were made of glass. "Because we need to discuss tonight."

"When we have that discussion," Marigold said, "will you finally look at me?"

The room chilled as his sharp gaze cut to her. "Excuse me?"

"I think I'll take a walk," Katya said, untangling herself from her brother's heavily muscled arm. "It was nice chatting with you, Marigold."

"You too," she said, without taking her eyes off Stone.

When the glass door closed, Stone snarled, "What the hell was that comment?"

She shrugged. "You've been avoiding me."

"I've been busy, tracking your piece of shit, brother."

"Whatever you say." She moved to stand, but he shoved her back into the chair, bearing down on the arms and caging her in.

"Are you calling me a pussy?"

"No."

"Then what? You think you saw something the other day that you understand? Trust me, you don't."

She tried to picture a weaker version of him, terrified and chained, beaten down by men forced to kill. Her hand slowly lifted as she cupped the side of his jaw where a long scar hid beneath his dark stubble, and she softly whispered, "Katya told me what happened to you."

His entire body stiffened. "That was a long time ago."

"But you still carry it with you, don't you?"

His nostrils flared. "It builds. Ash lets it out."

"That should have never happened to you."

"We can't undo the past, *Zayka*." He pushed back from the chair and turned away. "I survived. So did you. Our minds are better served by looking forward, which is why we must discuss your brother's arrival. We expect him in a few hours."

Rising from the chair, she quietly stepped behind him and banded her arms around his thick waist, resting her cheek on his back, her touch saying all she needed to convey.

Stone stiffened, then rested his hand softly over her interlaced fingers. He uttered something delicate in Russian that she didn't understand.

They stood like that for several beats, dredging through things that would only be cheapened by words.

Finally, he said, "Come to me tonight, when everything's over. I want to be with you. Alone."

She released him and nodded.

He caught her chin, and looked into her eyes. "We won't let anything happen to you."

"I know." She smiled. "I trust you."

CHAPTER 19

THROUGH THE KEYHOLE

Stone led Marigold through corridors she hadn't explored yet. The architecture changed as they walked, becoming more utilitarian. Service areas, she realized, the behind-the-scenes spaces that kept the fantasy of this gothic palace functioning.

They emerged into what appeared to be a security office. Banks of monitors showed feeds from every corner of the lodge, while communication equipment hummed quietly in the background. Hunter was there, along with Ash and several men Marigold didn't recognize—staff members, from their uniforms and bearing. In the corner, beside a rather intense-looking man she didn't know, sat Katya.

Hunter's smile held dark anticipation as he crossed the room to place a kiss on her lips. "Perfect timing. We were just going over the evening's schedule."

"Schedule?" Marigold asked.

"Your brother's visit isn't exactly social," Ash explained, moving to pull her against his side. "He's coming with lawyers and security. According to the messages we were able to hack, he's *anticipating* an unencumbered rescue. You see, you were kidnapped, and tonight, he'll find you having another psychotic episode."

Marigold sucked in a sharp breath. "You want me to act psychotic."

"No. We want you as far away from him as possible," Stone growled. "Hunter's only relaying what we've gathered from hacking your brother's phone. His words, not ours."

"But she wasn't kidnapped," Katya said, offended on her behalf. "Marigold has chosen to be here of her own free will."

"Well, sort of." She flinched when Ash pinched her ass.

"Watch it," he warned.

Hunter met her worried stare with unwavering confidence. "We're going to let him think whatever he wants. At least initially. That's how irrelevant his feelings are in tonight's outcome."

"What do you need us to do?" Marigold asked.

The brothers exchanged looks loaded with meaning. Whatever they had planned, it was complex enough to require careful coordination.

"Nothing dangerous," Hunter said finally. "We won't put either of you at risk. But your presence, your testimony, that's what makes this work."

"Jordan needs to understand exactly what he did," Stone explained. "Not just legally, but viscerally. He needs to feel what his victims felt."

"Powerless," Ash murmured.

"Trapped," Stone added. "Unable to escape what's coming."

The implications sent fear tunneling through Marigold's blood like ice chips. They were going to break Jordan the same way he'd broken others. There would most likely be violence, but also psychological domination. She tried to picture the slow, inexorable stripping away of his control. Wondered how he might act when cornered and outmaneuvered, laid bare, with nothing but naked vulnerability to protect him.

Just as she'd been unprotected and outnumbered when they strapped her to that table and sent one hundred and twenty volts of electricity through her. She hoped when the guys were through with him, Jordan experienced the same convulsing helplessness Katya suffered, plus the fear Marigold felt every time the doctors at Whitmore put her through those electric shock sessions.

"Where will we be during all this?" Katya asked.

"Safe," Stone said immediately. "Hidden. You'll be able to see everything, but he won't know you're there until we're ready."

"Until he's ready," Hunter corrected with a predator's grin.

The intimidating officer beside Katya stepped forward with a tablet. "Boat's approaching the harbor, sir. ETA twenty minutes."

The atmosphere in the room changed instantly. "Good job, Cole."

"Cole's the head of security," Ash whispered to Marigold, mouth warm against her ear. "He steps in when we're preoccupied with the guests."

The brothers moved with sudden purpose, checking equipment, confirming positions, as if preparing for battle. But it was Katya's reaction that broke Marigold's heart. The girl who'd been growing stronger by the minute suddenly went pale and rigid. Her breathing quickened, and her hands began to shake.

"He's here?" she whispered. "He's really here?"

All three brothers converged on her instantly, their protective instincts overriding everything else. The security officer looked back at her, appearing torn between his post and her response, but her brothers had her covered.

"Breathe, little bird," Stone murmured, his hands framing her face. "Look at me. Just at me."

"You're safe," Ash added, moving to her other side. "He can't hurt you. Won't hurt you. We won't let him."

"I know." But Katya's voice was thready, distant. "I know that. But my body... it remembers."

Hunter crouched in front of his sister, holding her trembling hands in his massive grip. "Do you want it to stop? We can handle this without you, in other ways."

"Or send you somewhere safe until it's over," Ash said.

"No." The word came out with reaffirmed strength. "No, I need to do this. I need to face him."

"You don't need to do anything," Stone said fiercely. "You don't owe him confrontation. You don't owe anyone your pain."

"I owe myself." Katya's chin lifted with stubborn courage. "I owe that scared girl who couldn't fight back. She deserves to see him brought down."

The love between the siblings was so intense it was almost hard to witness. These dangerous, ruthless men became something entirely different around their sister—gentle, protective, willing to move mountains to keep her safe.

Marigold envied their bond. Their loyalty for each other was the polar opposite of Jordan's disdain for her.

"Fifteen minutes," Cole reported. "If little bird wants to go back to her wing, I should take her now."

"What do you want to do, Kat?" Ash asked, brow pinched with worry for his surrogate sister.

Katya looked at the monitors, expression unsure.

Hunter stood, his expression shifting back to predatory focus. "Final positions. Remember, he thinks he's in control until he isn't. Let him get comfortable before we remind him whose territory this is."

"Before we show him what happens to unwelcomed trespassers," Stone sneered.

The staff, except for the lead officer, Cole, dispersed with military efficiency, leaving the family alone in the security office. Katya had stopped shaking, but Marigold could see the effort it cost her.

"Where will we be?" Marigold asked.

"The two of you will stay here, with Cole," Hunter said. "Then, when it's time, one of us will come to collect you. Do not open the door for anyone but me, Stone, or Ash. Do not leave this room alone or with anyone but us. Understand?"

Marigold nodded.

"Good. Cole's fully armed. He'll protect you."

Cole's gun cocked as if to confirm Hunter's statement. These men were not playing around. No flashlights and segways for them. They were fully armed with guns, silencers, Kevlar, and blades.

"Is that weapon even legal?" she asked, eyeing the massive bazooka-looking thing hanging inside the hidden closet built into the wall.

Stone slammed it shut and typed in a code. "Legal by our laws. That's all that matters."

It worried her that they were confronting Jordan in street clothes with only small pistols tucked under their suit jackets.

"What if I freeze?" Katya asked quietly. "What if, when I see him, I can't speak?"

"Then one of us will speak for you," Ash said simply.

"You still have the option of not seeing him at all," Hunter reminded. "But if that's your choice, you should make it now."

Katya glanced at the monitors tracking Jordan's approach. She worried her lower lip, unsure what to do.

"It's better if we stay together." Cole pointed to the monitors. "I can keep a better eye on everything with the women here."

"What do you want, sister?" Stone asked in a unique display of compassion and patience.

"I want it to be over. Can I stay in my room? I promise to lock the door."

"If that's what you want."

She looked up at Cole with apologetic eyes. "I'm sorry."

"It's fine," he said with militant formality. "I'll be watching."

Her smile was tentative.

"You're not alone in this anymore," Ash reminded. "You have all of us and nothing to fear."

"That's right." Marigold reached for Katya's hand, squeezing gently.

The Volkovs welcomed her into their private circle, a place deeply protected for family alone. They were as good as sisters now. And sisters protect each other.

Katya smiled despite her fear. Her grip tightened around Marigold's. Sturdier now. Calm. "It'll all be over soon."

"I'll walk you to your room," Ash said, taking Katya's hand. He paused and placed a kiss on Marigold's lips. "In case I don't see you before the big show."

"Ten minutes," Cole announced, gaze glued to the monitors.

Stone moved to a bank of computers, his fingers dancing across controls with practiced ease. The screens came alive with feed from the harbor, showing a sleek yacht cutting through dark water toward their dock.

"There," he said quietly. "Jordan Calder comes calling."

Even from a distance, even on grainy security footage, Marigold could see her half-brother's familiar figure standing at the yacht's bow. Tall, golden-haired, traditionally handsome in a way that made people trust him despite the screaming warnings of all natural instincts.

Beside her, Katya made a sound like a wounded animal, drawing Marigold's attention as she prepared to come face to face with her nightmare. "I can't," she whispered, all her earlier bravado crumbling. "I thought I could, but I can't. He's here and I can't breathe. I—"

"Get her out of here, Ash," Hunter ordered.

Katya's rambling broke into shallow gasps of panic. Her hands shook so violently she had to clench them to her stomach to still them.

Ash, always the nurturer, was beside her instantly, gathering her into his arms as if she were a child. "It's okay. He can't get to you."

Marigold went to her friend and hugged her tight. "Big breath in, Katya." She breathed with her friend. "Now, blow it out small." Her lips formed a small oh. "Just right."

Katya repeated the breathing, nodding in appreciation as her panic slowly calmed.

"Go with Ash. Go back to your room. And the next time you see us, this will all be over."

Ash's stare met hers over his sister's head, his eyes filled with admiration as he mouthed, *'Thank you.'*

Then his attention jerked to the monitors, the shift in his expression crystal clear. The enemy had landed in their territory, and a reckoning was about to begin. Katya's response only further cemented the need for justice. But it also meant, with Katya taking a step back, the endgame might come down to her testimony alone.

Panic welled up inside of her, but she shoved it back down. For Katya, and all the other girls Jordan hurt, she would be strong. And afterwards, when she fell to pieces, her three bears would put her back together again.

CHAPTER 20

ACTS OF CONTRITION

Jordan entered the lodge like he owned it.

Marigold watched from the hidden observation room as her half-brother strode through the front doors with the casual arrogance of a man who'd never been told no. Tall, golden-haired, and devastatingly handsome in his tailored Savile Row suit, he moved with the fluid confidence of someone who believed the world existed for his pleasure.

Behind him followed his entourage—a sharp-eyed lawyer in designer glasses, two private security consultants who looked like former military, and a man with a medical bag who could only be the bought and paid for psychiatrist meant to declare her mentally incompetent.

Stone appeared to greet them, immaculate in a designer black suit. His hair was perfectly styled, his expression professionally neutral. "Mr. Calder. Welcome to Kassel. I'm Stone Volkov, manager of *The Preserve*. We spoke on the phone." He shook Jordan's hand with firm confidence.

Jordan's handshake was aggressive, designed to establish dominance. Marigold had seen him do it a thousand times, the slight squeeze too hard, the moment held too long, the way he pulled others off balance like an insecure dictator wannabe with a small dick.

But Stone didn't move an inch further than intended and maintained higher ground through the brief exchange until Jordan let go, shaking his fingers to regain feeling.

"Quiet tonight." His exaggerated posh accent carried clearly through the speakers. His pale blue gaze, so like their father's, swept the foyer with calculating assessment.

"We thought a private setting might be more fitting tonight."

Disappointment flashed in his eyes. "Where are the women?"

"The Aurelius family is hosting their monthly gala." Stone's smile was sharp. "But don't worry. We've arranged something special just for you."

Jordan's eyes lit with interest. "You have my attention."

"Everything you need is in the playroom. But first, we must discuss the terms of your membership."

Jordan's brows lifted with cocky arrogance. "We'll see how the night goes."

Stone didn't flinch. Didn't step back. Didn't give Jordan the reaction he was fishing for.

"Quite a setup you have here," Jordan continued, strolling deeper into the lodge without invitation. "Private islands, exclusive memberships. You must cater to some very particular tastes. How many members did you say you had?"

"I didn't."

"Regardless, it's nice to find a gentleman's club that values discretion."

Hunter loomed behind them in silence, his lethal stare trained on Jordan like the scope of an AR. One wrong move, and Jordan would exist no more.

"Our clients understand the rules. We provide discrete accommodations," Stone replied, playing up the role of ultimate host. "Consensual play and privacy are our specialty."

"Privacy." Jordan's smile was sharp. "I imagine you see all sorts of... interesting behavior. Rich men with their hobbies and obsessions. Money does strange things to people, doesn't it?"

There was condescension in his tone, the subtle superiority of someone who believed himself above whatever degeneracy he imagined took place here. He was already categorizing Stone and his brothers as lesser beings, service providers for the truly wealthy.

"Indeed," Stone agreed mildly. "Shall we cut to the chase, Mr. Calder?"

"Which is?"

"Your sister's situation." Stone glanced back at his silent entourage. "Your guests won't be permitted past this point."

Surprised by Stone's directness, Jordan shifted gears. "I like a man who gets right to business."

"I understand you're concerned about her welfare."

"Concerned?" Jordan laughed, the sound rigid like breaking glass. "I'm fucking terrified. My sister's been unwell for some time. Delusional episodes, paranoid fantasies. When she disappeared from her care facility, I feared the worst."

The lie rolled off his tongue with practiced ease. Marigold's hands clenched into fists as she watched him execute a flawless performance, despite never wasting an ounce of true concern on her.

"She mentioned family troubles," Stone said carefully. "Perhaps we could discuss this more privately?"

"Of course." Jordan gestured to his companions. "Dr. Morrison here specializes in crisis intervention for patients experiencing psychotic breaks. And my legal team is here to handle any... complications."

Complications.

Those men were not on the right side of the law. Marigold had no doubt they would testify against her in court, acting as false witnesses to whatever took place here tonight. Jordan most likely paid them well to see the world from his perspective.

He was prepared to have her declared insane and dragged back to captivity before she could destroy his perfect life. She breathed deep in an attempt to mitigate the fury building inside.

Stone led them deeper into the lodge, past the common areas and ballrooms where members might normally gather. Marigold followed their journey on the monitors, Cole tracking with expert knowledge of the controls as the images alternated on the screens as they moved.

When Stone guided them to what looked like a conference room, elegant, private, with no obvious exits except the door they'd entered through, Ash was waiting. Her heart fluttered with uncertainty and an urge to see this through as quickly as possible.

The men entered casually, Hunter and Ash standing near floor-to-ceiling windows that offered views of the storm-lashed landscape. They looked exactly like themselves, wealthy, powerful men accustomed to getting their way.

"My partners," Stone said simply. "Hunter and Ash Volkov."

Jordan's eyes sharpened with interest. "I assumed the big one was part of security."

"No," Hunter said, his obsidian gaze narrowing on the target.

"Volkov, did you say?" Jordan was already calculating how to use these men, how to leverage whatever they wanted against his sister's inconvenient truths. Her brother moved forward with predatory confidence. "Family loyalty goes a long way in business."

"Indeed," Stone rumbled, his accent thick as honey. "Family loyalty is everything to us, Mr. Calder." Dark meaning seethed behind his words, but Jordan was too arrogant to think his statement might also include Katya. The fool probably didn't even realize they had a sister.

"Absolutely." Jordan's smile was brilliant. "Which is another reason why I'm here. Marigold's family, and family protects each other. Even from themselves."

The audacity was breathtaking. He was positioning himself as the protective brother while simultaneously planning to have her lobotomized into compliance.

"Stone's caught us up to speed after your brief conversation," Ash said. "But perhaps you could clarify your sister's motives for running away. She was rather distraught when she arrived."

"Was she?" His smirk proved he enjoyed any hint of a struggle. "I'd like to know how she gained entry to such an exclusive club in the first place. As her brother, I take her safety very personally."

"I'm sure," Hunter said with zero inflection, his jaw twitching with tension.

"Tell me," Jordan continued, settling into a leather chair like he was holding court, "what exactly has my sister told you about her situation?"

"She mentioned family conflict," Ash said quietly. "Some unpleasantness that led to her seeking treatment."

"*Unpleasantness.*" Jordan's laugh was bitter. "Is that what she called it? The poor thing has been having episodes for months. Paranoid delusions about... well, frankly, about me. She's convinced I'm some sort of monster."

"And you're not?" Stone's voice was perfectly level.

"Of course not." Jordan spread his hands in a gesture of wounded innocence. "I'm her older brother. I love her and only want the best for her. But Marigold has always been... mentally fragile. Emotional. She sees patterns that aren't there, conspiracies where none exist."

Inwardly, Marigold recoiled. Hunter's gaze looked directly into the hidden camera as if looking into her eyes and silently telling her not to listen, but she couldn't shut him out now. Jordan's words depicted her as an unstable woman who ran head-first into dangerous situations with no thought to consequences.

She stared at the screen, her vision blurring under tears of fury. She didn't want them to hear such horrible lies. What if they believed him? What if Jordan convinced them she was broken and they no longer—

Hunter shook his head. It was subtle and brief, but it was the command she needed. That single look grounded her as much as any verbal command could. He held so much authority in his stare, so much control. As she drowned in the depths of those obsidian eyes, she knew they weren't buying any of Jordan's bullshit lies and were still—one hundred percent—on her side.

Marigold sucked in an unsteady breath and blew it out slowly. This was about trust and justice. They trusted her. Believed her. And Jordan would pay for his lies and crimes. She believed that with all her heart, and trusted her men to protect her.

The lies rolled off Jordan's tongue with unhindered ease. He was a pathological con artist.

Leaning forward, he adopted the tone of a concerned sibling sharing painful family secrets. "The truth is, she's been obsessed with me for years. *Romantic fixations*, the doctors call it. When I started seeing someone seriously, something in Marigold broke. She started making wild accusations, claiming

I'd hurt other women. Total fantasy, of course, but a dangerous one."

The lies came so smoothly, wrapped in just enough truth to be believable. Nausea churned in her stomach as she listened to him twist the facts. He was using her attempts to protect other girls as evidence of instability.

"Romantic fixation," Hunter repeated slowly. "For her own brother?"

"Half-brother," Jordan corrected quickly. "Different mothers. But yes, the psychological dynamics are... complex. Dr. Morrison has extensive experience with such cases."

The psychiatrist, a thin man with cold eyes, nodded gravely. "Erotomania, combined with persecutory delusions."

"*Erotomania?*" Stone repeated.

"Excessive sexual desires," the doctor spoke in a condemning tone. "The patient becomes convinced that the object of their fixation shares their cravings. They often exhibit erratic, sometimes life-threatening behavior due to simultaneously desiring an unavailable bystander." He made it seem as if Jordan were completely innocent in this festering stew of lies. "They can create elaborate fantasies of... *shared* obsession."

Marigold's blood turned to ice.

"I'm sorry, did you say shared?" Ash cocked his head, his gaze drifting to Stone's

"At times, yes. They confuse pain with pleasure," Dr. Morrison continued as Marigold's breathing turned shallow. "Submission can be very pathological, which feeds the cravings. They seek out dangerous situations that strip away accountability. When reality and delusion blurs, sudden, unsafe outbursts can occur. Symptoms often spiral into increasingly risky sexual behavior—seeking validation through degradation, mistaking possession for love. It can be very dangerous if left untreated."

"Dangerous how?" Stone asked, the concern in his voice sharpening Marigold's doubts into razor sharp fear.

"Some patients have taken to self-harm and even suicide. They become addicted to taboo situations, interpret obsessions and compulsions as romance. In a sense, they're trying to rewrite their own trauma."

She closed her eyes, once more questioning her own sanity. Was that what she'd done? Was this entire experience one long delusion? Compulsions, manifesting in sexual aggression and captivity?

Everything is your choice... Their words came back to her and acid burned in her stomach. She chose this. Them. The bondage, the brutality. She couldn't breathe.

"Marigold can be very persuasive," Jordan warned. "When something threatens her objective, she'll do anything. Violence, deceit, she has no limit when it comes to getting what she wants."

"I see," Stone said, and Marigold's heart plummeted.

Did he see? Did he actually believe Jordan? He had to know this wasn't a game to her. She was the victim, here! He was the evil one! Her hands balled into fists tight enough to make her knuckles pop.

"Which is why," Jordan continued, "when she escaped from Whitmore, I knew I had to act quickly. Before she hurt someone. Before she hurt herself."

"How thoughtful of you," Ash murmured.

Ash... Marigold's gaze jumped to the screen. "Can you zoom in?"

Cole pressed a few keys and Ash's face expanded to full view, his expression unreadable.

She swallowed, throat dry as she tried to catch her breath. *"Big breath in. Blow it out small. Just right, baby. Just right."* Her mother's voice echoed as if from some distant corner of her mind.

You like visiting the library, don't you, Calder. Those sorts of privileges come with a price... She could smell the sweat on Willum's skin.

Hold her down, she's getting hostile! Her skin crawled with the fantom weight of the nurses and doctors strapping her to the table.

Blinking rapidly, she tried to stay present, but she was losing ground. Possibly losing them.

Jordan's smile was self-deprecating. "People often ask me how I stay so positive despite everything Marigold has put our family through. And I tell them, you can't wait for opportunities to present themselves. You have to create them. As soon as she went missing, I hired the best detectives, who then tracked her down here. Funny thing, though. I find myself wondering why she's still here and why authorities weren't contacted the minute she showed up uninvited."

Hunter's eyes narrowed on him. "Guess it doesn't matter, since you came to collect."

Her heart raced, hammering so erratically her shoulders seemed to vibrate. Did they change their minds? They were so convincing, so agreeable. In that moment, she knew, without a doubt, that she wanted to stay. Leaving, after all they'd been through, would devastate her to a point that they might as well put her in a padded cell and throw away the key.

"Please..." she muttered, bouncing her knee nervously.

"Did you say something?" Cole's question startled her, shattering whatever flimsy wall of fear was distorting her view of reality.

"Can you go to Hunter?"

He moved the lens and Hunter's face filled the screen. His eyes were pools of black, masking his ever-vibrating rage. When his jaw ticked, she knew he was boiling. He still hated him, which meant he still was on her side.

The image switched back to Jordan, naturally tracking the movement and sound within the conference room. He leaned back, folding his arms behind his head and stretching out his legs.

"See, I take action instead of waiting around for someone else to solve my problems. Marigold's my burden to bear."

There it was, the narcissistic core beneath the concerned brother facade. Jordan couldn't help himself. Even while discussing her supposed mental illness, he had to position himself as the superior being who understood how the world really worked, victimized by those who created challenges along the way, but never thrown off course.

Marigold closed her eyes and breathed through her irritation. He was such a performer, he even had himself fooled. Almost had her fooled. But Hunter, Stone, and Ash were smart enough to see through his lies.

"Wise words," Stone said with zero inflection. "Perhaps you could share more of your philosophies on success while our staff locates your sister?"

"Of course." Jordan settled back in his chair, already warming to his favorite subject—himself. "Success isn't about waiting for permission. It's about recognizing that most people are sheep, and sheep need shepherds. Men like us. The world will be inherited by those bold enough to take it. You have to go after whatever it is you want—at any cost."

"And what do you want, Mr. Calder?" Hunter asked with lethal calm.

"Excellence. In everything." Jordan's eyes gleamed with fervor. "Most people settle for mediocrity because they're afraid to reach for greatness. They make excuses, follow rules that don't apply to superior individuals. But true alphas? We create our own rules." He smirked at the three of them. "You guys get that. I've seen your little torture chamber downstairs."

Stone noticeably stiffened. "No one is tortured under our watch, Mr. Calder."

"Sure." Jordan laughed condescendingly.

Ash cleared his throat and leaned forward, setting a thickly muscled forearm on the table. "Before moving on, it's crucial that you understand how serious we are about our rules. Everything that happens under our roof and on the premises of *The Preserve* is one hundred percent consensual. We bring fantasies to life, not nightmares."

Her brother laughed, as if hearing an inside joke. "Until one of those sweet cherries want to get taken against their will, am I right?"

Hunter's shoulders shifted with each breath. He looked ready to snap like the pencil he just crushed in his grip. "Excuse me." He pulled out his phone. "I need to take this."

Marigold watched the brothers exchange subtle glances as Hunter took his leave. Was this part of the plan, or was he truly that disturbed that he needed to exit the meeting room before snapping Jordan's neck?

Her brother was giving them everything they needed—his arrogance, his belief in his own superiority, his conviction that normal moral boundaries didn't apply to him.

"Fascinating perspective," Stone said, drawing the attention back to Jordan. "You sound like someone who has experience leading, what did you call them? Sheep?"

"You know the type. Delicate, young, big-eyed waifs looking for an experienced Daddy to fix their issues and give them the long-overdue spanking they need."

Tell me," Ash said through clenched teeth. "How does one identify these...*sheep* who need shepherding?"

"Experience." Jordan's smile was sharp with cruel amusement. "You learn to read people. Their weaknesses, their desires, their pressure points. Most people desperately want to be led, even if they don't admit it. They crave someone strong enough to make decisions for them."

"And if they resist this... guidance?"

"Then you teach them." Jordan's voice dropped to something that made Marigold's skin crawl. "Everyone's got triggers. Vulnerabilities. The key is getting your finger on the gauge at just the right moment and then applying a little pressure."

"Such as?"

"Depends on the individual." Jordan was fully in lecture mode now, drunk on his own perceived brilliance. "Fear works well with most people. But sometimes you need something more... personal. Something that breaks down their defenses entirely."

The room had gone very quiet. Even Jordan's own team looked uncomfortable with the direction of his monologue.

"Like what?" Ash pressed.

"Shame." Jordan's smile was winter-cold. "Public humiliation. The threat of losing everything they think defines them. And for women..." He paused, his reptilian smirk slithering across his face as he grinned through beady eyes. "Well, women are different. They respond better to intimate pressures, if you know what I mean."

"I'm afraid I don't." Stone's voice had gone dangerously quiet.

"Physical vulnerability," Jordan said simply. "Once a woman understands that she's completely powerless, that no one will hear her scream, that her choices have been taken away, she becomes remarkably compliant."

The words hung in the air like a death sentence. Jordan had just confessed to sexual assault in a room full of witnesses, and he was smiling about it.

"Interesting," Ash murmured. "You sound like you speak from experience."

"Life experience," Jordan corrected smoothly. "I understand human nature. Most men are too weak to do what's necessary, too *woke* to acknowledge the beast within. If nature wanted men to be subservient, they would have made them the weaker sex. There's a reason females are so breakable. I do what I gotta do, and I don't get squeamish about it."

Marigold, like everyone else in that room, stopped breathing. The silence was deafening. How could anyone admit something so monstrous?

The door to the security room opened, and Marigold flinched, startled by Hunter's intrusion.

"Sir?"

Hunter held out a staying hand. "Everything's fine," he said to Cole, then turned his gaze to Marigold.

She was on her feet and in his arms in two seconds flat. As if sensing what this was doing to her, his arms tightened protectively around her.

His lips pressed to her hair. "You okay?"

"No, but I will be when this is over." Her hands fisted in his shirt, taking comfort in his strength.

"They're only words," he whispered. "We know the truth."

"If they were just words, we wouldn't be here. They're confessions." She looked up at him, noting the way tension radiated through his form.

"He's going to pay." He placed another kiss on her head. "I have to get back."

Had he only come to check on her? She smiled up at him, unable to express how deeply she appreciated his concern. "Thanks for checking on me."

He traced a gentle knuckle along her jaw. "You're my number one concern, now."

She covered his hand with hers, wishing he didn't have to go. "Be careful."

With a silent nod, he left the room. She looked back at the monitors. Something fundamental had altered in the room's atmosphere, something that ordinary people would interpret as unsafe. But Jordan was so high on his own ego, he missed the shift.

"Mr. Calder," Stone said quietly. "I think it's time you understood exactly where you are."

Jordan's confidence faltered. "I'm sorry?"

Hunter quietly returned to the meeting room, reclaiming his seat at the head of the table.

"This isn't a resort." Stone's voice was silk over steel. "And it's more than a private club. Our very exclusive memberships invite people into our home. They trust us to keep them safe at all times. That level of security requires consent. Real consent. Informed consent. The kind that can be withdrawn at any time."

"Unlike what you described," Hunter added. "Which sounds more like assault."

Jordan's face went pale, then flushed angry red. "Now wait just a damn minute—"

"No," Stone interrupted smoothly. "You wait. You see, Mr. Calder, we've been recording this conversation. Every word. And what you've just described, using 'intimate pressure' until women become remarkably compliant, that's what we call rape."

"I never said—"

"You did," Ash confirmed calmly. "In detail. Along with your philosophy about taking what you want from those too weak to stop you."

"Waifs, I believe you called them," Stone said.

"And sheep," Hunter reminded.

"Yes, young and big-eyed. Aren't those the exact words you used?" Ash looked at his phone, then shrugged. "Eh, we have it all recorded. We can fact-check later."

"We also have surveillance footage from your last visit," Hunter said with lethal calm.

The monumental implication of Hunter's words set in and Jordan exploded, "This is entrapment!"

The lawyer bolted to his feet, his briefcase clutched like a shield. "You guaranteed anonymity. My client never admitted to any specific crimes!"

"Didn't he?" Hunter's smile was predatory. "Because it sounded very specific to me. Almost as if he were describing a particular incident. A particular victim."

"This is a goddamn fantasy club for Christ's sake! You think I'm the first man to get a little rough with a woman in your halls. Give me a break—"

Hunter had him by the back of the neck and bent over the table in half a second. "Think back. Last time you were here, you met someone." He leaned down, dropping his voice dangerously low as he growled in Jordan's ear. "She had an accent... Just. Like. This."

Jordan's eyes went wide with sudden understanding. "You know her? The Russian girl? That's what this is about?"

"Ah," Stone said softly. "You do remember her."

"I thought she was part of the staff! A perk!"

"Her name is Katya," Hunter growled, tightening his grip on Jordan's neck. "But if I ever hear you speak her name, I'll personally cut your tongue right out of your fucking skull."

Jordan tried to break Hunter's hold, but he was outmatched in strength and rage. Desperate, his voice pitched, "Whatever that little bitch told you—"

"Careful," Ash warned, murder buried in his tone. "Be very careful how you finish that sentence, comrade."

The room's atmosphere shifted from predatory anticipation to barely leashed violence. Jordan finally understood he wasn't in control here. That these weren't men who could be bought, intimidated, or charmed.

"Gentlemen..." The psychiatrist looked ready to run. "I think there's been a misunderstanding."

"No misunderstanding," Ash interrupted. "Perfect transparency, actually. Mr. Calder came here to retrieve his sister. To have her declared insane and dragged back to the facility where she'd been silenced. He came seeking justice, which he'll have, but he's not judge and jury here."

"You see," Stone growled. "This is our territory. We make our own rules. And there's a price for breaking them."

"Get off of me, you grizzly fuck!" Jordan's voice went shrill with hysteria.

Hunter lifted him by the neck only to smash his head down on the table. "Be still."

"Fuck! You think you can touch me? Do you have any idea who my father is? What kind of power the Calder name carries?"

Stone cocked his head and dramatically tapped his chin. "Calder? Does that name have any meaning here?"

Ash rubbed his jaw. "I don't think so. Hunter, mean anything to you?"

Hunter's slow grin was full on salivating as he came closer and closer to vengeance. Fisting Jordan's hair, he yanked his head back. "On this island, in this room, where no one can hear you scream, the only name that matters is Volkov. You're in my den now, and you've woken the bear."

Ash and Stone pushed their chairs back and slowly stood. Color drained from Jordan's face as understanding finally dawned.

"I think it's time for your friends to leave," Stone said, moving to the door.

"No!" Jordan snapped as his entourage rushed to their feet. "Sit the fuck down. I paid you!"

"Money talks," Ash said, rolling up his sleeves. " But violence is louder."

"I'll show you out, gentlemen." Stone escorted the men through the door.

"You can't do this!" He thrashed under Hunter's grip. "People know where I am. My security team—"

"Will wait patiently for your return," Ash finished.

"Stop!" Jordan yelled as his attorney and paid doctor followed Stone, but it was too late. They were already gone and he was alone with two angry bears. *They kidnapped my sister!*

"Only a desperate man lies." Ash tsked, sleeves rolled to the elbow as he flexed his fingers wide, then made a tight fist that caused his knuckles to pop. "You see, Mr. Calder, we believe in hands-on education. And you have so much to learn."

"Wait—" Jordan's plea was interrupted by Ash's fist.

They moved in perfect coordination, every step purposeful, like dancers who'd rehearsed this routine a thousand times. Their techniques, the subtle psychology behind each word and gesture spoke of experience, years of survival honed through silent communication.

From the observation room, Marigold watched her half-brother's world collapse in real time. The golden prince who'd never faced consequences, who'd built his life on others' suffering, was finally learning what it meant to feel utterly powerless. And they were just getting started.

On another monitor, she could see into adjacent rooms—glimpses of equipment and furniture that spoke to the club's true purpose. Leather and silk, restraints and toys, all beautiful and sophisticated and clearly designed for consensual exploration of power and submission.

The contrast was stark. Consensual versus coerced. Predator versus prey. Mutual pleasure versus selfish violation. Jordan had played the predator. He'd coerced and forced. Now, he was going to pay.

"You see, Mr. Calder," Hunter snarled close to his ear as blood trickled from his nose. "You've hurt two women under our protection. Women who hold a special place in our hearts."

Jordan shook violently as the full reality of his situation sank in. "I didn't know! Whoever she was to you—"

"*Our sister!*" Stone roared, his mask of self-control gone. In its place, a bloodthirsty protector set on vengeance.

Marigold had been so engrossed in Hunter's hold on Jordan, she missed the moment he returned. If she thought Stone had been frightening before, she'd poorly misjudged. The man on the screen now was an unapologetic killer.

"But that word means little to you, doesn't it?" Stone sneered, slamming his fist into Jordan's ribs as Hunter and Ash held him up.

Jordan gasped and sputtered blood, his head hanging limp as his knees softened.

"All your bullshit about family loyalty. You make me sick!" Another punch. "Meaningless words. Sounds strung together with zero emotion so you can fantasize you're a decent man."

Ash grabbed him by the hair, lifting his head so he could look in his unfocused eyes.

"And I bet most people gobble your lies right up."

Stone sank his fist into him one more time. Jordan crumpled like a paper doll, falling to the floor.

"You can't do this," he gasped, holding up a hand.

"I think we can," Ash said with an indifferent shrug. "Probably from the years of torture and abuse we endured, from sociopathic pricks just like you." He fisted his hair, lifting his head. "Tell me, did you always lack empathy?"

Stone slammed a fist into Jordan's back, and the breath whooshed out of him. He leaned close to his ear. "That was your kidney, by the way."

"Please," Jordan whispered, all his arrogance stripped away. "Whatever you want...money, connections, anything—"

"What we want," Stone said quietly, "is for you to under-stand exactly what you did to those innocent girls." Stone quietly removed his tie and tossed it on the table. "What you stole from them. What you broke."

The men hoisted him onto his feet, but Jordan was too weak to hold himself up. They threw him down on the table as Stone slammed his knee into Jordan's thigh.

"We're going to enlighten you tonight. And then," Hunter added with a smile depraved enough to make a monster shiver. "We're going to make it so you can never hurt anyone ever again."

Stone kicked his feet, and Jordan's legs gave out. They dragged him back to the table.

Marigold had seen enough.

She wanted Jordan to know he'd caused his own downfall, that his lies didn't destroy her, and she would go on to live a full and happy life, free to do whatever she chose.

"Where are you going?" Cole was on his feet, his eyes darting between her, the door, and the monitors as chaos unfolded on the screens.

"I need to be there."

"Those aren't the rules. You heard what they said. You stay here, unless one of them comes to get you."

"That was before. Everything's different now."

"The rules stay the same."

"Look, I'm a part of this."

"I can't let you leave—"

"*No!*" She screamed when he grabbed her, fought as he tried to restrain her.

Cole was fast and professionally trained, twisting her into a restraint hold before she made it to the door.

"Let go of me!" It was just like when they held her down at Whitmore. The feeling of helplessness, the fear of having no choice over her body. Something inside of her snapped. "You can't do this! *I'm not crazy!* You can't keep me here!"

"I don't want to hurt you." He tried to restrain her, but she was through being confined against her will. He reached for something on his belt. Silver flashed as she lifted her feet, trying to slide through his arms as dead weight. When that didn't work, she slammed her feet down and swung her head back.

He grunted. Silver handcuffs glinted in the blue glow of the monitor screens. "You're giving me no choice—"

"*No!*" She twisted and spit, dropping to dead weight again. Slithering out of his grip and shoving him back. The cuffs fell and he fumbled to catch them. When they clattered to the floor, she snatched them up then—*CLICK*.

Cole looked at her with wide eyes, jerking his arm from the desk bolted to the wall. "What did you do?"

"I..." She rushed forward and snatched the keys off his belt, tossing them into the closet. "I'm sorry. But I have to go." Against every rational instinct, she left the observation room.

"Marigold!"

She rushed out of the room and raced down the hall, her footsteps muffled by thick carpet as she raced toward the conference room. From the corridor, she could hear the sound of heavy fists slamming into battered flesh. Jordan's pleading was lost against the grunts of pain.

She pushed open the door and rushed inside. "Stop!"

The room fell silent.

All eyes turned to her, but it was Jordan's reaction that made her blood sing with dark satisfaction. His face went white with shock. "Mari—gold," he coughed. "You have to help me!"

She folded her arms deliberately over her chest, showing him that she had no intention to intervene on his behalf.

"Please," he begged.

She let the sight of him sink into her mind, giving it a permanent home. Maybe she was disturbed because, in that moment, whatever loyalty she felt for this man was gone. His blood was not her blood. They were no longer family. He was nothing.

She slowly rounded the table, her eyes never leaving him as the other men watched her carefully, deferring to her lead. "I begged too," she confessed softly. "When they dragged me away, my bare feet sliding helplessly on that cold linoleum floor, I pleaded for them to listen." She paused to let that sink in. "And when they strapped me to that table, and forced that rubber guard in my mouth, I screamed for you or father to come save me. Do you know what they told me?"

Jordan's panicked gaze settled on her, but even now, beaten and bloody, he'd never tell the truth. He would always put himself before others, choose that self-serving hate over love or trust, because *he* was the one that was broken. Not her.

She stood before him, as he panted on his knees, Hunter holding his head up by the hair so he could look at her. "They told me you and Father ordered it. That you requested every level of treatment, no matter how controversial or cruel."

Understanding dawned. He was not only powerless here. He was at *her* mercy now.

"You fucking bitch," he seethed. "You set this up."

"Language," Hunter warned, smashing his face into the table.

Jordan sputtered blood and gasped for breath. "I'll fucking kill you."

"No, you won't." She waited for him to look at her. "You'll never hurt me again. Or anyone else for that matter. I'm not going back, Jordan. But you're going away for a very long time."

He dragged his sleeve under his nose, ruining his jacket, and sneered. "You think the world will just open for you if you spread your legs?" He laughed and spit blood on the floor. "You're not that pretty. And you've never been special."

Stone and Ash cocked back but she held up a hand, ordering them not to strike. "Doesn't that make this that much sadder for you? Imagine, being brought down by an ugly, unremarkable female."

"You're a whore!"

She smiled in the face of his fury. "Maybe I want to be."

"I'm not the only one looking for you. They know you killed that guard."

She swallowed at the memory of Willum. "Self-defense."

"Your word against theirs."

"In a month, Whitmore won't exist. Your sister wasn't the only one being abused," Ash informed. "It, and all its complacent benefactors are going down."

"You're done," Stone said.

"Fuck! You!" Jordan went ballistic, thrashing, spitting venom and blood. Until he was on the floor, the echo of Hunter's fist resounding like a gunshot through the room.

That time, Jordan didn't get up.

Hunter crouched beside Jordan's unconscious form, checking his pulse with clinical detachment. *"Ona Moya,"* he said, making his claim on her clear. His dark eyes found hers, unapologetic, but no longer cold. In those obsidian pools, she found endless warmth and safety. "We protect what's ours."

Ash's arms came around her, anticipating the moment her knees went weak. "I've got you."

She turned into his strength, hugging him tight.

"Me too." Stone came to protectively cover her back, his hands sweeping over her in calming strokes.

Sheltered and safe, they held her as two security guards appeared with the bearing of former military personnel. They moved with practiced efficiency.

"Take him to Room Seven," Hunter instructed, straightening as he brushed off his hands. "Strip him down, tie him spread-eagle to the bed. Then piss on his chest until he wakes up." His smile was winter-cold as he closed the distance between the guards and his brothers. "I'll be along shortly to finish this."

The guards lifted Jordan between them like he weighed nothing. His head lolled back, hair matted with blood.

As they dragged him out, Hunter pulled Marigold into his arms, his demeanor instantly softening as he inspected her for any sign of harm. "I told you to stay put until one of us came for you."

She bit her lip and wrung her hands, failing to appear the least bit contrite. "I didn't listen."

Ash and Stone prowled to her like wild animals. Hunter framed her face with his massive hands. Their surprising gentleness shocked her, and when they kissed her, their touch was soft and reverent, nothing like the violence they'd just displayed.

"Clever little fox," Hunter whispered against her lips. "How did you get past Cole?"

Stone's laughter spiked as he swiped his finger over the screen of his phone. "Goddamn, Goldilocks. How'd you manage that?"

Ash pulled her close, pressing his lips to hers as soon as

Hunter snatched the phone. When she broke away from the kiss, Hunter looked back at her with equal shock.

Ash frowned. "What?" He took the phone and looked back at her, wide-eyed.

She stepped back, holding her hands up defensively. "He was going to restrain me! I needed to be here, with all of you."

Hunter laughed. "One of you go unlock him."

"On it," Ash said.

"The keys are in the closet," Marigold called after him.

"His ego will never recover from this," Stone laughed, then eyed her with dark intent. "Neither will your ass."

Her smile vanished. "Why?"

Stone took a predatory step closer, his hand sliding possessively between her cheeks. "There are consequences for breaking the rules, *Zayka*." He captured her mouth in a punishing kiss. "Consequences I can't wait to reveal," he murmured against her lips like a wicked promise.

"How do you feel?" Hunter asked, stroking a gentle hand down her arm.

"I'll be fine." It was the truth, but her voice still shook. "The things he said—"

"Meaningless lies, *Lisichka*. The desperate lashing out of a cornered animal," Hunter finished firmly. "He knew he lost, so he tried to wound whatever he could reach. Don't give him that power."

"What are you going to do to him?" The question came out smaller than she'd intended.

Hunter's smile was sharp as a blade. "Only what he deserves. He'll wait, imprisoned by his worst fears, powerless without his autonomy. But you need not concern yourself with that."

Stone rubbed her hands, which were trembling and cold. "In the end, Katya will decide his punishment."

"But if you have any suggestions, we're happy to listen."

"He'll live?"

"Yes," Hunter assured. "Scarred but breathing."

"Reformed," Stone added.

She accepted Jordan's fate, finding Katya's role in his punishment fair and just.

"Then he goes to the authorities," Hunter explained, pulling her back into his arms. "Katya has agreed to press charges. With your testimony supporting hers, he'll spend the next decade in a cell where his daddy's money won't protect him."

"If we're that lucky."

Hunter frowned. "What does that mean?"

She shrugged. "Men like Jordan go to prison all the time, but their sentences are reduced to a mere slap on the wrist. Powerful men rarely face the punishments they deserve."

"You forget, *Lisichka*, Jordan might be wealthy, but he will never be as powerful as us."

"And don't forget, there is only one Jordan, but *three* of us to bear."

Capturing her face again, Hunter pressed his lips to her forehead. "We have connections. We vowed to protect you, and I promised he would pay. There will be no slap on the wrist for your brother."

They had a vicious thirst for justice, but she shared their hunger. To think, she never had to see him again unless from a witness stand.

The weight of her relief, weeks of running, months of fear and helpless rage, a lifetime of being gaslit and controlled by men who cared only about themselves. She was finally free. Finally safe, surrounded by men who'd moved heaven and earth to protect her peace.

CHAPTER 21

AFTERCARE

After leaving the boys, Marigold checked in on Katya, who had been frantically pacing in her bedroom behind locked doors. She was relieved by the visit, but curious about everything that had taken place with Jordan.

"He's still here?" she said, twisting the gilded lock on the door for safe measure.

"He's downstairs, but detained. You're safe."

"I'll be safe when he's in prison."

Marigold took her trembling hands in hers. "Jordan will get what he deserves."

A delicate V formed between Katya's brows. "Did you see him?"

She dropped her gaze. "Yes."

"Was he...hurt?"

"Yes. And it will probably get worse before he's removed. But you don't need to think about that, now."

She nodded, but then contradicted herself by admitting, "I want him to see me. I suppose that means I have to find the courage to face him."

"You don't have to do anything you don't want to do, Katya."

"I want him to suffer the way he made me suffer." She pressed a trembling hand to her narrow waist. "Not just me. The others too. Including you."

"Jordan hurt a lot of people. That's how he got into this mess. Your brothers will make sure he pays a just price, whether you're involved or not."

"I can't spend my life running from my past."

Marigold admired her tenacity. "Just remember that everyone heals at their own pace."

She looked up at her with stormy green eyes. "Have you healed? Did it help? *Seeing* him?"

"I'm...healing. It's going to take time."

"Because he hurt you." Her words were the quiet acknowledgement she'd been waiting for.

Marigold nodded, her throat tight. "Yes," she rasped.

Knowing this nightmare was coming to an end made the emotions that much more intense. It was as if she could finally count her scars and review the damage.

"I'll never be the same after this," she realized. "I've lost my home, my father..."

"But you've found a family in us." Katya's hands closed around her arms. "You're a Volkov now."

Emotion seemed to tumble out of her in the form of a laugh. "I've always wanted a sister."

"Well, you have one." She hugged Marigold so tight emotion continued to rattle out of her in laughter and tears.

"Okay, that's enough," she said, pulling back and wiping her eyes. "I've cried enough tears over these last few months to fill an ocean. We have to focus on the positive."

Katya dabbed the corner of her eyes and nodded. "That's a good plan for both of us."

Marigold let out a breath she felt like she'd been holding for the last year. "I think I'm going to take a long bath and think about what I want the rest of my life to look like, now that I know I'm free and I don't have to run anymore."

Katya walked her to the door and twisted the lock, but when she opened it, Cole was on the other side. His expression darkened to a scowl the moment he saw Marigold.

"You."

"Cole." She smiled nervously. "You're out."

His eyes narrowed. "I came to check on Ms. Volkov ." When he turned his attention to Katya, his gaze softened with concern. "Are you all right, *ptichka*?"

A smile teased at the corner of Katya's mouth like a secret. "Yes," she said, almost breathlessly. "Thank you for checking on me."

The radio on his belt chirped and a voice crackled from an unknown connection. "Grizzly Bear is heading to The Cave. Polar Bear is close behind. Do you have an update on Little Bird?"

"Safe and sound. Where's Black Bear?"

"Already with our guest."

Cole cut off the radio and glanced at Marigold.

She suddenly felt like an intruder. "I'll talk to you later, Katya."

She scurried past Cole, wondering what her official security nickname was. Hard to choose when she had three. Depending on her mood and situation, she was sometimes a skittish rabbit, sometimes a clever fox, and sometimes a pampered princess. But today, she felt as powerful as a queen.

When she reached the other end of the hall and looked back, the officer was still standing at Katya's door, his arm was reaching over the threshold.

Was something more than a security check going on

between those two? She wondered if the boys knew anything. On second thought, she decided to keep her suspicions to herself. A secret among sisters.

After her bath, Marigold curled under the fur blankets and dozed off. The fire had gone low, and she awoke to a gentle caress along her cheek. Peeking through her lashes, she made out Stone's silhouette as he looked down at her, stroking her face softly.

"You were supposed to come to me." His skin smelled of fresh soap, and his chest was bare.

"I fell asleep." The snap of kindling drew her attention to the fireplace, where Ash added more wood. Hunter entered and closed the door.

If they were all here, that meant... "Is Jordan—"

"He's gone," Stone said. "For a long, long time."

"He can't hurt you now," Ash said, stripping off his sweater and coming to sit on the other side of the bed.

Hunter flipped the gilded lock on the door, moving toward the bed.

"Have you slept?"

They each shook their head.

"We're wired," Ash said.

"Need to burn off some adrenaline before we crash." Stone stripped and crawled under the covers.

Hunter prowled closer, but kept his motions under tight control. "Any regrets?"

She hid a smile as he stepped closer to the bed, nothing but stark intensity and dark intention in his eyes. "No."

"Good." Hunter pulled off his shirt and tossed it to the chair.

The fur blanket pulled away, and her nipples tightened in the cold air. "What do we have here?" Ash teased, bending to capture a tight bud in his mouth.

"And here." Stone scooted lower, crouching between her thighs as he pressed a slow, devastating kiss on her sex.

Marigold's breath hitched as her eyes closed. The soft press of Hunter's mouth to hers was the delicate welcome home she needed. Their combined touch heated her into a fury of desire, limbs twisting and passion building as little gasps and moans escaped. Her body was overwhelmed by the three of them, a docile treasure they all wanted to cherish.

"I need you," she rasped, then moaned as Stone's fingers delved inside of her. "All of you."

"Ours," Hunter said, dragging his lips down her shoulder to capture her breast.

Ash's ice-blue eyes darkened with understanding. "Does this mean that you're finally ready?"

"I'm ready. This is where I want to be," she confessed, arching against the bed as they broke her apart bit by bit. "Please," she breathed, gasping as Stone devoured her slowly.

They exchanged looks, silent communication that spoke of years of shared understanding.

"We'll always take care of you," Hunter promised. "*Ona Moya*. Ours."

The trials of the day, the week, the months she'd struggled to find a safe place to rest felt so distant now. Her body was thrumming with leftover adrenaline, with relief so intense it felt like intoxication. She needed grounding. Needed this feeling of safety, so cherished and protected, consensually powerless. Theirs.

When she was with her three bears, surrendering her choice, and trusting them to take care of her, she was truly free.

"Kiss me," Ash commanded, smile soft with affection and eyes dark with promise. "We'll take care of the rest, *printessa*." He took possession of her mouth, driving her passion higher.

When he pulled away, she was breathless and her heart fluttered as he whispered against her lips, "We'll never hurt you."

He kissed her with infinite patience as hands roamed her body with reverent exploration, finding every sensitive spot and lavishing attention where she needed it most. This wasn't the singular desperate claiming she'd experienced with Hunter or the unique driving pressure to submit that she'd felt when alone with Stone. Nor was it the gentle comfort she and Ash shared.

This was something more profound. Trust as tangible as flesh, power exchanged freely. Four unique souls tied into one.

"I saw your curiosity," Ash murmured against her throat. "In the observation room, when you saw me with Stone. Were you curious?"

Heat flooded her cheeks, but she didn't deny it. "Yes."

"We'll show you everything you desire, *printsessa*. Every fantasy you've ever dreamed, we will bring it to life for you."

The control they had over her body and mind left her in a drug-like haze. The way they moved together, coordinated everything, the trust it took to let them make all the decisions, it should have been terrifying, but it only felt heavenly. She was floating on a cloud of pleasure, as soft caresses and teasing licks and kisses drove her higher and higher.

"Look how beautiful she is," Stone said, glancing up from between her thighs. "Such trust in us." His soft breath teased over her damp flesh. "Tonight, you're going to let go of everything that came before and embrace your future."

These men wanted control. Their brutal past demanded it. But they would never take without permission. When she looked at them, truly watched them, she saw strength offered in service, dominance that existed to protect and pleasure rather than harm.

"I trust you," she whispered.

"Good girl." The praise came from all three men and sent heat spiraling through her core.

"Relax, and let us take care of everything." Stone's mouth returned to her sex, and she arched against the bedding, hips tipped toward his talented tongue as Ash and Hunter caressed and suckled her breasts.

She fell apart in their arms, waves of pleasure crashing over her until her skin was dewy with sweat and trembling with aftershocks.

"My turn." Hunter took Stone's place between her legs, pressing her thighs wide to make room for his broad shoulders, and licked deeply. "Mmm," he growled. "Sweet, warm honey."

Stone appeared at her side, naked and stroking his engorged cock. "You know what I want."

She turned her head, gasping from the pleasure Ash and Hunter delivered. Stone traced her lips with the wet tip of his cock, teasing her playfully until he anchored her with a gentle fist in her hair.

"Open that beautiful mouth for me."

She cried out as her insides caught fire, and Stone slid into her mouth. Slow, deep strokes kept pace with Hunter's probing fingers and devious tongue.

Ash disappeared for a moment, but quickly returned. The startling tightening of her nipples told her why as he cinched the tips into studded clamps. "Look at that, boys. Jeweled like royalty in gold."

"Perfect." Hunter praised.

"So fucking hot," Stone agreed, licking around the diamond clamp.

She yelped as Ash tightened the second gilded lock, but her cry quickly shifted to a moan as Hunter returned to his post. Stone shifted, straddling her so he could thrust deeper into her mouth.

"Now, the eyes," Ash said, placing a soft red ball in her hand and a silk blindfold over her eyes. "You remember what we taught you? If you need a break, drop the ball." He kissed her temple and tightened the silk scarf. Her fingers closed around the familiar softness of the ball.

Stone stroked faster, in and out of her mouth. "Fuck, I'm close."

"So is she," Hunter growled. "Give me all that honey, *Lisichka*." He closed his lips around her clit and sucked hard as his fingers thrust in time with Stone's cock.

"That's it," Ash whispered close to her ear. "Come all over Hunter's tongue for him."

Stone grunted, his thrusting cock jerking out of rhythm as his hot release spurted down her throat.

"Swallow it like a good girl," Ash commanded as she, Stone, and Hunter all moaned at once. As soon as Stone withdrew, she gasped and panted for air. His weight lifted off her chest, but Ash quickly took his place. "My turn."

She didn't know where Hunter and Stone went until she felt them stretching her legs open. One man bound her ankle to the left bedpost, while the other bound her ankle to the right. The silk ties were soft and comfortable, but inescapable.

"Leave her arms free," Stone said.

"You like sucking our cocks," Hunter whispered close to her ear.

Unable to speak, Marigold could only moan.

"Such a good girl," Stone praised, stroking her blonde curls. "Ash is going to come all over your pretty tits when he's done.

She whimpered as both he and Hunter teased her clamped nipples. Ash's thrusts sped up as he lifted over her, rocking forward with rapid agility.

"Don't forget her little stunt in the control room tonight,"

Stone reminded and Ash pressed deep, holding himself at the back of her throat as if to send a message.

Marigold cried out, the sound muffled. Her eyes widened, but all she saw was black.

"That's right. You broke the rules," Stone teased with a flick to her nipple. "And there are always consequences."

Ash pulled out of her mouth just as someone's hand slapped down on her clit. She gasped then screamed, "Fuck!"

"Such a dirty mouth." Hunter's low chuckle rippled with amusement. "Better shut that mouth for her, Ash."

He pushed his cock back into her mouth as another slap landed on her clit and her shoulders lifted off the bed, her body naturally bolting forward.

"No, no." Hunter's hands pressed her back down. "You take your licks like a good girl." He held her shoulders, making sure she stayed flat on the bed.

Stone—she knew it was him by the strategic way he mingled pain and pleasure—slapped her again.

"Asshole!"

"We'll get to that," Stone teased, tapping her actual asshole in a sort of promise.

"You should probably add an extra spank for her calling you that," Ash joked.

"I'm pretty sure she was referring to Hunter."

"I was talking to you," she said through gritted teeth.

"Well, in that case—" Three quick slaps landed in rapid succession.

The strange thing was, the more he hit her the less it hurt. And when the last swat landed, she moaned.

"Ah, I think our little thief is stealing pleasure from all this pain."

"Good."

"Fuck," Ash grunted. It was the only warning before his hot release splashed over her ribs, dribbling down her side.

"You're gonna be covered by the time the night's over," Stone promised.

She lost track of how many slaps he delivered, but in the end, there was no pain. Her entire body was a raw, vibrating nerve of pleasure, so much so, that when he dropped the last smack, she climaxed.

She hadn't realized that the men were touching themselves while Stone dished out her punishment, but as she trembled through the confusing release, they painted her skin in their own. Masculine grunts and heavy panting filled the room as she became the sole target for their pleasure.

Limbs weak, she hardly protested as they moved her body, repositioning her like a doll, perfectly built for their desires. They propped her up, as Hunter's broad, hot chest slipped behind her, cradling her comfortably. She shivered against the heat of his body as Ash and Stone untied the binds at her ankles.

They scooted her this way and that until they had her exactly where they wanted. Then Ash pulled her forward to lay on top of him. She instinctively straddled his hips as Stone guided hers up. Ash aligned his cock with her sex, and gently pulled her down, filling her in one fluid motion.

"Give her a second. She's still clenching from her last orgasm." Ash moaned as her body naturally tightened around him with each pulsing aftershock.

Stone's firm hand guided her shoulders down, and Marigold rested her cheek on Ash's chest. A drawer opened and closed, then oil was drizzled over the base of her spine.

"I'll get her ready for you," Stone said, dragging his oiled finger down her crack. He climbed behind her, bending over her back and whispered, "Remember how I taught you to relax." His finger pressed into her ass and her spine stretched, instinctively trying to escape the intrusion.

"Don't try to avoid it," Hunter said, applying pressure to her shoulders to keep her anchored to Ash's chest.

"It's too much."

All three men caressed her until she calmed, giving her as much time as she needed to come to terms with the inevitable. She clutched the ball in her fist, determined to prove she could be their everything in every imaginable way possible.

"Ass up," Stone instructed once she stopped trying to squirm away. He hitched her hips higher. "That's a good girl."

Her labored breathing sped up as he pressed his finger inside of her. Hunter and Ash continued to pet her, whispering words of praise.

"That's it. You take it like a good girl. Tell me what you feel, *Lisichka*."

"Pressure. Tightness."

"She's very tight," Stone confirmed.

"She's tensing," Ash informed. "You have to relax, or you'll never fit all three of us."

"*Three?*" As in...down there?

The men softly chuckled.

"That's impossible." They were going to rip her in two.

"Not impossible. You just have to be patient, do as we say, and trust us to take care of everything else." Stone slowly pumped a finger in and out, finding a rhythm that countered Ash's easy strokes.

She moaned, her face tightening, as he inserted a second finger.

"A little more oil," he said, drizzling more over his talented fingers. "We have to get you nice and open. Hunter's cock's a hell of a lot bigger than two fingers."

"I should fucking hope." Hunter laughed.

She couldn't think beyond the tension building in her body and the idea that he thought all three of them were going to fit inside of her at once. All of her concentration focused on not screaming.

The pressure eased with the addition of more oil, and by the time Stone had three fingers inside of her, she'd somewhat adjusted to the pressure.

"Now, for the fun part." He kept his fingers buried inside but stopped thrusting, as did Ash. Shifting closer, the crinkle of the hair on his thighs brushed her skin, sending shivers down her arms. "Hold her."

Hunter's grip tightened on her arms, and he whispered, "You're doing very good, *Lisichka*."

Her lips parted on a cry as Stone's cock slid alongside Ash's, trying to fit inside of her. *"Wait!"*

They paused. "If you need to stop, drop the ball."

Oddly, her fist tightened, making sure the ball was secure in her hand. They slowly started to move again. She gritted her teeth, moaning as her body stretched to accommodate them both.

"Almost there."

Ash slid out so that Stone could slide in, then he returned, pressing into her from his position on the bottom.

"Ah! Oh, my God!"

As soon as they were in, Hunter's grip on her loosened. "Beautiful," he praised, stroking her spine as she gasped and panted.

"How do you feel?"

"Full."

A low rumble of amusement vibrated from Ash's chest. "You're about to be even fuller."

"And tighter." Hunter pressed a kiss to her cheek. "Forgive me for this."

When he moved away, her panic spiked. "Where are you going?"

"I'm right here, *Lisichka*."

Ash pulled the blindfold off her eyes, and she blinked, the dim room too bright for her dormant senses.

"Look at me," Ash commanded, as he lay on his back beneath her, feeling her body's every twitch.

She gripped the ball tight in her fist as Hunter climbed over her, between her and Stone.

"She's nice and open for you," Stone said, leaning back. Every muscle he moved had a resulting effect on her body. They were so connected, locked in as one.

"Beautiful," Hunter praised, aligning the broad head of his cock where Stone's fingers had been minutes ago.

Stone thrust into her, slow and constricted by Ash's buried cock. "Take your time. She's tight."

"Eyes on me," Ash reminded, and she looked at him with all her worry as Hunter seated himself over her.

The first press of his engorged cock made her whimper, in fear more than anything else. He poured oil down her back, massaging it into her body and over his length. "Just think, *Lisichka*, you will never know possession as all-encompassing as ours." He pressed forward, and she squeezed her eyes shut.

"Don't hide from it, *printsessa*." Ash stroked the hair away from her face. "Feel it. Face it, with eyes wide open. You're not running anymore. Every day, every moment, from this day forward, is a choice. You chose this. You hold all the control."

She blinked her eyes open and stared at him through spiked lashes. Breath jutted out of her as Hunter nudged deeper.

"I need more room."

Ash shifted, withdrawing so that Stone could shift lower and Hunter could ease himself in. His absence should have brought relief, but she wanted him back inside of her. "Come back."

"First Hunter."

Her lips parted on a silent scream as Hunter's tight, overwhelming possession became all she could feel.

"I'm in." His hand stroked softly down her spine. "*Velikolepnaya, Lisichka.* Magnificent."

"Look at me," Ash said, stroking her cheek. "You have to breathe."

Exhaling hard, she tried to speak, but words failed her. Ash held her stare, slowly lifting his hips.

"You're all too big," she finally managed.

But Ash only laughed. "Maybe you're too small."

Stone shifted, partially withdrawing so that Ash could slide fully into her again. When all three of them were finally seated, they shared a communal sigh.

Stone groaned. "I think you're just right."

"I knew you could do it, *printessa*."

She preened under Ash's praise, unsure how she managed to fit them all, but now that they were inside of her, she felt like she'd fall to pieces if they pulled out. "Don't let go."

"Never," Ash promised, as the three of them started to move.

Hunter's first full thrust brought her body to life. Sparks of pleasure zapped up and down her spine as the incredible sensation of being stretched by three cocks overwhelmed her. Stone moved slowly, restricted by Ash's thickness, but once they found an alternating rhythm, they were moving steadily in and out.

Their touch was everywhere and nowhere. They had complete possession of her, ownership in a way no one else ever had. She held nothing back and let them do as they wished, taking the extreme pleasure with the intense challenge that came with loving three men.

She trembled, but this time her shaking had nothing to do with the building sensation and everything to do with her realization. She loved them. Not one more than the other, but all three, differently and equally.

The ball dropped, and they froze.

"Marigold," Hunter's firm command pulled her from her thoughts. "Are you hurt?"

"No," she rasped.

"Pull out slowly—"

"Wait."

They stilled, surrendering to her full control.

"You dropped the ball."

She needed to catch her breath. "An accident."

"You're sure?"

"Positive." She was in shock. Was it possible to love three men at once and in such a short time? Her heart said yes. "I..."

When she didn't finished, Stone's voice went firm. "You have to communicate, Marigold, or we don't know what's going on. Do you want us to stop?"

"No," she said, stronger than before. "Don't stop."

Ash was the first to move, but stopped when Hunter snapped, "Don't move." Softening his voice, he said, "Talk to us, *Lisichka*."

"I just realized, you were right."

"About?"

"This. It's just right. Perfect, actually. The three of you."

Ash stroked her cheek. "I'm glad you see it our way."

"I do."

"Good, because I think I can speak for my brothers when I say, none of us are letting you go."

"Promise?"

Hunter bent forward, stretching her in a way that made her gasp, as he pressed a kiss to her shoulder. "I swear with my life."

"Mine, too."

"And mine."

She knew then, if she could trust them with her heart she could trust them with anything. "I love you."

"*Ya tebya lyublyu*," Hunter said fiercely in Russian. Stone quickly repeated the phrase. Ash smiled up at her. "We love you, too."

When they started to move again, the energy of the room shifted. The intensity and raw possession remained, but there was also tenderness and pure vulnerability. Whatever veil they'd been holding was finally down, and she saw them in their truest form.

Hunter, her avenging angel. Stone, the lone predator who gained immaculate control. And Ash, her cuddly teddy bear that loved to break her simply so he could put her back together again.

They didn't ask for authority. They commanded it. And this life that they welcomed her into, it wasn't merely something they chose to live. It was a brutal path they survived. Together. The three bears. And she was now their Goldilocks, locked between three passionate men who would die defending her and do anything to keep her safe and protected.

She gave them everything, and they took it proudly, keeping their promise to the very end as they drenched her skin in sin and left her in a thousand pieces that needed to be collected and put together again.

Stone carried her to the shower, passing her gently into Hunter's arms. "Rest now, precious *Lisichka*. Let us take care of you."

The three of them washed her hair and gently bathed her body under the hot spray of water. They carried her back to bed in a thick towel, which was soon replaced with lavish furs they'd warmed by the fire. Hunter pulled her close, and Ash lay between her legs with his head upon her belly. Stone curled into her other side.

"*Ya tebya lyublyu*, Marigold—tonight, tomorrow, and every day after."

As she drifted toward sleep, warm and sheltered in their strong arms, she savored the fact that she was finally safe, cherished, and gloriously free.

CHAPTER 22

SACRED VOWS

One month after Jordan's arrest, they finally got the news Marigold risked her life for. Hunter, Stone, and Ash waited for her in the library, after texting that the lawyer had called.

She found them sitting before the gaping fireplace in a circle of leather chairs, the atmosphere heavy with unspoken possibilities that hung like incense in a cathedral when lifetimes of worry were laid to rest. Outside, snow had begun to fall. Fat, lazy flakes transformed the world beyond the windows into a crystalline wonderland, and reality softened at the edges. But inside, the air pulsed with tension.

"What is it? Is Katya okay?"

"She's perfectly safe," Stone assured. "As a matter of fact, she just posted pictures from Sardinia." He flashed his phone screen, showing Katya posing in a white string bikini against the Mediterranean backdrop.

Hunter growled. "They don't have dresses in Italy?"

Ash chuckled. "She looks good. Happy."

Cole must be loving his time off if that was the dress code, Marigold thought.

Katya had escaped the winter to visit friends in the States, then decided to extend her trip with a vacation off the coast of Italy. It was the first time she'd left since the assault, not counting her time at the clinic, and her brothers were glad to see her back to her former, cheerful self again.

"You said you heard from the lawyer?" More than anything, Marigold feared Jordan would get off on the charges and be set free. She wasn't worried about him coming after her again. She had her three bears to protect her. But she feared what that might do to Katya's peace of mind.

"Sit." Stone ordered, then tacked on a kinder, "Please."

She dropped into an empty leather chair. "I see your manners are improving as fast as my Russian."

"Sorry." He apologized. "That was rude."

She crossed her arms over her chest. "You're forgiven."

"I better fucking be."

She stuck out her tongue, and Stone arched a brow as if accepting her challenge.

"Jordan's lawyer called this morning," Ash said, breaking the tension.

"I'll deal with your attitude later," Stone promised.

"As I was saying," Ash's voice carried the satisfaction of a man who'd waited patiently for justice. "Formal charges have been filed. Between Katya's testimony and yours, the prosecutors are confident of a conviction."

The fire crackled in the enormous hearth, casting dancing shadows across faces that had become as familiar to her as her own reflection. They dominated the vaulting space with the casual authority of men who'd never doubted their right to command.

"How long?" Marigold asked, frustrated with the drawn-out

sentencing process when Jordan had already pleaded guilty to several charges, but the attorney representing Katya said the case against him was still developing.

"Ten to fifteen years, if he's extraordinarily lucky," Hunter's voice rumbled with deep satisfaction. "More likely twenty to life. Other women have come forward."

Relief flooded through her like warm honey, but it carried complications in its wake. "When's the trial?"

"They haven't set the date."

"Yet," Stone said, easing her tension. "But we should have an answer by the end of the day."

"There's something we need to discuss," Ash said gently. "It's about your family."

"You're my family."

Hunter took her hand. "Yes. But this is about your father," he said, keeping his tone especially delicate.

Her pulse quickened like a hummingbird's wings. "Is he sick?" She could tell by their expressions it was something else, so she braced for the worst. "Just tell me. I can take it."

"He's officially disowned you," Hunter said with blunt honesty that could have shattered glass. "He released a statement yesterday calling you mentally unstable and severing all ties. You're persona non grata in their world now."

"Oh," she stared down at her lap, supposing part of her had expected something like this happening. "I guess that's better than health problems."

"Fuck his health," Stone said sharply. "Don't waste your empathy on that piece of shit."

The words should have devastated her, should have left her feeling hollow and abandoned, like an empty church on Monday morning. Instead, they felt like the final chains falling away from her ankles, the last prison door swinging open to reveal endless sky.

"Are you all right, *Lisichka?*"

"I'm fine," she said with surprising conviction. "I never wanted their world anyway. I belong here. With you." She scanned all three ruggedly beautiful faces.

"We agree, but now that you've had time to settle in, we need to align the past with the future," Stone said carefully, his voice carrying undertones that made her skin tingle with anticipation. "Our life here isn't conventional. Our relationship isn't something most people would understand or accept."

"I'm not most people."

"No," Hunter agreed with a predatory smile that could have melted arctic ice. "You're not. But you need to understand what we're asking. What it would mean to be ours—completely, irrevocably, eternally—"

"Publicly," Ash finished.

Marigold laughed nervously. "Are you planning on leaking the surveillance footage?"

"No, but keeping you safe, keeping the lodge staffed and fully functional, requires a great deal of money."

She sat back, confused, her humor fading. "But I have nothing."

"We aren't asking you for money, *printsessa.*"

She frowned. "Then what are you asking?"

"It's time to re-open our doors," Hunter explained. "We haven't hosted a party since you arrived, and now that things are settling with your family, we figured it was time."

"You want to have a party?"

"Not just any party. The kind of gatherings that people pay millions to attend."

Her eyes widened.

"That's what we do," Ash explained. "It's why we have so many rooms."

"And so many toys." Stone's smile was pure mischief.

Hunter shifted closer, his eyes intense. "Do you remember what it means to belong to all of us?"

"It means trust," she said as if reciting sacred vows.

"Absolute trust," Stone agreed. "Trust enough to let us make decisions for you, to guide you, to push your boundaries in ways that might terrify you even as they set you free."

"It means surrender," Ash finished, his voice carrying the weight of mountains. "Real surrender. Not just in bed, but in life. Letting us take care of you, protect you, and provide for you."

She understood that they were trying to do what was right, what they knew, but they would only do so with her consent. "Will I be invited to the party?"

Stone laughed and Hunter shot him a silencing glare. "Some, but not all."

She frowned. "Why not all?"

"They can be dangerous."

"For you?"

"No, not for us. But you know what happened to Katya."

"You said that would never happen again."

"It won't." Stone's tone had shifted from playful to serious. "You're safe here. We have Cole and the guards watching the cameras twenty-four-seven."

She flushed, not liking the idea of anyone watching the things they'd done, especially Cole. "Then why can't I come to the party?"

"There are some you can attend, but there will be rules."

"*Strict* rules," Hunter emphasized. "None of these escaping games you like to play."

"Look, I can't help it if your lead security guy was outmaneuvered by little old me."

"This is serious, Marigold."

She dropped the sass, fully trusting Ash and the others to put her safety above all else. "Sorry."

"Some parties are controlled. Those, you can attend—"

"As long as you follow the rules."

"Which are?"

"You are always with one of us, and never go off on your own."

"No one, besides us, touches you."

"And if anyone even looks at you wrong, you tell us immediately."

"Okay." She nodded her agreement. "Does that mean I can go to the party?"

"Yes, as long as you're fine with being fucked in front of the guests."

Her eyes went wide again. "Um…"

"Take time to think it over."

"Will other women be there?"

"Yes."

"Naked?"

"Yes."

She scoffed. "Then I'll be there. And I'll have some rules of my own."

Hunter smirked, a low chuckle rumbling from his chest. "Those women do not interest us, *Lisichka*."

Ash took her hand. "You're everything we need."

"In the spring though, you're going to have to sit some festivities out."

"What's in the spring?"

"We host the annual Feast of the Fallen."

She sat back. "What's that?"

"It's organized by Jack Thorne, and it's not anything you need to attend."

"But what is it?"

The men exchanged glances. "It's an exclusive party with a strict guest list. You're not on it."

She scowled at Stone and turned her gaze to Ash. "What aren't they telling me?"

He sighed. "Wealthy men, from all over the world, pay two million dollars to attend. The first million goes toward the house. The second million goes toward one of the hunted."

She tipped her head, certain she had misheard him. "I'm sorry, *the hunted?* What, exactly, are they hunting?"

"Women," Hunter explained. "Guests."

"Volunteers."

"You're saying these women want to be hunted?"

"Yes. There's actually an extensive waiting list to get invited to the Feast."

"Are they shot?"

The men all laughed. "Hell no," Stone said. "No one is hurt beyond a scraped knee."

"Or a chafed wrist."

"Or a sore ass."

She held up a hand. "I get the picture. So, these men pay a million dollars to use the property, and they hunt the women like they're some sort of *Hunger Games* tribute?"

"Pretty much."

"What do they do when they catch them?"

"Whatever the hell they want. Everyone on the guest list is fully aware of the possible outcomes and no one attends without full comprehension of the rules and total consent."

Her breath caught as she imagined what some men might do to a woman with limitless consent.

"They have twenty-four hours, and the women are paid whether they get caught or not. The entire Feast is surveyed closely. No one is hurt. We take all necessary precautions."

"I think I'm okay with sitting that one out."

Hunter's dark eyes narrowed on her in that way that made her skin tingle as if he were already touching her. But he hadn't moved an inch. He just stared at her, dominating that leather wingback chair as if it were a throne.

"Good, because you'll be in your room," Ash said.

"With the doors locked," Stone added.

"And this time, Cole will keep you there."

"Speaking of Cole, how's he enjoying his vacation?"

"He's not on vacation. He's working a job. We sent him with Katya for protection."

Marigold smirked. "And, by the looks of that string bikini, he must really have his work cut out for him."

The three of them grumbled various words of disapproval in Russian.

"We're done here," Stone announced, rising from his seat. "You're coming with me."

"Not so fast." Hunter's voice cut through the library like a blade through silk. He remained in his chair, sprawled with deliberate casualness, but his onyx eyes tracked Marigold with predatory focus that made her stomach drop.

Stone paused, one hand still wrapped around Marigold's wrist. "Problem?"

"Yes. Our little fox needs to understand *why* women might volunteer to be hunted."

Marigold drew back. "No, I think I'm set—"

Hunter held up a silencing hand. "Our clients come to The Preserve with a certain expectation. Our exclusivity and impeccable standards maintains an elite clientele. Beyond absolute discretion, we provide a judgement free space for them to explore their darker...*proclivities*. We do not judge that which is done with safe and sane consent."

"I wasn't—"

"You were." He glanced briefly at his brothers then back to her with dark promise in his eyes. "Now, you need a lesson."

Her heart skipped a beat. "Wh—what kind of lesson?"

Hunter rose slowly, unfolding from the leather chair with the lethal grace of something wild barely contained in human skin. Each movement was calculated, deliberate, a predator preparing to strike. "If you can't comprehend the appeal of a hunt, I think it's time for a demonstration."

Marigold's pulse kicked against her throat like a trapped bird throwing itself against cage bars. "What are you talking about?"

"You sat there, so fucking judgmental, questioning why anyone would enjoy being hunted." Hunter's voice dropped to a growl. The threatening implication of his words vibrated through her chest, settling low in her belly where it bloomed into liquid heat. "That's an arrogant position for a trembling little fox to hold."

"Hunter—" Ash started, but the warning died when Hunter's gaze cut to him.

"She needs to understand what we offer. What we protect her from." He turned back to Marigold, and her breath caught at the dangerous glint in his eyes.

Every instinct screamed *run* even as her body softened in refusal to move. "You won't hurt me," she said, reminding herself as much as the others.

"Are you sure?" He took a step and she immediately mirrored it with a backstep of her own.

"Out there," he pointed to the tall window, "at the Feast, women are prey. They beg for the opportunity."

She shook her head, finding his claim impossible to imagine.

"You don't believe me?" He looked at his brother. "Tell her, Stone."

Stone shrugged with zero misgivings to such claims. "Our

office is littered with applications. Essays from women all over the world pleading to attend the next feast."

"You see, *Lisichka*, they want to be one of the fallen."

"Why?"

Ash's low chuckle distracted her, but she quickly returned her focus to Hunter. In the split second she took her eyes off him, he moved closer without making a sound.

"They're chased by men who paid millions for the privilege, men who don't know them, don't care about anything beyond the thrill of a catch. Here?" He stepped closer, and she felt the heat radiating off his massive frame, smelled the masculine scent of cedar and something darker, something that whispered of violence barely leashed. "Here, you're mine to hunt. Mine to catch. Mine to claim. And, like them, you're going to love every fucking second of it."

Stone released her wrist, stepping back with a dark smile that sent electricity crackling across her skin. "You better get going, Goldilocks."

"Going where?" Her eyes widened as all three men began rolling up their sleeves and loosening their collars.

"Thirty seconds." Hunter cracked his neck, the sound sharp as breaking branches. "That's all the head start you get."

"To do what?" Marigold staggered back, her head shaking in protest, but arousal already pooled low in her belly, mixing with genuine fear in a cocktail that made her dizzy, made her thighs clench.

"*Run.*"

Her wide eyed stare turned to Ash, but there was no sign of teasing in his eyes. Only raw hunger.

She backed into the door, her hand fumbling behind her back for the brass knob.

"Tick-tock, *Lisichka*. That's the sound of time running out." Hunter's smile was all teeth, all threat, all promise. "Because when I catch you—and I *will* catch you—I'm going to fuck that pretty little ass until you scream my name loud enough that even the servants will hear."

Heat flooded her face, her chest, between her legs—everywhere at once. Her mouth went dry while other parts of her grew wet with twisted curiosity. "You can't be serious."

"Do I look like I'm joking?" He tilted his head, studying her like a wolf studies a rabbit, calculating which way she'll bolt, how fast she'll run, exactly how she'll taste when he tears into her soft flesh. "Clock's started."

Frozen between arousal and disbelief, between the urge to run and the equally strong urge to surrender right here, she couldn't move.

"Twenty-nine."

"Hunter, this is insane—"

"Twenty-eight."

Ash stood, moving to block the other exit with his considerable frame. "You'll want to get moving, *printsessa*. Unless you're trying to make this easy for him."

"Twenty-four."

Marigold's survival instincts finally detonated. She bolted, her bare feet slapping against cold marble, the sound echoing through the corridors as loud as her panicked heartbeats.

Blood roared in her ears, drowning out everything except Hunter's distant voice—steady, relentless, counting down her freedom like an executioner marking time until the blade falls.

"Nineteen."

She'd barely started running and already her breath came in ragged gasps, harsh pants that tasted of fear-sweat and adrenaline, burning her lungs. Her hand caught the banister as she made a sharp turn down the east corridor. She could no longer hear Hunter's voice, which should have comforted her, but it only made her situation more terrifying.

She'd been living at the lodge for over a month, but she still didn't know all the hidden passageways. He could be anywhere. And, he had steady access to every motion sensor camera on the premises.

Her gaze darted to the small bear head on the wall as she panted. Stepping back, hand on her racing heart, she turned and continued to run.

This was crazy. This was dangerous. This was, God help her, exhilarating.

She'd been hunted before. By orderlies at Whitmore, their meaty hands grabbing at her hospital gown. By her family's security, cold professionals with dead eyes. By the cold itself on her journey here, death's icy fingers reaching for her throat. But this was different. This wasn't escape. It was play. Dark, twisted, primal play that made every nerve ending in her body sing with anticipation, every cell vibrate with the certainty that being caught might be better than getting away.

A slow whistle carried from the west corridor and she stilled. That taunting melody triggered fear in her as much as a speeding bullet might, and she doubled her speed.

"Little fox…" His voice carried through the corridors like smoke, curling around corners, finding her even as she fled. She realized with a thrill of terror that he wasn't even chasing her yet. He was giving her time, letting the anticipation build. Like a lion with a playful mouse under its shadow, he let her believe she was free, but he already had her in his sights and she was as good as done. Any second now, he'd have her under his paw.

She rushed down a darkened hall as he strolled after her. The madness he triggered with his slow pace only emphasized his confident hunger. Like the men coming in the spring, he was set on a feast and she was to be the meal.

She flew through the great hall, her feet barely touching ground. Past the enormous fireplace where she'd nearly died that first night. The memory felt like a lifetime ago, belonged to a different girl entirely. That girl who'd stumbled in from the cold had been determined to escape. Hunted and scared at the time, she never would have believed she'd one day be running through these halls because she *wanted* to be caught. Voluntarily choosing to get hunted again.

Though, she hadn't volunteered for this.

Another slow, taunting whistle echoed through the cavernous halls. "Marigold...I can smell your perfume in the halls."

She dove into the shadows of an alcove, heart pounding as she caught her breath.

"I can smell your sweat." The lanterns turned on, exposing her hiding spot. "Your fear."

She bolted from the shadows, rushing away from his approaching voice and into the next dark hall.

Her heart hammered against her ribs like a rabbit's—rapid, frantic, impossibly fast. She could feel it in her throat, her wrists, behind her eyes. Every pulse point in her body throbbed with awareness, with fear that tasted like copper and felt like lightning.

The east wing opened before her, offering a maze of possibilities that suddenly felt like too many choices, like being lost in a forest with a grizzly on her trail. The wine cellar? No, too obvious and no escape routes. She'd be cornered, trapped, easy prey. The billiard room? Too open, nowhere to hide, she'd be spotted immediately.

The solarium! The thought struck like lightning, illuminating everything. Katya's sanctuary, that humid jungle hidden behind glass walls. It was far from the library, full of places to hide among the tropical overgrowth, and most importantly, Hunter might not think to look there, since Katya's wing was typically preserved for his sister's privacy. He'd expect her to run to the upper floors, to lose herself in the maze of bedrooms.

"Come out, come out, wherever you are..."

She changed direction, her feet finding purchase on the cold floors as she sprinted toward the glass-walled paradise. Her thighs burned. Her calves screamed. But fear—exquisite, arousing fear—drove her forward.

His echoing steps stopped, and she grinned, sensing that she'd confused him.

When she entered the solarium, the shift in temperature, exacerbated by her sweat-dampened skin, caused her to overheat instantly. Pausing to catch her breath, her sense of hearing was deafened by her heavy breathing. But she could sense him. Even here, through the closed door and down the long corridor, she could feel him, the phantom sensation of being tracked crawling up her spine like fingers, like breath on the back of her neck.

Sprinklers kicked on, and she flinched. They hissed quietly beneath the leaves, adding to the already humid air. The trickle from the fountains in the koi pond added to the white noise, making it harder to hear.

The solarium air was thick with vapor, moistening her lips as she rapidly breathed. Opening and closing her fists, she struggled to control her trembling hands. Swallowed by tropical heat that wrapped around her like a living thing, the temperature shift felt almost violent. Her skin coated with moisture, and her clothes clung to her dewy flesh. Breathing felt like drowning in warm honey.

Leaves rustled, startling her. But she saw nothing. Sometimes birds got trapped in the solarium and she wouldn't be surprised to find other small critters scurrying around in the dirt. Or maybe it was him, already here, biding his time before he pounced on his prey.

She moved deeper into the solarium, past the orchids that preened in jewel tones of purple, sapphire, and crimson. Past the palms with their massive fronds that whispered secrets as she brushed by. Past the wicker furniture where she'd sat with Katya, discussing monsters and survival.

Almost certain she was alone, she moved to the far corner where massive ferns created a natural alcove, their branches cascading like a living curtain, and she wedged herself behind them, trying desperately to control her ragged breathing.

The sprinklers cut off.

Silence.

The sudden absence of sound was somehow worse than his haunting taunts. Her heart didn't slow. It accelerated, rabbit-fast, hummingbird-frantic.

She pressed her back against the glass wall, the cool surface a shocking contrast to the humid air, to her overheated skin. Condensation formed where her body touched the glass, outlining her in moisture.

Where was he?

Seconds crawled by like hours, each one an eternity. She strained to hear anything over the hum of the fountain, over the drip-drip-drip of condensation falling from leaves like rain in a miniature jungle. Over her own pulse thundering in her ears like drums, like thunder, like the end of the world approaching.

Maybe he'd gone the wrong direction. Maybe she'd actually—

The solarium door opened.

Not with a crash or a bang, but with a soft click that might as well have been a gunshot for how it made her entire body jerk. The soft snick of the latch seemed to echo forever in the humid space, bouncing off glass walls, reverberating through her bones.

Marigold's hand flew to her mouth, palm pressed hard

against her lips to stifle the gasp that wanted to escape, the whimper building in her chest. Through the fern fronds, she could see the doorway, but couldn't make out if anyone stood there. Just shadow and light, reality distorted by tropical foliage and her own fear.

Then she heard it. A low, rumbling sound that resonated in her bones, in her teeth, in the base of her spine as Hunter took a long, deep inhale and let out a satisfied growl.

"I'm getting warmer, *Lisichka*." His voice was pure gravel, rough as stone scraping stone. "Your scent's intensified... Fear and arousal. Such a pretty combination. Like honey and smoke."

She pressed harder against the wall, making herself as small as possible. Her thighs trembled, muscles quaking with the effort of staying still, of not running, of not making a sound. Whether from fear or need, she couldn't tell anymore. They'd merged, become the same thing. A dark wanting that pulsed between her legs and squeezed her lungs.

Heavy footsteps punched into the stone floor, slow and deliberate. He was taking his time, drawing it out, savoring it. The hunter enjoying the hunt, the certainty of the catch more intoxicating than the capture itself.

"You chose well," he continued, and his voice seemed to come from everywhere and nowhere, bouncing off glass, filtered through plants, impossible to locate. "The heat...makes your scent stronger. I could track you blind in this climate, even with the perfumed air around the flowers. I know the smell of your wet cunt by heart." He lifted a palm leaf as he strolled closer, his body a flawless compass to hers. "Could track it straight to wherever you're hiding."

Marigold bit down on her knuckle, teeth stabbing into skin, the sharp pain grounding her as she fought to keep silent. Through the ferns, she caught a glimpse of him—shirtless now, all brutal muscle and scarred skin, moving through the garden like violence barely leashed, like a bear prowling through forest undergrowth.

His bare broad chest was already slick with sweat. The humid air beaded on his shoulders, his arms, highlighting every ridge of muscle, every old wound that decorated his skin like a roadmap of survival. He moved with surprising grace for such a massive man, each step deliberate, controlled.

"Found your footprints in the condensation." His laugh was dark amusement wrapped in threat, the sound vibrating through the humid air. "You went left at the orchids. Smart. But not smart enough." He flicked loose the top button of his jeans, drawing her attention to the massive bulge in his pants. "You should know by now, that I'd track you to the end of the earth. You'll never escape me."

He was getting closer. She could feel his nearness in her bones, in her blood, the way prey senses a predator closing in. Her body tensed, muscles coiling like springs ready to release.

She closed her eyes, willing herself to stay silent and small. Every survival instinct screamed at her to run, to bolt, to move, but her body refused to obey, frozen in that terrible space between terror and anticipation. Knowing he'd lunge at the first sound.

"There are rules to a good hunt," Hunter said, voice closer.

Maybe twenty feet away, maybe less.

"The prey always runs. First, they freeze. That's the fear. But eventually, survival instincts kick in and that same terror makes them bolt. The predator chases. And when the predator inevitably catches the prey..." His shadow spread across the damp stone, just by her feet. He parted the ferns with one massive hand. "The predator gets to feast."

She couldn't help it. A small sound escaped her throat, half whimper, half moan. Hunter's head snapped in her direction.

Need and fear tangled so completely in her belly she swayed.

Those obsidian eyes locked on her hiding place, and his mouth curved into a slow wicked grin. "*Poymal tebya*."

She exploded from behind the ferns, pure instinct overriding logic. The second her feet pushed off the wet stone, she launched into a dead run, sprinting toward the far side of the solarium where another door promised escape until his arm banded around her waist, yanking her back to his chest and knocking the wind from her lungs.

"No!"

He was faster. Always faster.

His hand closed around her wrist like a manacle, pinning her flailing arms down with enough force to startle a cry from her throat. His other hand covered her mouth, the arm around her waist tightening like an iron bar, like a bear trap snapping shut.

"Caught you," he growled directly into her ear, his breath hot against her sweat-dampened skin.

"Hunter, please," The words came out breathy, desperate.

"Please what?" He spun her around, backing her against the thick trunk of a palm tree. The bark bit into her shoulders, rough and textured, grounding her through the delicious bite of pain. His body caged hers completely, his chest heaving, eyes wild with triumph and lust. The darkness radiating from him made her core clench. "Please let you go? Please be gentle?" His hand fisted in her hair, tilting her head back until her throat was exposed, vulnerable. "That's not how this works, *Lisichka*. I hunted you. I caught you. Now you're mine to do with as I please."

Unhinged desire swirled in her belly like a tornado of mixed sensations she couldn't rationalize. It was a game. Only a game. But he'd triggered her adrenaline in a way that heightened every pulsing response her body was having in that moment.

All she had to do was breathe the word *'stop'* and the game would be over, but what fun would that be? Dear God, she was as twisted as him, as unhinged as every name on the stacks of applications in his office.

His hand closed around her neck, forcing her wild eyes to focus. Hunter would never accept less than her full attention.

"Whose pussy is this?" His other hand clamped between her legs, massaging firmly.

"*Tvoya,*" she gasped, the Russian word for *yours,* causing him to growl and tighten his grip another degree.

"Fucking right, it is. *Moya.* All mine."

"Yes," she breathed, the word synonymous for her surrender and his invitation all at once.

His kiss was brutal, claiming, all teeth and tongue and dominance. He devoured her mouth like a starving man presented with a feast, like he could consume her entirely and still not have enough. One hand remained tangled in her hair while the other roamed her body with rough possession, squeezing her breast hard enough to make her gasp, then softer, thumbing her nipple through the fabric until it peaked painfully.

When Hunter touched her, he demanded her full focus. To him, when they were alone, she belonged solely to him. It seemed to be a requirement they all accepted and no one dared to challenge.

"My *Lisichka,*" he growled, his voice thick with absolute possession.

The primal taste of his desire caused her to moan into his mouth. His scent surrounded her, overwhelmed her—cedar and sweat and raw masculine hunger that was more intoxicating than any drug they'd forced down her throat at Whitmore.

"Pants off," he commanded against her lips, the words vibrating through her. "Now."

Her hands shook as she fumbled with the button, fingers clumsy with need and adrenaline. She shoved the fabric down her legs, the air against her bare skin feeling cool despite the tropical heat. He didn't wait for her to step out of them completely before spinning her around with bruising force, pressing her front against the trunk.

The bark abraded her breasts, her belly, her thighs, intensifying every sensation until each nerve ending sung with awareness.

"Don't move." He pushed her hands to the trunk, silently commanding her to stay.

She gripped the tree, her nails biting into the bark. Behind her, something snapped and she turned. Hunter fisted the stem from a nearby aloe plant.

"What are you doing with that?"

He bit into the green branch, peeling open the leaf to expose the gel-like flesh on the inside. "Don't you worry." Scraping the natural liquid out of the plant with one hand, he tugged down his zipper with the other, that metallic rasp impossibly loud in the humid space.

Her eyes went wide as he fisted his swollen cock, stroking the aloe gel up and down his shaft until he was slick and fully coated. The heat of his hard body pressed against hers, his now lubricated cock hard and demanding.

"Hunter, wait!" Fear spiked through the arousal, sharp and clarifying.

"*Nyet.* You want me to stop, say the word."

She bit down on her lips, knowing if she even mouthed the word stop he'd let go in a heartbeat. But the truth was, she lived for his wild domination. "Just...be gentle."

"I'd slit my own throat before causing you pain." His voice

gentled fractionally, his hand stroking down her spine with surprising tenderness. "But you're going to take it for me. You're going to let me claim every part of you, mark you inside and out." His fingers found her center, stroking through her slickness, finding her swollen and soaked, ready despite her protests. "And you're going to love it. Aren't you, *Lisichka*?"

"Yes," she whimpered, the word torn from somewhere deep inside.

"That's my good girl." He worked her carefully, his fingers sliding through her wetness before moving to that forbidden place, circling, pressing, preparing. One finger breached her and she gasped at the foreign sensation—the burn, the stretch, the overwhelming fullness. He added a second finger and she whimpered, torn between wanting more and wanting mercy.

The aloe definitely helped. Despite his rough words, his touch was measured, patient. He worked her open slowly, thoroughly, his other hand reaching around to stroke her clit in maddening circles that made her hips buck against the tree trunk.

When he finally withdrew his fingers and positioned himself—the broad head of his cock pressing against that tight ring of muscle—she could taste copper in her mouth where she'd bitten her lip, could smell the rich earth scent of the solarium mixed with their combined arousal, could feel every atom of her body focused on that single point of contact.

"Breathe," he commanded, one hand reaching around to stroke her where she needed it most, fingers slipping through her wetness with obscene ease. "Breathe and relax for me. Let me in."

She did, pulling air into her lungs, air that tasted of orchids and sweat and sex. And, as she exhaled, he pressed forward. The burn was immediate, intense, stealing her breath. Her body fought the intrusion even as her mind screamed *yes, yes, more*.

"That's it." His voice was ragged now, control fracturing with each inch he gained. "Fuck, you feel incredible. So tight. So perfect. *Moya.*"

Inch by torturous inch, he filled her. The pain transformed into something else, something darker and sweeter that made her moan against the tree bark, the rough texture scraping her lips, her cheek. She felt split open, impaled, claimed in the most primal way possible.

When he was fully seated, they both stilled. Her pulse throbbed through every inch of her body. In her throat, her wrists, her core, around his cock buried so deep inside her she couldn't tell where she ended and he began. The humid air coated their joined bodies, making every movement slick, making her skin hypersensitive to every sensation.

"Say my name," Hunter growled, his hips drawing back slowly before pressing forward again, establishing a rhythm that was both punishment and pleasure. "Make them jealous."

"Hunter!" It tore from her throat, half scream, half prayer.

"Louder." He slammed into her harder, his fingers working cruel magic between her thighs, rubbing her clit with just enough pressure to keep her on the edge.

"Hunter!" His name echoed off the glass walls, bounced through the tropical foliage, carried through the lodge like a declaration.

He pistoned into her with increasing urgency, each thrust driving her against the tree, the bark scraping her sensitized skin in a way that added to the overwhelming sensation. She could hear the wet sounds of their coupling, smell the musk of sex beyond the floral sweetness of the orchids, taste blood from her bitten lip and feel... God, she felt *everything*.

Her orgasm built like a tidal wave, pressure mounting at the base of her spine, in her core, throbbing between her thighs. When it finally crashed over her, she shattered, splintering into a thousand ruined pieces that might never come back together the same way.

"That's it, come on my hand," Hunter snarled, his control disintegrating. "Come while I fuck this tight little ass. Soak my fucking fingers."

She did, her whole body convulsing with the force of it, clenching around him so hard he roared, an actual roar that echoed through the solarium like a bear claiming its territory. He followed her over the edge moments later, his release pouring into her, marking her from the inside out.

They collapsed against the tree, both trembling, their bodies slick with sweat and condensation, their breathing ragged and synchronized. Hunter's weight pressed into her, grounding her, keeping her tethered to earth when she felt like she might float away.

She closed her eyes, saving her strength to catch her breath as he held her upright.

"How do you feel about hunts now?" he murmured against her hair, his voice rough as gravel but threaded with amusement.

She laughed breathlessly, the sound turning into a moan when he shifted inside her. "It all depends on who's chasing me, I suppose."

He slapped her clit and she gasped, the sharp shock bordering on tight pleasure that nearly had her sliding over the edge again. "Greedy little fox."

He pulled out slowly, his gentle care a complete contrast from the way he'd handled her moments ago, and she whimpered at the sudden emptiness that came in his absence. Turning her in his arms, he gathered her against his chest with surprising tenderness. His heart thundered against her cheek, proof that he'd been as affected as her.

The solarium door crashed open with enough force to rattle the glass walls.

Stone stood in the doorway, Ash behind him, both wearing expressions of dark amusement and barely restrained hunger. Their eyes tracked over Marigold's disheveled form—her sweat-dampened hair, her flushed skin, the marks blooming on her shoulders and breasts, the way she wilted in Hunter's arms.

"You couldn't wait your turn?" Stone asked, but there was no real anger in his voice, only anticipation.

Hunter grinned, holding Marigold possessively against his chest like a prize he'd won. "To the best hunter goes the spoils."

"She's not spoiled yet." Ash's ice-blue eyes burned as they traced over her, his gaze lingering on every mark, every sign of what had just happened.

Marigold met his gaze, then Stone's. Both men watched her with shameless hunger banked in their eyes. "Boys?" Her voice trembled as her racing heart tripped out of beat. She whimpered, unsure if she could take much more so soon.

Ash came to cup her face delicately. "You're shaking." He kissed her gently, his love pouring over her as Hunter held her in his arms.

"I'm cold." She shivered, the sheen of sweat now chilling on her body despite the heat.

Stone stepped forward and pulled Marigold from Hunter's arms. "I'll warm you up."

Knowing that there would be no deterring him now, she shut her eyes and rested against Stone's hard chest as he hauled her out of the solarium, not stopping until they were shut inside his room with the door locked.

He dumped her onto the bed, and she curled into the fur blankets. "Are you upset?"

"No, but I'm not giving you a pass, either." Stone was already shucking off his clothes.

The fire crackled, casting the warm room in an amber glow. He caught her ankles, yanking her to the edge of the mattress. "Now, I have to mark my territory as well." He shoved inside of her and they both moaned.

Like a beast needing to be sated, once he buried himself in her heat, he instantly calmed. Bending closer, he kissed her gently. "Do you like making me jealous, *Zayka*?"

"You had me just last night."

"Not to myself."

That was true.

While each of the men loved to share, they were also incredibly territorial and liked to steal moments when it was just the two of them, one on one. Marigold liked that too.

"Are you growing tired of us yet?"

"Oh, I'm tired," she teased as he pounded inside of her with selfish need. "But I don't think I'll ever tire of being the center of three men's attention."

"Us, not just any men."

"Yes," she clarified. "Only my three bears."

"That's right. Ours. And right now, you're mine." His hand closed around her throat as he held her down, fucking her hard.

Stone loved to play games and challenge her. He used his hands, his mouth, feathers, ice, whips, basically, anything he could find to heighten the experience. And when she begged for more, he gave her less. When she tried to rush toward release, he slowed everything down. It was always a power play and he never gave up that hard earned control.

"Please," she gasped, tugging uselessly at his arm as he teased and tormented her in that twisted way they both adored. "Stone, please—"

"Please what?" His voice was amused, indulgent. "Use your words, *Zayka*. Tell me exactly what you need."

"I need to come—" She broke off as his fingers found her

center, stroking with maddening expertise as he thrust in and out of her.

"In Russian. How else will you ever learn?"

Her brain scrambled for the right words, *"Pozhaluysta, pozvol' mne konchit'."*

"You're so fucking sexy when you speak my language. Especially when you get the words wrong."

"Did I get it wrong?"

"No, that was perfect."

As soon as she was about to climax, he pulled his hand away.

She growled in frustration. *"Bastard!"*

He slapped her ass and laughed. "You need to learn patience," he murmured. "Good things come to those who wait. And you're going to be very, very good for me, aren't you?"

"I thought I was being good."

"Say pretty, pretty please, Stone—in Russian."

"Nu pozhaluysta, pozhaluysta, Stone."

"Beautiful. You make me a greedy prick. When I hear such pretty words from your mouth, I want to fuck it." He fisted her hair, pulling out of her as he dragged her to the floor and forced her to her knees. "Suck me off, and then I'll make you scream so loud my brothers will come running."

Loving the fact that she could drive him to the edge of his control, she looked up at him with big brown eyes and said, *"Da, ser."* He was groaning before she even took him into her mouth. She finished him in a few short thrusts and then he was burying his face between her legs, keeping his promise as she screamed at the top of her lungs.

In the end, Ash came bursting through the door as predicted, Hunter following closely behind. By the time Stone was through, she needed to be held, and Ash was right there, happy to serve. He praised her and brought her back to that safe place she often found in his arms. When he finally took her—slowly, thoroughly, with complete control over every aspect of her pleasure—she was incoherent with need. He orchestrated her final release like a symphony, building and backing off until she was sobbing with frustration before finally allowing her to shatter in his arms.

"How do you feel?" Ash asked, gathering her against his chest as aftershocks rippled through her.

"Perfect." She breathed in the familiar scent of them on her skin. "Absolutely perfect."

"Good." He pressed a kiss to her temple.

Hunter pressed another to her shoulder.

And Stone bit playfully into her thigh.

Their absolute entitlement should have terrified her, should have sent her running toward whatever scraps of freedom she'd managed to claim. A month ago, they would have triggered every defense mechanism she'd built while fighting for autonomy. But after everything she'd experienced—Jordan's downfall, her father's rejection, their unwavering protection, the exquisite surrender she'd discovered in their arms—she found herself craving exactly what they provided.

Their fingers lingered over her skin with deliberate intent, skin against skin like electricity seeking ground.

Together, they led her toward a future that promised to be everything she'd never dared to dream. And she realized, through the deepest trust she'd ever known, in her surrender, she found her true worth. Not as their submissive, but as their salvation. Hunter, Stone, and Ash needed her as much as she needed them. Apart, they could be too violent, too cold, too consuming. Separately, they were everything wrong. Together, they were just right.

Spoiled didn't begin to describe Marigold's new life. Being doted on by three powerful men at all times could have that effect.

But it wasn't just their attention. It was the endless luxury. Her three bears made her feel like a queen every single day she promised she was theirs. And for that, they treasured her above all else.

Her closets were filled with designer clothes. Silk and cashmere, leather and lace, everything in colors that would complement her skin tone. But as beautiful as the day wear was, it was the intimate apparel that made her breath catch.

Lingerie in every style imaginable—delicate lace that would barely cover anything, silk that would cling to every curve, leather pieces that spoke to darker fantasies. And in the back, hanging like promises of things to come, were garments she couldn't quite categorize. Beautiful restraints that looked like jewelry, corsets that were works of art, things that were clearly meant to enhance rather than conceal.

They thought of everything.

Her days were spent doing whatever she pleased. If she showed an interest in a hobby, she'd find herself surrounded by resources within hours. Books, crafts, and obscure ingredients whenever she had a craving to bake something. They indulged her every whim.

And she indulged them much the same. Though their desires were less tangible than hers and more often of the carnal sense.

And on the mornings after those exceptionally long nights, she found herself pampered beyond anything she'd ever known. They had a team of discreet specialists at their disposal, and often spoiled her with spa treatments that redefined her understanding of indulgence.

They instructed the massage therapists to work every knot out of her muscles with oils that smelled like heaven, until her skin glowed like moonlight and she felt like a living goddess. She even had a personal aesthetician to perform a long list of beauty treatments until her skin appeared reborn, transformed into something that belonged on marble statues rather than mortal women.

She had stylists to take care of every inch of her grooming. Every hair below her neck had been removed with precision that bordered on artistry. She let the staff buff and polish her until she gleamed like smooth, precious marble. They shaped and painted her nails, lathered her skin in lotions, and basically transformed her into living velvet.

And then there was her very delicate, very thorough nurse, Elena, who saw to the more intimate preparations that often made Marigold's cheeks flame. Her approach was clinical but professional, and mortifying beyond description. But Elena's matter-of-fact methods made the process bearable, and afterward, Marigold always felt cleaner and more prepared for whatever intimacies awaited in the darkness ahead.

These rituals, which were once so foreign and strange, now felt like necessities. She shouldn't become so dependent on luxuries, but whenever she uttered the slightest hint of guilt, the men chastised her in a way that made her remember their corrections every time she sat down the next day.

"We like taking care of you. Leave it at that," Hunter had *growled the last time she worried she was taking advantage of their kindness.*

Stone drove home his point by planting another reminder on her bare ass.

"Okay!" She squirmed under the sharp sting. "I won't complain anymore."

Ash tsked. "What kind of woman complains about being spoiled anyway?"

"A naughty one." Stone spanked her ass again.

Suffice it to say, after that night, she never felt guilty about accepting their gifts again. She simply accepted that she was their greatest treasure, and no matter what they gave her, they would always wish they could give a little more.

Ash said she needed to learn her worth.

Hunter said she was priceless.

Stone said she needed to be spanked more.

Maybe they were all correct on some level.

But after months of running and narrowly escaping a life sentence in a padded cell, it was hard to believe anyone would want her, let alone love her as deeply and completely as Hunter, Stone, and Ash.

While some people waited their entire life to find a single good man, she'd managed to fall in love with not one, but three gorgeously generous, doting—often demanding—men. Despite their rough edges, at their core, they were all honorable and kind.

And tonight, they were officially marking her as their own, a commitment she'd requested, and a gift they couldn't resist granting. She was not just theirs. They were hers, and she wanted to make that claim for all the world to see.

Knowing dinner wasn't for a few hours, Marigold drew a bath and grabbed a novel from the nightstand. She sank into the tub with a sigh that bordered on ecstasy. The water was perfect, hot enough to melt the tension from her muscles, and scented enough to make her feel like a goddess. When her eyes got heavy, she set the book aside and floated peacefully.

This was what security felt like—not just physical safety, but emotional sanctuary. A place where she could explore desires she'd never dared acknowledge, with men who would push her boundaries while keeping her absolutely safe.

When the water had cooled, she finally emerged, wrapping herself in a soft towel. In the mirror, her reflection held a radiant glow—relaxed, like a woman who'd finally found her place in the world.

A soft knock interrupted her thoughts. "Come in," she called, as she combed through her damp curls.

Ash entered, carrying what appeared to be a jewelry box. His eyes tracked over her towel-wrapped form with evident appreciation, but there was something deeper in his stare—possession mixed with reverence.

"I hope you don't mind the intrusion," he said, taking her comb and setting it on the vanity. "But we have something for you."

"What is it?"

"Open it and see." He handed her the small package, and she lifted the lid.

Inside the box, nestled on black velvet, was the most beautiful necklace she'd ever seen. Not gaudy or ostentatious, but elegant in a way that spoke of old money and older power. The centerpiece was a pendant, chiseled with raw diamonds.

"Is it a bear paw?" The piece sparkled and gleamed as she turned it in the soft glowing light.

"The Volkov family crest," Ash confirmed. "Worn by women who have given their hearts to Volkov men, dating back centuries before you or I ever existed."

Like her, Ash had once been an outsider looking in. This wasn't just jewelry. It was another claim. A public declaration of ownership that would mark her as theirs to anyone who understood the significance.

"Ash, it's beautiful."

"May I?"

She nodded, lifting her hair as he fastened the necklace around her throat. The pendant settled tight around her throat, a collar, warm against her skin like a brand.

"Perfect," he murmured, his hands settling on her shoulders. "It looks good on you, like you were born to wear it."

In the mirror, she could see how the necklace transformed her. She no longer looked like a refugee who'd stumbled into luxury. She looked like she belonged here. Like this life, this room, these men were always meant to be hers.

"How do you feel about tonight?" Ash asked softly.

"Scared," she admitted. "Excited. Like I'm standing on the edge of a cliff."

"Are you getting cold feet?"

She met his eyes in the mirror, seeing patience and desire and something that could only be love. "No," she whispered. "I want this more than words can say." Her finger brushed over the diamond-crusted pendant. "I'm yours."

"*I ty moya. Nasha.*" *And you are mine.* "Ours." His smile was radiant.

Before she could respond, there was another knock then Stone let himself in, impeccably dressed in a dark suit. "Dinner's ready," he announced, then stopped short when he saw the necklace, tracing an adoring finger from the pendant to her exposed collar bone, he gave her that predatory grin. "It suits you perfectly, *Zayka*."

"Thank you." She touched the pendant self-consciously. "For everything. The room, the clothes, the…"

"The chance to spoil you properly?" Stone finished with a smile. "Marigold, we've been over this—"

"I'm not complaining."

"You better not be," Ash admonished.

"I'm only trying to say thank you."

Stone kissed her softly, gracefully accepting her gratitude as long as she accepted their gestures of love. "You're welcome."

Ash, not one to be outdone, pulled her into his arms and kissed her deeper.

Stone crowded her back, pulling loose the towel to run his fingers over her bare hips. "I can't wait to get inside of you." He pulled her hand to the bulge at his crotch. "Tonight can't come fast enough."

Marigold twisted out of their grip and covered herself with the towel. "Soon." Seeing both of them in her room made Hunter's absence that much more palpable. "Is he still angry?"

"More so…resigned."

She hated disappointing any of them. "Maybe I'm making a mistake—"

"No," they both said at once.

Ash took her hands, kissing her fingers. "You want this. *We* want this. Deep down, Hunter wants to fulfill your every desire. He just can't bear the thought of you in pain."

The pain was the most challenging part to imagine. "How bad will it hurt?"

Stone nudged Ash out of his way so he could frame her face and look into her eyes. "We have ways to manage the pain,

Zayka. In Russia, we have a saying—*Chto dayotsya legko, ne imeyet vesa*—what comes too easily holds no weight."

"He's right. Pain is the price that transforms a simple act into a sacrament. Without the ache, without the burn, it's merely touch. But with it?"

"Every mark becomes scripture written on your skin." Stone dragged her hand over his face, where a jagged scar disrupted his beauty. "It's a permanent reminder of what you were willing to sacrifice."

She shivered with a mixture of fear and excitement. "I'd give you anything," she whispered, leaning into his strength, and he wrapped her in the shelter of his arms.

Stone placed a gentle kiss on her head and whispered, "The body remembers what costs us most. We will remember as well."

Dinner was served in the private family dining room, an intimate, candlelit space with a table that seated exactly four. The food was exquisite, but she barely tasted it. She was too aware of the three men watching her every movement, their eyes tracking each bite, each sip of wine, each gesture.

"You're staring," she said finally.

"We're memorizing," Hunter corrected. "The way you look right now, in our home, wearing that necklace—our mark. It's enough, *Lisichka*."

She glanced nervously at Stone and Ash, but this was her battle to fight, not theirs. Her choice. "Hunter, please don't be upset with me."

"I'm not upset with you. But you can't blame me for wanting to save you a moment's pain."

"One moment to make a permanent statement."

"The necklace is a statement."

"And it's beautiful," she agreed. "But I want this too, Hunter. Please don't refuse me."

Reluctance battled in his eyes, but he could deny her nothing.

She moved from her seat to his lap, wreathing her arms around his neck so she could lay her head on his broad shoulders. Beneath all that hard muscle hid softness at his core.

"Please let me have this," She whispered. "I don't want it if it comes without your blessing."

Pressing his lips to her brow, he sighed. "Your choice, as always. You have my blessing."

"Thank you, my love." She smiled.

"Tomorrow you might not look so kindly at us," Stone teased.

Her belly swooped with nerves. "Stop trying to scare me."

Ultimately, like everything else, it was her choice. And she wasn't going to let fear change her mind.

The conversation shifted to lighter topics, volleying between flirtatious banter, personal stories, and details of their day. She could barely taste the food through her anticipation, too nervous to have much of an appetite, so she eventually switched from food to champagne.

"You've barely eaten," Ash said with a disapproving stare.

"I'm nervous."

Stone set down his glass, and Ash pushed back his chair. "Does that mean it's time?"

Her empty belly made her jumbling nerves that much more pronounced. The significance of the evening approached like a storm on the horizon.

"Yes," she breathed. "I'm ready."

"Good," Stone said with a predatory smile. "Because I'm still hungry."

The champagne gave her liquid courage. She drained the

glass in several quick swallows, feeling alcohol spread warmth through her limbs like liquid starlight, then she pushed back her chair.

"We've planned something special first," Ash said, leading her from the table.

Hunter followed, already loosening his tie.

The promise in their eyes sent shivers of anticipation racing through her like competing symphony orchestras. When they didn't go directly to the playroom, she frowned.

"Where are we going?"

"The ballroom. Like I said, we wanted it to be special." Ash led her to the massive double doors and paused.

"Once you walk through those doors, there's no turning back." Stone gave her a moment to let the gravity of this moment set it. "You sure this is what you want?"

"Positive."

Her hand shook as she reached for the door handle, fingers trembling with anticipation. This was it—the point of no return she'd been approaching since the moment she'd entered their world.

She pulled open the heavy doors and stepped into her future, ready to become exactly what she was meant to be.

Theirs.

Completely, irrevocably, eternally.

Taking in the sight of their preparations, she gasped. Massive didn't begin to describe what was clearly a platform built for gods and carnal pleasures. Candles flickered from crystal chandeliers suspended from a glass dome in the vaulted ceiling. Alcoves were adorned with oil-painted murals of erotic orgies that boasted appetites for the flesh. The architecture was designed for worship, draped in champagne silks that stretched to the ceiling.

But it was the restraints that made her pulse race like thoroughbreds at the starting gate. Golden cuffs attached to each corner of the enormous bed, a spreader bar positioned with mathematical precision, everything beautiful enough to be jewelry but clearly functional as sacraments.

She stepped further into the room, anticipation trembling through her legs. The door closed behind her with a soft click that sounded like destiny sealing itself.

They emerged from the darkness like ancient gods made flesh, materializing from shadows where candlelight couldn't reach. Three sets of eager hands untied her dress and pulled away her underclothes like she was a gift to be unwrapped.

In the mirror, she saw a goddess—polished, perfected, ready for worship by those who understood her true worth. Her hair fell in perfect waves that caught light like spun gold, framing her face. She looked like a virgin sacrifice prepared for worship.

Tracking every detail of her appearance with the focus of men memorizing scripture, fingers trailed over her bare curves reverently. Their touch was the most exquisite torture she'd ever experienced, a systematic dismantling of every defense she'd ever built.

They exposed her in ways that transcended physical nakedness. They saw the vulnerability in her soul, open to possibilities that terrified and excited her in equal measure.

"Beautiful," Stone breathed, his pale eyes drinking in every curve like a man dying of thirst. "Absolutely fucking beautiful."

They guided her to the bed with hands that were gentle but implacable, movements so coordinated they might have been dancers performing choreography rehearsed in dreams. When she lay back against the champagne silk, they positioned her on the bed the way they wanted her.

Their movements spoke of ritual rather than simple restraint. Gilded cuffs closed around her wrists with soft clicks that echoed through the room like wedding bells. The spreader bar locked her ankles apart, holding her open and as vulnerable as an offering on an altar. But instead of feeling trapped, she felt... cherished, prepared for worship by those who truly understood her full worth.

"How does that feel?" Ash asked, testing the restraints with clinical precision that somehow felt like caresses.

"Strange," she admitted, truth flowing from her lips like water from springs. "But not bad."

"That's the champagne talking," Stone said with amusement that held darker undercurrents. "And the endorphins. Your body knows what's coming, even if your mind hasn't caught up yet."

They stepped back to admire their work, and she saw herself through their eyes—golden hair spread across dark silk like spilled honey, pale skin glowing in the candlelight like polished marble, completely helpless and completely theirs.

Her gaze found Hunter's. His resistance to this evening had vanished, replaced with bone deep hunger she felt at the core of her soul.

"I love you," she mouthed.

"*Ya tebya lyublyu*," he mouthed back, with a nod that communicated great pride.

Ash approached the bed, dragging a finger slowly from her hip to her rib. "Tell us you want this."

"I want this.

"Good," Stone said, giving the restraints a tug. "Now close your eyes and center yourself. Forget everything else. No thinking, no analyzing, no trying to control anything. Just feel what we give you."

She closed her eyes with a nod, anticipation amplifying every sensation.

They began with touches so light they might have been imagined—fingertips tracing patterns on her skin like artists sketching masterpieces, breath ghosting across sensitive places like secret promises, the whisper of fabric as they shed their own clothes.

Peeking through her lashes, she caught glimpses of them in the golden light—pale scars and dark tattoos that told stories of violence survived, muscle and sinew built for war but dedicated to pleasure. Each was beautiful in his own way, dangerous enough to make her pulse race, but loyal enough that she felt truly safe in their care, despite her helpless position.

Hunter's hands were rough from years of fighting, calloused in ways that made every caress a study in contrasts. Silk and sandpaper. Gentleness wrapped about barely leashed power.

Stone's touch was clinical and precise, mapping her responses with scientific accuracy that resonated with more intimacy than poetry. Whenever toys or restraints were present, he became the puppet master.

Ash was pure seduction made flesh. He knew instinctively where to touch her, how much pressure to apply, and when to retreat and leave her gasping for more.

They worked in perfect synchronization, three parts of a whole dedicated to her complete undoing. When one mouth left her skin, another appeared like magic. When fingers withdrew, they were replaced by something else—lips, tongue, the edge of teeth that never quite crossed the line into pain but promised they could if she wanted them to.

"Please," she gasped when the teasing became unbearable, when pleasure built like storm clouds gathering on horizons. "I need..."

"What do you need?" Stone asked, his voice calm despite his own arousal pressing against her hip.

"More. Everything. I can't bear the teasing."

"You can." Hunter's firm tone brooked no argument. "You can take more than you realize. We're going to prove it to you."

They gradually increased the intensity of their slow seduction, systematically pushing her toward the highest degree of human pleasure. Hands that had been gentle became demanding. Mouths that had whispered became insistent. They were unraveling her, bit by bit, and she was coming apart at the seams, a symphony composed of sighs and surrender, conducted by them and them alone.

When the first climax hit, she screamed out in pleasure and desperate relief, a sound torn from her throat that echoed off the golden walls like prayers offered to darker gods. But they didn't stop, didn't give her time to recover or catch her breath. Instead, they built her toward another peak, higher and more intense than the first.

"That's it," Ash murmured against her throat, his voice rough with desire and something deeper. "Let go completely. Show us how beautiful you are when you surrender everything. To us."

By the third orgasm, she was incoherent, words dissolving into sounds that had no meaning beyond pure sensation. By the fourth, she was begging for mercy, for more, for them never to stop, for release that felt like dying and being reborn in the same breath.

Her body felt like it belonged to someone else, like she was watching from outside herself as they took her apart and rebuilt her according to their specifications.

"Now," Stone said finally, the single word carried the weight of destiny and desire fulfilled. "She's ready."

They positioned themselves around her with the same careful coordination they'd used for everything else, movements that spoke of planning and patience finally reaching fruition. Stone at her head, his pale eyes holding hers as he guided himself into her mouth with gentleness that belied his obvious need. Hunter pressed between her thighs, spreading her wider as he pushed forward with steady pressure that made her gasp around Stone's length.

"Relax," Ash whispered, his hands gentle on her skin as he prepared her with oil. "Trust us to take care of you, to make this perfect for you."

The sensation of being filled completely, claimed by all three of them simultaneously, was an art form of its own, requiring great coordination and communication. They knew how to prepare her body, and that moment just before they all entered her, every nerve ending was on fire, every breath so intense it bordered on pain. And then...*peace*.

Theirs.

One.

Her heartbeat synchronized with theirs until she couldn't tell where she ended and they began.

"Look at us," Stone commanded, his voice rough with restraint. "Keep your eyes open. We want to see you, all of you."

She obeyed, meeting each of their gazes in turn, finding different gifts in each stare. In Stone's jade eyes, she saw possession and something more profound. Love, fierce and protective as winter storms. In Hunter's dark gaze, she found acceptance and hunger that matched her own. And in Ash's ice-blue eyes, she discovered home, a safe haven wrapped in passion.

They moved together like they'd been born to pleasure her in precisely this way. Her heart ached with joy. The perfection of their claiming was unmatched.

Their rhythm harmonized with her desires, each moan a song in ecstasy. When one withdrew, another pressed forward. When the intensity threatened to overwhelm her, they eased back. When she needed more, they gave it without request.

"This is what you were made for," Hunter growled, his hands gripping her hips hard enough to leave marks that would remind her of this moment for days. "This is where you belong, *Lisichka*."

"With us," Stone added, his thumb tracing the column of her throat as she worked to accommodate him, reminding her of the diamond collar now locked around her neck. "Always with us."

"Ours," Ash finished, pressing deeper until she gasped around Stone's length.

The pleasure became so intense her mind seemed to float outside her own body.

"Completely and forever ours."

Their words broke something inside her, the last wall falling away as she surrendered completely, giving them everything they asked for and more. Her body, her heart, her very soul offered up like a sacrifice on an altar, built from trust and desire.

When the final climax hit, it was a crescendo of sensation that erased the past and made room for a future filled with abundance and joy. She shattered and reformed like glass. Stronger. More confident. And absolutely certain she belonged with them.

They held her afterward, their bodies forming a protective cage around her as she trembled through endless aftershocks. Stone stroked her hair, murmuring words of praise in Russian that sounded like poetry even though she couldn't understand them.

Ash's hand traced soothing patterns on her skin, tracing where the brand would go.

Hunter stared into her eyes. "Do you know how perfect you are to us?" he whispered. "We're so proud of you, of how you've exceeded our highest expectations."

She kissed his scarred fingers, nuzzling against his palm. "You've opened my eyes to a life I never could have imagined on my own."

"We knew, the moment we saw you, that we couldn't let you go."

"And here you are," Ash added. "Ours forever."

"How do you feel?" Stone asked, his voice gentler than she'd ever heard it.

She rolled to her back so she could see his eyes. "Relaxed."

"Good."

Ash quietly left the bed and returned with a medical kit, his movements careful and precise. The sight of the syringe made her tense involuntarily, but Stone's hand found hers and squeezed. His sturdy grip grounded her.

"Just lidocaine," Ash explained, showing her the vial. "We'll numb the area completely first. You'll feel pressure, heat, but the worst of the pain will be manageable."

She nodded, watching as he prepared the injection with the same meticulous care he brought to everything. She sat up so they could clean her shoulder with an alcohol swab, then she looked forward into Hunter's eyes, careful not to gasp as the needle slipped beneath her skin.

"That's one."

"How many are there?"

"Four."

She swallowed back another hiss as another syringe emptied into her. Ash worked around her right shoulder blade, each injection spreading blessed numbness through the area. By the time he placed the last injection, she felt nothing at all.

"Can you feel this?" Hunter asked, tracing a finger down her back.

"No." Her voice came out steadier than she felt.

Stone appeared holding a strip of soft leather. "For your protection. Something to bite into."

Her gaze dropped to the strap, memories of Whitmore flashing to the forefront of her mind. She didn't want to bring that ugliness into this beautiful moment, but there it was. A part of her.

"Give her a minute," Hunter said, sensing her hesitation.

She gave the trauma the space it deserved, recalling how the doctors and orderlies had to wrestle her down and force her submission. But there was no force here. She remembered them shoving that rubber mouthguard between her teeth and tightening straps to her head. But she was completely unbound now. Free.

She looked back to Stone. "I'm ready now."

"Open."

The leather was butter-soft, nothing like the hard rubber that tasted of fear and chemicals. She breathed in the natural, wild scent, reminding her of many toys he'd used on her before. She clung to those memories, those moments of pleasure she controlled as much as him, and the images of her body bowing on a table, electricity coursing through her skull without her consent faded away.

This was not that. This was her choice. This was them, giving her exactly what she wanted.

Stone placed the leather strap between her teeth. "Good girl," Stone murmured, pressing a kiss to her temple.

Such a profound difference. No gagging. No straining. No tears. At least not yet.

She bit down gently, accepting this small protection they offered.

Her vision blurred as the full weight of the moment settled over her. This was her decision. Her declaration. Her permanent claim on them as much as theirs on her.

She met each of their gazes in turn—Stone's deep emerald stare, Hunter's fathomless, intense stare, Ash's comforting ice-blue eyes.

Then they lowered her onto her belly. She shivered as the cool silk sheets pressed against her heated skin.

"Still okay?" Hunter asked and she nodded, keeping her bite tight around the strap.

Ash took her left hand. Hunter mirrored the position on her right, stretching her arms out wide as she turned her head to rest on her cheek. Their touch anchored her. Kept her present and grounded against the turbulent emotions erupting inside.

"We've got you." Hunter's thumb traced circles in her palm. "We won't let go."

"Breathe," Stone instructed. "Deep and steady. In through your nose, out through your mouth, around the leather."

She heard the click of the heating element and smelled the metallic tang of hot iron mingling with the candle smoke. Her heart hammered, but not from fear. Her anticipation was for the transformation. She was claiming her life back, becoming the woman she was meant to be.

"Last chance," Stone said softly. "You can still—"

She squeezed Ash and Hunter's hands, shaking her head firmly. The leather muffled her words, but the intent was clear.

"She's good," Ash said, speaking for her. "Do it."

The first touch of heat made her whole body tense despite the anesthetic. Not quite pain, but pressure and warmth that went deeper than skin. She bit down harder on the leather, her pained groan intensified to a scream and their grip on her hands tightened.

One second. Three. Six. The pain mounted until her toes curled and her feet kicked. She sobbed into the leather, in agony, but also from the overwhelming perfection of it.

And then the pressure was gone, but the burn remained.

Stone worked with surgeon's precision, treating the area with whatever salve he applied next.

"You still good?" Ash asked, but breathing was all she could manage, so he brushed a finger along her temple where a tear had slid. "It's done."

The scent of burning skin should have horrified her, but in her mind, that was the smell of commitment. This was the wedding they could never have, the promises written in flesh that nothing but death could dissolve.

They removed the strap from her mouth and gently helped her sit up. Stone brought her a glass of water which she gratefully sipped. They hovered at her side, watching her cautiously, as if waiting for her to condemn them.

When the glass was empty, she handed it off to Ash and asked, "How does it look?"

"Perfect," Hunter growled, his thumb stroking over her cheek to wipe away a tear. "So fucking perfect."

She smiled, glad to see he'd come around. "See, I knew you'd like it."

"How could I not?" He gently kissed her eyes and whispered, "It's only the sight of your pain that rips me to pieces, but your bravery...that's a sight to behold, *Lisichka*."

The pain would fade, but the mark would remain forever. Evidence of her choice. Proof of their claim. A testament to something that transcended ownership—mutual possession, complete and irreversible.

They'd given her what the Whitmore and her family had tried to steal—agency, choice, and the power to make her own decisions.

"Fuck. Look at that. Look at her." Stone's voice was heavy with reverence. His hands were infinitely gentle as he dressed the wound, applying more of the cooling salve to the brand.

"Wait, I want to see."

Ash carried a mirror closer, angling it toward the one hanging on the closest wall. Outside the gilded ballroom, snow continued to fall, blanketing the world in pristine white that spoke of new beginnings and clean slates. But inside, Marigold had never felt warmer.

"Can you see?" Ash tipped the mirror.

Her lips parted at the distinct outline of a bear. "It's just like yours."

"Ours," Hunter said roughly, voice thick with emotion.

Her gaze found theirs in the mirror. *"Moi tri medvedya,"* she whispered. *My three bears.*

Three sets of eyes shimmered with moisture.

Three dangerous men brought to tears by her surrender.

They were now etched into her skin. Permanently linked by beautiful scars.

As they held her, careful of the fresh brand, she felt the truth of their love settle into her bones. She was theirs. And they were hers. Together forever. Just right.

And they lived happily—and wickedly—ever after...

THE END

Did you like visiting the Isles of Kassel?
If so, this is your exclusive invitation back.
CLICK HERE to find out which wicked villain is up next in the
Villains of Kassel series!

BOOKS BY SERIES
Many first-in-series books are FREE
Grab them here!

MCCULLOUGH MOUNTAIN
Almost Priest *
Beautiful Distraction
Irish Rogue
British Professor
Broken Man
Controlled Chaos
Hard Fix
Intentional Risk

JASPER FALLS
Wake My Heart *
The Best Man
Love Me Nots
Pining For You
My Funny Valentine
Side Squeeze

CALAMITY RAYNE
Calamity Rayne Gets a Life *
Calamity Rayne Back Again
Calamity Rayne Gets Hitched
Calamity Rayne Over the Moon
Calamity Rayne Knocked Up

THE SURRENDER TRILOGY
Falling In
BreakingOut
Coming Home

Ruthless Billionaires
One Billion Secrets *
Two Billion Enemies

MASTERMIND
Blind
Untied

NEW CASTLE
First Comes Love *
If I Fall
Shattered Vows
Remember Me

ADDICTED TO YOU
Crush *
Bang
Throb

THE ORDER OF VAMPIRES
Original Sin *
Dark Exodus
Prodigal Son
Immortal Bastard
Primal Kill
Blood Moon

VILLAINS OF KASSEL

Hush Darling
Gilded Locks
Feast of the Fallen

STAND ALONES
La Vie en Rose
Simple Man
Sugar
Breaking Perfect
Hurt
Protege

About the Author

To receive Lydia's Newsletter and 7 FREE Books, click HERE !

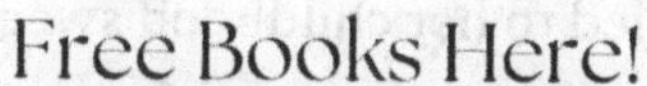

Lydia Michaels is the bestselling and award-winning author of more than fifty novels. She writes heart-clenching, unpredictable romance with dark elements and high heat. Her work is character-driven and bursting with broken heroes and badass females. With a sweet spot for overbearing, territorial types, her deeply emotional books are spicy, emotionally satisfying, and guaranteed to leave readers with many book hangovers.

Lydia is the consecutive winner of the *2018 & 2019 Author of the Year Award* from *Happenings Media* and the recipient of the *2014 Best Author Award* from the Courier Times. She has been featured by *USA Today*, *Romantic Times Magazine*, the *Women in Publishing Summit*, and more.

Michaels started her author career in 2007, becoming a recognized presence and advocate within the publishing industry. She is the CEO of LMC Consulting, a certified author coach specializing in character and plot development, and the founder of the *East Coast Author Convention*, the *Behind the Keys Author Retreat*, and www.LydiaMichaelsBooks.com.

She is happily married to her childhood sweetheart. Her favorite things include cooking Italian cuisine, hosting extravagant dinner parties, sipping espresso martinis, listening to her husband play piano, and escaping to her coastal home on the Jersey Shore. She's an LGBTQ ally, a BLM supporter, a firm believer that the patriarchy must end (women's rights are human rights), and an advocate for pediatric cancer research.

LYDIA

Follow Lydia Michaels on social media!
Facebook | Instagram | TikTok

FOLLOW LYDIA!

Do you follow LYDIA?
TikTok @LydiaMichaels
Instagram @lydia_michaels_books
Facebook @LydiaMichaels
Goodreads
BookBub

Show Your LOVE & Support the Book Community!
If you enjoyed this story, please tell your friends about it and/or leave a review.

THANK YOU FOR YOUR REVIEW!

Reviews help authors so much! If you left a review for this book, I greatly appreciate it!
Thank you,
Lydia

Where can I leave a review?
Goodreads
BookBub
Lydia Michaels Shop
Learn More!